WHAT COLOR JUSTICE

WHAT COLOR JUSTICE

Andrew P. Baratta

iUniverse, Inc.

New York Lincoln Shanghai

What Color Justice

iUniverse books may be ordered through booksellers or by contacting:

iUniverse
2021 Pine Lake Road, Suite 100
Lincoln, NE 68512
www.iuniverse.com
1-800-Authors (1-800-288-4677)

ISBN-13: 978-0-595-36967-6 (pbk)
ISBN-13: 978-0-595-67439-8 (cloth)
ISBN-13: 978-0-595-81374-2 (ebk)
ISBN-10: 0-595-36967-7 (pbk)
ISBN-10: 0-595-67439-9 (cloth)
ISBN-10: 0-595-81374-7 (ebk)

Printed in the United States of America

CHAPTER 1

▼

Spring—1992

The thin red light bleeding out from the crack under the door and over the tattered hallway carpet was a familiar sight to the boy. He hardly hesitated to simply walk in to the dingy, tenth floor apartment. But what he saw when he entered the almost completely dark room stopped the breath in the back of his throat. He tried not to show his fear, knowing from terrible, recent experience that any sign of weakness on his face would only make things worse. Instead, he gritted his teeth, gripped tightly the worn, rubber basketball clutched in his skinny arms like a life preserver, and made his way warily across the room.

"Shut the fuckin' door," the man snarled. The voice was deep and breathy; it's timbre suggestive of both the man's physical enormity as well as his present activity. It was a voice the boy had heard many times in the previous year, and it terrified him.

The boy pushed the door behind him, making sure not to slam it. Hidden now in the swath of darkness on the edge of the red light's circular glare, he crept sideways towards what in any other home would have been a bedroom, but in this apartment, in this place, was just another four walls and a ceiling, with a filthy mattress on the floor. The boy knew that he if he could just stay here, in the shadow and clear of the red light, the man might simply forget he was there.

It hardly mattered anymore what was happening just a few feet away. It didn't even register. No, all that mattered was that the man not do to him what he was doing to her.

The boy tiptoed under the greasy curtain hung listlessly across the doorway to the bedroom. The shafts of moonlight creeping around the bars in the room's lone window provided just enough light so that the boy could tell it was empty. Breathing a sigh of relief for small favors, he flopped himself onto the dirty mattress. He lay there on his back for a few seconds, staring at nothing, trying to think of the same.

Absentmindedly, he began shooting the ball directly in the air towards the ceiling. His form was perfect, the ball rising in a straight line, with perfect rotation, just brushing the ceiling every time. Although it was dark, the boy had taken so many shots from that position in his short eleven years of life that he didn't need to see to know exactly where the ball was going.

Not that he would have seen it anyway. No, what he saw were his friends, Michael Jordan and Larry Bird and Magic Johnson, and himself, sweating and running and shooting and passing their collective way to NBA title after NBA title. The roar of the crowd in his head his only shield from the noise in the next room.

It's a tragedy that an eleven year old boy should even know what the phrase "crack whore" means. It's an abomination that he should consciously realize his mother is one. The red light he had crept around meant the dingy apartment on the tenth floor of the Raymond Rosen Housing Projects in North Philadelphia was open for business, and the woman the boy knew as his mother was working. The light was emitted by a shadeless lamp in a corner of the apartment's main room, which stood next to the room's only piece of furniture; another threadbare mattress. The blare of its red bulb was mom's special touch, her way of setting the mood.

If the man fucking his mother had been simply one more anonymous stranger, the boy would hardly have batted an eye. But tonight's visitor was different. "Clark" was what she called him, but who knew what his real name was. Even in these projects, where one's life was in danger at every moment of every day, no one had yet dared challenge the man the boy's mother called Clark. His presence was still new and unexpected, and his capacity for cruelty and violence unsurpassed.

In fact, he was more like a ghost than a man, with people afraid to even mention his name. The boy had only heard his mother use it once, as she begged him to stop beating and raping her one evening. Her entreaties had gone unheeded, and only seemed to increase the man's anger, and the viciousness of his attacks. He was very tall and very fat, but not sloppily so, with smooth skin which always seemed to be glistening and shiny with sweat. Clark was one of those men whose girth portends immense physical strength, as well as appetite, and he had made the boy suffer greatly as the result of both.

But the boy's suffering had not begun with Clark. Despite several attempts by various child welfare workers since his birth, none had had any success in helping him. The mother's addiction was too powerful, and the workers too overburdened to follow up as necessary. So what started out as threats to terminate the mother's parental rights, dissolved over time into the morass of a system which could not even keep track of a child's existence, much less his welfare.

So the boy's file was passed from worker to worker, department to department, until it found itself lost inside some file cabinet somewhere, where it and the boy simply ceased to officially matter to anyone. He was on his own, unprotected by his crack-addicted mother, easy prey for the monsters who fucked her.

Neighbors within the Project saw what was happening and some tried to help. But they were beset with their own sets of problems, most equally as bad. And whatever help they had been able to offer, evaporated almost immediately after Clark barreled into all of their lives.

Clark did not ask permission to come and go as he pleased, and almost from the first day, took ferocious liberties with the boy's mother. He plied her with the drugs she so desperately craved, and abused her both physically and sexually. She had neither the strength nor the will to resist.

Tonight was obviously no exception. As the boy lay there, convinced of the future glory the ball in his hands would someday bring him, he listened just enough to his mother's muffled grunts, and Clark's expletive-laced sex talk, to gauge both the level of her effort, and the force of Clark's ardor. The boy knew all too well that if the former were not enough to fully sate the latter, his turn would be next.

The first slap was a bad sign, although not necessarily definitive. Most of the men beat her. It was almost considered part of the package. It wasn't as if the sex was satisfying to either party involved. Of course the boy had no real comprehension of this. All he did know was that the woman in the next room had apparently given birth to him, that she was a strung-out junkie, and that as far as he knew, she hadn't had two consecutive coherent thoughts in his lifetime.

She didn't care for him in any way except to absentmindedly allow him to sleep on the mattress and forage for what little food might find its way into the apartment. He survived by going down to Temple University's campus every day and hanging around outside the law school, begging for loose change. The white girls thought he was cute and pitiable, so most days he was able to scrounge up just enough to get at least one small meal at McDonald's.

"Wake the fuck up, bitch!" yelled Clark suddenly. The sound of repeated punches and slaps filled the apartment. "You ain't earned your shit yet!" More punches, then a thud as the boy's mother was thrown into the corner, where she lay in a bony, unconscious heap.

Tears involuntarily leaked from the boy's eyes as he stifled the urge to run and scream with the rising terror he felt. He'd tried that the first few times, but that had only made it worse. So, instead of running, the boy simply rolled onto his stomach, making sure to tuck his ball under a mound of dirty clothes and garbage that lay next to the bed.

He didn't have to roll back over to feel Clark's immense presence as it filled the doorway to the bedroom. Although the man had been coming around less frequently, his presence was a constant weight on the boy's heart, a weight that dropped like an anvil into the pit of his stomach every time Clark appeared.

It was at these times that the boy wondered why it was that everyone in the projects feared this man so. It was confusing because he instinctively knew that the people who lived the way they did feared nothing. And he knew this because he too feared nothing. What is there to fear when you have absolutely nothing to lose? Yet they feared Clark. The boy assumed it was because Clark did to all of them what he often did to the boy. It would be many years before he would look back and realize he was more right than he could have known.

Clark stood in the doorway, sweating and breathing heavily from the exertion of beating and fucking the boy's mother. Completely naked, he stroked his immense erection while staring lasciviously at the boy, his eyes red-rimmed and vacant.

Without a word, Clark lowered his enormity to a kneeling position behind the boy and pulled the tattered dungaree shorts he was wearing down to his slender ankles. He laced a thick forearm under the boy's quivering stomach, lifted his tiny body, and maneuvered himself into position.

It was at this point that the fear always left the boy, replaced instead by a great nothingness inside him. The pain was excruciating, but he had learned from the very first time that screaming only made Clark enjoy it even more. And even though the boy knew from experience that a few quick screams would certainly have the effect of making his suffering end sooner, he had learned to gain a measure of small personal revenge by not letting Clark enjoy himself as much as he otherwise could. So the boy steeled himself against the pain as his tiny body jerked back and forth repeatedly, gripped as it was in Clark's giant, sweaty arms.

As the boy suffered in silence, he stared through burning tears just off to his left, and focused on the basketball. It was the only thing he knew he could count on, the only thing in the world that would never betray him, and the only thing which might someday save him.

CHAPTER 2

▼

Philadelphia has always been a geographically large city that wants to be thought of as Big, but will always be nothing more than a vast collection of neighborhoods sharing the same negative self-image of all the things it is not, namely New York or Washington D.C. Nothing attests to this better than the fact that the city's main artery, from Cheltenham at the North end, down to South Philly and the Navy Yard at the other, is called "Broad Street." In reality, Broad Street is nothing more than the 14th in a grid of numbered streets crisscrossed by smaller streets named after prominent Philadelphians who no one outside of Philly ever heard of.

At the epicenter of town, where North Broad becomes South Broad, sits City Hall, occupying 4 city blocks, the largest and most expensive municipal building ever built in the United States. It took thirty years to build, so long that by the time they were finished, the original mode of architecture and the technology available to put inside it were completely outdated. Prior to the early 1990's, Philadelphia had been losing the same fight against the advancement of style and progress for the previous hundred years.

One area in which Philly had not been left behind though was in the sophistication of its politics. But despite the location of the offices in City Hall of the Mayor and City Council, it was not the place where the really important political decisions in Philadelphia were made. No, those decisions were made by the men who paid for the right to make them, and because they could afford it, these men chose to meet and determine the future of their city in more luxurious surroundings a few blocks away from City Hall, at the Union League.

The classic French Renaissance-styled League building today still occupies an entire city block of its own in the center of Philadelphia's "cultural" district (which consists mainly of The Kimmel Center for the Performing Arts).

The Union League building sits just above the Kimmel Center on South Broad Street, its brick and brownstone façade fronted by massive twin circular staircases leading to the main entrance. Magnificent double oak doors open into a structure with nearly a quarter million square feet of space, spread out over eight floors, every inch of which is meticulously and expensively appointed with the richest leather, wood and polished marble. Its walls are adorned with one of the finest art collections in the world.

Of all its luxurious nooks and crannies, however, the largest and most exquisitely appointed is the Cigar and Reading room on the seventh floor. Behind a giant mahogany bar running the length of an entire wall, sits top-shelf liquor stacked to the ceiling. A gleaming brass pole edges the bar. Throughout the room are scattered plush sofas and chairs upholstered in imported Italian leather and suede. Along the two walls abutting the bar are floor-to-ceiling bookcases filled with rare and expensive books. Also available is a current copy of every major newspaper in the country. In addition, there is a round-the-clock wait staff of fifteen men (no woman has ever officially been allowed into the room, despite their having been allowed membership in the club itself for the first time in 1972). There is also a librarian and chef on duty twenty-four hours a day.

Directly across the cavernous room from the bar is what looks like a giant vault door, made completely of oak and over three feet thick. Through this door is the room's walk-in humidor, stocked with literally thousands of the world's finest cigars (the Cuban trade embargo is not recognized in the seventh floor Cigar and Reading Room). Inside the humidor, there are exactly fifteen lockers. Just as the temperature in the humidor has been maintained at a steady sixty degrees for over a hundred years, so has the number of lockers allowed: fifteen. There have been fifteen lockers in that humidor for over one hundred and forty years, and it is in the charter of the club that there never be any more than that.

Ownership of a locker is, to say the least, a mark of distinction. There have been rumors of six figure offers for the transfer of a locker's title, and it is said that both Teddy and Franklin Roosevelt were denied their own. Amongst that most rarified of air breathed only by the super-rich and super-powerful, to be a "locker owner" is the ultimate status symbol, not just in the city, but in the world.

Despite its magnificent square footage, the furniture and shelving of the room managed to make each little area seem intimate and secluded. It was on a warm spring day in 1992 in one particularly segregated and dimly-lit corner that George Cohen leaned back into the soft leather of the armchair only he was allowed to sit in, and puffed contentedly on one of the thirty-five dollar Winston Churchill cigars the waiter had retrieved from his personal locker. Cohen was careful not to let any ashes fall into the lap of his hand-made, silk trousers. Through the smoky haze in which they sat, Cohen studied his protégé, seated in the chair facing his, and smiled.

That smile of yours always makes me nervous, George, thought Ashland Wilson as he puffed away on the other Churchill. Short and pudgy, with a round, pleasant face topped with sandy blonde hair, Wilson's less than imposing physical presence belied a peerless intellect.

Cohen regarded Wilson impassively as he looked around the room. There were pockets of men, in groups of varying sizes, situated throughout. Dressed uniformly in business suits, drinking and smoking, they all, to a man, appeared very serious and involved in important conversations. Most were in their fifties, sixties, and older, making them significantly younger than George Cohen, and significantly older than Ashland Wilson.

Wilson followed Cohen's gaze around the room and took the opportunity to regard the man who was both his mentor and best friend. Wilson was a man with many friends, and a multitude of acquaintances, all of whom, if they could, would certainly help him achieve his goal of becoming the next District Attorney of Philadelphia. But no matter how much all of those people liked, or even loved him, George Cohen was the only one of his friends who could, and would, make it so.

At eighty years old, Cohen had the vitality of men a third his age. He was still a handsome and intimidating man. Standing six feet-four inches tall, with a thick shock of silvery hair, square jaw and deep-set brown eyes, he could be found lifting weights and jogging on a treadmill at five-thirty every morning in the sprawling gym located in the basement of the Union League. He had been a standout forward for the University of Pennsylvania basketball team in the early 30's, and took great pride in maintaining the physical fitness of his youth.

Pride was at the root of every success Cohen had ever enjoyed, and like most great men, also the cause of every mistake he had ever made. The sheer force and magnitude of the man's determination and brilliance however, insured that the former had always greatly outnumbered the latter.

Cohen shifted in his chair and looked directly into the eyes of what he believed to be his greatest accomplishment of all.

"I've been thinking lately," he said seriously, "that there is a certain futility which exists in the lives of the men in this room…and all men really, who are like them."

Wilson smiled. "Is this going to be another stand-up philosophy lesson, George?"

Cohen chuckled softly. Wilson was the only man on the planet who dared speak to him in such a fashion, and the old man loved him for it. "Hold your tongue, son, and listen."

Cohen's eyes traveled back to the room. "Unbeknownst to them, these men are all involved in a futile quest...for satisfaction. Not power, not money, and not fame." He looked back at his younger friend who was trying not to smile. "You know as well as I do that every one of the men in this room in fact already possesses a large measure of one or more of those things, or they would not be in this room."

"So do you, George. You just happen to have considerably more than they all do...combined."

Cohen smiled patronizingly. "Once again, in your typically myopic way, you have unwittingly made my point for me. You see, Ashland, the very thing that leads men such as these," Cohen swept his hands toward the room, "and yes, even myself, to accomplish the things we have, is the very thing that keeps us from ever being satisfied with what we've achieved."

Wilson took a savory sip from a glass of Tinta Roriz port "Yeah, yeah, I know, the thrill of the hunt, the alpha male, blah, blah, blah."

The older man furrowed his brow and lightly shook his head from side to side. "Where did I ever find you?" he asked while staring down the length of his patrician nose.

Wilson laughed. "I found you, George, don't you remember?"

"So you did," sighed Cohen as he leaned forward and placed his cigar into the ashtray. He waited in that position until Wilson got the hint and leaned in as well. Their knees and heads were almost touching.

"I'll admit that there is some validity to the theory that certain men are never satisfied with what they have, and are always searching for their next challenge, whether it be more money, a new career, or even a prettier mistress. This is an affliction, however, which cuts across all boundaries of class, education and wealth. That particular phenomenon, however, the 'alpha male syndrome' as you call it, is not why these men are dissatisfied with who they are and what they have accomplished."

"Are we getting to the part about their futile quest for satisfaction?" Wilson smiled as he reached out and squeezed Cohen's calf.

Cohen gave an exasperated sigh and leaned back into his chair. "I am about to give you the benefit of eighty years of experience in the ways of the world, about to teach you what life is truly about, and you make jokes."

Wilson sensed that Cohen was actually serious. "I'm sorry, George. I do want to hear what you have to say. But you know that every day since I was fifteen years old you've taught me what life is really about. I am who I am because of you, you know that."

The old man shook his head. "Ashland, you were born who you are. I've just been lucky enough to be around for the past twenty-three years as you've grown into the man you've become."

Wilson blushed with the compliment. "I didn't give you much choice, did I?"

"No you didn't," acknowledged Cohen with a nostalgic smile.

Wilson returned his friend's smile. "So tell me. What's today's lesson?"

"The lesson, as you call it, is simple. So simple, in fact, that the vast majority of men who have been fortunate enough to learn it are not even aware that they possess the secret to achieving true happiness." Cohen glanced about the room and noticed the intensity with which everyone was pretending not to listen in on his conversation. He leaned forward again. "*Know yourself,*" he whispered, "that is the secret."

Wilson nodded seriously as if he had just been let in on a deeply spiritual revelation. He then raised an eyebrow. "Huh?"

Cohen rolled his eyes. "Kid all you want. But *know yourself.* These men will never be satisfied with themselves because they do not know who they truly are. Their entire lives have been dedicated to the pursuit of one goal after another, not because the achievement of the goal will in any way make them feel better about themselves, but rather, because they think it will change the way they will be perceived by those around them. To men such as these, perception is more important than reality. The problem is, as much as they might be able to fool the rest of the world around them into thinking that they are wonderful, they can never truly fool themselves. And thus their dissatisfaction."

"Ah, but George, isn't perception in fact reality?" Wilson responded.

Cohen sat back in his chair and puffed the cigar. "I am glad you asked. The answer is no. If perception were the same as reality, they would be listed as synonyms by Webster's. It is the man who understands the difference between the two who is most likely to be happy. The difference is a life of self-fulfillment, as opposed to a life of empty yearning. The difference is as stark as the differences between you and me, my friend."

That was an intriguing statement. "What's that supposed to mean?"

"I mean simply this. I became a lawyer because I realized that it was the best way, given my particular talents, for me to become a very wealthy man. I identified wealth as my goal. But what I really wanted was to be recognized by the upper crust as someone worthy of their circle…I wanted to be viewed as a successful man. I wanted all those Main Line, blue blooded society mavens to kiss my ass. And I knew that the only way a dirt-poor Jew from 48th Street and Osage Avenue was ever going to earn their respect, would be to have more money than they did. I wanted to create the perception in their minds that I was just as good as them."

Wilson frowned. The thought that anyone could consider himself superior to George Cohen, in any way, was an impossibility as far as Wilson was concerned. There was no greater man on the planet in his eyes.

Cohen ignored Wilson's expression. "But you know what, Ash? After all these years, after all the money I've made, the millions I've given to their charities, all my sophistication, my worldliness, I know, in my heart, that I'm still nothing more than that poor Jew from West Philly. No matter what I do, I can never change the perception I have of *myself.* It is for precisely this reason that for over the past sixty-plus years, I have not enjoyed a single moment devoted to the practice of law, or business…for the simple reason that they have not given me what I really wanted to get out of them."

Wilson sighed deeply and slumped back into his chair. He eyed Cohen wearily. "George, if you don't want me to run for D.A., just say it, don't give me all this pseudo-psychology crap."

Cohen frowned with frustration and shook his head vigorously from side to side. "You know, I think I might be the only person you don't really listen to. I am trying to tell you that I understand why you want to be D.A., and that I not only support your candidacy, I admire it."

Wilson gave a little snort. "Why?"

"Because of all the incredibly successful men I've met in my long life, be they Presidents, business leaders, entertainers, athletes…amongst all of them, you are the one man I believe in my heart truly knows himself."

Wilson raised an eyebrow again but did not interrupt.

"You are a very wealthy and powerful man, Ash. Lord knows that when I die you'll be counted amongst the richest men in the country. You love your wife and sons, and they love you back. You crave neither fame nor public acceptance. You have an ego, yes. In fact, it's quite large. But it is one which is created by the confidence you have in the rectitude of everything you do. You are supremely self-confident, but not because of the way other people see you. No, your ego derives from the belief you have in yourself. This is a rare quality.

"For instance, you're the happiest person I know. Yet, for the past few years, the only thing you've been able to talk about is becoming the District Attorney of this third-rate, corrupt, afterthought of a city, and turning it into something only you believe it can be turned into. And not because you want to be governor or a senator, or because you want people to recognize you when you walk down the street. You want to do it because you know you can, and believe you should."

Cohen leaned in and rested his elbows on his knees. He looked up to Wilson's eyes. "The reason I'm saying all of this is because I don't think you're even aware of how truly powerful, and lucky, you are. For men like you, Ash, success and true satisfaction do not depend on the achievement of a given set of circumstances. You are able to wake up every day and know that you will do your best, and appreciate the opportunity to do so. The men in this room cannot say the same."

Although it wasn't necessarily unusual for Cohen to be so candid and philosophical with Wilson, the younger man recognized that Cohen was attempting to reveal a bit of himself, as well as teach an important lesson. Wilson appreciated the effort, and loved the man even more for having given it. But he didn't need to hear it. Ash Wilson knew very well how fortunate he'd been in life, and how much he had to offer the world. And it was his intention not just to offer it, but to give it as well. Not because he wanted anything in return. For Ash Wilson, it was simply the right thing to do.

*   *   *   *

Philadelphia Daily News, August 31st, 1992
Wealthy Power Lawyer Wants to be Next D.A.
By: Jerome Allen

The loftiest heights of Philadelphia's legal community were rocked yesterday when Center City power lawyer, Ashland Wilson, announced his intention to relinquish the Chairmanship of Cohen & Elson, Philadelphia's most successful and politically connected law firm, to run for District Attorney.

Wilson has been a rising star over the past fifteen years in the city's legal circles. The personal protégé of millionaire and legendary local lawyer George Cohen, the founder of Cohen & Elson, Wilson, 38, is a graduate of the University of Pennsylvania, and Harvard Law School. He grew up in the Fairmount section of the city, and attended St. Joseph's Prep in North Philadelphia. He first met George Cohen as a fifteen year old high school sophomore, when the young Wilson literally stalked Cohen in order to con-

vince the uber lawyer that he should be given a summer job working as an intern at Cohen & Elson.

"*Ashland's goal was to be an attorney,*" *says Cohen, 80, in a rare interview.* "*He would wait for me every day outside my building. He'd be there at six o'clock in the morning when I arrived, and no matter what time I left, Ashland would be there. I tried to ignore him at first, but he was so determined that I eventually had no other choice but to give him a job in the mailroom.*"

According to Cohen, once he was hired, Wilson demonstrated a commitment to learning as well as a marked ability to get things accomplished. "*Ash Wilson is a special individual. I have never known anyone like him. Once he sets a goal, he allows nothing to interfere with the accomplishment of that goal.*"

Cohen's relationship with Wilson is so close that many City Hall insiders are worried that Wilson's run is just one more political maneuver by the super-powerful Cohen to exercise control over Philadelphia. "*George is tall and has long arms,*" *says one high-ranking pol,* "*and they'll have to be to reach up Wilson's butt all the way over in the D.A.'s Office.*" *This comment makes reference of course to allegations that Ashland Wilson is nothing more than a puppet of George Cohen, and that his bid to be Philadelphia's top law enforcement official is nothing more than a springboard to higher political office.*

When confronted with that question, Wilson laughed. "*If George wants to help me clean up the streets of Philadelphia, I'll accept his help willingly. As for my political ambitions, I have none. I want to be D.A. for the simple and sole reason that I want to make the world I live in, and the world my children live in, a better place.*"

Those who know Wilson well claim that such optimistic idealism is his trademark, as is his fervent, some would say fanatical, following of the University of Pennsylvania's Men's basketball team. By his own account, he was too "*short and dumpy*" *to play college ball while a student at Penn, so Wilson served as the team's manager and unofficial mascot for his four years there. Since then, he has rarely, if ever missed a game at the Palestra, the historic gymnasium at 33rd and Spruce which has served as Penn's home court since 1927, and the official home of the Big Five since the 1950's. He and the otherwise reclusive Cohen can often be seen sitting together at center court.*

Ash lowered the paper and took another sip of his coffee. He smiled at the petite brunette sitting across the table from him. "You know what's funny?"

"What?" asked Noelle Wilson.

"I don't even let you put your hands near my ass, and we've been married for eleven years."

Noelle laughed. "It's hardly as if I'm begging you to let me do it. You can't see it, but your ass is not really all that inviting a place."

"Well, goddammit, will you pick up the phone and tell the Daily News that!"

Noelle shook her head as she got up to clear the breakfast table. "First day of the campaign, and already worried about saving your ass."

"Hey, that's a pretty good line. I should have used that when they asked me the question. But seriously, you don't like my butt?" Wilson asked with a mock pout.

Noelle came over and sat down. At only five foot three, with a tiny little body, she fit easily into Wilson's rather ample lap. She pushed her short, black hair out of her face and smiled at her husband.

"Awww, honey, I love your ass. In fact, every time you leave the room, I'm happy to see it." She kissed him daintily on the cheek and popped up before her husband was able to realize that she'd zinged him.

Wilson laughed heartily. "You're funny. Lookin. Seriously, are you sure you're ready for this?"

They'd talked at length about it before the decision was made. Fortunately, they were incredibly well off financially due to Wilson's position at the firm, as well as George Cohen's generosity over the years. It was Cohen who had given them their beautiful stone, five-bedroom manse in Chestnut Hill. Cohen had also established a trust fund for the Wilson's two sons which would not only pay for their education, but also make them incredibly wealthy young men when they turned twenty-one. The boys considered Cohen their grandfather, and in fact called him Pop-Pop.

"I've told you how I feel," she said from the sink as she cleaned the breakfast dishes. "You're going to represent a real danger to the status quo out there. All politicians, but especially in Philly, make their livings exploiting the very system they say they're trying to change."

She turned around to face him. "But you're already a wealthy and powerful man who doesn't need the system. They'll be worried that because you don't need the patronage they do just to survive, you'll expose them for who they really are. They'll come after you because of that alone, and they'll be ferocious."

"I'm not scared of them," he said, his nose still buried in the paper.

"I know you're not," said Noelle, "and knowing you the way I do, neither am I."

Wilson smiled at his wife and picked up the most recent edition of Philadelphia Magazine with whom he had done an in-depth interview a few weeks earlier.

"Wilson is an accomplished trial lawyer. His most significant victory was in defense of Precor Savings and Loan in the class action suit brought by two thousand of its shareholders in 1985. It was alleged that the bank's directors had defrauded investors and regulators by not disclosing certain debts before they went public. Wilson was able to fashion a highly complex defense strategy, which involved attacking the credibility of so-called "whistleblowers" within the bank's hierarchy, while at the same time challenging the constitutionality of certain S.E.C. disclosure regulations. Wilson was able to convince the jury that the bank fully complied with existing laws at the time, and in the process, prevented an award which could literally have been in the billions of dollars. The trial lasted over six months and involved over one hundred witnesses and half a million documents. As lead attorney for the defense, Wilson won high praise for his organization

and advocacy skills. The verdict also heralded his emergence from the shadow of George Cohen."

He put the magazine down. Wilson knew when he made the decision to seek public office that his relationship with Cohen would be the thing most scrutinized. He would be seen as simply one more Cohen prop in a city filled with them. Everyone from judges to city councilmen to the Mayor himself had to go through George first if they had any hope of getting elected. That's because since forever, one thing and one thing only had controlled Philadelphia politics: money. Not just money for commercials or flyers or phone bank workers. A candidate needed street money, cash payments to ward leaders who on election day doled out the money.

The cash went to everyone who could conceivably control a vote. Sometimes this was as obvious as standing around the corner from the polling place and handing out twenties. Most times though, the money was given to volunteers, who would ensure that a certain candidate's name was at the top of the ballot card, or union reps who would have their members congregate outside election halls and basically threaten anyone who didn't vote for their guy.

Was the system crooked? Probably. But if you wanted to get elected, it was the only way to operate. So even if you were the most idealistic candidate with the strongest message and the best qualifications, someone who really wanted to do good, you still had to pay to play.

George Cohen recognized early in his professional life the realities of Philadelphia. As a struggling young lawyer with a small, solo practice, Cohen poured every dime he had, and some he didn't, into the candidacy of one Keith Johnston, who was running for State Representative in Northeast Philadelphia. Once elected, Johnston lobbied the state legislature to hire Cohen in the negotiations for several lucrative bond deals, the fees for which had run into the millions.

Cohen's firm grew larger and more and more successful, and he was able to pour even more money into the candidacies of men who, once elected, always brought a return on the investment. In addition to the savvy and early acquisition of key real estate up and down the East Coast, both Cohen's wealth and his political influence grew exponentially until there were few who possessed more of either.

All of this was no secret. Candidates were often lambasted in the press and by opponents as nothing more than shills for Cohen's personal and political point of view. Wilson knew full well that no one would be subject to that criticism more than he. But much of Wilson's professional life had been spent battling the accusations that whatever success he achieved in life was because it had been handed to him by George Cohen.

In moments of deep reflection, Wilson wondered if his desire to be D.A. was simply one more attempt to prove himself worthy of his success independent of the shadow cast over him by George Cohen. In those moments though, Wilson always realized that no matter what he did in life, that shadow would always color whatever success he achieved, in whatever arena. He had come to accept this fact and was able to move on from it, because as Cohen himself had observed, Wilson was a man content within his own skin, and confident in who he was.

CHAPTER 3

▼

Lionel Cooper looked at his watch. He was already five minutes late for his Secured Transactions class and the way this announcement was going, it looked like he wouldn't make it at all. It would be the first class he'd missed in three years of law school.

"Relax, Lionel," said Melissa Freer, the pretty secretary from the fifth floor whom Lionel had briefly dated during his first summer internship at Cohen & Elson. "Missin' one class ain't gonna' kill ya'. Besides, you've already got the job here. Take it easy."

Lionel smiled thinly through a contemptuous snort. *Take it easy*, he thought with a private sneer. *Easy for you to say, sweetheart. You don't get to be the first black man offered the first-year associate position at Cohen & Elson by taking it easy. Especially when you're the most qualified third year in the entire fuckin' city and you still have to worry about being called a token. I'll never take it easy*, thought Lionel bitterly as he checked his watch again.

The entire firm was gathered in the ornate lobby of the George Cohen building in the heart of Center City Philadelphia. Seventy-one lawyers and twice that many in support staff listened respectfully as Ashland Wilson made his farewell speech.

"As the Chairman of this firm for the past four years, and having worked here since I was fifteen years old, it is with mixed emotion that

I make this announcement today. I want you to know that aside from my immediate family...and George," Wilson looked to his right and nodded at Cohen, then waited for the polite applause to subside, "you all are the most important people in the world to me."

Lionel looked at the floor so no one would see him rolling his eyes. *Christ almighty*, he thought, *does he really think we care that he's running for D.A.? Who gives a shit about one more rich white guy running for office?* Lionel looked around the cavernous lobby where everybody but him seemed to be paying rapt attention. He chuckled to himself. *Looks like they do.*

"And I am counting on your continued support as I attempt to achieve my dream of making this wonderful city of ours a safer place to live."

Raucous applause filled the room, joined politely by Lionel's "golf clap" in which he lightly tapped the fingers of his left hand against the lower palm of his right. Melissa gave him a reproachful smirk, which he ignored.

"It is with a mixture of excitement, regret and fear that I take this step," Wilson was saying. "I am excited at the prospect of helping stem the tidal wave of crime and deviancy which has washed over the shores of this city. I believe that the rest of the decade of the 1990's will be one of prosperity and explosive economic growth. But in order for Philadelphia to fully realize the benefit of that growth, our streets need to be safe for everyone. I intend to make them safe."

Wilson paused until the applause subsided. "I am regretful of course, that I will have to leave all of you, my extended family, and that I will not get to work with all of you on a daily basis. And I admit to being just a bit afraid that the people of Philadelphia are not fully prepared for the type of leadership and vision I intend to bring to the law enforcement community of this city."

More applause and shouts of approval from the crowd. Always conscious that he stood out in this crowd, not just because of the color of his skin, but also because of his six feet, seven inches of height, Lionel went through the motions of joining in with the cheers. Though even as he did so, he felt a pang of guilt. Ashland Wilson seemed like a genuinely good man. Lionel had only met him once, during his final interview with the firm. Wilson had been more direct, honest, and at the same time respectful than any other…adult, had ever been to Lionel. And he knew all about Lionel's painfully abbreviated college basketball career. The guy was apparently a freak about college basketball. The meeting with Wilson was really why he had accepted the firm's offer over all the others. That and the starting salary of $85,000 a year, of course.

But no matter how nice a guy Ashland Wilson was, Lionel did not have time for this self-congratulatory soiree. Wilson being D.A. wasn't really going to do anything for Lionel's career, as Cohen & Elson didn't practice criminal law. Having realized that, Lionel was now prepared to move on. He didn't really care how nice a guy Ashland Wilson was or wasn't. If he wanted to piss away the millions he was making as the Chairman of the city's most prestigious law firm, that was his prerogative. It was incredibly stupid as far as Lionel was concerned, but hey, to each his own.

Sentimentality and fond remembrances were for women and children as far as Lionel was concerned. At least while there was work to be done and a career to build. It was the only way to look at the world for a man who fully intended to make his first million by the age of thirty. At twenty-seven, that didn't leave much time.

"Oh man," he muttered as everyone began lining up to shake the candidate's hand.

"What?" asked Melissa.

"I haven't got time for this. I can still make the last half of my secured transactions class if I leave now." With that, he snuck out the 16th Street door of the lobby, ignoring as he did Melissa's disappointed glance.

Despite the obvious quality of the suit he was wearing, and the fact that he had just emerged from the lobby of Center City Philadelphia's finest office building, Lionel was still a six-foot-seven black man in the city of Philadelphia. Three empty taxis passed him by before he was able to secure a ride back to the campus of Temple University Law School. The daily snub from cab drivers was hardly unexpected and was in fact built in to any trip Lionel planned around the city. He often joked about it with his friends.

But not so deep inside he knew that his difficulty catching a cab was just one more contributing factor to an ever enlarging chip growing on his broad shoulders.

As he sat squeezed into the back of the smelly taxi during the ten-minute ride back to school, Lionel thought seriously about the comment Melissa had made, and about the bitterness of his internal reaction. Why was everything with him increasingly about being black? It was something he noticed himself doing more and more. That is, attributing every slight, every injustice, no matter how minor, to his race. He had always scoffed at blacks who used their race as an excuse for their failures. Lionel felt that by doing this, black people impeded the very cause they sought to further.

But for some reason he had not quite figured out why, he felt himself every day becoming generally more hostile to white people, especially the lawyers at Cohen & Elson. What made it disconcerting was that for most of his life Lionel had been so successful operating amongst white people, deliberately 'playing the game' to get what he wanted.

Ever since he was a little boy, Lionel knew what he wanted out of life…money, and lots of it. But he also knew that he didn't want the kind of money that was so easily and often grabbed by his friends and other kids in the West Philly neighborhood where he grew up. It went as quickly as it came, and so did his friends, either to jail, or the morgue. No, Lionel was smart enough to know that to get the kind of money he wanted, to have "fuck you money," he had to be the guy people go to *after* they get in trouble, not before.

So he played the game. Got straight A's at William Sayre Middle School at 52nd and Market, smiled and said 'yes sir' and 'no ma'am' to all the do-gooder social workers who came every week to assuage their own kind of guilt. Excelled at basketball. And, best of all, he grew.

Every one of the prestigious prep schools dotting the suburban Philadelphia landscape wanted him badly to come to their schools. Not only did they offer full scholarships, they also had rich, white families offering to take Lionel to live with them instead of bouncing from foster home to foster home as he had been.

Even at his young age, Lionel saw the opportunity, and snatched it. He chose to attend the Shipley School in Bryn Mawr, in the very heart of the Main Line. He just knew that three things would inevitably happen if he went there. He'd be the best basketball player that school had ever had, he'd get a great education, and he'd be living in the middle of the largest concentration of wealth in the Philadelphia area.

Lionel had seen it all so clearly from such an early age: he'd treat these rich white people like the dealers in his neighborhood treated the addicts who came looking to cop. That is, like the marks that they were. He'd give them what they thought they wanted, all the while emptying their wallets before they realized they'd never really gotten anything at all. His only mistake along the way had been believing his own press, believing that he needed to go to a big-time basketball school if he wanted to play pro ball.

He took a full scholarship to the University of Tennessee, where he broke his leg in four places during the second practice of his freshman year. He never played competitive basketball again, and ended up getting his undergraduate degree at Temple. From the moment he broke his leg, Lionel vowed to himself never to waver again from achieving his goals.

But as he sat in the back of that cab with his knees pinned in the air, lamenting what his posture was doing to the crease in his Hugo Boss suit-pants, he came to grips with a realization which had been slowly creeping up on him for months. He'd been pretending to be a sellout for so long, that somewhere along the line he forgot he was only pre-tending. And he felt guilty. All of a sudden, he felt guilty.

The cab stopped at the corner of Broad Street and Montgomery Avenue, directly in front of the wide concrete steps leading to the front entrance of the square, six-story Temple Law School Building. A giant bust of Abraham Lincoln sat off to one side of the metal and glass doors. The cab's meter read $7.75.

Lionel unfolded himself onto the street, pulled out his wallet, and retrieved a ten-dollar bill. He had taken the same cab ride probably a hundred times while doing his second and third year internship at Cohen & Elson, and it always cost between seven and eight bucks. He couldn't remember a time when he hadn't simply handed the driver a ten and walked straight up those steps like he owned the place.

"Give me two back," he said instead, but he didn't readily know why. Lionel turned slowly from the disgusted look of the cabbie with-out looking, while replacing the two singles into his wallet. In doing so he almost tripped over the boy.

"Spare some change, mister?"

Lionel had seen the boy before, many times in fact. He'd just never noticed him. Yet seeing him at that moment stunned Lionel. Years later, Lionel would realize what it was about the boy that stopped him cold that day, and changed the course of two lives. It certainly wasn't the boy's distended belly, or lips cracked and peeling from dehydra-tion. It wasn't the knobby elbows and knees which portended explosive growth to come, but at the time simply provided joints for impossibly skinny arms and legs. It wasn't the tattered clothing hanging from the boy's body, or even the way he clutched the bald, rubber basketball that looked like an oversized circus balloon next to his emaciated body.

No, he didn't take notice of any of those things. That's pretty much what he and all the other kids from his neighborhood looked like at that age. What caught Lionel's attention, what actually caused him to stand on the sidewalk and stare at this pathetic little boy was...his eyes. This tiny, nothing of a boy, with the body of a six-year old child and the eyes of a sixty-year old man. They were dark and narrow, and suspicious and world-weary. But more than that, they were…shrewd. Lionel felt as if the boy were looking directly through him, past the fifteen hundred-dollar suit and three hundred-dollar shoes, right at the tattered little boy he himself used to be. It was unnerving.

Still staring, Lionel opened his wallet, took out the two ones, and handed them to the boy.

"Hey, thanks, mister!" the boy said as his face cracked into a wide grin. Half of his teeth were missing and the other half were green and rotted. Lionel had never enjoyed a smile more.

The boy began to literally skip away as he clutched the windfall tightly in his left fist, the basketball tucked securely under his right shoulder. "Yo, little man!" shouted Lionel. "What's your name?"

The boy turned halfway around as he continued to skip and yelled over his shoulder. "Darnell!"

*   *   *   *

Lionel sat in back of the lecture hall, ignoring the professor's incantations about the Uniform Commercial Code and how to perfect a security interest in chattel. His notebook, filled with detailed notes from every prior lecture on the subject of secured transactions, lay closed on the too small fold-down desktop. He stared vacantly towards the floor, over and over in his mind turning Darnell's image. Why was he so affected by this kid all of a sudden? Why did he feel the overwhelming need to run outside, find the boy, and…what? What was it that he felt the need to do?

Inside, he knew. Sometimes he felt like there were two people inside his head carrying on two separate conversations. One was asking why, while the other was telling him he knew the answer. *But I don't have anything to feel guilty about,* he thought. *No one gave me anything, no one showed me how to make it out. I earned everything I ever got. So what if I'm going to make a lot of money? I deserve it.*

But how are you going to make the money? One of the voices asked. Have you ever considered that maybe you *are* a token? Ever thought that maybe you've gotten played by them while you were patting yourself on the back, that all the while you thought you were fooling them somehow, you were in fact exactly what they wanted you to be?

Lionel shook his head and rubbed his eyes. *I am a fucking token*, he thought with sudden anger. No matter how much I achieve, no matter how successful I become, it'll only be by virtue of their good graces that I do so. Yeah, sure, Lionel, come join our firm, we're happy to have you. You'll work 70 hours a week and we'll pay you good money, and we'll get credit for being diversified. It's a win-win situation, right Lionel?

But what else am I to do? Lionel asked the voices. *I want the money, it's important to me.* Why? The voices asked in unison. Why is it important that you make a lot of money?

Lionel knew the answer. It confirmed his worst fears and was the real reason he felt so much guilt. He wanted the money so they...white people, would view him the way he thought he viewed himself. But as he thought it through in his mind, Lionel realized, for the first time in his life, that if he truly believed himself to be worthy of his success, he wouldn't need white people to share that view in order to make it real.

His desire to go find Darnell all of a sudden made perfect sense, and became an urgency. Lionel packed his briefcase and walked out of the lecture hall. He charged out the front doors and down the steps to the sidewalk. He looked in the direction that Darnell had gone, but had no real concept as to how to even begin looking for the boy. He sat down on the steps with his bag between his knees.

*   *   *   *

Darnell left the McDonald's two blocks away rubbing his swollen belly. With the two dollars Lionel had given him, combined with the three dollars in change he'd collected earlier in the day, he'd been able to eat a number 4 meal: a quarter pounder with cheese, fries and a Coke. But best of all, he'd been able to supersize it, and he even had a little left over for a small vanilla shake for dessert.

It was the first full meal he'd eaten in two days, and he'd done so way too fast. By the time he had walked a block from the restaurant, his stomach began to reject what his eyes had been unable to. Desperate not to vomit, he had no choice but to run the fifteen blocks home to the only toilet he knew. He just prayed that no one would be there.

The Raymond Rosen housing projects were located on three acres of land at 23rd and Edgely Streets in North Philly, its five high rise towers having been built in the mid-sixties. Each building was eleven stories high, with two buildings each facing each other across a courtyard, and the fifth building sitting at one end of that courtyard. The courtyard had evolved over time, or devolved as it were, and was infested with broken glass, discarded condoms, and all the other detritus of an indifferent human existence. Originally conceived as a playground, with a grassy area, jungle gym, and swing sets, it was now a dust bowl, with the children's playthings nothing more than the skeletal remains of a long ago lost dream.

The courtyard at the Rosen projects was perhaps the most dangerous two thousand square feet of open land in the city. Drug dealers and whores openly plied their trades, and young men boldly brandished guns of every size and caliber, which guns could be heard at any time during the night and day, any night and any day.

It was a place so foreboding and desolate that the police rarely, if ever, even bothered to investigate or patrol. This was due in part to the danger, but mostly to the acknowledgment that no amount of policing would ever make this place safe. The people who lived there then were left literally to the wolves, forced to fend for themselves in their own little war-torn part of the world.

Darnell's life was not really all that much more different from many of the young boys growing up in the projects. School was an afterthought to every day survival. Math and spelling and history had little relevance to an eleven year old boy whose challenges of every day living included finding enough food to survive and avoiding being raped or shot.

But Darnell didn't need school. He was going to make it out of this life because even at his young age and his slight build, he was already becoming something of a playground legend. At the outdoor courts at 23rd and Diamond Streets, he was at first scoffed at by much bigger and more talented players.

Gradually though, he showed everyone that no matter how small he was, he was so strong with the ball when he handled it that it could not be taken from him. He was too short to really get a decent shot off, so he made his reputation as a passer, someone who always got the ball to the guys who could score. Everyone wants shots on the playground, so when you find a guy who can play who's willing to give up the rock, he gets picked.

The basketball court was the only place in the world where Darnell had begun to be accepted by anybody, and where he was actually shown a modicum of respect. To a boy whose life was as devoid of both of those things as Darnell's was, they were like drugs, and he came to crave them so much that every waking moment was spent dribbling the ball, handling it, and making it a part of his body, so that when he went to the courts, he could get his fix.

The feeling he got when he played basketball, that realization that there was something he could do with his life that would make other people like and respect him, was the same exact realization that led so many young men in those projects to turn to selling drugs and joining gangs. For most of them, those were the only options available to achieve an identity.

At that moment, of course, Darnell was thinking about none of these things. His only priority was to get to the bathroom, quickly. He had eaten too much, too fast, and now he had to go. Unfortunately, no one was about to let such a raggedy looking young boy just use their toilet, including the McDonald's where he'd just eaten. His only choice was to sprint back to the apartment and pray no one was home.

Taking as much care as he could not to be noticed as he ran through the courtyard, Darnell entered the front door of the Northwest building, which led into a small vestibule. The smell of urine and vomit and trash was overpowering, but Darnell, having known no other smell, didn't notice. There was a broken elevator to the left of the vestibule, and the stairs were to the right.

If the courtyard was the most dangerous piece of open land in the city, the stairways of these projects were the most dangerous pieces of enclosed property anywhere. Darkened long ago by lights that had either been burned out or broken, and never replaced, the only light that came in was through the small barred windows at every landing. Even on a sunny day, the stairs were dimly lit at best. The only people who traversed the steps alone at night were the very people who made the steps dangerous in the first place.

Left with no choice but to go it alone, Darnell charged up the ten flights of stairs, clutching his ball and trying not to crap his pants. He raced past a couple of young teenagers having sex on the fifth floor landing, and an elderly man apparently passed out on the eighth. He burst through the fire door at the end of the tenth floor hallway and ran to the door of his mother's apartment.

Breathing heavily and sweating, Darnell put his ear to the door. It was quiet. His mother was either out, or asleep. And there didn't appear to be anyone else around. Quietly, Darnell opened the door. It was almost never locked (there was nothing in the place to steal). He took a few steps inside the darkened room, the fading sunlight providing only a hint of dusty light. Hearing nothing, Darnell let out a huge breath of relief and started towards the bathroom.

"Where you been boy?"

Darnell froze and promptly defecated all over himself.

"Goddamn!" yelled a shirtless Clark as he sprung from his position on the bed where he had been sleeping. "You filthy motherfucker!"

Clark punched the boy hard in the face, which sent him sprawling across the room and smearing feces all over his legs and the floor.

Clark eyed the boy with disgust as he put on a tee-shirt that barely covered his huge belly. He had not been around for months, and he sniffed the air with contempt, like he'd almost forgotten how badly it stank.

"I was waitin' for you, bitch," he snarled drunkenly at Darnell, who had curled himself up into a ball in the corner.

Clark stumbled across the room and stood over the boy watching him for a few seconds, his enormous left hand rubbing his crotch. Without a word, Clark unzipped his jeans, pulled out his penis, and began peeing on Darnell. The boy was too scared to move, and instead, simply closed his eyes and waited for it to be over.

When it was, Clark zipped up his pants and left without a word.

For the longest time Darnell simply lay there in the dark, covered in his own feces and Clark's urine, blood streaming down from the cut over his eye that had been inflicted by the punch. Knowing why Clark had really been waiting for him, the boy felt some mild relief with the realization that it could have been worse, but other than that he had no real conscious thought.

In a daze, he finally got up, the basketball still in his grip. He found himself wandering down the steps. The darkness didn't stop him. Maybe it was the wretched smell emanating from his body, maybe it was fate. But no one bothered the boy as he aimlessly shuffled down the ten flights to the courtyard, nor was he accosted as he wandered back towards Temple's campus. He wasn't going anywhere, he was just going.

Lionel had been sitting on the steps in front of the law school for about an hour and a half. He ignored the people going up and down the stairs, even some who would occasionally say hello. All he could think about was the boy…and himself. He was a young man struggling suddenly with who he really was. He had been so sure for so long that he knew the answer to that question, that he had stopped asking it.

And now he wasn't sure at all. **Lionel** felt intense fear rising in his belly, the kind you feel when standing **too** close to a dangerous precipice. The fear not just that you might **fall**, but that you might jump.

It was clear in his mind, the cliff over which he looked. Behind him, on safe and solid ground, was the path upon which he had embarked so long ago as a child. The path illuminated by the white skin of the people who had allowed him to travel it. Over that cliff though, was uncertainty. Down there somewhere, he suddenly felt sure, was the opportunity to forge a path of his own making, of his own design.

Each option held the allure of being able to give Lionel most of what he wanted, so he felt as if he really couldn't make a bad choice. But what kept luring his mind back over the cliff was the possibility that, if he jumped, the fall alone could offer him everything he wanted, and more, but only if he demonstrated that he was worthy.

In the penumbra of his consciousness, Lionel became aware of the boy. Perhaps it was the smell, maybe it was fate. Whatever it was, at the moment when Darnell came shuffling past him on the street that evening, Lionel made the decision that would change both of their lives forever.

He jumped.

*   *   *   *

For many years after that horrible first night, Lionel would wonder what it was that made him take the boy into his heart. It was only after many, many sessions with the therapist they would eventually see together that he realized his true motivation.

Lionel had created a life plan for himself, the sole goal of which was his own personal aggrandizement. Be it through the accumulation of wealth, professional accomplishment, or both, Lionel's dreams were about one person...Lionel Cooper. The feeling which had been growing inside of him for months leading up to that afternoon though, was more than just guilt for his selfishness. In fact, his selfishness didn't really trouble him all that much. Rather, it was the subconscious realization that even if his wildest dreams came true, he'd still be the loneliest person on the planet. Having been alone for his entire life, sometimes by choice, but most times not, Lionel needed more than anything to not be alone any longer.

But most of all, Lionel needed to feel essential to another human being's life. He needed someone to think of him and know that they couldn't live without him. Sure he was loved by people, maybe he was even important in the life of some. But he knew in his heart, without ever consciously thinking it, that if he were to die, no one's world would be destroyed. And there was no one out there who felt for him the kind of desperate love the starving man has for a morsel of food, or the drowning man for the life preserver.

For a man inclined to selfishness, it was the most self-centered emotion possible. Yet it resulted in the single greatest act of selflessness he would ever endeavor.

The smell of urine and feces about the boy was overpowering, but he seemed not to notice. Darnell was in a fog as he shuffled aimlessly past the law school steps, clutching the basketball rigidly beneath his reed-thin right arm, his dirty, wet tank top hanging listlessly along the sides of his distended belly.

"Hey," Lionel started to say as he rose from the steps, but the word got caught in his throat. He had to lick his lips and swallow hard before he could actually speak.

"Hey, Darnell."

The boy stopped walking but did not turn. Very few people ever actually called him by name and he sometimes forgot what it was altogether.

Lionel tapped him on the shoulder and smiled when their eyes met. His heart almost broke. The boy's eyes were as wide as saucer cups, and the richest shade of brown Lionel had ever seen. They were soft and vulnerable and terrified, like a beautiful baby seal who waits helplessly on the shore to be clubbed to death by marauding bands of whalers. The boy's helplessness served only to fortify Lionel's newfound resolve.

"You okay, little man?" Lionel asked, his huge hand still touching the boy's shoulder.

Darnell continued to look up at Lionel, but there was no hint that he recognized him from earlier that afternoon.

The smell of the boy seemed to get worse. It was obvious he had not bathed in quite some time, and his teeth were dingy from lack of brushing. Lionel wanted to take the boy back to his place just to get him cleaned up, but he knew how it would look if he suggested that. After all, a grown man picking up a little boy on the street and inviting him back for a shower…not a good idea.

"You hungry?"

Darnell still hadn't spoken. He nodded his head no, the look in his eyes though was transitioning from fear to confusion.

Lionel smiled brightly. "Well, I am, and I hate eating alone. I'm gonna' grab a hoagie and a soda from that truck right over there. You feel like joinin' me?"

Before Darnell could answer, Lionel kind of nudged him along as they walked the few feet to one of the food trucks lined up along Broad Street.

"Yo," Lionel said to the man bent over inside the moving kitchen. "Lemme' get an Italian Hoagie with oil and Provolone." He looked down at his bedraggled companion. "You sure you don't want anything?"

Darnell didn't respond. Rather, he simply stared hungrily at the row of TastyKakes hanging alongside the truck. Although he'd eaten heartily at McDonald's just a few hours earlier, his malnourished body craved food whenever it was available.

Lionel laughed at Darnell's look and plucked a French Apple Pie, a pack of Jelly Krimpets, and a package of mini-donuts, and handed all of them to Darnell. He took his hoagie, grabbed two Sprites from the ice box, and paid. He then went back over to the steps and sat down.

Darnell stood by the truck for awhile, not quite sure how to react. He obviously wanted more than anything to eat the snacks in his hand. But Lionel thought that he seemed confused by the generosity. Had no one ever done anything nice for this kid, he wondered. Rather than continue to stare at the boy though, Lionel unwrapped his hoagie and took a big bite.

Finally, Darnell slowly shuffled over to the steps and sat down a few feet away from Lionel. The big man pretended not to notice as he chowed down. Darnell tentatively tore open the Krimpets and eyed Lionel, clearly waiting for the catch. When Lionel said nothing, Darnell opened the package all the way and literally inhaled the three oblong Jelly-filled snacks.

"Goddamn!" laughed Lionel through a mouthful of hoagie. "You still got any fingers?"

Darnell quickly checked, and smiled. As quickly as it appeared though, the smile was gone, and the boy seemed ashamed to have let the expression occur and hung his head to stare at the sidewalk. "Why you give me this?" He asked softly without looking over.

Surprised to hear the boy's voice, Lionel shrugged and said, "I don't know. Looked like you needed it."

Darnell looked over. "Thanks."

Lionel smiled. "My pleasure…Now, I know you're thirsty, and that Sprite ain't getting' any colder."

The boy fought a smile and grabbed the soda. He chugged like a drunken sailor for a few seconds, then let out a huge burp.

Lionel cracked up. "How in the hell can such a little body produce a sound that loud?"

The boy smiled proudly this time, glad to have impressed his new-found benefactor, and the two shared a laugh.

The smile was all it took to seal the deal in Lionel's brain. "Darnell, where do you live?" he asked, ready to do something to start helping this boy immediately.

As soon as the question was asked, the smile vanished and the boy chewed his bottom lip. He looked at the food and drink still remaining and wondered if he could grab them quickly enough to run.

The change was obvious to Lionel and he saw that Darnell was looking to get away from the conversation. He had to make the boy understand, and quickly, what his motives were. Lionel leaned over and clasped Darnell on the shoulder. The man's hand literally engulfed the entire upper left side of the boy's body. Lionel lowered his head to try and look into Darnell's eyes, but the boy avoided the eye contact.

"Darnell," he said softly, "I know you don't know me. If I was you, I'd be really suspicious of some dude buying me food and asking me where I live and stuff. And you've got no reason to believe this...but I want to help you. You seem a little lost to me, and when I was young I almost got lost too. But people I didn't even know helped me find my way. They gave me food and a place to live and sent me to school, all because it made them feel good to do that. I know that's a difficult concept to understand, but I want to help you in the same way."

Darnell wasn't buying it. Of course, he had no frame of reference. No one, let alone an adult, had ever even treated him like a human being. Why would this complete stranger do so?

The look on the boy's face was easily read by Lionel. He wondered briefly if he should even bother. *What the hell am I doing?* He thought. But for some strange reason that he could not understand, that thought was quickly pushed out of his mind by the growing determination to make this boy trust him.

"C'mon," he said, "What do you have to lose?"

Perhaps it was the simple realization that this man could do nothing worse to him than had already been done. Or maybe it was the sliver of hope which exists in all human beings, that no matter how dire the situation there is a chance things might work out. Whatever it was, Darnell decided to let Lionel walk him home.

Lionel had begun his life in the projects and he'd seen firsthand the depravity that is bred by the hopelessness of these places. Given the boy's physical appearance, Lionel expected the worst. Somehow, Darnell's home exceeded his wildest expectations.

The dusk of early evening had crept over the city by the time they arrived, and the pitch-black stairwell awaited. Lionel was too street-smart not be wary, but he was also not afraid. "Act like you been there" had been a motto of his for a long time, and it was an attitude he found worked as well at the country club as it did in the projects. The secret to success, he truly believed, was realizing that ninety-nine percent of the people in the world have no idea whether or not who they are is who they should be. When confronted with someone who appears not to have that same doubt, most people are intimidated. This was as true of CEO's as it was of gangsters.

Darnell was impressed with how Lionel bounded up the darkened stairs as if he had not a care in the world, and how he was left alone by the stairwell denizen on the way up. Darnell found himself staying as close as possible to the older man as they made their way to the tenth floor.

When they reached the tenth floor and started down the hall towards the apartment in which Darnell slept, Lionel really had no idea what to expect. The boy had barely said two words to him. Even worse, though, was that Lionel hardly knew what he would say to whomever was in the apartment. He had not decided in his own mind exactly what it was he was willing, or able to do for this kid.

A red light seeped out from under the crack of the door in front of which Darnell stopped. "Is this it?" asked Lionel.

Darnell just nodded yes, but made no move to enter. All he did was reach up to grab Lionel's hand, which practically swallowed the boy's. Great loves are formed in an instant. This small gesture of the boy's made Lionel feel physically stronger than he ever had in his life, and made him want to use very ounce of that strength to protect this little boy with the old man's eyes. Lionel gripped Darnell's hand tightly and knocked firmly on the door. It wasn't locked, or even closed all the way. As Lionel knocked, the door creaked open about halfway. A low voice could be heard along with muffled grunts.

"Hello? Anybody home?" asked Lionel to the darkness as he slowly entered the room.

Nobody answered. As Lionel stepped forward, his grip on Darnell's hand tightened and his eyes hardened. In the corner was what appeared to be a woman, her hair a mottled mess down her back, completely naked and on all fours. She was so painfully skinny that she looked almost like a corpse. The man on his knees behind her was almost as skinny, and in the pale red light which surrounded them, they looked like two skeletons. Neither even appeared to notice Lionel and the boy. Or if they had, they didn't care.

Horrified for the boy, Lionel looked away in disgust, and in the darkness tried to see what other horrors abounded in this place. He saw that the mattress on the floor appeared to be the only furniture. He saw no refrigerator, no television, and trash strewn everywhere.

He was furious. "Is that your mother?" he asked through gritted teeth,

Darnell nodded yes.

Lionel let go of the boy's hand and took two giant steps towards the mattress. He raised his size fourteen Italian loafer and with all his might, kicked the skinny man in the ribs.

"Get the fuck outta here!" he screamed at the man who was writhing in pain on the floor. The man didn't even look up. He simply crawled away and into the hallway like the wounded jackal that he was. Darnell's mother just rolled over onto her back, barely conscious of what had happened. Lionel looked down on her in disgust.

He took out his wallet, extracted a business card and a hundred-dollar bill, and threw them both onto the mattress. "Your son is coming with me. If you want to speak with him or see him, call me at that number."

She offered no response, nor did Lionel wait for one. He grabbed Darnell's hand and pulled him from the apartment. They were down the stairs and blocks away before the mother even moved. When she did, it was to grab the money.

Clark had watched the entire scene unfold from the other room. He walked over to the mattress, picked up the card and read it. He then punched the woman in the face, knocking her unconscious. He put both the card and the hundred into his wallet. As far as anyone knew, that was the last time Darnell's mother was ever seen alive. No matter how it actually happened, it was Clark who killed her.

Darnell hadn't spoken a word since they left the projects. They caught the 33 bus which took them within a few blocks of Lionel's apartment in the Dorchester Building, at 20th and Walnut. Lionel ignored the horrified stare of the doorman, as well as that of several co-tenants in the lobby. It wasn't until Lionel was actually putting the key into the door that Darnell finally spoke.

"What are you gonna' do to me?" he asked quietly.

Lionel knelt down beside the boy and looked up to him. He bit back tears as he looked into Darnell's eyes. "I'm not going to do anything to you," he said, the lump in his throat growing, "I'm never going to let anyone ever do anything to you again."

CHAPTER 4

▼

"STEEERRRIIIKE!"

John Ryan exploded from his seat in the front row of bleachers along the first base line. "Yo, Ump! No way that's a strike. C'mon, open your eyes!"

Linda Ryan covered her eyes and lowered her head while simultaneously tugging on her husband's shirttail. "Will you please sit down," she whispered. "He's nervous enough without you screaming."

Ryan sat down, but not without an angry glare in the direction of the umpire. Several of the other fathers sitting around the Ryans gave him supportive, albeit covert nods showing that they agreed with his assessment of the umpire's call.

"STEEERRRIIIKE TWO!"

Ryan practically leapt from his aluminum seat. "OH MY GOD! You can't be serious! That's a baseball bat in hands, not a nine iron!"

"Yeah, Ump, whassamatta' wif you! Open yer' eyes!" yelled the little girl sitting next to Ryan's wife. Her hair was blindingly blonde, and she had the most perfect set of crooked baby teeth. Her chubby cheeks, red from the sun, were spread wide by a proud smile.

"That is it." Linda turned to her left and looked sternly at her daughter, Kelly. "Young lady, you do not yell at the umpire. He deserves your respect." She turned to her right and yanked her husband back down into his seat. "Are you satisfied? You've taught your daughter how to be a cretin just like you."

Ryan looked at his wife and smiled broadly. He reached across her lap, grabbed his daughter and pulled her squealing and giggling over to him. He gave her some light noogies and said, "Whassamatta wif *you*?"

Mrs. Ryan shook her head, pretended to be annoyed, and turned her attention back to the game. "C'mon, honey, you can do it!" she shouted to her son.

"Jesus Christ, Babe," John whispered to his wife. "You don't call a twelve-year old boy 'honey' in front of his friends. You're gonna' get his ass kicked."

She brushed him aside and concentrated on the field. Linda Ryan came to every one of her son's games, whatever the sport, and she promised herself after each one that she'd never come to another. It was too nerve-wracking.

Joey Ryan stood tall in the batter's box and held his hand up towards the pitcher, just like he'd seen his dad do a million times in the F.O.P. softball leagues. With his back foot he kicked at the hard dirt, which on the somewhat dilapidated field, did not yield much of a foothold and served only to raise a small dust-storm. Pretending not to notice it, the batter resolutely dug into his stance like Mark McGwire, his skinny left arm tucked close to his side. He brought the bat above his shoulders and glared malevolently at the pitcher. The one thing he was determined not to do was strike out in front of his dad. And given the way the ump was calling the balls and strikes, he was pretty much set on swinging at anything.

The pitch was low and outside. Joey closed his eyes and swung as hard as he could. He heard the crack of the bat before he felt the sensation in his hands of having hit the ball perfectly. As he sprinted towards first base, he could see out of the corner of his eye his parents and little sister jumping up and down wildly on the flimsy aluminum bleachers. As he rounded second, he saw the third base coach swinging his arm excitedly in a wide circle. He had no idea where the ball had gone and all sound seemed to have ceased to exist. Joey rounded third and sprinted towards the plate, his arms and legs pumping as hard as they possibly could. Barely conscious of the throng of his teammates crowding into the opening between the dugout and the metal cage surrounding home plate, he closed his eyes and slid. In the billowing cloud of dust he saw the umpire spread his arms wide. Only then did the happy roar of twenty-five little league parents and their fifteen sons come crashing over him like a wave. Joey Ryan jumped into his teammates' arms, a hero for the first time in his life. He didn't even know that the right fielder was still running after the ball across the basketball courts on the far side of the playground.

The whole Ryan family was hugging each other and any other Falcon parent within arm's reach. "Way to go, Joey! Atta, Boy!" yelled John, beaming with pride. Linda pumped her fists like she'd just won game seven of the World Series, and Kelly just jumped up and down, happy to have a reason to yell wildly with no repercussions from Mom or Dad.

"That's the way to swing the bat, boy!" a gravelly voice along the third-base line boomed loudly above all others.

Amidst the celebration in the bleachers, Linda's smile momentarily left her face as she caught her husband's ear. "I thought you said he wasn't coming."

Ryan pulled his wife into an even tighter hug. "C'mon, sweetie," he soothed while throwing wink at his buddy. "It's the championship game and Joey is his Godson. There was no way he'd miss it. Besides, I promised him he could come as a reward for how well he's been doing with his rehab."

Linda Ryan sighed deeply and pulled away. She located her boy amongst the swath of his teammates and beamed a smile, which he returned covertly through the unruly mop of thick, black hair that he inherited from his father, and which no baseball cap seemed able to contain.

Every time she looked at her son, Linda Ryan's heart melted. At twelve years old, he was the spitting image of his father. The most piercing set of blue eyes, the hair, and a short, wiry frame coiled with energy. Like his father, Joey Ryan was a tremendous athlete, but unfortunately for any potential professional athletic career, he had also inherited his father's height, which is to say his lack thereof. Linda knew that her son was now at the age where his advanced athleticism and coordination were becoming surpassed by the sheer size and strength of his classmates, a fact which her husband was determined to ignore. He still expected Joey to be the best athlete on the field and there was no excuse for anything less.

John Ryan had never let his own physical shortcomings prevent him from becoming a highly decorated cop and detective, and he simply expected the same drive from his only son. As only a mother can though, Linda keenly appreciated how difficult this was for Joey, not just because of his size, but because of his burning desire to please the man whom he viewed as the world's biggest and strongest.

She scooped her squealing daughter up in one arm and along with her husband, the Ryan family made their way down the bleachers to congratulate the hero. Her heart was so all at once full of pride, relief, happiness, and love, that a few tears snuck down her smooth cheeks.

Joey Ryan sprinted towards the family and jumped into his parents' arms. "Did you see that shot, Dad? Man, I never hit a ball that far before!"

"I know!" John laughed happily as he squeezed his son mightily. "I am so proud of you." Ryan lowered the boy to the ground. He too fought tears. "Go say hi to your Uncle Joe and then we'll all go get some pizza to celebrate."

With that, the boy wheeled and sprinted towards Joe Fullem. He attempted to jump up into the man's arms, but experienced the same difficulty Sir Edmund Hillary must have encountered during his historic ascent of Mount Everest. Even in his current debilitated state, Joe Fullem was a mountain of a man, with a huge round belly, big, muscular arms, and a thick, bald skull that always appeared sunburned. He bent down, and with his free hand roughly ruffled Joey's hair. His other hand he kept firmly planted on the cane he still needed to walk.

"That's the best goddamn hit I ever saw, boy," he growled. "Just like your Uncle Joe taught ya'."

Fullem looked up and saw Mrs. Ryan approaching warily. "Hey, Linda," he said sweetly as the rest of the Ryan clan approached. The big man's eyes twinkled mischievously. He was convinced that deep down, despite everything she said about him, Linda Ryan really loved him.

"Joseph," said Linda Ryan as politely as possible.

John Ryan rolled his eyes and shook his friend's hand. "Chip off the old block, huh?"

Fullem gave a loud, sarcastic laugh. "Yeah, right. You've never hit a ball that far in your life, much less with the game on the line, and forget about ever doing it in the championship." Fullem gave his former partner a friendly punch in the arm.

"Easy, now," said Ryan as he rubbed his arm. "You wanna' get some pizza with us to celebrate?" Ryan asked the question quickly and without looking at his wife. Joe Fullem had not often in his life turned down food, but one look at Linda Ryan's expression when she heard her husband make the invitation was enough to make him do so.

"Nah, I'm not hungry. You guys go, enjoy. I'll see you later." He turned to Joey Ryan and smushed his hat on his head. "I'm real proud of you, buddy, you did great!" He then leaned forward and gave Kelly a kiss on the cheek. "I'm proud of you too, kiddo."

Kelly smiled broadly. "Thanks, Uncle Joe," she beamed.

Fullem then gave Linda a smack on the butt but he moved his face away quickly enough to avoid the slap she attempted to throw. "I'm proud of you too!" He said with a Cheshire grin and limped away laughing. John Ryan and his children enjoyed the moment immensely, and only stopped laughing with Linda's withering look.

*   *   *   *

"I don't want him around the kids anymore."

John Ryan looked over his glasses at his wife who lay reading in bed next to him. "Well that only took six hours," he said as he lay down his case notes on a homicide, the trial for which John was preparing to testify.

"I didn't want to say anything at all. I know how much they love him," said Linda Ryan, still looking at her novel but seeing an entirely different subject.

"And how much he loves them," her husband reminded her.

Instead of responding, Linda just snorted. Joe Fullem was the rare subject that the Ryans vehemently disagreed about, and one of the few things over which they argued at all.

John took off his glasses and rubbed his eyes. "You know, you can snort all you want, but that man would literally give his life for the kids, me, *and* you. You may question certain things about him, but do not ever question that." John felt himself getting hot already, and the discussion had barely even begun.

Linda was angry too. She had felt strongly for a long time that the man was a bad influence on her children and it had always made her uncomfortable when he was around them. She had kept quiet for so long because she admired her husband's loyalty to the man, and had acquiesced in John's personal rehabilitation and reclamation project that had literally brought Fullem back from the dead. But he appeared to have mostly recovered, from his physical injuries anyway, and Linda could hold her tongue no longer about what she truly felt given what she knew Fullem to be capable of.

As angry as she was though, she had to tread lightly. Linda Ryan knew her husband better than anyone else in the world, and she loved him fiercely. He was kind and patient and gentle and loving and handsome. He was almost perfect as far as she was concerned. For the life of her, though, she could not and had not ever understood her husband's devotion and loyalty to his friend. John had told her many times the story of how Fullem had literally saved Ryan's life. But as grateful as she was for that, Linda was unwilling to excuse Fullem for the monstrous act of violence she, along with the rest of the country, had witnessed him commit.

"Hon, you know as well as I do that the man is a violent racist."

Ryan rolled his eyes and let out an exasperated sigh. "Christ. Not this again."

"You can roll your eyes all you want. I still get ill just thinking about what he did to that kid. You always defend him, but I think you're being a bit naïve, John."

Ryan shook his head and chuckled with irritation. "That's such a funny word coming from someone who's always had the luxury of not having to live in the real world."

Now it was on. "Yeah, I guess you're right. I guess I don't see babies left out on doorsteps by teenagers, or kids who are so beaten and battered by foster parents that you can't even recognize their faces, and I guess I don't have to explain to kids every day why their mother or father doesn't want them, why they're worthless human beings. I guess you're right. Only big bad cops know what it's like in the 'real world'. Thank God for them."

Ryan said nothing at first. His wife was an extraordinary woman. He had truly 'over achieved', as friends had often pointed out in jest over the years. Beautiful and blonde, with the brightest smile, Linda Ryan could have made a career as a model. Instead she chose to spend her days as an adoption social worker, helping kids who no one wants find homes. She was smarter than Ryan, and he knew it. She had the infuriating ability to say things which to most people would sound only mildly insulting, but to Ryan were deeply offensive and attacked him exactly where he was vulnerable. It was a talent he did not possess, and the main reason he hadn't ever won an argument with his wife. She was simply too good at it.

But he would never stop trying. "That's right, sweetheart." He always called her sweetheart when he was angry. "You should thank God for cops. And I got news for you. That 'kid' that Joe beat the shit out of had a criminal record longer than my arm. He's an animal. He raped an eighty-three year old woman while her husband, who that mutt had knocked out of his wheelchair, was forced to watch. He then left both of them there to die on the floor of their kitchen. The only bad things about that beating were that it was caught on tape, that Joe didn't kill the fucker, and that he had to lose his job for it. Joe's life has been destroyed, and that kid's driving a Lexus and living the high life because the city paid him off."

Linda shook her head. "What that kid had done is horrible and he deserved to be punished. But by a judge and a jury, who sit and hear the evidence against him. That's our system and it's the only way we can ever hope to live in a civilized society. Besides, you know as well as I do that the little bastard was acquitted because of what Fullem did to him."

John laughed out loud. "Bullshit. You and I both know why that mutt got off, and it had nothin' to do with Joe. And where did you ever get the impression that we live in a civilized society? You of all people know damn well we don't. I got some bad news for you, sweetheart. I've thrown my share of punches at suspects. I've not played by the rules all the time when I knew the system would end up letting a guy get off if I did.

"Do you know how many guilty guys I've arrested who've been let go because some scumbag lawyer gets evidence tossed? You're telling me that because I only wait ten seconds, instead of fifteen as the law requires, before kicking a door in, that the six pounds of coke I find on some mope's coffee table has to be suppressed? That's some system you place your faith in, Pookie." He called her Pookie when he was really mad.

Linda held back whatever comment was about to come flying reflexively out of her mouth and took a deep breath. "Look, I don't want to debate this with you. We always end up fighting about something else whenever we talk about Joe. The bottom line is, the man's a racist and I do not want that kind of influence around my children."

It drove him crazy when she called them 'her' children. But it was late and his heart wasn't in the fight. He knew he'd never convince her that he was right, and he knew that she'd never convince him that she was right. "I don't want to fight about this anymore. The honest truth is that I don't really care either way if he's a racist or if he's not a racist.

"The man has saved my life on more than one occasion, and is the one person in the world, outside of this family, that I know I can count on one hundred percent. He's never been anything but wonderful to our children, in fact he dotes on them. He's smart enough to know that his personal views are just that, and I know he would never, ever, try to foist them onto the kids."

Linda didn't want to fight either. She rolled towards her husband and put her arm across his chest. "All right, let me say this last thing and then I'm done. It's not that I think he'll have them in some shack in upstate Pennsylvania wearing brown shirts and arm bands and goose stepping down Main Street."

John let go an involuntary chuckle.

"The problem is that when he's around them, he can't help himself from saying 'nigger' or 'rooster' or 'schwoogie'. And kids pick up on that, especially when it's someone who they look up to, like their 'Uncle Joe', and they think that that's the right way to talk and think. That's what worries me."

John raised his left arm so that he could put it around his wife's back. Softly, he said, "Do you know why I know he'll never say anything like that around the kids?"

Linda shook her head no.

"Because no matter what he says about black people in anger, or in jokes, no matter how loud he might argue that they're an inferior people, he knows that he's wrong. We've talked about it. He admits that the way he feels emotionally about black people is intellectually wrong and that white people are just as bad as black people, or good, however you want to look at it. And not only does he know it's wrong, he knows full well that it makes him look stupid and uneducated when he says racist things. Because of that, he's ashamed of the way he feels, and he's embarrassed by it. He loves those kids too much, and values too deeply how they look at him, to ever look stupid or uneducated in front of them. That's why I'm not concerned."

As she lay there with her head on her husband's chest, Linda thought about what he had just said. She took great pride in her marriage and in the relationship itself. One of the things she felt made the union so successful, and truly happy, was that they really did listen to each other. John had just given her a new slant on an old story, and if it was true, if Fullem really did know that his views were fundamentally wrong, maybe she couldn't simply file him away in a certain category, and having done so, ignore him completely. It was something for her to think about.

For his part, John hoped what he said would end the discussion. He had certainly meant it and truly believed it. But what concerned him were the things that Linda didn't know about Joe Fullem. Either way, John Ryan knew the true measure of the man, and it was good. There was no one he trusted more.

CHAPTER 5

▼

"You need any money?"

Joe Fullem looked with a bemused eye upon his much shorter best friend. "Johnnyboy, would you stop worrying about me, please. I'm okay."

John Ryan pursed his lips and stared at the worn Formica table in Amici's Diner. The two men had shared many meals at Amici's, even after they had been partners patrolling the hardscrabble streets of Kensington, specifically the eastern Philadelphia neighborhood affectionately nicknamed "the badlands." Despite the fact that Ryan no longer lived anywhere close to the diner, they still met there regularly.

Fullem took a swig from his espresso and smiled. "I appreciate the offer. I do. But I'm okay financially, so really, you don't have to worry about me."

It's a funny thing about male friendships, especially very close, long-standing ones. The better two men know each other, and the more they trust one another, the less they want to appear vulnerable to each other. Women of course are exactly the opposite. They judge the depth and genuineness of their friendships by just how vulnerable they can safely appear in front of one another.

Perhaps this trait of men goes back to the relationships most had with their fathers. No son ever wants to look like a failure or show any weakness in front of Dad. Implicitly, boys are taught that to be vulnerable is to be both a failure and weak. And even if a man should feel vulnerable, the last person he would ever show that to is another man in whose eyes he wants to be seen only as strong and successful.

"Okay, I'll stop asking…So what are you doing for money now?" Considering the favor he wanted to ask of Fullem, Ryan had to know.

Fullem just shrugged as he accepted a corned beef Reuben sandwich with a huge side of onion rings from the waitress. "Don't forget the chocolate shake, sweetheart," he said with a wink to the septuagenarian server.

Ryan just shook his head in amazement at the sheer volume of food Fullem was able to put away.

Fullem ignored Ryan's look and took a huge bite of the sandwich, which he barely chewed before swallowing and diving back in for more. Within seconds, the entire sandwich was a distant memory, and the onion rings were right behind. If it had been any other human being in the world, Ryan would have thought his question was being evaded. But he'd shared enough meals with Joe Fullem to know that the man ate like an animal, and there was no talking when food was on the table.

"You know, the usual bullshit. Security work, mostly part-time. No big deal."

"Sounds kinda' boring," said Ryan worriedly. "You might need something a little more challenging, something to keep your mind occupied."

Fullem shook his massive head from side to side. "Not me, amigo. I had my share of challenges. All I wanna' do now is lay low and relax."

Ryan was skeptical. "You don't know how to relax. You forget who you're talkin' to. I'm the guy who was on the streets with you back in the day."

"No, you forget who you're talking to. The only reason you got to walk the streets at all was because of who was walkin' next to you."

Both men shared a knowing smile. It was true. Ryan had only been a cop for two years when he was thrown into a squad car with Joe Fullem. Even though the big man had only been on the force a little bit longer than Ryan, he had by that time already earned the reputation as being the toughest and meanest cop in Philly.

It had taken exactly ten minutes before Fullem challenged the manhood of his diminutive new partner. It had taken exactly ten minutes and one second for Ryan to punch Fullem in the head. In that moment, three things happened: John Ryan broke three bones in his right hand; Joe Fullem felt a slight twinge of discomfort in his left temple; and a lifelong friendship was sparked.

They partnered together for four years. Fullem not only taught Ryan how to be a great cop, he literally saved Ryan's life, and in doing so, changed the course of both of their careers. They were doing a foot patrol on Kensington Avenue when Ryan saw a corner drug buy. It was hardly an unusual sight in that neighborhood, but Ryan was too stupid to realize that only the winnable fights were the ones worth engaging in. He sprinted towards the dealer, expecting the man to run. That didn't happen.

When Ryan began to tussle with the much bigger dealer, Fullem charged in and got between the two. The dealer was physically almost as big as Fullem, which was scary enough, but he was also strung out on PCP, and possessed the freakish strength only that drug can endow a human being with. Ryan never even saw the knife, but Fullem did, and moving more quickly than his size should have allowed, Fullem slid in front of his partner, allowing all ten inches of the rusty blade to be plunged into his chest.

Unfortunately for the dealer, he didn't kill Fullem. With the knife's hilt sticking out of his massive chest, the enraged behemoth literally threw the dealer face first into a concrete wall. Any other man in any other state would have been rendered unconscious, if not killed immediately. But with his PCP-fueled resolve, the dealer simply bounced off the wall, ignored the blood and mottled mass of bone which had been his face, and charged back at Fullem. It was in this moment that the legend of Joe Fullem was truly born.

As the dealer barreled blindly towards him, Fullem reached up to his chest, yanked out the knife, and promptly plunged it into the left eyeball of the dealer. The very large, very high dealer was killed instantly. It had happened so fast that Ryan barely had time to understand what he had just seen. For his part, Fullem simply picked up his radio and calmly asked for a body bag and an ambulance. He spent six weeks recovering at Temple University Hospital, three in an infection-induced coma.

Newspapers around the country ran with the story. At first the stories focused on Fullem's heroism and bravery, and incomprehensible toughness. But as reporters asked more questions, they began to hear stories about Fullem that changed the complexion of the story, literally. Stories about Fullem calling suspects niggers, telling black jokes, bragging about his ability to intimidate the toughest drug dealers with violence.

So what had started as "hero cop saves partner while defying death", became "racist white cop brutally kills defenseless black suspect." By the time Fullem was released from the hospital, he was lucky to still have a job. With one death defying act he had become a legend and a hero amongst his fellow officers, and at the same time a rogue cop who represented everything that was wrong and racist about the Philadelphia Police force. It caused great embarrassment to the department brass, and only the strength of the police union prevented Fullem from losing his job altogether. But the entire episode did effectively end any chance he would ever have at advancing in his career anywhere beyond beat cop.

For the longest time, Ryan felt personally responsible for Fullem's predicament. His way of assuaging his own guilt was to decline all opportunities for advancement in his own career. Ryan was prepared to remain a beat cop for the rest of his own career just to show Joe how much he sincerely appreciated what he had done. It was only after four such declinations over the course of a year that Fullem had finally threatened Ryan with bodily harm if he didn't take the offer of a promotion with East Detectives in the Narcotics Division.

After Ryan's ascension, Fullem was relegated to a solo foot beat in the badlands. It was an assignment designed specifically to drive him off the force. The rationale was that he would either quit or get killed, with no preference amongst his superiors for one alternative over the other. What the brass hadn't counted on though was the sheer force of Joe Fullem's will, his discipline, and his absolute determination never to lose. He decided that there was no way he would ever give them the satisfaction of either his death or his resignation. So, mostly out of spite for his superiors, he became super-cop.

Fullem created police mini-stations throughout the neighborhood. He personally visited every business owner along Kensington Avenue and gave them each his home telephone number with instructions to call him immediately for any trouble they were having. And he kept a most watchful eye on the elderly folks who had lived in Kensington for decades, having moved there in the twenties and thirties and never left.

One old Polish couple in particular, the Krinsky's, became almost like surrogate parents to Fullem, something he never had as a kid. Mrs. Krinsky was eighty-three and her husband almost ninety, yet they always made sure to have some snack or small meal prepared for Joe when he happened by. Their welfare became so important to Joe that he would come on his off days and take them to the grocery store and the pharmacist. They had a car, but after Mr. Krinsky had a stroke, which paralyzed the entire left side of his body and rendered him barely able to speak, he was confined to a wheelchair, and his wife refused to drive. So Joe took them everywhere they had to go.

It was the Krinsky home that seventeen year old Frank Cheeseboro decided to rob in the hopes that he might score enough cash or pawnable loot to feed a wildly uncontrollable crack habit. High as a kite, and while he was stealing what meager belongings the Krinsky's possessed, Cheeseboro decided on a whim to rape Mrs. Krinsky as well.

Her husband, who was less than five feet away while his wife of sixty-three years was raped and beaten, tried to defend her. He succeeded only in capsizing his wheelchair, leaving him prone and helpless, and most horribly, forced to watch the brutalization of the only woman he had ever loved.

Fullem found them lying dead on the kitchen floor three days later. Despite its physical impossibility, Mr. Krinsky had somehow managed to crawl across the floor and get close enough to his wife to clutch her hand. In all likelihood she was dead already when he did that. The coroner guessed that the old man lived for about two days in that position, unable to cry for help, all the while squeezing his wife's dead hand.

Whatever self-restraint had existed in Officer Joseph Fullem before the couple's death, died along with them. For two weeks an enraged and frothing Fullem terrorized the entire neighborhood. He beat and threatened every two-bit punk, street hustler and dope dealer he could catch. By the time he got Cheeseboro's name, everybody knew what Fullem would do.

Unfortunately, so did Cheeseboro. He may have been seventeen, but he was as street-smart as they come.

Knowing he had no chance of escaping Fullem, Cheeseboro had a friend stand across the street from Fullem's mini-station with a camcorder while Cheeseboro made a big show of surrendering. If it worked for Rodney King, Cheeseboro had schemed, maybe it would work for him. It was quite an event, with Cheeseboro walking across the four lanes of busy Tioga Street in the middle of a summer afternoon, hands in the air, shouting "I surrender, I surrender!"

The only station that showed the full seven-minute video was Channel Six Action News, and that was only once. After that a public outcry was heard denouncing the station for showing such graphic violence on television. Thereafter, only short clips were shown, and even then only with a sternly worded warning from the anchormen that what was about to be shown was incredibly violent.

The unedited video started out with Cheeseboro's back to the camera, his long arms straight up in the air. He can be heard yelling, "I surrender," over and over again. In what appears to be slow motion, but is not, Fullem emerges quietly from the darkened mini-station into the sun-drenched afternoon. His face is absolutely devoid of all expression. As Cheeseboro approaches, Fullem just stands in front of the doorway, motionless, his shirt sleeves rolled up onto massive forearms. He wears no gun belt nor is he carrying a nightstick.

"I'm here to surrender," Cheeseboro shouted over his shoulder towards the cameraman. "I don't want no trouble."

Of course trouble was exactly what he wanted. He expected Fullem to beat him up, that's why he was there. He figured the beating on tape would not only get him off the hook for his criminal case, but might make also make him some money in the process. What he hadn't counted on of course was the fact that every scary story which had ever been told about Fullem in the neighborhood, was absolutely true.

As quick as a cat, Fullem raises his left foot, clad in a steel toed work boot, and slams it with all his might in the exact middle of Cheeseboro's right shin.

"AAAAAHHHHH MY GOD MOTHERFUCKER JESUS FUCKING CHRIST MOTHERFUCKER!" screamed Cheeseboro in agony as he collapsed to the ground and stared in wide-eyed horror at the jagged piece of bloody bone sticking out of his lower leg.

Fullem's face is expressionless as he steps towards Cheeseboro, who is trying to wiggle backwards away. But he's in too much pain and Fullem is quickly standing over top of the prone criminal. Fullem lifts his leg again and stomps directly onto the exposed piece of bone.

"Oh Jesus," the cameraman is heard to mutter as the view goes out of control while he vomits. By the time he recovers and rights the camera, all that can be seen is a prone and unconscious Cheeseboro, and a few bystanders creeping in to get a closer look.

They scatter a split second later though as Fullem reemerges, this time with a ceramic coffee cup in his hand. He calmly walks over to

Cheeseboro's body, leans over him, and is heard clearly to say, "wake up, you fucking monkey." He then turns the cup and splashes obviously hot coffee into Cheeseboro's face. It's obviously hot because Cheeseboro immediately reaches up to his face, wailing in pain.

Over the course of the next two minutes and eleven seconds, Fullem slowly and methodically stomps, punches, spits on, and otherwise degrades the body of Frank Cheeseboro.

"Take that you filthy fucking nigger!" he screams, over and over again while raining vicious kicks and punches down on Cheeseboro's body and face. One hundred and fifteen total blows are inflicted, until finally, mercifully, three police cars roar up. The officers in the cars take their times approaching Fullem though, and it is determined that seven more kicks are inflicted between the time they arrive and the moment they pull Fullem away.

For even the most hardened veteran police officers, many of whom had seen intense combat in Vietnam and Korea, the entire video was almost impossible to watch. Fullem had methodically and with increasing fervor, broken every major bone in Frank Cheeseboro's body. The blood and exposed bone were only slightly more unsettling than the freakish cries of pain emanating from Cheeseboro's mouth. Miraculously, Fullem stopped short of killing him.

He was of course fired, and charged with attempted murder, aggravated assault, official oppression, and a litany of other crimes.

Cheeseboro's semen was found in the anus and mouth of Mrs. Krinsky, and he was charged with two counts of capital murder, rape, and robbery.

Because of the nationwide publicity garnered by the videotape, and threats of rioting and violence towards Fullem, his trial was moved to Pittsburgh. A jury of eight whites, three blacks and one Hispanic, acquitted Fullem by reason of temporary insanity.

Cheeseboro's lawyers did not seek a change of venue, so his trial was kept in Philadelphia. After six months in the hospital recovering from his injuries, his trial began. The Judge in the case admitted into evidence the beating by Fullem, and Cheeseboro was acquitted by a jury of nine blacks, two Hispanics, and one white.

Throughout the entire ordeal, from Fullem's arrest, through the trial, and after, John Ryan stood by his friend. He felt that he understood why Joe had done it, and in fact, was glad he had. While the media and the rest of the country chose to focus on the words coming from Fullem's mouth as evidence of the motivation behind his brutality, Ryan knew better. He knew that Fullem called Cheeseboro a nigger simply as one more way to inflict pain.

If Cheeseboro had been Jewish, Fullem no doubt would have called him a filthy Kike, or Dago, or Spic…whatever. At that moment, Officer Joseph Fullem was conscious of only two emotions: rage and hatred. His actions, and his words, simply reflected that fact.

Of course, this was something that Ryan had understood without an ability to explain it to anybody else. How could he? And what difference would it make? The bottom line for Ryan had not been how to prove to everyone else what a good friend he was to Joe Fullem, but rather, how to prove that to Fullem himself.

It wasn't easy. After his acquittal, Fullem literally disappeared. He left the Pittsburgh area by train, and no one saw or heard from him again for almost eleven months. No one Ryan knew was able or willing to tell him where Fullem had gone. He heard isolated rumors here and there, the most persistent of which were that Fullem had actually gone insane and was living on the streets. Finally, he received a call from the emergency room at Jefferson Hospital.

Fullem had been shot fifteen times in the legs, butt, and right arm. Whoever shot him had tried to get him in the face, but he had only graze wounds on either cheek. In addition to being shot, he'd also been beaten badly. The only reason he was alive was because an actual paramedic crew had discovered his body behind a dumpster they were using to dispose of some hospital waste. They had rushed him to the hospital. Another five minutes and he'd have been dead.

He'd had no identification, money, and was only wearing one shoe. But the policewoman who responded to the report of John Doe homeless man having been shot, recognized him. After a few phone calls, she was directed to Ryan's desk at Northeast Detectives. He assumed the case.

When Fullem regained consciousness six days and three surgeries later, Ryan was there at his bedside, reading a magazine.

"I was dreaming about you," Fullem said groggily to his friend.

Ryan nearly fell off his chair. "Jesus, Joe, you scared the shit out of me. How do you feel?"

Fullem smiled faintly. "Probably about as good as I look."

"What happened, Joe? Who did this to you?"

Fullem turned his head away on the pillow. "I don't know."

"Get the fuck outta' here," said Ryan as he rose from his chair. Ryan assumed that someone had sought revenge against Fullem for the Cheeseboro attack. "Where have you been for the last ten months anyway? I looked all over for you."

A tear escaped Fullem's eye. "I wish you'd found me sooner, John," he said softly to the window.

Ryan sighed and sat down on the edge of the bed. "Well…I've found you now. That's all that matters."

And for the six months leading up to their meeting at the restaurant that day, it had been all that mattered. Ryan got no further information from Fullem about who might have shot and beaten him, even though he was sure that Fullem knew exactly who had done it and why. He also was unable to learn where Fullem had gone for all that time. Ryan stopped asking after awhile, content just to be pushing his friend past whatever he'd been through.

He had brought the big man home to stay with the Ryans, where he lived for four months after getting out of the hospital. He also pushed Fullem, who had developed a raging addiction to alcohol, through a dramatic and mercurial detoxification process. It was only after Fullem had finally acknowledged that he was an alcoholic who needed help, and was finally able to walk with just a cane, that Ryan allowed him to move into an apartment, the first year's rent to which Ryan insisted on paying for.

All told, it was more love, generosity, and kindness any one human being had ever shown Joe Fullem. John Ryan had literally raised him from the dead, and in the process, earned the man's undying love and devotion.

But in reality, it was the kids, more than anything, which Ryan believed made Fullem's life possible again. The big fellow had always had a soft spot in his heart for kids. He saw in them hope and a future. Although he had always generally been around since they were both born, it wasn't until Fullem moved into the house that he and the kids really got to spend great lengths of time together.

The three of them developed an intensely close bond, and Fullem spent as much time as he could with the kids. They seemed to be the only people in the world he could believe really loved him and did not judge him. Although Linda was not happy about the relationship her children developed with Fullem, her husband did not share her concern. Like any father, John Ryan's greatest fear was that harm would ever befall either of his children. With Joe Fullem around them, he knew that they would always be safe.

Which was why he had arranged for Joe to meet him at Amici's in the first place. "I'm glad things are working out, Joe," said Ryan sincerely.

Fighting back a sudden lump in his throat, Fullem responded quietly, "I couldn't have done it without you, John." The big man leaned forward and looked down at his empty plate. "We're even, you know," he said without looking up.

Ryan knew what his friend meant. "That's not why I did it. We're friends, Joe. I named my son after you for Christ's sake. I'm there for you no matter what, and I expect the same from you. Besides, no one's keeping score."

Fullem nodded silently. After few seconds of uncomfortable silence, he said, "So what's up? Why did you want to see me tonight?"

Ryan smiled. "I need a favor."

Fullem returned the grin warmly. "Anything."

Ryan held up his hand. "You do not have to say yes. I'll understand, believe me. I'm planning on surprising Linda with a cruise to Bermuda for our thirteenth wedding anniversary next month, and I need someone to watch the kids. Her parents live out of state and you know I haven't seen or heard from my mom in about ten years…"

Fullem was shaking his head from side to side and smiling. "John, asking me to watch those kids is a favor to me, you know that. I love spending time with those little rug rats. I guess I'll come stay at your house while you're away?"

Ryan laughed aloud. "Well, you don't think I'd let my kids set foot near your rat-trap of an apartment, do you?"

"Good point," Fullem acknowledged. "Did you clear this with Linda?"

"Don't worry about her. Once she gets on that boat she'll forget all her troubles. Do yourself a favor, though. Take good care of Joey and Kelly."

Fullem nodded seriously. "That's the last thing you'll ever have to worry about."

Not the last thing, Ryan knew. Although Fullem's physical injuries had healed for the most part, the one lingering effect of whatever he had been through was a serious dependency on alcohol. It was the one demon Ryan was concerned had not been corralled.

"One last thing, Joe," Ryan said somberly.

"What's that?"

"No booze."

Fullem did not flinch, nor did he look away. "You have my word."

CHAPTER 6

▼

The Philadelphia D.A.'s race of 1993 wasn't even close. With George Cohen's considerable backing, both financial and political, Ash Wilson won by a two-thirds margin over the incumbent. The two men decided to celebrate by watching Penn play Harvard at the Palestra the night after the election.

Sitting at center court in the seats Cohen had held for over forty years, Wilson barely saw the game. It seemed as though every person there had voted for him, or at least so they said as they shook his hand and congratulated him. A mid-November Penn-Harvard contest was not a big draw in the city, and there was probably only about two thousand people in what was lovingly called college basketball's most historic gymnasium. The sparse crowd, and less than scintillating game gave Wilson and Cohen a chance to catch up after a long campaign in which they'd deliberately kept their distance.

Wilson picked at a greasy bag of popcorn and chuckled. "Well, we won...now what the hell do I do?"

His eyes following the action on the court, Cohen patted Wilson on the knee. "Do what you've always done. Do what you know in your heart is the right thing to do."

"George, C'mon. Aren't you the one who always says that morals and politics don't mix?"

Remembering he had in fact said just that on more than one occasion, Cohen nodded and smiled. "It's true I have said that. I've meant it too. But I do not see you as a politician, and you and I both know that you were not motivated to seek the office you've now attained by political ambition." Cohen leaned over and snuck a handful of popcorn.

"I hope you understand," said George after he had fully chewed and swallowed his pilfered popcorn, "that I have supported your candidacy for precisely those reasons."

Wilson threw the last handful into his mouth and crumpled the bag. "I know," Wilson mumbled through a mouthful of popcorn, "but now that it's here, I'm all of a sudden wondering if it can really be done. Especially in this city."

Cohen grimaced as a Harvard lay-up increased the Crimson lead to twenty-two points. "If it were any other man, I might share your trepidation. But because it is you, Ash, I know in my heart that you will always do what you believe to be the right thing, that you will never compromise out of political expediency. Your choices may not always be correct, but they will always be right."

Wilson searched the older man's eyes to see if what he had just said was an expectation or a command. He saw no answer, only disappointment at the poor performance his beloved Penn Quakers were putting on down on the floor. With the subject seemingly closed, Wilson was left to wonder if he'd ever feel the same confidence in himself as D.A. that Cohen felt so strongly.

The actual decision to run for District Attorney had been hatched one late night at the offices of Cohen and Elson a few years earlier, just after the verdict in the Precor case. There Wilson sat, in his fifty-seventh floor, corner office, with three walls made entirely of glass providing a panoramic view of the entire city. His feet, planted firmly upon the lip of the giant mahogany desk behind which he sat, were shod comfortably in a pair of expensive Italian loafers, and the drape of his linen trousers was made just right by their perfectly weighted cuffs. He puffed lightly on a small Romeo et Julieta cigar, thought about his life, and was happy. Ashland Wilson was running the most successful law firm in the city that literally gave birth to the practice of law in America, and he was running it well.

But having achieved such success running Cohen and Elson, Wilson had grown restless in recent years as the job became less challenging. His mind would often wander, and he wondered what new professional venture he might tackle. As he sat there in his office that one night, smoking his cigar, Wilson thought about his next career move seriously for the first time, determined to make a decision on his future.

It was at that moment that Cohen had walked in. "Savoring your victory?" he asked as he helped himself to a cigar from Wilson's desktop humidor and sat down on the leather couch in the corner.

"Actually no," said Wilson as he tossed a lighter over. "I was actually trying to decide what I should do next."

Cohen and Wilson had discussed the younger man's growing restlessness with his position at the firm, and knew what he meant. "Come up with anything?"

Wilson swivelled his chair to look out the window. "Well, I've thought about the possibility of going into business. But one thing I have come to realize is that the accumulation of more money is not a goal of mine, and in business, that is the only goal. Lord knows I have more money than I know what to do with as it is anyway."

Cohen did not respond.

"I've thought about philanthropy, you know, charity work and stuff like that. But I must admit that I find no vocation in the idea of simply giving money away to people. Rewards so easily obtained, no matter how well-deserved, are hardly ever appreciated, and never used properly."

"Maybe," said Cohen in a wistful tone which suggested he did not necessarily agree. "Clearly you've decided what you *don't* want to do...so my original question still stands."

Wilson turned in his chair and sat forward, resting his elbows on the desk. "I think...after really considering it all, George, that I am at heart a trial lawyer, and I love practicing law more than anything in the world."

He was regarded as one of the better trial lawyers in the city, and felt most alive when trying cases in front of juries and arguing in front of judges. His litigation style was not flashy. Where some, if not most lawyers rely on grandstanding and dramatics, Wilson instead took a more dispassionate approach.

He was famous for the meticulous and exhaustive preparation of cases for trial, refusing to believe that he could not anticipate every conceivable variable that can occur in the course of a trial. Wilson would spend a month before every trial working on nothing else. He would not open his mail, speak on the telephone with anyone not directly involved in the trial, and he would spend days upon days preparing his witnesses to testify. It was a grueling and exhausting process for all involved, but ultimately successful in every case he had ever tried to a jury.

"So I think that I will always be a trial lawyer, and no matter what, I will always make my way in this world as one." He leaned back. "But the problem is, how could I possibly practice law anywhere else than at Cohen and Elson, here, with you?"

Cohen smiled. "There are other law firms who would be ecstatic to have you, Ash, you know that."

Wilson shook his head. "This is the best firm in the city, George, there's nowhere to go but down."

It was at that moment that Wilson thought of becoming District Attorney. Although he had only tried a few criminal cases over the years, all as pro bono counsel for indigent defendants, Wilson had always been intrigued by the practice of criminal law. Compared to civil litigation, which could drag on for years and years and generate literally tons of paper, only to settle with neither side really satisfied, criminal cases were fast-paced and streamlined, with the issues and law clearly defined, and invariably there was a winner and a loser. No other arena in the law provided as much a forum for pure advocacy skills than the criminal courtroom.

As he thought more about it, the idea of becoming District Attorney really began to appeal to Wilson.

"You know," he said, "the D.A.'s Office is really just another law firm in this city when you really think about it. Of course, no ones ever run it like a law firm, with a focus on the bottom line. Rather, they run it like just one more department of city government, with all the baggage necessarily attendant to bureaucracy. But what if someone were to come in and do just that?"

Cohen chuckled. In a town as thoroughly corrupt as Philadelphia, running any department of government with a legitimate focus on the bottom line, would be nearly impossible.

"If anyone can do it, Ash, I believe you could."

They spent the rest of the evening and the early morning hours of the next morning brainstorming all of the different ways Wilson could better run the D.A.'s Office. Those discussions however, had remained confidential between the two of them, even during the campaign.

The morning after Penn lost to Harvard by fifteen points (a result which in recent years had become routine), Wilson sat nervously behind his desk in his new fifth floor office at 1601 Arch Street, a block from City Hall, and waited for his eight o'clock appointment, which would be the first step in Wilson's master plan to revamp the office. The meeting was with Roger Queenan, the chief deputy in charge of the homicide division, the highest profile unit of lawyers in the office.

Queenan had been an assistant D.A. for over twenty-five years. When he first began his career as a prosecutor fresh from Howard University School of Law, he had been a firebrand; aggressive, driven, and determined to let no crime go unpunished. He was good, and he quickly gained a reputation as a top-notch trial lawyer.

Over the years though, the sheer volume and incomprehensibility of the crime and degradation he had to deal with every day eventually overwhelmed Queenan. He continued to show up for work, but that was about it. He was promoted to Chief Deputy of Homicide by the former D.A. to both re-ignite the fire which had once existed in the man, and also to help win the black vote in an election year. The promotion failed on both accounts.

Wilson intended to fire a lot of people immediately, and Roger Queenan was one of them. What did not have to be explained to Wilson was that there would be an immediate political and media backlash for the unceremonious dismissal of an experienced, high-ranking, seemingly competent attorney, who was black. It was for precisely that reason that Wilson chose to meet with Queenan first. He wanted to send the immediate message that no one was safe, that politics would not interfere with his vision for the office, and that only those who carried their weight would be welcome in the Wilson administration.

Queenan arrived fifteen minutes late. "Sorry," he mumbled as he shuffled through the door and helped himself to a seat in front of Wilson's desk. Queenan was wearing a suit that appeared two sizes too small and the tip of his clashing tie was barely within shouting distance of his belt buckle. That particular fashion faux paus was a pet peeve of Wilson's.

"You're fired, Roger," said Wilson as he busied himself with some papers on the desk.

Queenan said nothing for a few seconds. Then he smiled and replied, "Seriously, what did you want to see me about?"

Wilson pretended to write something important. Finally he put down his pen, removed his reading glasses, and took great care in laying them upon the desk. When he finally looked up at Queenan, his face was absolutely expressionless.

"Roger, you were a good lawyer once. In fact, there was a time when you represented everything that could be good about this office. But you haven't been that person for a long time now. This place is about to undergo a sea change, Roger, and it's beginning with you. And just so you know, it's not ending with you. Everyone I'm meeting with today will be hearing the same thing from me. You'll receive two months severance. Thank you for your service."

Wilson stood up to signal that the meeting was at an end. Queenan remained seated. He was, in spite of everything, a seasoned trial lawyer, long accustomed to maintaining an absolutely unruffled appearance in the face of even the most shocking surprises. He showed no reaction whatsoever, his only physical motion the leisurely crossing of his legs. Wilson was struck by the same emotion that many a criminal defense lawyer had felt when facing off with Roger Queenan at his best…doubt. It was the same emotion felt by a prize-fighter when he lands his absolutely best punch to the temple of his opponent, and the guy hardly blinks. Queenan's ability in this regard was legendary, and it made Wilson wonder whether or not he was doing the right thing.

Finally Queenan spoke, and quickly erased all doubt from Wilson's mind. "You'll get crucified," he said with a smile as he slowly rose from his seat.

Queenan was not a big man, but he still towered over the stubby Wilson. "I'll be the first to admit that I may not be the lawyer I used to be. Hell, I consider that a compliment. But I'm still the highest-ranking African-American law enforcement official in this town. I win most of my cases, and I have four guys on death row. The fact that your first official act as District Attorney is to fire me, will be seen as pure racism."

The word hung in the air between the two men like a sudden fog. The mere mention of the word created a whole new dynamic, on several levels. On the first level there was the moment occurring between the two men in that room and the words each would use to advance their positions. Queenan had thrown a haymaker, and waited for Wilson to duck, hit back, or go down.

The second level was the thinly veiled threat made by the mere mention of the word. By making the accusation so boldly, and so quickly, Queenan showed that he had prepared himself for this, and was telling Wilson that he intended to very publicly repeat his incendiary charge.

The last, most subtle level of the conversation was occurring within the minds of each man. Wilson had known the accusation would come, even if he had been unprepared for Queenan's audacity. He was completely comfortable and confident that his decision was in no way motivated by the color of Queenan's skin. But with the moment at hand, Wilson suddenly doubted himself. If Queenan was white, Wilson thought briefly, would he have made the same decision?

For his part, Queenan fought to stifle the pang of guilt he felt. He knew full well that he had stopped trying years ago. A broken marriage and a budding addiction to pain killers due to the resultant depression had deprived him of all motivation. Queenan avoided tough cases, assigning them instead to his young assistants, and took only those cases for himself that were sure to result in guilty pleas. His personal appearance had also suffered. Queenan had once been considered a clothes-horse, but could not now remember the last time he'd bought any new clothes or shoes. He knew he deserved to be fired.

But whatever self-esteem he still had left was tied up directly with the fact of his position, and he couldn't let that be taken from him. If that meant for the first time in his life hiding behind his skin, he was prepared to do that. And besides he thought, for all he knew, Wilson really was a closet racist.

All of these thoughts went through each man's mind in the split second it took for Wilson to respond.

"Fuck you, Roger. You do what you have to do. But first, clear out…now."

Queenan smiled unconvincingly. As he turned to leave, each man wondered if they'd handled the situation properly, and if they had made a mistake, who it would hurt more.

CHAPTER 7

▼

John Ryan had been right about his wife's reaction to the surprise vacation. She was very upset about the idea of leaving the kids with Fullem and at first refused to even go on the trip if he was to be the babysitter. It had taken Ryan the better part of a week to convince her, with a little help from Joey and Kelly, who adored their Uncle Joe and were excited at the idea of spending the week with them. She agreed finally, but not without serious reservations.

As soon as she set foot on that cruise ship though, all was forgotten. The six night, seven day cruise to Bermuda was like a second honeymoon for the Ryans, and the first time they had been on vacation alone since Kelly had been born nine years earlier.

Linda Ryan had in fact never been outside the country, and had only left Philadelphia once, when she had honeymooned with John in Colorado for a short ski vacation. She marveled in Bermuda at the sky-blue waters off of Horseshoe Bay, and the multitude of colorful fish that schooled just beneath the surface. They rode mopeds around the island with abandon, struggling and laughing at each other as they tried to steer the unfamiliar little motor bikes and stay on the right side of the road, which was of course the left. For a girl whose only first-hand contact with the Atlantic Ocean had been on the Jersey shore, it was a wonderful and eye-opening experience.

For John, it was an opportunity to see his wife in a way he hadn't seen her in a long time; completely relaxed, tanned and rested. Although he didn't really need reminding, he was hit full force once again with how strikingly beautiful she was. And it wasn't just the appreciative stares of other men on the ship and island who openly stared as Linda walked by in her white bikini. It was her smooth skin, deeply tanned, offset by a gleaming white smile. It was her long blonde hair, lightened even more by the sun, which flowed over her toned shoulders.

But most of all, it was her laugh, loud and hearty and unreserved. They made love like newlyweds and talked like high school kids. For two people who appreciated just how happy their lives were, it was as happy as they'd ever been.

They had such a good time that when Fullem picked them up at the airport, Linda actually gave him a hug and a kiss on the cheek.

"That musta' been some trip, tiger," Fullem said to John with a wink as he gave Linda a squeeze. "Jesus, you two look great! I feel like I'm picking up a couple of movie stars."

The Ryans smiled demurely, pretending not to know how good they looked.

"It's a good thing I can transport you in style." Fullem led them to the curb, where his not-so-luxurious ride idled with the trunk open.

"You still driving that piece of shit?" asked John.

Fullem took all four of their suitcases and threw them into the trunk at once. "Hey, take it easy on the Skylark. She's a classic." He slammed the trunk, and the whole car shuddered.

"Well, how are my babies?" asked Linda as they made their way up Northbound I-95 towards the Ryan home in Northeast Philadelphia.

"Everybody's fine" said Fullem. "I let 'em stay up late every night, gave Joey his first beer, and taught Kelly how to curse like a sailor. All-in-all, we had a very productive week. By the way, that son of yours drinks like a fish. He owes me a case of Rolling Rock."

John just shook his head and smiled. "You were on such a roll there for a minute. Linda hugged you and even gave you a kiss. Now, before it's too late, tell my wife what a wonderful job you did watching her children so she stays in her good mood."

Fullem looked in his rearview mirror and smiled at Linda's arched eyebrow.

"Aw, C'mon, Linda," he said with as he caught her eye. "You know the only person in the world I'm actually afraid of is you…those kids are angels. I didn't even have to hound them to do their homework or anything. They even did all the chores on the list you left. They're fine."

They drove in silence for a few minutes as the Ryans each breathed silent sighs of relief, both for different reasons.

"By the way," Fullem said finally, "Joey's at practice for the summer league all-stars up in Upper Merion." Fullem found Linda's eyes in the rearview. "He asked me to have you pick him up, Lin. He's real anxious to see you."

Linda sat back contentedly with the knowledge that her son had missed her and wanted to see her right away.

John put on a mock pouty-face. "Yo, my boy doesn't want to see the old man? What's up with that?"

Fullem laughed. "He knows you've got to work tonight. I don't know why you let them schedule a shift for you on the same day you got back from vacation."

"I've got too much shit to do," said Ryan. He hadn't taken a week off in nine years and as much fun as he he'd had on vacation, he was itching to get back to work. Ryan was secretly glad that Joey wanted Linda to pick him up. It made him feel less guilty about going right back to work.

"Daddy! Mommy!" screamed little Kelly as she came running out the door to greet her parents. She flung herself into her father's arms and gave him a tight hug. Kelly then turned and grabbed her mom so her little arms somehow managed to be grabbing both of them at the same time. She had never been away from them for more than a day, and she began to cry. Involuntarily, so did her parents.

"She's been sitting by the window since Mr. Fullem left for the airport," said Mrs. Russell, the Ryan's next door neighbor.

"Thanks so much for your help, Diane," Linda said through smiling tears over Kelly's shoulder.

"Hey, kiddo," said John, "You wanna' see what Mommy and Daddy brought you from Bermuda?"

"Yeeeaaah!" shouted the little girl as she scrambled down from her parent's hug and ran towards the trunk, where Fullem was lifting out the bags.

"Okay, but first I want you to go inside with Mommy while your Uncle Joe and I bring in the bags."

Kelly grabbed Linda's hand and walked with her towards the house.

"So," asked Ryan as Fullem stood up with all the bags, "how was it?"

"It was fun, John. They really are great kids." Fullem was walking without his cane and was able to carry most of the bags himself. Ryan had always marveled at his friend's brute strength, and was glad to see that it had returned.

Fullem dropped the bags in the foyer with a thud, which Kelly immediately set to rummaging through in search of her presents. Linda tried to slow her down with no success.

"Um, listen, John," said Fullem quietly to Ryan as he pulled on his elbow to lead him away from the girls a bit. "Joey's mad at me because I wouldn't let him go out with his friends last Saturday night. I'm sure you would have let him go, but I just didn't want to take a chance of letting either one of them out of my sight unless I knew exactly where they were at all times."

Ryan laughed at the seriousness of Fullem's tone. "Yeah, you kind of get over that after a while. Sometimes you don't even wanna' know where they are at all, you're just happy they're gone. Right, honey?" he asked Linda, who'd caught most of what had been said.

"You bet," she agreed as she put her arm around her husband's waist. "Thanks a lot, Joe," she said sincerely. We really appreciate it."

Fullem nodded.

Linda gave Ryan a kiss on the cheek and headed for the door. "I've got to run if I'm going to get Joey. The Schuylkill's going to be a nightmare as it is."

"Okay, be careful," said Ryan, his eyes already turned towards his daughter. "I'll get dinner ready and deal with this one."

"I've gotta' run too," said Fullem, following Linda towards the door.

After they had both left, Ryan knelt down and gave his daughter another tight hug. It never stopped amazing him that his capacity to love his children grew exponentially every day. Being without them for a week had been incredibly difficult. It made him realize just how much his life was wrapped up in theirs.

"So, did you have fun with Uncle Joe?" asked Ryan.

Kelly nodded absentmindedly, presumably preoccupied with whatever gift she was about to get. "I guess so," she said as she pulled her Daddy towards the luggage, "but Joey's really mad at him."

"Oh, yeah? What for?"

Kelly was already picking through her dad's open suitcase. "I don't know," she said absently, "all he said was that he couldn't wait to tell mom about it."

The Schuylkill Expressway in Philadelphia is a notorious stretch of highway. It has several nicknames, such as the "willkill expressway" or the "dokill expressway." Connecting the western suburbs with the city, it is a two-lane highway for most of its length. Given the amount of traffic it sees on a daily basis, four lanes would not be enough. Besides the fact that the two lanes are separated by a high concrete median, there are several dangerous curves which, when taken too fast, cause cars, and more significantly tractor-trailers, to overturn on a regular basis. Worse yet, most people treat it like it's the Autobahn. There is at least one serious crash a day.

In order to get to her son's practice in Upper Merion, Linda had to travel along Roosevelt Boulevard, out to the Schuylkill Expressway, and exit at Route 202 North in King of Prussia. Although she knew the way, she was unfamiliar with it, and uncomfortable driving on the expressway. She was almost relieved to be sitting in bumper-to-bumper traffic the whole way there.

Joey Ryan and his mother had an especially close relationship, and he wasn't yet old enough to be embarrassed by it. Linda knew that day was coming fast though. Soon, teenaged girls would be the only females her son would have time for, and the long, personal conversations which were practically a ritual between the two of them would be a thing of the past. She savored every revelation of himself her son made to her, and Linda had earned Joey's trust over the years by never betraying one of his confidences, even to her husband.

When Linda arrived at the ball field, Joey was the last kid there. All of the other kids on the team lived on the Main Line, so their parents had far fewer distances to travel. Dusk was beginning to fall when Linda pulled her station wagon into the parking lot.

"Hey, kiddo!" she shouted cheerfully out the open window as she parked. "Didya' miss me?"

Joey was not nearly as effusive as he simply shrugged his shoulders. "Yeah," he said flatly. He threw his gear into the back seat and walked slowly around to get into the passenger's side.

"Well how 'bout a kiss for old mom?"

Joey leaned over and gave her a half-hearted peck on the cheek. He then turned and looked out the window.

"Hey, I'm sorry I'm late, okay? I left as soon as I got back from the airport," said Linda as she wheeled out of the lot. The entrance ramp for the Schuylkill was only a minute away, and before she had time to probe for a response, she busied herself with merging onto the highway.

The traffic was gone, replaced in the Eastbound lanes with zipping cars, some with headlights on, some without. Gripping the wheel tightly, Linda waited for a gap and gunned the engine. The old wagon lurched with effort and managed to successfully merge into the right lane, but not without an angry beep from the car which had to slow from eighty to seventy because he got stuck behind her. Joey flipped the bird, and received no rebuke from his mom, who would have done the same had her hands not been glued to the wheel.

When finally she felt comfortable enough to relax just a bit, she sneaked a glance at her son. Despite the fact that he was staring to his right, his whole body seemed angry and rigid. "Honey," Linda said soothingly, "you can't be this mad because I'm late…can you?"

Joey sat quiet for a few seconds, simply staring out the window with his arms crossed. "I hate Uncle Joe," he said finally.

Linda had overheard Fullem telling John about Saturday night. Linda smiled to herself, secretly relieved that her son wasn't mad at her. "Sweetie, it was just one night. I'm sure your Uncle Joe was just doing what he thought was best for you."

Real anger flashed to Joey's face, but just as he began to respond, a beat up old car cut directly in front of the station wagon and screamed down the Manayunk exit ramp to the right side of the highway. "Watch out!"

There was no time to react. Linda slammed on the brakes as she spun the steering wheel to avoid hitting the car that had cut them off. Unfortunately, at that moment, an eighteen wheel tractor trailer was speeding down the left hand lane just as the wagon careened to the left. The trucker did not even have time to slam on his brakes as the huge rig rolled right over top of the wagon, crushing it.

Linda and Joey were killed instantly.

CHAPTER 8

▼

The first few weeks had been incredibly hard. Lionel had to literally teach Darnell how to bathe properly and brush his teeth. It amazed Lionel that a human being could exist in the fifth most populous city in the United States, yet appear to have gone so completely unnoticed and neglected. What was truly amazing was that the boy had lived as long as he had.

Lionel explained to his neighbors and friends, and employer, that Darnell was the son of a long lost sister who'd been overcome by an addiction to drugs, and that the boy would be staying with him for the foreseeable future. It was a story that allowed Lionel to tell the truth about Darnell's situation without really doing so. Everyone was supportive, even the folks at Cohen & Elson, who gave him three months before he had to start work full-time after graduation, with pay, in order to get Darnell's life on track, the only stipulation being that he pass the bar exam the first time he took it.

Lionel used the same story with the doctor and the dentist he took Darnell to see, and blamed the lack of previous medical records on the fact that his sister was simply incapable of remembering even where the boy had been born. Based on their physical examinations, it was estimated that Darnell was eleven years old, but his physical development was that of an eight year old.

As the weeks became months however, and Darnell was treated for the first time in his life to a steady and balanced diet, as well as quality medical care, he literally began to sprout. Within months he had grown three inches and put on thirty pounds.

And the boy could play ball! It had been years since Lionel himself had played any basketball. His injury and his bitterness over it had doused what had been a burning love of the game. But nothing it seemed could diminish Darnell's desire to play. His ability to handle the ball, with such strength and confidence, made him seem like a totally different person.

But it was the person that Darnell was when not playing that worried Lionel the most. What little snippet Lionel had seen firsthand of Darnell's life, combined with the limited information Darnell was willing to discuss, made Lionel realize that the boy's entire life had been literally torturous. And Darnell had not even told him about Clark.

Lionel knew that Darnell needed school badly, but he had no idea where to start. He was not in any position to simply walk the boy up to the nearest school and ask them to take him in. He didn't need a law degree to know that he had basically kidnapped the boy, even if it had been in his best interests. He knew also that if he took Darnell to a city agency, the very first thing they would do is put the boy in foster care. Then they would try to see if he could be given back to the mother.

Lionel had seen enough of Darnell's mother to know that he was not going to allow that to happen. He'd also read enough about the state of the city's child welfare agencies to know that they were ill-equipped to do anything right by any child, much less one Lionel had come to care about so deeply.

Feeling therefore for the very first time in his life that he was absolutely doing the right thing, he deliberately and willingly broke the law.

The internet in 1993 was not yet the tool it is today, which turned out to be both a blessing and an obstacle. Because while Lionel was unable to simply go on-line and figure out how people fake identification papers, the computers of the agencies he would need to fool did not have the ability to communicate with each other adequately enough to catch him when he did.

Left with nothing but his own resources to figure out how to essentially create a brand new identity for Darnell, the first thing he did was call a friend from law school who'd gone to work for the Immigration and Naturalization Service in Harrisburg.

"By the way," he had said after ten minutes of small talk, "the firm I'm working for has a big client, owns a bunch of mushroom farms in the Kennett Square area. You know how many Mexicans work on those farms. He's worried that he might be unwittingly hiring illegals. They all seem to have birth certificates, but...".

The friend laughingly cut him off. "That doesn't mean anything. Tell him to be careful. Forged birth certificates are a huge business. They're pretty easy to get apparently."

"Oh, yeah? How?"

"Well, I ain't been here that long, but I know there's a movement afoot to start investigating these auto tag dealerships in Philly and Pittsburgh that advertise in the Spanish newspapers. Apparently there are hundreds of blank birth certificates stolen from the department of vital records in Harrisburg every month, and they've made they're way onto the black market flowing through those places."

"Hmmm," Lionel had replied. "I'll let him know."

"Well, don't tell him where you heard it, because nothing's been done about the problem yet."

Five minutes after promising to get together for a drink and hanging up, Lionel was paging through the yellow pages. He found four auto tag places with parts of their ads in Spanish. Three hours later, at the third one he visited, he hit pay dirt. It cost him 400 dollars, but he had three blank official birth certificates, all bearing the official seal of the Philadelphia Prothonotary.

He waited that night until the last lawyer had left the offices of Cohen & Elson before sneaking in and setting up shop in front of a secretary's typewriter. He practiced on blank copies of the birth certificates for hours, until he was finally ready to create the official birth record of the boy he'd met just a few short months earlier.

He paused a moment as the enormity of what was he was about to do hit him full force. Slowly and deliberately, each peck of the key like a sledgehammer against the page, Lionel realized that he was creating a whole new person. At that moment, the boy Darnell had been ceased to exist anywhere but in the memories of three men.

Born anew was an eleven year old boy named Darnell Cooper, his past a clean slate, his future whatever he wanted it to be. When he finished all three certificates, Lionel wiped away the tears which had been streaming down his face. He suddenly knew exactly the feeling shared by every new father as they watch their child born. It was the most overwhelming emotion he had ever felt, both invincible and helpless, all at the same time.

In the next few days he'd been amazed at how easy it was to establish a legal identity for the boy with just a birth certificate. Within a week, Darnell Cooper had his own social security number, health and dental insurance, and an official mailing address. Having thus learned who he now was, both Lionel and Darnell set out to understand who the boy was supposed to be.

They went to see Dr. Clint Charles at Children's Hospital. He was a child psychologist who had been used as an expert in pediatric neuropsychology by some of the partners at Cohen & Elson in a very big case, and he agreed to see Darnell upon their request. Over the course of three days, Charles tested and evaluated Darnell. On the third day, when Lionel arrived to pick the boy up, Dr. Charles asked to speak with him alone.

Charles ushered Lionel down a corridor and into his cramped first-floor office. He sat down heavily behind his desk, and beckoned Lionel to have a seat, which he did. They sat staring at each other for a few seconds before Charles finally spoke.

"Lionel, I have been a psychologist for over thirty years. I've treated and evaluated thousands of patients. Your nephew is, without a doubt, the most extraordinary individual I have ever met."

Lionel had only known the boy for three months, but he wasn't surprised to hear the doctor say this.

"I administered to Darnell what's known as the Weschler Intelligence Scale for Children-Third Edition. Lay people would refer to it as an "I.Q." test, but in reality, there isn't any reliable way to measure a person's intelligence." Charles leaned forward onto his elbows, his eyes wide with excitement as he explained the science to Lionel.

"There are twelve sub-scales within the test that contribute to the evaluation of a Full Scale IQ—a Verbal IQ, and a Performance IQ. The Full Scale IQ is the global and aggregate measure of cognitive abilities. The Verbal IQ deals with vocabulary and verbal mechanisms. The Performance IQ is designed to be a nonverbal measure of intelligence and requires the individual to manipulate objects rather than answer questions."

As Charles was speaking, Lionel reached into his bag and pulled out a yellow note pad. "Okay," he said as he jotted down a few notes.

"Now, I'm not going to bore you with the different kinds of testing and how it's scored. Suffice it to say that there are all kinds of different sub-tests, everything from picture completion to coding to arithmetic and vocabulary."

Lionel held up his hand as he continued writing. "Wait a minute, what's 'coding'?"

The doctor was obviously excited about what he was saying, and seemed almost annoyed to have to stop along the way and answer questions. "Coding is a sub-test in the performance sub-scale which requires the child to copy symbols according to a specified pattern as quickly as possible. The child needs visual perception and short-term memory skills in order to copy the symbols effectively. The sub-test also measures degree of persistence, speed of performance, and fine motor skills."

Lionel nodded understanding.

"Actually, I'm glad you asked that question because it allows me to tell you what the bottom-line is." Charles paused for dramatic effect.

"Darnell has scored the highest in what I would call 'raw IQ'...of any patient I have ever tested." The doctor sat back and smiled.

Lionel raised both eyebrows. "I'm not sure I know what that means, Doc."

"Let's put it this way. The scores on these tests range from 40, which is essentially mental retardation, all the way up to 160. I have never heard of anyone ever testing above a 150. The mean is 100. In the performance sub-scale, Darnell scored a 157."

"Holy shit," said Lionel.

Charles laughed. "Yeah, exactly. But the most amazing thing is, with regard to his verbal, math and reading skills, he would be considered mildly retarded if simply given a conventional IQ test. The Weschler is perfect for him because it measures not only what you know, but also how you process information and react to tasks. He's really quite remarkable."

Lionel felt his chest puffing up with pride. "So the kid's a genius," he marveled.

"Well...yes and no," said Charles, a frown overtaking his wide face. "The Weschler's a one day test. I've been talking a little bit with Darnell over the past two days, as well as administering some personality testing. I gave him the Rorschach, which I'm sure you've seen in movies, and the Minnesota Multiphasic Personality Inventory, or MMPI."

Lionel wrote the names down. "Okay. Why does your expression tell me that he didn't do nearly as well on these."

Charles nodded and pursed his lips. "As you know, Darnell has been through hell in his life. In addition to the obvious neglect he has suffered, he has also been physically and sexually abused, probably over a period of years. I don't know if he's talked to you about this, but there was one particularly brutal man in the projects where he used to live named 'Clark.'"

Lionel's blank expression told Charles that Darnell had not shared with Lionel the things Clark had done to him.

"Apparently this man was greatly feared throughout the projects. He was a drug dealer who used Darnell's apartment as kind of a sentry point slash safe house. He abused both Darnell and his mother, sexually and physically, on a fairly regular basis. In fact, Darnell told me about the night that he came to live with you. Apparently, the mere sight of Clark had led Darnell to defecate on himself, and when Clark was unable to abuse Darnell as a result, he urinated on him."

Charles leaned back in his chair and sighed. "I must tell you, though, as absolutely harrowing as that story is, the way Darnell tells it leads me to believe that it pales in comparison to some of the other torture this poor boy has been put through."

Lionel balled his fists and gritted his teeth in absolute frustrated rage. He could not stop the images his mind immediately conjured up of this 'Clark' animal ravaging Darnell's tiny body. Adding to his anger was the guilt he involuntarily felt, sitting in front of this white doctor, knowing that it was a black man, someone like him, that had done this to Darnell. It was an irrational thought, and Lionel did his best to purge it.

"Well, do those other tests you gave him give you any insight as to how he'll be able to cope with all of it in the future?"

Charles shook his head. "Unfortunately, there is no test that can be done which can accurately predict human behavior. For instance, I administered the Trauma Symptom Inventory, or TSI. That's basically three scales designed to predict behavior which might occur as the result of serious trauma. Darnell's scores indicate that he frequently feels out of control. He often describes anger as an intrusive and unwanted experience, and sometimes sees his angry thoughts or behavior as not entirely under his control.

"For instance, he scored very high on the anger/irritability scale. This means that he experiences pervasive feelings of irritability, annoyance, or bad temper, such that minor difficulties or frustrations can provoke contextually inappropriate angry reactions."

Lionel nodded. "I've already seen a little bit of that. I've been trying to impress upon him the need to keep his room clean and do his dishes, little stuff like that. But the fact is he's never had anyone try to discipline him in any way, so he gets frustrated so easily. The other night he started crying and screaming just because I told him to pick up his coat off the floor. When he finally calmed down, he said he didn't even know why he had gotten so angry."

Charles nodded. "That kind of behavior is perfectly consistent with his test scores. For instance, the impaired self-reference scale measures a variety of difficulties associated with an inadequate sense of self and personal identity. ISR items include problems in discriminating one's needs and issues from those of others, confusion regarding one's identity and goals in life, an inability to understand one's own behavior, an internal sense of emptiness, a need for other people to provide direction and structure, and difficulties resisting the demands of others. His score on the ISR shows him to be easily excitable and less functional under stress."

Lionel just listened and continued to take notes, his face registering the growing fear that he was in way over his head.

Charles read his expression, but figured he'd give him all the bad news, then let him know he wasn't alone.

"Now, the tension reduction behavior score is the most troubling. The TRB measures an individual's tendency to externalize distress through suicidality, aggression, inappropriate sexual behavior, self-mutilation and activities intended to forestall abandonment or aloneness. Because TRB reflects a tendency to act out negative affect, this scale can be seen as a gross indicator of Darnell's relative risk for behavior potentially injurious to himself or others when stressed or dysphoric."

Lionel put down his notepad upon which he'd been scribbling furiously and scratched his head. "Jesus Christ, Doc, is this kid doomed to be some kind of mad genius, a guy whose smarter than everyone else but has no control over what he does?"

Charles smiled sympathetically. "Not at all. In fact, all of these indicators are actually normal considering the trauma he's been through.

The amazing thing really is the impact you've had on him in so short a time. This boy soaks up love like a sponge. I think, with a proper regimen of medication, your continued support, and therapy, he could turn out to be someone quite extraordinary."

"But is there a specific diagnosis?" The lawyer needed to name the problem before he could solve it.

"Well, there's no question that Darnell has Borderline Personality Disorder."

"Okay?" Asked Lionel, as in 'what the hell's that mean?'

Charles smiled. "BPD," he said patiently, "is a descriptive term for a person who is characterized by things such as frantic efforts to avoid abandonment, unstable relationships, impulsivity, which usually manifests itself in the abuse of drugs or alcohol, difficulty controlling anger, sometimes self-mutilation, and suicide attempts. It usually does not manifest itself until later in life. But given the extraordinary circumstances Darnell has been subjected to at such an early age, all of his neuroses are accelerated."

Lionel leaned forward in his chair and rubbed his face. What the hell had he gotten himself into? He wasn't equipped to handle this kid, to give him the life he needed. *Christ*, he thought, *I'm just a kid myself. I'm going to have to go back to work soon…if I pass the Bar that is.* He'd only been studying a few hours a night after Darnell went to sleep. *Who's going to watch him? Who's going to make sure he doesn't go batshit?*

Dr. Charles quietly watched Lionel's internal struggle. He was incredibly intrigued by the whole situation. Darnell had not only told Charles about Clark, he'd also told him the truth about how Lionel came to be in his life, and what he'd done for him so far.

Charles had also spoken with the lawyers he knew at Cohen & Elson about Lionel. Though they expressed concern that Lionel was just a little too confident, bordering on cocky, they spoke glowingly about his legal acumen and his ambition. They predicted big things for their new associate, whom they painted as ambitious and shrewd. But that image did not jibe with what Charles knew Lionel was doing with this boy. Not an overly superstitious man, Charles believed that something special was happening, and that it was not simply coincidence that the three of them had met.

"Lionel," Charles said, "I'd like to help in any way I can with Darnell's treatment. He's a special kid, and I think there's a lot I can learn from him. Would you mind if I saw him as my patient?"

"Aw Jeez, Doc, that would be unbelievable," said Lionel with a huge sigh of relief. "When can we start?"

Right away was the answer. And as time progressed in therapy, Darnell came to understand where his anger came from sometimes, and found ways to channel it into constructive areas. He also came to believe that Lionel was not going to abandon him, a feeling which was the source of much of his frustration early on.

There were many, many setbacks, and there were more than a few times during which Lionel threatened to send Darnell back to where he came from. Darnell would scream back that he didn't care, that he didn't really need Lionel, or Dr. Charles, or anybody else. He could make it on his own.

But in the end, these conflagrations were always quickly quelled. Both Lionel and Darnell grew quickly to depend almost completely upon one another, becoming true brothers. Lionel came to love Darnell, so much so that he could no longer seriously contemplate the boy's absence from his life. And the mere thought that Darnell would ever set foot in the projects again, anywhere near the clutches of men like Clark, was enough for each of them to put aside whatever momentary anger they had and realize just how fortunate they were to be in each other's lives.

Where Clark himself was concerned, Darnell and Lionel rarely spoke of him. Darnell had gradually shared with Lionel and Dr. Charles, through their many joint therapy sessions, the full panoply of horrors Clark had subjected him to. Even to a man like Dr. Charles, who had witnessed firsthand over his career the depths to which humanity can sink in its treatment of itself, the raw and remorseless brutality of Clark was something with which even he was unfamiliar.

Dr. Charles tried to explain to Lionel the emotional scars left by such treatment, and how they manifest themselves throughout the course of life, in sometimes uncontrollable ways. Although he felt it important to confront the demons created within Darnell by Clark, he also recognized Darnell's torment every time he was forced to discuss the man. Lionel saw this too, and deliberately avoided the subject.

They talked about Darnell's mother even less, which was a deliberate choice on Lionel's part. Every time his phone rang during the first year they were together, Lionel literally cringed, expecting every call to be Darnell's mother wanting her son back. He had no idea how he'd deal with that situation should it arise. He had committed several felonies in creating Darnell's new identity, and were he to be exposed, he'd not only face possible jail time, he would most certainly lose his recently obtained bar card.

But the call never came, and as they both relaxed into each other's lives, they were happy together. Each brought to the other a unique facet of personality which somehow managed to perfectly complement the other. Lionel gained a maturity which he had been lacking, a different outlook on life. It made him more humble as a person, and more effective as an attorney. With Dr. Charles guiding him, he was able to shepherd Darnell's life where it needed to go, and at the same time take control of his own. After passing the bar, Lionel quickly became a rising star at the firm, and earned the right to work on important cases.

As for Darnell, once he was exposed to quality education and health care, he literally blossomed. He grew four inches in the first year, and gained forty pounds. By the beginning of his second year living with Lionel, Darnell was getting A's and B's, and had become a phenomenally gifted basketball player. In fact, much as Lionel had done, after completing eighth grade in a center city public school, Darnell accepted a full scholarship to a prestigious Main Line prep school. The only difference…Darnell's was both an academic and athletic scholarship.

It was because everything was going so well for them both that Lionel never told Darnell about the call he had gotten from Clark. For the first year and a half there had been no communication at all. But he happened to be working at the office late on the night when a two-page article on Darnell had appeared that day in the Daily News about the best young players going into high school the following year, and the possibility of great things happening for Darnell if he continued to improve. Darnell's picture accompanied the article, thrilling the boy, and terrifying Lionel.

"Lionel Cooper," he'd answered, hoping it was Darnell on the other end demanding a pizza for dinner, and not someone who'd recognized Darnell Cooper from his former life.

"Hello, Counselor," slurred a deep, gravelly voice.

Immediately Lionel sensed a malevolence in the man's tone. He sat up straight at his desk and leaned towards the phone. "Can I help you?" he asked cautiously.

"You stole my little bitch," said the voice, "you owe me some money."

Lionel's eyes narrowed and the blood rushed from his face as he realized immediately who he was talking to. A sudden fury welled up inside and he forgot ever being concerned that this man might call. Lionel leaned into his desk and gripped the receiver tightly in his fist.

"I think you're right, motherfucker," he said through gritted teeth. "Why don't you come on down to my office and I'll give you what you deserve."

Clark laughed and coughed into the other end of the phone. "I'm sure I'll get what I deserve, brotha'…someday. But that's not yours to give. What you're gonna' give me is what I want. And what I want is three grand."

Lionel was too mad to know he had no other choice. "Or what? You piece of shit. If I ever get close enough to hand you money, I'll be too busy fuckin' you up to reach for my wallet."

"You talkin' a lotta shit for somebody who ain't in no position to be no talkin' at all, replied Clark angrily. "You and I both know where you got that kid from. You kidnapped that little brotha' from his momma then went and changed his name." Clark was obviously drinking something even as he spoke. Lionel could hear him gulping as he paused.

"Now, I don't necessarily blame you," Clark continued, "I mean, that boy could suck the chrome off a trailer hitch."

"You MOTHERFUCKER!" Lionel screamed. "I will kill you if I ever see your nappy ass," he hissed.

"Yeah, well, get in line. You should calm down though. You got bigger problems than me, and you and I both know it. As unbelievable as it is, that little crack ho' went and got herself all cleaned up, off drugs, off the welfare. Shit, she's a true Bill Clinton success story. And it's you who did it. She finally realized about two months after you snatched the kid that he was gone. Something finally clicked in her brain because of that. She thought he ran away or got kilt," Clark stopped talking to let out a wheezing cough, then he started laughing again.

"She has no idea that he's even still alive. She up and moved to Florida, started a whole new life…Now, don't you think she'd be interested in knowing that her little boy is still alive? How pissed off would she be knowing that some uppity brother came in and stole her son? I ain't no lawyer, but I bet that'd be one bitch of a lawsuit. Not to mention about six different federal offenses."

Lionel was too stunned to speak. He'd spent every day for a year and a half falling in love with Darnell. He thought of the boy at that point as his own brother, if not his son. He could not fathom losing him now. Of course, Lionel had know way of knowing that Clark was lying. Darnell's mother was dead.

"I guess I'll just give her a call and let her know where he is."

"No wait!" said Lionel more quickly than he wanted to. He took a deep breath. How could he know if any of this was true? Could he risk it being so?

He didn't think he could. The next morning Lionel withdrew three thousand dollars from his checking account. He knew it was stupid to pay the man, and that if he did, Clark would keep coming back for more. But he had little real choice. Not paying meant the possibility of losing his career, his freedom, and worst of all, Darnell. At least if he paid he'd buy himself time to figure out a better solution.

Lionel never saw him. He left the money in a brown paper bag in an abandoned building not far from the Rosen, just as he'd been instructed. He'd waited for a few hours, hiding behind a dumpster across an alley that gave him a view of the spot where he'd left the bag. But it was no place to be alone at night, no matter how tough you are. And as badly as he wanted to lay his eyes, and his hands on Clark, he rationalized that it would all have been for naught if some gangbanger rolled up and liked his shoes enough to kill for them.

Lionel also figured that he'd hear from Clark again soon enough. He immediately resolved to never pay the man any more money. Lionel was convinced he had done the right thing by Darnell, and he would just have to let himself be exposed if that was what was necessary to protect the boy. He had to have faith that if there is any such thing as justice, everyone would understand.

But there had been no further contact from Clark. Even as Darnell's talents exploded and he developed over time into one of the best high school basketball players in the country. Every time a new article appeared in some paper or magazine, or Darnell's highlights ran on television, Lionel cringed just a bit. He was comfortable with what he knew he would do if Clark or Darnell's mother called him out, but he wasn't anxious to do it.

Although Darnell did not know about the blackmail of Clark, he too feared that his mother might someday just decide she wanted to be back in his life. His concern was more bitter though, believing the only reason she would do so was because of his budding celebrity.

So as soon as Darnell Cooper turned sixteen, on the birthday Lionel had given him, Darnell petitioned the family court to become an emancipated minor. The petition was based on the real fact that Darnell's true parents were not involved in his life. Given that there is no formal procedure in Pennsylvania for obtaining emancipated minor status, a call to a friendly family court judge from George Cohen was all that was necessary. Cohen did not ask why Lionel had needed the favor.

Having in this fashion avoided the possibility of Darnell being sent back to his mother, Lionel breathed a little easier. And as time wore on and the statutes of limitation on his various crimes expired, he began to go whole days and then weeks without even worrying about Clark.

As Darnell neared completion of his senior year in high school, Lionel's major concern was what college he would attend.

Darnell was the number one recruit in the country. He had grown even taller than Lionel, and weighed 240 pounds. He was compared often to Kobe Bryant, but thought to have more potential because he was more physically mature. He had excellent grades, had scored a 1530 on his SAT's, and was popular with his teammates and classmates. The only big name schools that didn't recruit him were the ones who thought he might go pro out of high school. Even the Ivy League schools had all called, offering generous aid packages in lieu of athletic scholarships.

Lionel and Darnell had spoken at length about what college Darnell would attend.

"Well, what's it gonna' be?" Lionel asked over dinner one night during the spring of Darnell's senior year. His team had won the state title for the first time ever, and Darnell's future plans were highly anticipated.

Darnell chewed thoughtfully on a hunk of cheesesteak and shrugged with a smile.

Lionel chuckled. "Yeah, keep smiling and shrugging. If you don't make a decision soon, all the scholarships will be given away."

Darnell nodded and took a sip of his Pepsi. "You might be right. But what if I'm not worried about getting a scholarship?"

Lionel sat back in his chair and shook his head. "Look, just because I said I'd pay your tuition, doesn't mean I'd rather not have to!" Money was not really a problem. Lionel was making over two hundred thousand dollars a year working at Cohen & Elson.

That was why both of them laughed. Darnell leaned forward though, and looked seriously at Lionel. "Who was the last great NBA player to come out of the Ivy League?" he asked.

Lionel thought for a second. "Bill Bradley."

"And that was in the sixties. Don't you think they're due for another one?"

Inside, Lionel's heart jumped for joy. For Darnell to have gone through everything he had, and overcome it the way he did, to then go on and get an Ivy League degree would be the culmination of a dream. But as he always did, Lionel probed Darnell with questions to make sure that his choices were thought completely through before they were made.

"Why the Ivy League?"

Darnell's eyes sparkled and he smiled. "Here's why," he said with obvious passion. "I am blessed. I am blessed to have been taken from where I was, and to have been lucky enough to be where I am, with the choices I have. You have always taught me not to limit myself, to think as big and as outside of the box as I can. Well, I am not just a basketball player. I want to be more than just an athlete. I want to use basketball, just like Bill Bradley did. I want to use it as a vehicle, a platform, and nothing more."

Darnell put down his sandwich and paused as tears welled up inside his throat. He had thought long and hard about what was truly important to him, and the deep appreciation he had for just how lucky he had been since Lionel had saved him. It was something he was often very emotional about.

"I *have* to give something back, Lionel. I owe it to you, and everything you've given me. I can't waste this on myself. I have to go back and find more kids like me back where I came from and lift them out the way you did. The Ivy League's where I'm going to start that whole process."

Lionel fought his own tears as he listened to Darnell speak. He considered the day he met Darnell to be the luckiest of his life. Their

chance encounter led to both of their lives being immeasurably different, and infinitely better.

The young man was so extraordinary, so talented. Lionel too wondered how many more kids lived and died in those projects with the
same gifts, but without the opportunity to utilize them. He gave himself no credit for the man Darnell was becoming, and obviously still yet
wanted to be. Rather, Lionel was just grateful for having been allowed
to be a part of it's happening. He didn't doubt for a second that Darnell would accomplish everything his mind could imagine.

"What are you thinking about?" Darnell asked.

"I'm thinking that I love you…that I admire you, and that I think
you could not have made a wiser decision."

Darnell blushed. "You know I love you too, Lionel. And I know
that you gave me my life. Absolutely everything I am, or will ever be, I
owe to you."

Tears sprang to Lionel's eyes and they both laughed at each other.
"Jesus," said Lionel as he wiped away a tear. "Enough of that maudlin
shit. So what's it gonna' be, Superstar? Princeton, Yale, Harvard?"

Darnell shook his head no. "Penn."

CHAPTER 9

▼

Pain.

For the first few months after Linda and Joey's death, the only conscious feeling Ryan had was of the pain. It was literally as if someone had knifed him in the belly and he was slowly bleeding to death. Many nights, as he lay awake sobbing to himself, bewildered and furious, he seriously contemplated killing himself. He did not want the life with which he was now confronted, a life without Linda, or his son.

Like everyone else, Ryan had envisioned the life he would lead. He planned it, worked to achieve it, and was in a lot of respects simply sitting back and happily watching it happen. Everything to the point of the accident had gone accordingly to plan. But now, confronted with the reality of creating a new plan, a new life, Ryan found himself unable, and unwilling to do it. He felt that his life had ended on that highway too, at least the life he wanted, and there seemed to be no sense going through some other existence simply for the sake of being alive.

Generally these morbid thoughts would be pushed from his mind by Kelly's soft breathing as she lay sleeping beside him in bed, which she did for the first six months after the accident. Ryan would watch her at night, afraid to close his own eyes, terrified at the prospect of her ever being out of his sight again.

She was a gorgeous child, somehow even prettier than her mother had been. Before the accident, Kelly had been a bundle of boundless energy, whose face seemed creased into a permanent smile. Her girlish giggle announced her presence in every room she had ever been in, and she seemed to be friends with everybody she met. Ryan had always marveled at his daughter's confidence, even as a toddler, and the way that people were drawn to her because of it.

The death of Linda and Joey had changed her instantly. There had been of course, the tantrums and crying and acting out fueled by her anger and confusion. That had been expected. But between the outbursts, Kelly withdrew into herself, seemingly lost inside her head, with no willingness to let even her daddy come inside. Nothing Ryan did could seem to make her emerge from her shell. He even took her to a therapist, but she too was unable to get Kelly to open up.

Which is not to say that father and daughter were not close. In fact quite the opposite was true. The entire existences of both Kelly and John Ryan collapsed in on each other after the deaths of Linda and Joey. Neither was willing to be away from the other for a second, as each saw in the other the one person in the world who made life worth living.

There was only one person who John trusted enough to watch Kelly when he couldn't, who was conversely the only person whom Kelly was willing to be alone with other than her dad. After the funeral, Joe Fullem practically moved in to the Ryan home. He cooked every meal, did the laundry, paid the bills (many times with his own money), and generally provided John and Kelly the opportunity to grieve full-time for their losses.

The hardest part about personal tragedy is that the world does not stop along with it. No matter the personal devastation in one's life, others lives will always continue. Although she was too young to compose the thought, it was infuriating and confusing to Kelly that the sun continued to rise every morning, classes at school were the same, and even the commercials on television didn't change. John felt the same emotions. Although Linda (and he) had substantial life insurance policies on themselves, he still had a job that we was going to have to return to eventually, there were still bills to pay and grass to cut and clothes to wash. It was impossible for them to grasp how life around them could on as if nothing had happened.

Joe Fullem understood loss, and guilt, and he knew exactly the feelings that Kelly and John were having. Hell, he was having them himself. But he knew the best way he could help John and Kelly recover was to allow them the freedom to grieve without the worry of living.

When Kelly returned to school two months after the funeral, and John had returned to work, it was Fullem who picked Kelly up from school every day. He bagged a lunch for them both every morning and hoped that they'd remember to eat. Every night for a year after the accident, dinner was on the table at 6:30 sharp. There were many, many nights, especially in the beginning, that Fullem would sit at the kitchen table by himself eating. But after such nights, the Tupperware with the leftovers was never full the next morning. Giving John and Kelly the freedom to do something as simple as eating when they felt like it made Fullem feel as if, in some small way, he was helping things gradually get better.

And they did, over time. Kelly slowly rebounded and eventually developed into an incredible athlete. By the time she was a senior in high school, she was five feet, eight inches tall, and the star of the 2001 state-champion swimming team. She was also a National Merit Scholar and scored a 1430 on her college boards. Every Ivy League school recruited her heavily, and she was accepted early-admission to Yale, Harvard, and Penn.

She was an extraordinarily beautiful young woman, the kind whose beauty alone stops a room when she entered. Her smile, whenever it made a rare appearance, stopped hearts.

But she was a different person after the deaths of her mother and brother. Whereas before she had been bubbly and vivacious, with a smile for everyone she met, after the accident she was withdrawn, reluctant to expose herself to anyone. She had also lost her confidence, no longer was she so sure of herself.

Combined with her beauty, these traits had the effect of making her seem mysterious and alluring, and all the more attractive. Her fundamental sadness however had prevented her from ever forming any close relationships with anyone other than her father and Fullem.

Ryan had changed as well. Having lost the softening influence of his wife's sensitive liberalism, he too became hardened in a way he had not been before. The unfairness of his loss, and the natural cynicism engendered by his job, worked together to create in him a bitterness that no amount of healing could take away. But Ryan was careful not to expose this side of himself to anyone other than his daughter and his best friend, and only they knew just how permanently he'd been scarred, and how fragile his psyche was.

When it came time for Kelly to finally decide where she'd attend college, she sat at the kitchen table with Ryan and Fullem and asked their opinions.

"Sweetheart," said Ryan, "I don't want to unfairly influence you towards one school or another because of what I want for you. Whatever you decide is fine with me, as long as it makes you happy."

Kelly looked to her Uncle Joe.

"Hey, don't look at me, kid," he said with a smile. "This is something you've got to decide on your own."

Kelly shook her head in mock frustration. "I'm not asking you to make the decision for me, I'm asking for your input. Now, I've narrowed it to two choices, Harvard or Penn. What do you think?"

Ryan's heart jumped with joy when he heard that Penn was in the finals. He desperately wanted Kelly to stay close to home, but he sincerely did not want to do anything to influence her towards that direction. If there was one thing John Ryan was determined would happen, it was that his daughter be happy. And he didn't want her to stay close to home just to make him happy.

"Why those two?" he asked.

"Well...I think Harvard's the best school in the world. I can pretty much study anything I want and I'll be guaranteed a great education. The only problem is their swim program kinda' sucks."

"What about Penn?" asked Fullem.

"I like Penn a lot. Obviously, reputation-wise it's not Harvard, but they have a real commitment to athletics there that I really like. All of their programs are successful. Plus it's close to home."

Ryan reached out and touched his daughter's hand. "You're not adding that in there because you think I want you to stay close to home, are you?"

Kelly shook her head no. "Close to home is where I want to be, Dad," Kelly said as she squeezed her old man's hand. She also reached out and grabbed Fullem's hand as well.

"There's one more reason that I like Penn," she said as she looked them both alternately in the eyes. "They have a really well-respected school of social work." She looked at her father with tears pooling in her eyes. "I think that's what I want to do when I graduate."

Ryan looked at his daughter through his own tears and leaned forward to hug her. How he had ever managed to raise such an extraordinary young lady was beyond him. He loved her so much it hurt.

"I know Mommy would really have loved that," he was barely able to say.

"So, is Penn the choice?" asked Fullem through tears of his own.

Kelly pulled back from Ryan and nodded yes. Father and daughter embraced, lost in mutual love and need. Neither of them noticed the nervous look on Fullem's face.

CHAPTER 10

▼

"Ash Wilson is a racist and a liar," Roger Queenan proclaimed the day after his firing. He was standing at a press conference which had been hastily called by the Black Clergy of Philadelphia.

"Why do you say that?" asked an Inquirer reporter.

Queenan had been told by several former colleagues about Wilson's day one staff meeting where he'd outlined the policy initiatives he intended to implement.

"Because he never told anyone about his true intentions. He knew he'd never have gotten elected if he did. Why do you think the first thing he did when he showed up was fire me?"

The press collectively waited for Queenan to answer his own question.

"I'll tell you why. Because, in addition to firing a third of the lawyers who work for him, his plan is to start invoking the death penalty in every first degree murder case he's legally allowed to."

"Okay, so he's conservative on the death penalty. What's that got to do with you?" Asked a pretty blonde from channel ten news.

Queenan sneered at her, as did several members of the Clergy, who were situated behind Queenan. "That's exactly the kind of question I'd expect from someone like you." He said 'like you' as if they were curse words.

"The death penalty is disproportionately sought and imposed on young black men. Wilson knew there was no way I'd stand for that kind of racist policy. So he fired me."

The Daily News reporter jumped in. "I've been told by sources that you were fired because of your poor performance over the last several years."

Queenan eyed him suspiciously. "Oh yeah, your sources…you must mean the Jims…you know, Jim Crow and Jimmy the Greek." The reporters all laughed.

"So why are we here, Roger?" somebody asked. "What are you going to do about it?"

Queenan straightened up and paused for dramatic effect. "I'm not going to stand for it," he said quietly. "I'm announcing today my intention to fight the racism of this District Attorney's Office with every ounce of talent and experience that I have. I want the young black men of this city to know that through me, they have a voice. It's 1994 for goodness sake. I cannot allow a man who is so clearly living with a pre-1960's vision of civil rights to wield unfettered the power he hoodwinked the people of this city into giving him."

It was a bold coming out party for the law offices of Roger Queenan, which technically didn't even exist yet. But before the end of the day, he was getting calls on his home phone from people looking to hire him.

Wilson too was being inundated with calls, mostly from the press who were anxious to get his rebuttal.

He hated publicity though, and always had. Wilson felt strongly that nothing good can come out of injecting the public eye into an adversarial situation. And although he had not viewed Roger Queenan as his adversary when he fired him, his press conference certainly made him one.

Wilson was not naïve, though. He knew that if his administration was to have any credibility at all, he had to answer Queenan's accusations…quickly, vehemently, and publicly. He scheduled an interview with an Inquirer reporter in his office two days after Queenan's remarks had been publicized.

"I fired Roger Queenan for the simple reason that he was no longer performing anywhere near the level he once had, or the level I expect from my prosecutors," he said in response to the reporter's first question. "Roger's race had about as much to do with his firing as it did with his performance."

Wilson rattled off a series of statistics he'd memorized showing the decline in the number of cases handled by Queenan, and the decline in the murder conviction rate since he'd been chief of homicide.

"But what about all those changes Queenan says you're going to make. Were you honest during the campaign if you did not disclose them to the voters?"

Wilson shook his head no. "Of course I was honest. It's true I have a vision for the office which is drastically different than any of my predecessors. But what I said during the campaign was true. I will do everything within my power to fight crime in this city. Now that I'm in office, that's what I'm going to do."

"What about the death penalty issue?"

"I'm glad you asked," said Wilson with confidence. "I do intend to make changes in the way the death penalty is utilized. But that is only one of the initiatives I'll be implementing.

"For instance, as you know, I made a lot of money in private practice. I'm very proud of that fact. So I have decided not to accept a salary as D.A. Instead, I'm going to take that money and divide it amongst all of my deputies equally. Also, I have put over one million dollars of my own money into a trust to be managed by the city treasurer, with the sole caveat that it be used to increase the salaries and benefits of the prosecutors in my office. Salaries will be raised across the board for those who have earned it.

"As for those who have not, like Roger Queenan, they have already been fired. The people of this city, especially crime victims, deserve the best lawyers in town protecting their interests. That's my vision for the office. If Roger Queenan doesn't approve, he can go pound sand."

The reporter reviewed his notes and realized he hadn't gotten an answer to his question. "But what about the death penalty?"

Wilson smiled. "You know, I must admit to being very surprised by Mr. Queenan's accusations of racism with regard to the death penalty, considering that back when he was actually a good prosecutor, Roger put four murderers on death row…all of whom were black.

"Look, I'll be the first to admit that the death penalty has historically been sought and imposed in an inconsistent fashion, and that as a result, more blacks have been executed than whites. In fact, it is precisely for that reason that I am making the changes I am.

"I want every prosecution this office undertakes, be it for shoplifting or first degree murder, to have one, and only one concern…justice. Not race, not politics, not ego…justice. By making the blanket policy that my office will seek the death penalty in every first degree murder case where there are aggravating factors, as the law allows, that's exactly what I'm going to accomplish."

Having gotten his rebuttal, the reporter ended the interview. Wilson thought about what he had said, and while he believed it all, he knew it was not entirely truthful. He did not personally believe in the death penalty. But it wasn't his job to decided which laws he liked and didn't like.

The reality was that the death penalty was a valuable prosecutorial weapon. When it is invoked, the jury selected to hear the case must be "death qualified." That is, each juror must be able and willing to vote for a sentence of death, if the law allows it. The selection process for such a jury is much different than a normal murder case. Normally, only the judge gets to ask questions of the jurors, and the lawyers have to decide how to use their peremptory strikes based on questionnaires filled out beforehand.

But where the death penalty is concerned, both the defense lawyer and the prosecutor get to question each potential juror individually, and ask directly whether or not they will be able to vote for someone to die. If a person says no, or even expresses hesitation about their ability to do this, they may be stricken for cause. Additionally, in death cases, each side gets considerably more peremptory strikes.

The value of this process is that the jurors who are eventually picked are those people who can visualize and verbalize a willingness to impose a death sentence upon another human being. Statistically speaking, people who can do this are more prosecution friendly, conservative, and more likely to convict. It was for these reasons that Wilson felt so strongly about using the death penalty as a tool to help his prosecutors convict murderers. In an adversarial system, where each side has its own advocate, he saw it as simply making oneself the most effective advocate possible.

The Wilson-Queenan feud remained a front page story for about two weeks before petering out. As time went on though, Wilson's office began earning high marks from victim's advocacy groups, judges, and cops, and the tide of public opinion began to roll favorably towards Wilson, and away from the nay sayers.

But when the first opportunity to invoke the death penalty crossed his desk two months into his term, Wilson was confronted with doing what he knew was right, even though he thought it was wrong.

He decided to meet with the one person in the world whose judgment he trusted more than his own to discuss it. Cohen invited him to the Cigar and Reading Room for drinks and a cigar.

"Why are you having second thoughts?" asked Cohen between puffs.

"Because I don't believe in the death penalty," Wilson replied with a sigh. "I think that by allowing ourselves to seek retribution, or revenge, we demean the victim. It's as if we are saying that the life of some dirt bag criminal is equal to an innocent life lost, and that once the murderer has himself been murdered, justice has somehow been done. Well, that's a load of crap. There can be no justice for a murder victim.

No amount of punishment to the killer will ever bring the person back."

Cohen cocked his head. "Okay, but isn't there something to be said for the argument that by deliberately taking another human being's life, which you will agree is the ultimate crime in our society, one forfeits his right to his own life within that society? If not, how else can order in the society be retained?"

Wilson put down his cigar. "Order is retained just as much by removing the criminal from society as it is by killing him."

Cohen shook his head no. "Wait a minute. Just because a person is in prison, does not mean that they are no longer a part of our society. They may not move in the same circles as most other people, but they remain nonetheless.

"You see, Ash, what critics of the death penalty fail to conceptualize is that our 'society' is not a thing. It is not a set of people, nor is it a place from which one can simply be removed and forgotten about. Our society is an idea, a shared commitment to civilization. When one kills another human being, when they renege on their portion of that commitment, like a loose thread in a lace bonnet, their very existence threatens to unravel the entire order of things. We cannot deal with people such as these by simply putting them someplace where they can't be seen. As long as they exist in the world, they poison us all, and erode the idea to which we are all committed."

Wilson eyed Cohen with a smile. "You really believe that?"

"Not really," said Cohen with a wink. "But I can see the logic to the argument. And I can see why we have laws that allow for the implementation of the death penalty. Isn't that your job, by the way, to uphold the law? Is it really your province to decide which laws you like and which you don't?"

"Of course not," said Wilson with a sigh. "I know that in order to do my job, the death penalty is a necessary and important tool. It's just hard to know what is right."

"Again, I don't think you have the luxury to make that decision in your present position," Cohen said with an 'I told you so' smile.

"Feel free to lobby Congress and the state legislature to change the law when your term is up. But for now, the right thing to do, is what your job calls for you to do. Yours is an important position, Ash. Your decisions carry great weight and significance. As a taxpayer, I expect you to do that which you were elected to do, which is take criminals off the street by utilizing every legal weapon within your arsenal…But I must admit that as your friend, I am glad to see that you are personally struggling with this decision. It assures me that whatever you decide, it will be the right thing to do…even if it's not correct."

Wilson just smiled in response to Cohen's cryptic counseling. Like most people confronted with a difficult decision, he wanted someone else to tell him that he was right, or that he was wrong. But he had not had that luxury in years. He was the one who had to tell everyone else what was right and wrong.

He left the Union League that night not sure of the distinction. But in the face of his uncertainty, he vowed simply to do his job the best way he knew how…and not ask the question again.

Over the next three years of Wilson's first term, the District Attorney's office invoked the death penalty twenty-eight times. It was actually imposed seven. Seventeen defendants pled guilty to first-degree murder and received life in prison, one was acquitted, and three were found guilty of lesser offenses. In all twenty-eight cases, the accused was black.

In addition to his stance on the death penalty, Wilson did one more thing unheard of in the world of prosecution; he tried cases. No other big city D.A. in the country actually goes into court and does this. But Wilson felt that in order for his philosophy to have credibility, he had to be willing to go into court, look jurors in the eye, and convince them to apply the law as dispassionately and consistently as his policies intended.

Besides, trying cases was what he loved to do, so it was also a selfish decision too. In the beginning of his first term, Wilson started himself in the charging unit, where the assistant prosecutors work twelve hour shifts at a time in a trailer parked outside of Police Headquarters, deciding what charges apply to every arrest made. It was where all new assistant district attorneys began.

Wilson did not spend much time in the lower ranks, however. He was after all an accomplished trial attorney. By the beginning of his second term in 1996 he was trying murder cases exclusively. Of the twenty-eight death penalty cases that came through in his first term, Wilson had handled seven of them. He was the prosecutor in two of the cases in which the jury voted for death.

CHAPTER 11

▼

In the latter part of the first half of the 18th Century, after London, Philadelphia was the center of the English speaking world, home to a uniquely cosmopolitan and well-educated citizenry. One of those citizens was Benjamin Franklin.

In 1749, Franklin founded the College of Philadelphia, the colonies' first secular college (the other existing schools: Harvard, William and Mary, Yale, and Princeton, were actually seminaries). In 1751, classes began, and continued up until 1775, when the Revolutionary War interceded. The College reopened in 1779 as the University of the State of Pennsylvania, the first University in American history. In 1791, the school became a private institution, and was known from thereon as the University of Pennsylvania.

From its inception to the present day, although expanded considerably, the University has been located in the same area in West Philadelphia. Today, it occupies 262 acres of land, which run from 32nd Street to 45th, and from Chestnut Street to Baltimore Avenue. It is widely considered one of the top educational institutions in the world.

The first African-American was admitted to the undergraduate program at Penn in 1879. Since that time, few students, black or white, had caused as much of a stir upon their matriculation as Darnell Cooper.

He was six feet, eight inches tall, quick as lightning, and strong as an ox. His vertical leap was measured at 46 inches, he could run the forty yard dash in 4.3 seconds, and he could bench press 300 pounds. After stories about him appeared in Sports Illustrated, Time and on ESPN, Darnell became one of the most highly visible young athletes in the country, and there was speculation that he intended eschew college altogether and declare himself eligible for the NBA draft.

So when Darnell announced at a packed press conference held in his high school's gymnasium that he would not only be going to college, but that he would be attending an Ivy League School, it made national headlines. Almost overnight, Darnell became something of a national icon. A young black kid from the streets with great grades and an unlimited future, chose academics as more important than athletics. It was a great story.

Especially for the University of Pennsylvania. In the decade of the nineties, Penn athletics experienced a rebirth. After struggling in the late eighties and early part of the nineties, the university's administration committed itself to improving every area of its athletic department. The shift in focus was spurred by a desire to energize the campus, to inject a different kind of pride amongst the student body.

But by the time Darnell arrived on campus in the fall of 1999, the rest of the Ivy League had caught up with Penn by copying its formula for success; that is, by crediting the contribution a recruit could make to the school athletically as well as academically, and ignoring the critics who complained of lower admission standards. As a result, of the best basketball recruits who could gain admission to an Ivy League school, many were beginning to choose Yale and Princeton, which also had young, aggressive, black coaches.

So as big a deal as it was across the country that Darnell had chosen to attend Penn, it was a significantly bigger deal on campus. Season ticket sales for the basketball team increased by four hundred percent within two days of the press conference. Immediately, the bookstore began selling Cooper jerseys with Darnell's high school number, and the admissions department began to think of ways to incorporate Darnell's pictures into its promotional brochures.

Despite this enormous pressure and a constant spotlight, Darnell managed to shine. He quickly demonstrated an athletic skill that had not been seen in the Ivy League for a long time. He was the consensus Ivy League rookie of the year, as well as the league's MVP. Penn went 14-0 in the Ivy League that season, and lost a tough game to eventual champion Arizona in the second round of the NCAA tournament. Darnell averaged 27 points, 7 assists, and eight rebounds a game. With his size, ball handling ability and character, had he chosen to enter the NBA draft he would have been selected with the first pick.

But Darnell had no intention of leaving college early. He was too busy learning, and having fun. His grade point average for his freshman year was 3.8. He was well-liked on campus and considered to be humble and gracious to everyone he met. To the world at large, he was perfect.

Only Lionel and Dr. Charles knew what a struggle it was for Darnell to perform in all areas of his life as well as he managed. Darnell continued to treat with Dr. Charles at least once a week throughout his freshman year. Oftentimes, Darnell would simply sit on Charles' couch and cry with frustration and anger that he could not make go away. The most frustrating thing about his mercurial emotions was the fact that he couldn't truly understand why he felt the way he did.

Sometimes he would berate his teammates for the simplest mistakes, and later wonder what it was he was so upset about. As highly thought of as he was, those who knew him well learned to fear his temper.

Over time, his blow-ups became more and more infrequent though, and by the time he was ready to begin his junior year at Penn, Darnell was both a consensus first team All-American, as well as an Academic All-American. He spent that summer working as an intern in the offices of Cohen & Elson, sorting and delivering the mail. Darnell had become something of a favorite son of the lawyers in the firm, and everyone there followed his career with an extra special interest. The partners marveled at the humility of a kid who, if he so chose, could have gone out as a twenty-year old and made five times as much money as they ever had.

His humility notwithstanding, much like his mentor, Darnell suffered from no shortage of confidence. In fact, if not for a brilliant smile that he always wore for the world, his confidence would have been mistaken for cockiness. As it were, his self-assuredness was considered part of his charm, more Michael Jordan than Kobe Bryant.

Being who he was, Darnell also did not have any trouble meeting girls. Although he never let it interfere with his workouts or his studies, he always found his fun. He hardly had to look very far. Women of all ages literally threw themselves in his direction. It wasn't just that he was smart, and a world-class athlete, he was very handsome too. The easy access to women though, made him even more distrustful of them.

Darnell had never once consciously missed his mother, and believed that she had not impacted his life in any meaningful way since he was 11 years old. But he was wrong. Darnell had a deep-seated distrust, and fear, of the opposite sex. Dr. Charles recognized the source of these feelings, but Darnell wasn't convinced. Rather, he felt that Charles did not give him credit for being smart enough to be wary of women.

It was his determination not to let another woman ever hurt him again that prevented Darnell from ever forming any kind of close relationship with a woman. While there had been "girlfriends," they were really nothing more to Darnell than a series of one night stands. None had ever lasted more than a couple of months.

In August of the summer before his junior year at Penn, all of that changed. In fact it was at 2:33 p.m., on August 11th, to be precise. After that, nothing in Darnell's life would ever be the same. Because at that exact moment in time, Darnell was walking by himself up Locust Walk towards his apartment at 41st and Walnut, when he was struck by lightning. Not literally, of course. Lightning would not have made nearly the same impact.

It was at that moment that Darnell saw Kelly Ryan for the very first time.

The lightning had come in waves. The first wave to crash over him had been the sheer force of her beauty. Darnell had never seen a more beautiful face. Kelly's golden blonde hair seemed to absorb the sun-drenched day, and it shot out in beams like an aura. Contrasted against her deep tan, honed as it was by a summer of days spent as a lifeguard on the 25th Street beach in Ocean City, New Jersey, her blond hair and dark eyes were a vision unlike Darnell had ever encountered.

Once Darnell was able to catch his breath from the sight of Kelly's face, he drank in the rest of her body. Tall and lean, Kelly had her mother's breasts and smooth, Italian skin. From her father she'd inherited naturally muscular arms and legs, chiseled by hours spent in the pool. She wore a red cotton tank top, light brown khaki shorts, and leather sandals. Her calves rippled when she walked past him, and her face betrayed no recognition of Darnell, or his open-mouthed stare, as she walked seemingly obliviously away.

He stood still for at least five seconds, staring at the airy space she had just occupied. When he finally regained his senses, his first thought was to run after her, fall to his knees and beg her to spend every waking minute of every day with him until they were old and dead. And he almost did. But then he remembered who he was. So instead, he chilled.

Darnell fought the sudden courtship impulse with the self-discipline that made him a great student, and a great basketball player. Nothing good ever happens, either in an exam or in a game when you rush, he thought to himself as he made his way aimlessly back to his apartment. Along the way he ignored the stares and whispers of the people who recognized him. Freshmen. Classes were still weeks from beginning, and the only people on campus were athletes, who are on campus year-round, and the freshmen, there for orientation meetings, tours and seminars.

Whereas normally Darnell would have given everybody a big smile and put them at ease, that day he did not even know they existed. The only thing he could see was the angelic face of Kelly Ryan. If there ever was such a thing as love at first sight, this is it he thought.

As for Kelly, even though she had done her best to completely ignore Darnell when she saw him on 'The Walk', it was all she could do not to stop and stare right back at him. Kelly was a huge sports fan, basketball especially, and she and her dad had been to many a Sixers game together. They had also attended a fair number of Penn games since Darnell had arrived on campus, and they were equally in awe of his talents as the rest of the country.

But it wasn't his fame that had nearly cracked her famous cool when she saw him. She had never realized how handsome a man Darnell was. His close- cropped hair, smooth caramel colored skin, and dark brown eyes, on top of a powerful physique, formed a combination that she had never encountered before.

Kelly was very proud of herself for the way she was able to walk right past Darnell without appearing to even notice him. It was a skill she had picked up as a young teenager, when she had first begun to develop into the stunning looking young woman she had become. Kelly learned that even the slightest hint of recognition given to a leering man is like some sort of unwritten invitation to him. She learned to therefore ignore all of the stares wherever she went, so as to avoid even the possibility of strangers approaching her. As she headed to Gimbel Hall for a workout however, Kelly felt certain that she and Darnell would connect.

The opportunity presented itself sooner than either could have hoped. The University of Pennsylvania is home to two historic sports arenas. Franklin Field has been the home of the football team since the early part of the 20th century, and in fact, until 1970, was the home field for the Philadelphia Eagles as well. Prior to the creation of the Ivy League, Penn was a national football powerhouse, regularly taking on and beating teams like Army, Notre Dame, and Southern Cal.

Hall-of-Famer Chuck "Concrete Charlie" Bednarik was a two-way star there in the forties, in addition to a myriad of other old-time NFL greats. Aside from its rich history, the facility itself is an impressive stadium, with 65,000 seats. Located at 33rd and Spruce Streets, it is the largest on-campus football stadium in the country.

Sharing a parking lot with Franklin Field is Penn's even more historically significant basketball arena. The 'Palestra' was built in 1927, and up until the mid 1980's, was not only the home of the Penn basketball teams, but also Philadelphia's famous "Big Five." Consisting of the five division one basketball programs in the city, Penn, LaSalle, Temple, Villanova, and St. Joseph's, the Big Five is recognized around the country as college basketball's most intense intra-city competition. Over the decades, each school has taken turns in the national spotlight, yet always, the most satisfying title has been winning the Big Five "championship." In addition to these locally significant games, the Palestra has also played host over the years to more NCAA and NIT tournament games than any other arena. It is for these reasons that the public address announcer at basketball games always welcomes the fans to "college basketball's most historic gymnasium."

At the base of the parking lot which separates the Palestra and Franklin Field, is a small brick building known as the "Teahouse". In this building are some assorted Athletic department offices and storage areas. But most significantly, there is a dining hall, used almost exclusively by Penn athletes, located as it is where all of the athletic facilities are situated. In early August, aside from the Freshman Quadrangle, Teahouse is the only dining hall open on campus. It was in the Teahouse that Kelly came to eat dinner after her swimming workout that day. Darnell was already halfway through his dinner when she walked in.

He'd been thinking about her all afternoon, wondering who she was, what she was about, all the while turning over in his head the image of her perfect face. The impact his fleeting glimpse had had on him was like nothing he'd ever experienced before, the sudden desires and feelings he was having confused and thrilled him at the same time.

For her part, Kelly had shifted focus as soon as she'd hit the pool. There was no distracting her during a workout. She had been a state champion in the 400 meter butterfly in high school, and she fully intended to be a collegiate champion as well, and maybe even shoot for the Olympic team. Like attending an Ivy League school, the Olympics were a dream Kelly could afford to chase. Before leaving for Bermuda, both John and Linda Ryan had taken out rather enormous life insurance policies.

After Linda and Joey's deaths, Ryan had taken all of the money and put it into an account for Kelly. The stock market boom of the late nineties had made it possible not only to pay Kelly's tuition at Penn, it provided what she hoped would be seed money towards training full time for the Olympics after she graduated. Or so they had been led to believe by Joe Fullem.

As she made her way from the food line into the almost empty dining room, Kelly had yet to see Darnell sitting in a corner eating by himself. But he had seen her. At first, he just stared at the food on his plate, feeling a pressure he had rarely felt, and certainly never experienced on the basketball court. He could feel his cheeks getting hot and his feet seemed to tap up and down all by themselves. He had to speak to this girl, but for the first time in a long time, he was scared a girl would not be interested in him.

Kelly saw him sitting there, looking down at his plate and her heart skipped a beat. She suddenly regretted not showering after jumping out of the pool, but Teahouse only serves dinner until 7:30, and she had barely made it as it was. There were about fifteen empty, round tables in the room, with lone diners at three of them. Darnell's was all the way in the corner. Kelly chose a table directly in the middle of the room, pretending not to notice that anyone else was around. She sat so that only her profile faced Darnell. Subconsciously she knew that both her back, and her front, would send the wrong message. She was open to him approaching her, but she wasn't going to make it easy for him either.

Before he could talk himself out of it, Darnell pushed himself up from his seat and walked over to Kelly's table. "Hi," he said, immediately regretting how cheery he sounded. "Mind if I join you?"

Kelly looked up, his height requiring her to crane her head all the way back. She pretended to be surprised he was there, as if she'd just then realized that there was anybody else in the room. "Sure," she replied, immediately regretting how unenthusiastic she sounded.

Darnell grabbed a chair all the way on the other side of the table. "I'm Darnell." He tried to smile, but couldn't quite stretch his dry lips over his teeth.

"I'm Kelly," she replied. He was obviously nervous, and it charmed her more than his looks possibly could have.

"I, um, saw you earlier today on the walk. What team are you on?"

Kelly smiled. "Swimming. How 'bout you, what team are you on?"

It was Darnell's turn to smile. He was literally famous. It had been a long time since he'd had to tell anyone who he was. "Now, I'm 6'8 inches tall, I'm wearing high-top sneakers, and I'm black. What team do you think I'm on?"

Kelly laughed and held up her hands. "Okay, don't get touchy, I never knew how sensitive you chess players were."

It was official. He was in love. "Funny," he said with a smirk. Although Darnell was a superstar athlete, a Dean's list student, and overall big man on campus, he never simply expected of other people that they would automatically be impressed by him. At least he had fooled himself into thinking as much. Sitting there at that moment though, looking at Kelly Ryan, he wanted desperately for her to be impressed by him, and for the first time in many years, he felt totally unimpressive. It was unsettling for him to realize that his sense of self worth had become intertwined with, and dependent upon, his athletic and academic success.

Confronted with the prospect of charming this beautiful girl without the benefit of his celebrity, drained the confidence right from him. He suddenly doubted that Darnell Cooper, just the man, was not in this girl's league.

Watching his face, Kelly sensed his trepidation. She was nervous as well, but it wasn't the same thing. Her nervousness was the excited kind, the kind that flutters in your chest when you realize something really cool and fun, but also scary, is about to happen. Regardless of who he was, Kelly could only look at Darnell's face and marvel at how handsome he was. His obviously increasing nervousness only made him more handsome, as it stripped away the hale-fellow-well-met façade, and showed the real person underneath. Kelly had expected cocky, but was seeing vulnerable. She liked him instantly, and was anxious to like him even more.

But the silence had grown, and although Kelly was happy to let Darnell take the lead in the conversation, she was about to say something just for the sake of saying it when Darnell asked, "So, where are you from?"

"Northeast Philly," Kelly replied, relieved to have fought back the silence.

Despite his nervousness, Darnell was warming to his self-assigned task. "What year are you?" he asked.

Kelly nodded. "I'm a freshman." She blushed after she said it, embarrassed not to be older.

Normally such an admission from a pretty girl would have put Darnell in a position of power within the dynamic between the two strangers. As a junior, but more importantly, as the most famous guy on campus, Darnell would otherwise be the pursuee of a freshman chick, not the pursuer. But somehow, the fact that Kelly was a freshman only made him more nervous. His immediate fear was that a girl like this probably already has a boyfriend, and if she doesn't, it's only because she doesn't want one so that she can experience the college social scene without being tied down.

The long pauses were beginning to bother Kelly. For someone so strikingly pretty, and who possessed the athletic prowess she did, Kelly had remarkably little social experience. She understood all too well the concept of loss, and it was both her intentional and subconscious choice to avoid having anything to lose, so as to never feel the pain she felt when Linda and Joey were killed. In high school, her emotional detachment had earned her a reputation as a snob. Nothing could have been further from the truth. In fact, she was jealous of the close friendships her classmates and teammates seemed to enjoy, and felt that her inability to have the same kinds of relationships was due to some character flaw within her.

But in spite of her self-constructed emotional shell, Kelly realized that she was suddenly intensely attracted to Darnell, despite his bumbling. She couldn't say exactly why, though. He was very handsome, there was no doubt about that. But it was more than his physical attractiveness that was intriguing to her. Looking at him, searching for things to talk about, she realized what it was…his eyes. All of the boys, and men, who hit on her always had the same, hungry, insecure, shallow look in their eyes. And although Darnell's face betrayed insecurity, his eyes seemed… older, and deeper. He seemed to exude the kind of intelligence that is born of experience, as much as it is by books. Kelly recognized this look from somewhere, but she could not put a finger on where.

Darnell caught her staring at him, and it took his breath away. It was more than he could take. "Kelly?"

She laughed unintentionally at his sudden seriousness. "Yes, Darnell?" she replied in a deep voice, mocking his serious tone.

Darnell had accomplished some extraordinary things in his young 21 years, and every time he had, it was because he had set a goal for himself and simply kept working until he achieved it. He suddenly did not want to work for this girl. He wanted her to be his at that moment.

"I know you don't know me," he said, looking directly into her pale, blue eyes, "and given my witty repartee up to this point, you probably don't want to."

Kelly smiled.

"But I would very much like to take you on a date, somewhere very nice where we can both get all dressed up and I can bring you flowers and hold doors open for you and hold your hand as we walk down the street…and kiss you goodnight. And then call you when I get home to tell you what a great time I had, and then do it all again the next night."

Kelly looked down at her plate where her dinner had long since gone cold.

Before she could reply, Darnell said, "I want you to know that I have never said anything remotely like that to a girl before. But I have never felt the desire to before now. So whaddya' say?" He sat back in his chair, ready for rejection, but glad he threw his best pitch.

Kelly looked up, unable to contain her smile. "I would **love** to."

*   *   *   *

There is no more intensely pleasurable experience for human beings than falling in love for the first time. It is a feeling of euphoria that few who have experienced it ever forget, and one which many spend their entire lives trying to recapture. It is the feeling that has inspired the world's greatest art, as being in love makes even the simplest person see the world around him as lyrical and beautiful.

When love happens, it physically hurts to be away from the other person and the rest of the world ceases to exist. The silliest, nonsensical things become personal and hilarious secrets, and even the smallest transgression can spark vicious arguments. And when two young people who have fallen madly in love with each other make love for the first time, it is as if every ounce of their beings are poured into the other, and it is an explosion of pleasure like no other physical experience on earth. When in love, it is impossible to imagine a world without the other by their side, and it is equally impossible to ever imagine that they would part.

Darnell and Kelly were no exception to this time-honored tradition. By the time classes started, they were inseparable. They ate every meal together, studied together, and even worked out together. Darnell's friends and teammates rarely ever saw him, and when they did, he was with Kelly, who had gained immediate notoriety on campus as the girl-friend of Darnell Cooper.

Although they had fallen in love relatively quickly, it had not happened instantaneously. In fact, their feelings for one another did not truly begin to intensify until both Kelly and Darnell each discovered from the other that they both shared a deep pain which they hid from the world. Although he did not share the gory details, just the broad strokes of his childhood were enough to shock and awe Kelly. And for his part, Darnell understood all too keenly just how fresh the pain from Linda and Joey's death could still be, even after nine years, given that every day since he'd escaped the clutches of Clark and his mother's drug dependency, the emotional wounds were still as fresh as they had ever been.

Horrified at the abuse Darnell had suffered as a child, Kelly not only understood his continued pain, she was truly amazed at his ability to overcome it and accomplish as much as he had. Kelly quickly came to realize what an extraordinary human being Darnell Cooper truly was, and she both loved and respected him for it.

In short, Kelly and Darnell found in each other someone they could let inside the walls they had constructed to protect themselves emotionally, someone who could come inside and be trusted not to cause the other any more pain.

The absence of their pain when with each other was as joyous an experience either one of them had ever hoped to experience. While it lasted.

CHAPTER 12

John Ryan had known little of finance or investing. All the money he ever made had always been spent on his family, and his only real investment had been the down payment on the three-bedroom Cape he and Linda had purchased in the Northeast just before Joey was born. So when he was left with almost a hundred thousand dollars in Life Insurance proceeds after Linda's death, Ryan's thought had been simply to put it all into a savings account, and let it simply accrue interest until Kelly's eighteenth birthday. He had no intention of using any of the money for himself, even though he was the first named beneficiary of the policy.

But Joe Fullem had explained that a lump sum of money such as that could be invested in such a way that the principal would be protected, and steady growth guaranteed. Mourning the death of his wife and child, Ryan had turned over control of the money to Fullem, trusting that no one else would have Kelly's interests at heart more than he, and that no one would work harder to insure that Kelly's money was protected.

Fullem did work hard. He researched every possible avenue of investment, and keyed in on the upcoming dot-com revolution. He invested heavily in start-up technology companies, and in the first few years, had almost doubled Kelly's money. Every month, Fullem dutifully handed Ryan a statement of the investment accounts, proud to be helping the man who had done so much for him over the years. Ryan marveled at his friend's alacrity with investing, and was deeply touched yet again by the big man's loyalty and love for what remained of the Ryan family.

But like so many others, Fullem's luck eventually ran out, and the dot-com crash not only erased in a matter of weeks all of the gains he had made, but practically decimated the principal, to the point where less than five percent of the original sum remained. Horrified at the magnitude to which he'd betrayed John's trust in him, Fullem could not bear to have his friend know the extent of the losses. Ryan's friendship was the most precious thing Fullem had, and in many ways was the one thing that kept him sane. He could not let John know. To do so would be to lose Ryan's trust, a prospect too frightening for Fullem to contemplate.

So he assured Ryan that the losses were minimal, that he had seen the crash coming and had transferred the funds to Municipal bonds and CD's. Fullem even made up phony monthly statements which showed that the money was all still there. He had scrambled to come up with cash at one point so that Ryan could make a surprise birthday gift for Kelly of sending her to an elite overnight swimming camp in Connecticut.

But later, after Kelly had started classes at Penn, the first overdue notice for Kelly's tuition arrived in the mail. Fullem knew then that he had to either come clean, or do something drastic to correct the problem. Given that it cost $35,000 a year to attend Penn, with room and board factored in, he had few options.

Fullem intercepted the bill and clutched it in his left hand for an entire day. In his other hand was a succession of beers, shots, and mixed drinks. It was only after he was as drunk as he could get that he picked up the phone and dialed a number he hadn't called since he'd taken his last drink six years earlier.

"Evidence Room," the man answered.

"What's up, Sarge?" he said quietly into the receiver, his eyes closed, the alcohol on his breath hovering in front of him like a poison cloud.

A split second elapsed. "Fullem?!" the man asked excitedly. "Jesus Christ, man, what's it been, five years?'

"Something like that," he responded glumly.

The man on the other end of the phone knew there was only one reason Joe Fullem would be calling him.

"Don't tell me you're back in the game? I never thought I'd see that happen."

Fullem shut his eyes tighter. "Yeah, well…"

"I can't even believe you're alive. Those niggers really did a fuckin' number on you, boy."

Fullem hated that he had to be talking to this man again. He represented a time in his life when he had let his demons run out of control, a time spent drinking his life away. Fullem hated who he was then, and abhorred the thought of becoming that man again.

"I need a quick hitter," he said softly.

"Let me call you back from my cell phone," the man replied. He was the Sergeant in charge of the Philadelphia Police Department's evidence room during the overnight shift, a position he'd held, and exploited for ten years. More drugs and illegal contraband flowed through his hands on a nightly basis than all of the drug dealers in the city combined.

"All right," he said after walking outside of Police Headquarters and calling back on his cell. "I didn't recognize the number on my phone. Where you livin' now? How ya' doin'?"

Fullem wasn't in the mood for catching up. "Whattya' got for me?"

The Sarge was okay with eliminating the small talk. It was a relatively easy one time score, for which they could both clear fifty grand easy, he said. It was Ecstasy, or X, the "club drug" of the eighties that in the late nineties exploded back into the party scene, most prevalently amongst white teenagers. While the use of heroin and cocaine, and even marijuana decreased significantly, Ecstasy use, and deaths resulting from it, skyrocketed, especially among kids in 8th through 10th grades.

There was so much X on the streets that the cops could barely keep track of the stuff they confiscated. The evidence room was literally overflowing with the little white pills. At twenty bucks a pop, they represented real money.

But the problem was that he couldn't dump it where he normally would his other stuff, because X simply had a different market. It was the rich, white kids in the suburbs who took X, so that they could dance all night at their rave parties and have casual sex with strangers. X was a drug that the kids took so they could enjoy themselves more. Inner city kids had no use for such a drug. They needed their drugs to help them forget who they were.

"I got a hundred grand sitting in my basement, but no way to get at it," the Sarge had said.

This was the point of no return. "Give it up, I'll get rid of it for you."

Knowing that Fullem had never stiffed him before, the Sarge arranged to give him five thousand pills, with an agreement that they'd split evenly whatever he could sell.

As he sat there in his apartment a week later, a brown paper bag filled with a hundred thousand dollars worth of pills sitting between his legs, Fullem cursed his very existence and fought hard with himself as to why he shouldn't commit suicide. It was one thing to have lost all of Kelly's money and lied to John about it, it was quite another to do what he was contemplating doing. After much agonizing though, he realized two things: first, he couldn't, under any circumstances, bear Ryan's enmity. And second, he was too chickenshit to kill himself.

But he truly had no way of selling the pills. The market was white, middle-class teenagers, and they didn't exactly hang out in Fullem's old stomping grounds. No, Fullem only knew one white, middle-class teenager. She was his only choice.

Kelly had come home to do laundry and raid the fridge one late September Saturday afternoon while her Dad was working. Fullem offered to take Kelly to dinner at Wendy's.

It hadn't been difficult for Kelly to realize that there was something on Fullem's mind. Whenever he was troubled, his face clouded over like a little boy who's been denied dessert.

"Whatsamatter, Uncle Joe?" asked Kelly through a mouthful of chocolate frosty.

Although he'd made the decision to tell Kelly everything, and give her the choice of what to do, his conscience put up one last stand. He said nothing.

"C'mon, you know you're gonna' end up telling me anyway, so let's hear it. Why the long face?"

Fullem let out a deep sigh and looked over both shoulders. He then brought his enormous shoulders towards the tiny table and leaned in towards Kelly. "Do you know anyone who uses X?" he whispered.

Kelly snorted. "Uh, yeah," she said sarcastically. "Just about everybody's tried it. It's all over the place. That's one of the reasons I never go out. Everybody's so high on X on the weekends that unless you're high too, it's miserable. Why?"

Fullem looked down at his untouched burger and fries. "Do you know anyone who sells it?"

"Why, you looking to score?" Kelly asked with a laugh. But her smile evaporated as soon as she saw that Fullem wasn't kidding around. "Seriously, Uncle Joe, you're freakin' me out. Why are you asking me these questions?"

Fullem looked slowly up to meet Kelly's gaze. He slid his left hand across the table and placed it on top of Kelly's, making it disappear completely. "I'm in trouble, kid," he said softly. "I screwed up."

Kelly brought her right hand over and placed it on top of Fullem's. "How?"

"I lost your money."

"What do you mean, you lost it?"

Fullem shook is head. "I lost it. I mean, everything was going great, the original amount your mom had left was literally doubled at one point. But I made some bad choices, let it ride in places I shouldn't have, and guessed wrong in others." Fullem squeezed Kelly's hand. "You have got to believe me, kid, that all I ever wanted was for you and your old man to be proud of me. I'm so sorry."

Tears began to fall down Kelly's cheeks. She had never seen her Uncle Joe so vulnerable before. Heck, she didn't even know it was possible. But here he was, practically crying, laying himself open to her. The loss of the money hardly even registered in comparison to her surprise at Fullem's demeanor.

"Okay," said Kelly as she let out deep breath she'd been holding. "Let's just tell Dad. I know he'll be mad, but he'll understand that you meant well."

Fullem pulled his hand back and shook his head. "We can't tell your Dad. There's too much baggage there. He'll never forgive me, Kel. In his eyes that money was your mom's legacy to you, the way she was able to be a presence in your life forever. Now that it's gone, it'll be like I killed her all over again."

Her head hung low, Kelly pondered what Fullem had said. He was right, she realized. Ryan often talked about the money reverentially, treating it almost like another person in their lives. Ryan's dreams for his daughter were totally wrapped up in that money. It would crush him to know that it was gone, and that his best friend had lost it. Worse yet, Ryan would blame himself for letting Fullem manage the money in the first place.

Kelly knew all of this, and realized that Fullem was right. They couldn't tell Ryan unless they absolutely had to. "So why were you asking me about X?" she asked without looking up.

Fullem hesitated one last second. "I have a way of getting enough money to pay all your bills this year. I need you to help me set up a rave party. In one night I could clear enough cash to replenish the account so I can start getting it back to where it was."

Kelly looked up to her Uncle slowly, then out the window at the traffic. Everything seemed to be moving a lot slower all of a sudden.

CHAPTER 13

▼

It had been easy for Kelly to put Fullem in contact with the right kids, the stoners from her high school days who were still hanging out on the same street corners. They had eagerly joined the conspiracy to throw a rave and be Fullem's runners at the giant party. Afterwards, Kelly never spoke about the subject further with either Fullem or the kids from her high school when she saw them. In fact, the kids seemed a bit afraid of her after they had made whatever deal they had with him. Although she never attended any of them, Kelly knew there had been more parties, and more X being sold with Fullem as the supplier.

Fullem's revelation of himself and her complicity in his scheme affected Kelly deeply. She certainly felt differently about Fullem. They had always been close, but after that day at the Wendy's restaurant, things were never the same. Despite her genuine affection for the man, the real reason Kelly had decided to help him was because she knew it would absolutely wreck her father to find out the truth. Fullem was right about how Ryan felt about the money. It was his Earthly link to Linda, and his son, and gave them both a tangible presence in Kelly's life and her future.

Even while she had ignored her own failure to adequately deal with the deaths of her mother and brother, Kelly recognized in her father the continued torment and pain which he did his best to hide from her. From the moment he had been told of the accident, John Ryan had been an utterly broken man, but not in some clichéd, soap opera sort of way. In fact, everyone besides Kelly and Fullem thought he had recovered remarkably well, returning to work, encouraging Kelly to pursue her own dreams.

But all of Ryan's outward indications of normalcy were a complete charade. Only Kelly could hear him, late at night, years after the accident, crying in his bedroom. She knew about the pictures of Linda and Joey that her dad kept hidden under his bed, and more than once had found him clutching them in his sleep. Deep inside his heart was irreparably torn in two.

But the one thing that propelled Ryan forward in life was his beautiful and talented daughter, in whom he saw Linda more and more every day. Ryan's entire emotional existence, his very grip on reason, was bound up in his love for his daughter. He was a man with an infinite capacity for love, and he was dedicated to loving, and protecting, his precious daughter.

Thankfully for Kelly, though, Ryan was smart enough to know not to smother her with his love. Despite a fierce urge to follow her wherever she went, make her check with him every fifteen minutes, and prevent her from doing anything which might possibly cause her harm, Ryan fought mightily to restrain himself from doing so. It was in fact the truest measure of his love for Kelly that he never did anything to prevent her from blossoming into the rather extraordinary young woman she had become. Although he was terrified every time she walked out the door, he was even more terrified that he might do anything to stand in the way of Kelly's dreams.

For her part, Kelly not only recognized how painfully difficult this was for her father to do, but was also deeply appreciative and respectful of it. In fact, she was so sensitive to her father's concerns that growing up, she had done everything she could to insulate herself from the things he desperately wanted her to avoid. It was Kelly's way of expressing her appreciation, and her love, for everything her dad was to her. They were very much committed to one another, to the virtual exclusion of the rest of the world.

Except Fullem of course. He had been a constant presence in their lives. Over time, he became really the only person in the world, besides Kelly, that Ryan would allow himself to trust at all, and he came to rely on Fullem for many things. Kelly knew exactly what it would do to her father's already fragile psyche were he to learn that this man, in whom he had placed his trust, had destroyed the very things Ryan held most sacred: the memory of his wife and son, and the future of his daughter.

So Kelly had gone along with Fullem's deception for her father's sake, even though she hated herself for doing so. And although she believed that Fullem's intentions had been good, she couldn't stop herself from hating him too.

Fullem had not only betrayed her father's trust, but he'd seriously jeopardized, if not destroyed, Kelly's Olympic dream, not to mention her education. In a young girl already emotionally walled off, her Uncle Joe's actions had added a few more bricks.

It was in the aftermath of Fullem's betrayal that Kelly began to seriously question her relationship with Darnell, which had become for her an all-consuming passion. Jarred by the reality of being hurt by someone she had held so close, and trusted, Kelly's instinct for self-preservation caused her to doubt whether or not she could trust any man, particularly one she loved as deeply as she loved Darnell.

She struggled mightily with these doubts, and her rational mind told her to pull back from Darnell, that he would end up hurting her too. She believed he loved her, it wasn't that. But she had allowed him into her heart, a place that since her mom and Joey's death, had been a locked vault to which only Fullem and her father held the combination. Despite her diligence in keeping all others out, she had still been hurt. How could she possibly expect that Darnell would not do the same? She knew she couldn't.

It started the Friday night after her dinner with Fullem, when Kelly told Darnell she couldn't see him because she had to go grocery shopping. Next, she couldn't study with him because she was too tired from practice, and so on and so on. These things she did despite a burning desire to be with the man.

Darnell was, of course, emotionally wrecked, as only a twenty-one year old kid in love can be, by Kelly's sudden aloofness. But he was too intelligent (and had spent too many years in therapy), to brood, or pretend he wasn't bothered. He had even gone back to see Dr. Charles to speak with him about his feelings, something he hadn't felt the need to do since meeting Kelly.

Not able to bear being out of her presence any longer, Darnell sat down, uninvited, at Kelly's table in Teahouse one night after both had finished practice. But for a lone crew team member at the next table, she was alone in the room.

"Hi," he said cheerily.

"Hello," said Kelly, looking up in surprise. "I think some of the girls from the team are coming in to eat," she said coldly, as in, no room for you, buster.

Darnell was having none of it and ignored the raised eyebrow of the rower. "Great! I'll get to eat my dinner with a bunch of hot chicks instead of my usual one."

Kelly smiled weakly. "So, what's up?" As in, what can I do for you so you can then leave?

Darnell wrapped his arms around himself and shivered. "D'you feel that icy breeze that just came through here? Looks like winter's coming early this year."

"May be," said Kelly as she shoveled some mashed potatoes into her mouth.

Darnell was quiet for a few seconds, weighing his next words. A lot of men would get angry in a situation like that, where they had done nothing wrong and yet are being snubbed by the woman they love. Others would get apologetic, even though they had nothing to apologize for. Most, however, would demand answers as to why they were being given the cold shoulder. Such demands inevitably lead to vicious fights from the defensive posture each combatant has automatically put the other in, and more often than not, is the thing that prevents relationships from developing.

Darnell's emotions swung back and forth between anger and sadness, and he desperately wanted to grab Kelly by the shoulders, shake her, and yell, "What else do I have to do? Why are you blowing me off? Do you all of a sudden not love me anymore?" He wanted to both cry and storm off angrily, undecided as to which would be more effective in breaking down the wall she had thrown up around herself.

But Darnell fought all of those urges, seeing clearly how he had to pretend to feel, in order that Kelly might once again appreciate how he really did. He simply smiled, reached out and touched her hand lightly, and looked as deeply into her eyes as could when she looked up.

"I love you, Kel." The words filled his brain and the emotion flooded his heart. There was nothing he wouldn't do for this girl, including wait forever while she worked out whatever it was that was bothering her. "Call me when you're ready."

He squeezed her hand and smiled warmly at her. He then got up and walked away quickly, hoping that the tears in his eyes had gone unnoticed.

Kelly gritted her teeth and pretended to be eating, fighting her own tears. A few runaway drops streaked down her face and into her mouth, making her food wet and salty. Her heart ached, and she wanted only to run after Darnell and squeeze him tightly to her. A fierce internal struggle waged within her, her conscious desire to give herself totally to Darnell regardless of the consequences, fighting her subconscious defense mechanisms.

One by one those defenses were defeated, like a series of alarms and laser beams and vicious guard dogs around a great work of art in a museum, until very suddenly she realized that she was ready. Not just to love Darnell completely, but to let herself be loved back.

Kelly sprang from her seat, abandoning her tray of half-eaten dinner, and sprinted up Locust Walk. She could see Darnell walking in front of Van Pelt library, between the giant statue of Benjamin Franklin and Claes Oldenburg's famous "Button" sculpture. Darnell's head was hung low and he was walking very slowly.

"Darnell!" yelled Kelly.

He was running before he even finished turning around. They embraced fiercely, each squeezing the other, burying their faces into each other's necks, which became wet with the other's tears.

"I'm sorry," said Kelly as she pulled back to look him in the eye. "I don't know what's wrong with me. But I love you, and I want more than anything to just be with you. I've got issues, I know…".

Darnell smiled and pulled her close into him. "We all have issues. All that matters is that we love each other. Everything else will be okay."

They held hands and began walking towards Darnell's apartment, where Kelly had yet to spend the night. "Why are you so scared of this?" asked Darnell quietly.

Kelly thought for a few seconds before answering. "I would say I don't know, but I'd be lying." She chewed her bottom lip, debating that last step over the cliff. "It's hard to explain." Tears began to roll down her cheeks. Darnell simply waited, and listened.

"I haven't been able to talk about my feelings, really talk about them, since I was a little girl. Especially my dad. I feel like for all these years I have been carrying this weight with me wherever I go, that every time I smile or feel good or laugh, I feel guilty. And whenever someone tries to get close, and I start to want them to, I just kind of lock up emotionally." She snuck a look to her left. "Pretty weird, huh?"

Darnell stopped and looked Kelly in the eyes. He lifted her chin so that she was looking back. "No. It's not." He bent down and kissed her lightly.

As they continued walking, they did so mostly in silence. When they reached 40th Street, the choice was to turn left towards Spruce and walk Kelly home, or turn right towards Walnut, and head towards Darnell's place. They had not yet spent an entire night together.

Against every physical instinct he had, Darnell said, "How 'bout I walk you home?" He had not even seen the inside of her apartment, and by making this suggestion, knew he was essentially inviting the night to end.

"Will you stay over?" Kelly asked unexpectedly.

Darnell knew what she was asking. He also knew that Kelly was a virgin, and very much a product of an Irish Catholic upbringing by a very protective Irish Catholic father.

"You sure?" he asked, more hopefully than he wanted to sound.

Kelly nodded yes, and smiled mischievously. "You can stay over…but only if you beat me there!" With that, Kelly took off running, and Darnell gave chase. He had almost caught up with her as she bounded up the front steps of her apartment building onto the front porch.

Kelly's apartment occupied the first floor of a three story, stone house that had been converted to apartments on each level. Her bedroom was in the very back of the house, and the back door to the building, which led out into a very small alleyway between Spruce Street and Baltimore Avenue, also led directly into her bedroom. Kelly enjoyed her little private entrance, and used it often, much to her roommate Anita's dismay, who always complained that she never knew whether or not Kelly was even home.

That night though, with Darnell hot on her heels and breathing heavily from the run, she strode up onto the front porch and through the front door. She felt so happy and excited. But as she neared her bedroom, nervousness took over. They had to pass in front of Anita's open bedroom door to get to Kelly's room. But Anita was hardly shocked to see Darnell following Kelly down the hall to her bedroom. She had known the two were an item, everyone on campus did, and had suspected it would only be a matter of time before Kelly brought him around.

"Hey, Kel," Anita said as she buzzed by.

Kelly peeked her head back around the door frame. "Hey," she said with forced cheer, not wanting to talk.

Anita smiled knowingly. "Just wanted to let you know that some guy called earlier looking for you. Said he was a friend of your Dad's. Name's Joe?"

The message raised immediate alarm bells in Kelly's head. Fullem knew how much she hated lying to her father, and had been too ashamed to even speak to Kelly since asking her to do so. Kelly worried that he was calling because he needed more help, something she had no intention of giving. "Did he say anything was wrong?"

"No. He said he'd try you later. Hey, Darnell."

For some reason he blushed as he rushed past the door. "Hey," he said over his shoulder.

Had it been any other moment in her life, Kelly would have obsessed over why Fullem had called. But she was too happy, and too distracted, to think about it. She led Darnell by the hand down the narrow hallway to her bedroom door and closed it tightly behind her.

It wasn't what Darnell had expected. The walls were essentially bare, except for a large poster of Albert Einstein's face which hung directly over the double bed. The bed was (thankfully) devoid of the usual stuffed animals and extraneous fluffy pillows he had found in every other girl's bedroom he'd been invited in to. In fact, if Darnell hadn't been led into the room by the most beautiful girl he'd ever seen, he would have thought it was a guy's room. There were books everywhere, on the floor, on the bed, and overflowing in a leaning bookcase in the corner. In addition to books, clothes were strewn haphazardly about the entire room.

"You're a slob!" Darnell said laughing.

Kelly's face reddened. "I know, but in all fairness, you're the first guest I've had." She cleared the bed of books and clothes and sat down. Her nervousness was obvious.

Darnell sat next to her and pulled her long, tanned legs over so that they were resting across his lap. "Kel, relax." He grabbed her hands and sat quietly for a moment. There was something important he wanted to express, and he wanted to say it exactly right.

"Let's be different," he finally said in a rush of words. "Let's promise each other never to let there be any pretense between us, any secrets. Let's be so confident in each other that we can share our absolute darkest secrets, and know with total certainty that neither of us will ever do anything to take advantage of that knowledge…," His voice trailed with the realization that it wasn't coming out like he wanted it to.

"You mean let's trust each other."

It really was as simple as that. "Yeah…You think we can?"

Kelly pulled her legs back and sat Indian style on the bed. "I don't know. I've never tried. Have you?"

Darnell shook his head slowly. "I've only ever trusted one person in my life. He literally took me out of the garbage when I was eleven years old. Everything I am today I am because of him. He's the only person I've ever trusted."

"You're talking about Lionel?" Kelly had met Lionel on two occasions, once by coincidence when he and Darnell had been walking up campus together, once on purpose when Darnell had invited her out to dinner with the both of them. He was certainly very nice, and obviously successful. But Kelly had never pried into the relationship, figuring that Darnell would tell her what he wanted her to know, when he wanted her to know it.

"Yeah, I am, Kel." Darnell took a deep breath. "Do you want to know about me? I mean really know everything about me?"

Kelly nodded. "Yes," she said, and she meant it.

So he told her. He told her about his mother and Clark and the apartment and the beating and the sexual torture. He told her about being raised like a wild animal, foraging in trash cans for food, his baby teeth rotting away, and his flea-ridden skin. He told her about that horrible, wonderful day that he had met Lionel. He told her how

Lionel took him in, fed him, cleaned him, educated him, and brought him to life. He told her about the years of psychotherapy with Dr. Charles, about the transition from barely human to boy genius, to superstar athlete, to American Icon. He spoke without interruption for over an hour. It was the first time he had ever told anyone the whole story besides Lionel and Dr. Charles.

It was the scariest, most heart-rending, and uplifting story Kelly had ever heard. She was terrified at how much more it made her love him.

They sat in silence for a few minutes after Darnell had finished speaking. They were both emotionally exhausted. Darnell flopped back onto the bed and began laughing. It started as a giggle, evolved into a chuckle, then exploded into a full-blown, tears-in-his-eyes guffaw.

Kelly wiped the tears from her eyes and involuntarily began laughing too. "What's so funny?"

Darnell shook his head and wiped his own eyes. "I don't know. I just felt like laughing."

Kelly laid back and propped her head on her elbow so that she could look at Darnell. The bottom half of his legs were hanging off the bed, but his upper body alone took up most of it. His smiling profile, with his white teeth and granite chin, was about the most handsome thing she had ever seen. Kelly reached out and rubbed his muscular chest. "No one knows that story, do they?"

Darnell nodded no.

"Except for Lionel and Dr. Charles," he turned his head to face her, "and you." *And Clark*, a voice inside his head whispered. As he had always done, Darnell ignored the voice.

"Thank you for telling me," Kelly said, and she meant it.

"Thank you for listening," he replied, and he meant it too.

Darnell had never felt so elated. His true past was something he deliberately kept buried and hidden from everybody he knew. It wasn't that he was ashamed of it, but rather, he did not want anyone's pity, nor did he ever want to give people a ready-made excuse should he ever fail. Lionel had always pounded into him the belief that once Darnell had been taken out of his early environment, taught right from wrong, and given the opportunity to succeed, his past was rendered irrelevant. His successes and his failures, Lionel taught him, would be from that point on the product of his own deliberate choices, and nothing else.

Lionel also convinced him that if Darnell's true story were ever to become known, every foible, every misstep, every mistake, would either be excused by, or blamed on, his past. For the same reason that Lionel and Darnell did not believe that was a legitimate thing for them to do, so too did they believe that it would be illegitimate as well for the public to do it.

They had also talked of course over the years about what Lionel had done to create Darnell's identity as his nephew. Although Lionel had never once asked Darnell to keep it a secret, the boy knew that he could never tell anyone the truth…and he never would.

So he had told no one, save for Dr. Charles. But more importantly, he had never had even the slightest desire to share his story. Newspaper, magazine and television reporters always asked about his mysterious early years, with nary a response from Darnell or Lionel. Darnell explained his reluctance to be candid in this regard by claiming, truthfully, that it was too painful to talk about. Lionel would simply defer to Darnell.

But for some reason, Darnell had wanted to tell Kelly the story the first time he met her, and now that he had, he felt so happy that all he could do was…laugh.

"Was that your way of showing me that you trust me?" Kelly asked in a serious tone that immediately made Darnell's smile disappear.

"I guess so."

Kelly gritted her teeth. This was so difficult for her. She had been bungee-jumping once when she was in high school. It had been a dare, offered mostly in the hopes that the "ice princess" would melt with fear and be knocked off her high horse. She had accepted the dare out of pride, determined not to let anyone ever have the satisfaction of thinking they had the upper hand on her.

It was a bridge, a very high bridge, at least two hundred feet over a fast running river. Kelly had stood at the edge, looking down at the water, feeling the eyes of her classmates upon her. She could feel their hope that she fail, that she quit, and be humiliated. Her mind presented her with two options: fail, or have faith in the cords wrapped about her body and in the complete strangers who had secured them. Knowing that she would literally rather die than fail, Kelly gritted her teeth and leapt from the bridge, prepared for the worst possible outcome, and satisfied with her choice, even if she were about to die.

As she lay there on the bed she was confronted with a similarly stark choice. She respected and admired everything about Darnell, and was incredibly attracted to him physically. He was smart, handsome, funny, honest, and confident enough in himself not to be outwardly cocky. If ever Kelly Ryan was going to be able to truly love another human being, Darnell Cooper was the man. The question was whether or not she was willing to take the leap, willing to open herself up to the possible pain he could cause her. Or would she turn around and quit, retreat from the bridge, humiliated perhaps, but alive?

"That man, Joe, who Anita said called earlier?"

"Yeah, what about him?"

"He's my father's best friend. Hell, he's my father's only friend. They're like brothers, those two. He saved my dad's life when they were partners…or so the story goes."

Darnell raised an eyebrow, wondering what that had to do with the price of tea in China.

Kelly sensed his confusion. "I want to tell you something about me that no one in the world knows. I have not even said it out loud."

"Okay," Darnell replied nervously.

"I helped him sell drugs about a month ago."

Darnell didn't know how to react. But when Kelly lay back and started crying, he rolled over onto his side and pulled her into a hug. Her sobs came heavy into his chest, her tears wetting his shirt. Kelly wrapped her arms around him and they lay there hugging each other tightly, neither willing or able to let go.

Finally, Kelly pulled herself back and looked intently into Darnell's eyes. She saw no judgment there, no disbelief, no skepticism. All she saw was tenderness and compassion, and she felt a rush through her body like nothing she had ever felt before. Her chest felt like it does when you come over the crest of a huge roller coaster and plunge head-long into the pure, joyous fear. They kissed each other passionately, groping suddenly at each other like the children that they were. Kelly had never felt such intense desire, nor had Darnell.

They were completely naked in seconds, barely pausing to drink in the sight of each other's perfect bodies. As fiercely as they wanted each other though, and as ready as she was to receive him, Kelly's eyes flickered with doubt just as Darnell prepared to enter her. Seeing her hesitation, he did his best to slow himself, posting his weight over her, his chiseled arms and chest hovering like a statue. Despite her eagerness, she was incredibly nervous, and not physically ready to receive him.

"Ow," said Kelly, upon Darnell's initial, anxious and powerful thrust, "easy."

"I'm sorry," he replied, mortified that he may have hurt her.

Kelly smiled to hide the burning pain she felt in her vagina. She had expected it to hurt the first time, and she was embarrassed by her inexperience. "It's okay, you just have to go slow for a little bit."

He was already about to explode. Darnell gritted his teeth and tried to focus on everything but the extraordinarily beautiful girl who lay beneath him. For a few seconds, he was successful. But the moment swiftly overtook the both of them. They made love quickly, furtively, that first time, Darnell unable to contain himself for long.

Darnell had never been so excited, emotionally or physically. They lay there, the two of them, breathing hard and sweating, squeezing each other in hugs and kisses. Within a minute, Darnell was hard again.

The second time they made love it was slow, and long, and luxurious, and Kelly experienced a physical awakening that was more pleasurably intense than any sensation she had ever imagined. When they climaxed together, she felt her heart and her mind and her body were like one big electrical current. She had never felt as alive, or as happy.

They lay there naked on top of the bedspread, sweating and breathing heavily, both lost in their own thoughts. "Wow," said Darnell finally.

Kelly laughed. "I was just about to say the same thing."

They giggled together and rolled back towards one another, each ready for more of the other, when the phone rang, rattling them out of the moment. Kelly sighed, got up and walked across the room to the phone. Despite the fact that all the lights in the room were on, and she was as naked as a Jaybird, she felt no self-consciousness. In fact, she found that she enjoyed being naked in front of Darnell.

Darnell was hardly complaining. Kelly was a gorgeous girl with clothes on, but naked, she was ridiculously perfect. Her tan lines accentuated her perfect breasts, rock hard abs, and long, muscular legs, all of which looked practically average when seen in conjunction with her perfect ass. Darnell found himself staring to the point of leering, but he couldn't stop looking at her.

"Hello," Kelly said with a smile that vanished as quickly as she heard the reply. "Is everything okay?" she whispered into the phone, turning her back to Darnell. "No. I don't want you to, that's why…Fine, whatever. I'll be here. Bye."

All of the joy which had been in her eyes just a few moments earlier was gone when she turned around and trudged back to the bed, where she flopped onto her stomach next to Darnell.

"Whatsamatter?"

"I don't know. Listen, the last thing I want is for you to leave, believe me, but I think you should."

"Why, who was that on the phone?"

She was clearly pained. "Nobody. It'll just be a lot easier on me if you're not here tonight. Will you meet me for breakfast tomorrow?"

Darnell was crushed, but he could tell she was too, and that made him feel at least a little bit better. Obviously there was someone coming over, and whoever it was, Kelly didn't want Darnell there to complicate things. "You don't have some other guy coming over here do ya?" he asked half-kiddingly. "Cause if you do, I will have to kill him."

Kelly hugged him. "There are no other guys. I don't want there ever to be any other guys."

He squeezed her tightly. "Me neither." He pulled back from the hug, embarrassed by the enormous erection which had sprung up between his legs. They both laughed as they quickly got dressed. Kelly walked him to the back door, where they kissed softly. "I'll meet you in teahouse at nine o'clock, okay?"

"You bet," Darnell said with a smile. As she was closing the door behind him he turned. "Kel?"

"I really love you," he said.

Kelly reached out and hugged him again, as tightly as she could. "I believe you. I love you too."

She locked the door behind her, threw on a terry cloth robe that had been on the floor, and floated over to her bed. The thought of Darnell consumed her. Kelly had never thought she could feel this way about a boy, never thought she could feel this strongly about anyone. She lay down on the bed, lost in her thoughts, forgetting about why she had asked him to leave in the first place. After a few minutes, there was a light tapping on the back door. Kelly smiled as she jumped from the bed, excited that Darnell couldn't stay away. She opened the door without even looking through the peephole.

"Did you just fuck that nigger?"

She was so taken aback by Fullem's appearance that what he said took a second to register. His enormous body filled the entire doorframe, and he wreaked of alcohol. His clothes were dirty and he was unshaven. His eyes were bloodshot and wet. He had never looked so haggard, nor so mean.

"Are you drunk?" Kelly asked him as he staggered into the room.

"Answer my question," he growled. Fullem was obviously upset and angry with her, and his demeanor scared her.

"What the hell is wrong with you? Does my dad know you're here?" She tried to sound angry, but it only made her sound unsure of herself.

Fullem didn't answer. Instead, he slowly paced the room, looking over the scene, as if he was trying to memorize it. Finally, he turned and glared at Kelly. "Is this what you do up here in the Ivy League? Bang these big fucking city coons?"

"Fuck you!" she yelled. She rarely cursed. "I don't know who you think you are, but don't you dare come in here and talk that way about someone I care about. Why are you here, anyway? You need me to help you sell some more drugs?"

With a violently swift rush, Fullem grabbed Kelly around the throat and threw her down on the bed, where she landed with a thump against the wall. "You better watch your mouth, little girl," he hissed.

Suddenly she was really frightened, remembering for the first time in years the last time she'd seen him in this state. But the sheer force with which he'd been able to throw her down took her breath away, and she was unable to speak. She'd never experienced that kind of brutal strength.

"That never happened," Fullem was saying, and Kelly didn't know if he meant the drug thing, or what he had just done.

Kelly sat up slowly on the bed and pulled her knees to her chest. It was all too much to absorb. She had refused for so long to even let herself think about Linda and Joey over the years, but now all at once, her brain was flooded with memories. Seeing Fullem as he looked, standing there with his heaving chest and stench of alcohol, she suddenly remembered hearing Fullem tell John Ryan that his son was angry because Fullem would not let him go out with his friends on the previous Saturday night. That had not been true.

"Why are you here?" she asked as calmly as she could.

Fullem was pacing the room like a hungry grizzly around a campfire. "Your old man's talking like he wants to put your account officially into your name." The account was currently in Ryan's name because Kelly had been a minor when it was created.

Kelly raised an eyebrow. "What did you tell him?"

"I told him it wouldn't be a problem."

Kelly shook her head sideways. "Don't you think this has gone too far? I mean, you really didn't come here tonight expecting me to continue to lie to my father, did you?"

"It's for his own good, Kel," he said softly.

"Oh, bullshit! Lying to him has never been for anyone's benefit except your own. You're really screwed up, you know that? Your entire life is for some reason wrapped up in my father's approval, and yet in order to get that approval you have to hide from him what a loser you really are. It must eat away at you at nights knowing that my father would spit on you if he really knew what you've done."

Fullem stopped moving and glared down at her. "You got a smart fuckin' mouth, you know that?" he slurred. "You're just like your mother."

"Don't you dare ever speak about my mother, you piece of shit!" she hissed at him. Hot tears began streaming down her reddening cheeks and she buried her face in her hands, her body wracked with sobs.

Fullem's shoulders slumped and he sat down heavily at the foot of the bed. But when he reached up to rub Kelly's leg, she recoiled as if she'd been bitten.

"Don't you TOUCH me!" she shouted as she crawled to the farthest corner of the bed. Her eyes narrowed and her lips curled in disgust at Fullem's surprised expression.

But her eyes suddenly widened. "That's what Joey said to you that night," she whispered almost to herself. "I remember…you were drunk…You went into Joey's room and I remember now…he said 'Don't you touch me.'"

Fullem stood up. "Shut your mouth. You don't know what you're talking about."

Kelly scrambled to her feet and stood on the other side of the bed.

"Oh yes I do, Uncle Joe," she sneered. "He said 'don't you touch me, and then the next day, right before you took him to baseball practice, he told me he was going to tell mom on you...But he never got the chance, did he?"

Fullem balled his immense fists. "What are you trying to say, little girl?" He whispered malevolently through clenched teeth.

"You caused that accident, didn't you? You must have followed my mom to the practice. I remember you left as soon as she did. You knew what a nervous driver she was...YOU MOTHERFUCKER!"

Kelly darted towards the front door of the bedroom, but before she even took two steps, Fullem took one long step to his left, grabbed her with one hand, and punched her in the jaw with the other. She was lifted off of her feet, and landed unconscious on the bed, her mouth bleeding profusely, her robe thrown open.

Fullem stood there in the room, his chest heaving, sweat pouring down his face, contemplating his next move.

He walked over to where Kelly's lifeless body lay, wrapped one huge hand around her thin neck, and squeezed. With the deprivation of oxygen, Kelly's body automatically fought back, her legs kicked and her arms flailed, but only briefly. Within a minute, she was dead.

CHAPTER 14

▼

The clanging phone woke Noelle Wilson from a deep, restful sleep, and it took her a few seconds to realize she wasn't dreaming it. "Hello?" she murmured groggily into the receiver.

"Noelle? It's Tony Sciolla," said a gruff voice. "Sorry it's so late, but I gotta' talk to Ash."

Noelle handed the cordless phone over to her husband, who by now had turned on the table lamp and was rolling over to see who it was. "What is it?" he whispered into the phone.

"Ash, it's Tony. I wouldn't bother you this late if it wasn't absolutely necessary. We're about three hours into a murder investigation of a Penn co-ed who was killed earlier tonight in her off campus apartment. It looks like she was raped, beaten pretty badly, and strangled. She was the daughter of a detective in the Northeast squad."

Wilson sat up in bed and rubbed his eyes with his off hand. "We got a suspect?"

"Darnell Cooper."

Wilson was now wide awake and suddenly aware of why it was necessary for Sciolla to wake him up at three o'clock in the morning. "How much of a suspect is he?"

"Well, we've got the girl's roommate who saw Cooper go into the girl's bedroom with her. She thinks she heard them having sex, and a little bit later hears Kelly yell 'don't you touch me' and a couple minutes later 'you motherfucker,' then she hears a thump, and then nothing. She waits a couple of hours before doing anything because she says the girl was really private and they weren't really that close. But finally she goes to knock on the door, and when there's no answer, goes in. The girl was dead on the bed."

"Wait a minute, did anyone see Cooper leave?"

"Nope. The apartment is on the first floor of one of those big old stone jobbies that got converted into apartments. The girl's bedroom had a second door which was apparently the original back door to the house. That door leads out into a little alleyway. The roommate says she would have seen anybody who came in or out the front door, because they would have to walk right past her bedroom door, which was open the whole time."

Wilson shook his head. As close as he was to the athletics programs at his alma mater, he was intimately familiar with Darnell Cooper, and in fact, had spent a fair amount of time with him over the preceding two years at fundraisers and banquets and post-game parties. Wilson had actually participated in a campaign by a group of prominent local business and political leaders to persuade Darnell that he should remain in school, rather than go pro after his sophomore year. Wilson believed that Darnell represented everything that was right with the world and one of the true role models out there. And he wasn't alone in those feelings.

"Any trace evidence?" Wilson asked.

"Crime scene says blood on the bed was the girl's. Hair, fiber, and semen were taken off the bed and are on their way to the lab. Fingerprints were obtained. Autopsy's being done now."

"Where are you?"

"I'm at the scene. So is the press. Right now it's just local print, but this is going to be national headlines in a couple of hours."

Wilson was already up and looking for his clothes. "All right. No one makes any comments to the press, on or off the record. Keep the scene free of all non-essential personnel. I will be in my office in an hour. I want a complete briefing, including autopsy results. And Tony?"

"Yeah?"

"Prepare an affidavit of probable cause to get a warrant for Cooper's hair and blood. I'm going to give him an opportunity to just give it to us, but in the event he says no, I want to have the warrant ready. Okay?"

"You got it."

Wilson hung up the phone and began rushing around, looking for his socks and shoes. Suddenly it dawned upon him the magnitude of what had happened, and what was about to happen. He shook his head and took a moment to calm himself.

"You okay?" asked Noelle.

"No."

Mrs. Wilson sat up behind her husband and rubbed his back. "What's happened?"

Ash let out a sigh and began pulling on his socks. "I think I'm about to charge the American dream with murder."

*   *   *   *

It was past 5 a.m. by the time Wilson made it to his office. It had been reported on KYW-1060 news radio that a Penn student had been found murdered, but no further details were given.

Wilson strode into his office and somebody handed him a cup of coffee. In the room were Tony Sciolla, a fifteen-year veteran of the D.A.'s Detectives, Alan Small, Wilson's top deputy, and Frank Grace, a long-time assistant D.A. whose function over the years had developed into a media-relations position; he was the only assistant not expected to try cases.

"What have we got at this point?"

Sciolla took the lead. He was not an attractive man. Standing about five feet, seven inches tall, he had a very round belly which rested on top of very thin legs, giving him what Wilson often joked was the "tomato on toothpicks" look. He had a big bushy moustache and he wreaked of tobacco from the pipes he collected and was rarely seen without. His suit jackets never seemed to match his pants, and they always appeared too tight. His white socks were a staple, no matter the outfit, and they were always visible under his usually ill-fitting pants.

Notwithstanding his physical appearance, Sciolla was the best detective in the city. He had handled some of the highest profile murders that had occurred over the last ten years, and Wilson relied heavily upon his input in just about every major investigation. He had been the lead detective on every one of Wilson's murder cases. Sciolla was as perceptive and well-educated as anybody, having graduated cum laude from Duke University with a Masters in criminal justice. He was one of those rare human beings whose absent-minded appearance somehow lent a greater air of intelligence about him, as if he was too smart and too focused on important things to worry about how he looked.

Sciolla took the unlit pipe from his mouth. "We dragged the on-call M.E. out of bed to help process the scene and do the autopsy. It's Maury Templeton." Sciolla paused at the roll of Wilson's eyes, but didn't comment.

"Maury says there are abrasions in the vagina consistent with rape. Her jaw was broken before she was killed. Time of death was between 10:30 and 11:30. Cause of death is manual strangulation, which occurred a short time after the injuries to the vagina were inflicted."

"How short?" asked Wilson.

"He can't say. Within an hour is the best he can do. There was also semen in the vagina and on the bed."

"Any way to tell if it's old?"

Sciolla shook his head. "Two things: First, roommate says that Cooper was the first boy the girl had ever brought back, and she didn't sleep around. Second, M.E. says there were spermatozoa present."

Grace spoke up. "What's that mean?" He'd have to explain it to the press.

Wilson answered. "Spermatozoa are sperm with their heads and tails intact. It means that the semen was probably deposited last night, not from some earlier sexual encounter."

"Last thing for now," said Sciolla. "Bruising pattern on the neck and jaw suggests that whoever killed her had very large hands."

"How 'bout fingerprints?" Asked Small.

Sciolla shrugged. "Right now we've got about fifteen different sets of identifiable prints throughout the room, which includes Cooper's. It's a college apartment. Apparently there was a cleaning service offered by the landlord, who also had a key, by the way. We'll see where that takes us, but my guess is we won't get anything from the prints other than that Cooper was in that room as some point during his lifetime."

"I was more referring to prints on the body," said Small without looking up from his notes.

Wilson sighed and gave Small a disapproving look. They had argued many times with the police commissioner about getting the equipment necessary to lift prints off of skin. But the Commissioner, ever conscious of staying within his own budget, had always refused. He told Wilson that as soon as a judge said such evidence was admissible in court, he'd approve the expenditure.

Wilson rubbed his face. "Frank, I think I know, but tell me how you see this playing out over the next few days."

A fastidious man in his late sixties, Grace had a clipboard in front of him with an outline of notes. Even though it was just after five in the morning, he was wearing a perfectly pressed blue suit with his customary bow tie.

"As soon as we go public with Cooper as our suspect, either by way of arrest or questioning, this becomes a national story immediately. We all know what this kid is about, and so does the rest of the country. The biggest thing we have to prepared for, Ash, is the race angle."

Wilson leaned back in his chair and threw up his hands. "No, absolutely not. We're not going down that road. You make that clear from the beginning, Frank. This is going to be about evidence, and it's going to go by the book. You got that?"

Small and Sciolla shared a skeptical look. "Ash," said Small, "we all know how sensitive you are about this subject, but we can't be naïve. I mean, it's breaking my heart to think what I'm thinking. I hate to be dramatic about this, Ash, but when we go after this kid for the murder and rape of an Ivy League white girl, who, by the way, is also the daughter of a Philadelphia homicide detective, we are going after every black American's dream of what is possible for them in this country, both good and bad. So let's not sit here and pretend we can avoid this issue."

Wilson felt his heart pounding with growing frustration. He could see it just as clearly as the other men in the room could, and had in fact seen it as he sat on his bed over an hour earlier. This poor dead girl was about to become a footnote in the personal destruction of an American icon, and Wilson would be the man holding the sledgehammer. But that was secondary, really, to Wilson's true dread; that in the smoky tumult which lie ahead, justice would be impossible to find…for either side.

"Go talk to him, Tony. See if he'll come in voluntarily. If not, show him the warrant and get the samples."

Sciolla had already found out Darnell's address and the fact that he lived alone in a one-bedroom, first floor apartment in a building at 41st and Walnut. He was there within twenty minutes. He had to knock several times before a light finally came on.

Darnell opened the door wearing nothing but boxers. He had clearly been sleeping.

The detective was unprepared for just how big Darnell was. At six feet, eight inches tall, and supremely muscular, he dwarfed the pudgy policeman, who was suddenly very grateful for the two Penn police officers sitting in a squad car just a few feet down the street. Sciolla took note of Darnell's huge hands as he showed his badge and asked to come in.

Darnell led him into the living room/kitchen area, which had a matching sofa and recliner. Darnell sat on the sofa, Sciolla remained standing. "Son, do you know a girl named Kelly Ryan?"

Darnell's heart jumped into his throat. "Yes, I do, is something the matter, is she okay?"

"Why do you ask me that, son?"

Darnell shot Sciolla an irritated look. He was tired, but not stupid. "Because it's like five o'clock in the morning and you're a cop and you just woke me up to ask me if I know Kelly. Don't let me slow you down here, Colombo, but could you please tell me what's happened to her?"

"All right, take it easy, kid. Were you with her tonight?"

Darnell gritted his teeth. He was suddenly very frightened. Something terrible had obviously happened. "Yes, I was. I was in her apartment until about ten-thirty. Will you please tell me what's happened?"

"D'you go out the front door when you left?"

Darnell stood up, and Sciolla took a step back. "Why? Does it matter?"

"Take it easy, kid," said the detective again, this time as a command as he brought his right hand up to his hip, "we're just talking. Is there anybody who can verify that you left there at ten-thirty?"

Darnell put his hands on his hips. "No, I came right home and went to bed. Now I'm not answering anymore questions until you tell me what's going on."

Sciolla put away his notebook and pencil, and looked hard into Darnell's eyes. This was always a very important moment in any murder investigation, and it was one Sciolla prided himself on being able to decipher correctly. "Kelly's dead, Darnell. She was raped and strangled last night."

Everything inside Darnell rushed downward. His face and shoulders and hands fell and he sat down hard on the sofa. His mouth was open and his eyes were blank. He said nothing, seemingly oblivious to Sci-olla's presence, and just shook his head slightly from side to side.

It wasn't the reaction Sciolla had expected, and he briefly considered that the kid didn't do it, but just briefly. "I need you to do something for me, Darnell," he said softly.

Darnell looked up at the detective, but there was little comprehension in his eyes.

"I need you to come down to Police headquarters with me and give me a blood and hair sample. Will you do that for me to help me catch whoever did this to Kelly?"

Darnell nodded blankly.

It took a few minutes for him to get dressed. Throughout that time, Darnell said nothing, and appeared lost within his own head. Sciolla watched this with great interest. The kid was either the greatest actor he had ever seen, or he was genuinely shocked by the girl's death. But Sciolla had arrested enough murderers over the years though to know that killers are often devastated when confronted with the reality of what they've done. In fact the more he thought about it, given that this kid wasn't some hardened killer, Sciolla realized that Darnell's reaction was exactly the kind he should have expected.

They drove in Sciolla's unmarked Mercury Grand Marquis, with Darnell in the back seat, and followed by the Penn cops. Darnell was not handcuffed, nor was he under arrest. When Sciolla checked his rearview mirror, the boy appeared to be crying.

"How well did you know her?" he asked, his voice low and compassionate.

Darnell seemed surprised to hear Sciolla's voice. "Huh?"

"How well did you know her?"

Darnell's bottom lip trembled and he bit it hard. He scrunched his face to fight the tears, but the dam had already been broken. He began sobbing uncontrollably, unable to answer.

To anyone else in the world, Darnell's behavior would have suggested that he cared too much about Kelly to kill her. But to a veteran homicide detective like Sciolla, it only convinced him all the more that Darnell was guilty. Love had put more guys on death row than greed or hate put together.

"You were boyfriend and girlfriend?" Sciolla asked soothingly.

Darnell nodded.

"How long were you two dating?"

Darnell was so sad. It felt good to talk about it. "Three months…," he suddenly blinked hard, as if a flash bulb had just gone off before his eyes. Tonight was the first time we made love, he was about to say, but at that moment, his shock and grief gave way to the fearsome reality of the situation. He was in the back of a police car, headed to the police station to have samples of his blood and hair taken because his girlfriend had been found dead last night, and he was the last person seen with her. Suddenly he was terrified, and even though he had done nothing wrong, he felt the urgent need to say something that would convince the detective that the obvious perception was not the reality.

"Listen," Darnell said as he leaned forward. "I love Kelly and there is no way I would ever do anything to hurt her."

Sciolla nodded with understanding into the rearview mirror. "Hey, I believe you, kid. It just looks bad, you know. Mind if I ask you a personal question?"

Darnell nodded yes, wanting to appear as cooperative as possible. His new focus was on making Detective Sciolla believe that he had done nothing wrong and had nothing to hide. Darnell leaned forward to hear the question.

"Did you and Kelly have sex last night?"

He felt like he'd been punched in the gut. There it was, the million-dollar question, but Darnell's brain was stuck, he couldn't figure out how to answer the question without making Sciolla think he was guilty.

"No," he replied quickly, not wanting to show any hesitation, but the doubt about how to answer which had crossed his mind had also traversed his face, and the detective had not missed any of it.

That's the ballgame, Sciolla thought to himself. If there's no semen match, then the kid walks. If there is, well, the kid just hung himself. Sciolla said nothing more, but the corners of his mustachioed mouth betrayed a smile, for nothing made Sciolla happier than to solve murder cases.

Seeing the hint of Sciolla's smile, Darnell sank back in his seat. It slowly, and suddenly, dawned upon him that this detective's perception was not important at all, and the lie he had just told to alter it had immediately served to create a whole new, much more unforgiving reality.

"Um, listen," he stammered, "I don't want to seem like I'm trying to hide anything, but I really think I should call a lawyer before I say or do anything else."

Sciolla shrugged nonchalantly. "Yeah, sure, kid, whatever you want. You can use the phone at the station." This time Sciolla didn't even try to hide his smile.

Police headquarters at 8th and Race Streets for years has been known informally as 'the roundhouse' for the simple reason that it is a five-story, concrete building with a circular design. It is where almost all those who are arrested for crimes in the city are first taken to be processed and arraigned. Once inside, Sciolla led Darnell into a small, fourth floor ante-room where he was able to use a telephone in private.

Lionel picked up on the second ring. He was just about to head to the gym.

"It's me," said Darnell flatly. "I'm at the police station." Tears unexpectedly rolled down Darnell's cheeks. "Kelly's dead. Somebody killed her, and…raped her." He grimaced, then wiped his eyes and took a deep breath. "They think I did it. They want to draw my blood and take a hair sample." Darnell cupped the receiver around his mouth and whispered, "Lionel, we had sex last night. It was the first time."

Lionel's heart jumped into his throat and he had a million questions, but he forced himself not to react. "Okay," he said so calmly that Darnell was sure he hadn't heard a word of what had been said. "Relax.

Everything will be fine. Do not speak to anyone, not even to tell them your name. I will be there in forty minutes. Do not say a word. Everything will be fine."

CHAPTER 15

▼

Before the deaths of his wife and son almost a decade earlier, John Ryan had been, by all accounts, a gregarious, popular man with many friends, most of whom he genuinely liked. He loved his family and his job, and he was happy.

After the accident though, he was a different person, suspicious of others, cynical, and bitter. He was like a stilted beach house ravaged by a surging tide, teetering on the wobbly foundation of two remaining pylons. It seemed, at least for a few years after the accident, that at any moment he might just give up the fight and keel over. But over time, Ryan allowed a new foundation to be built beneath him.

At first, Kelly, and Fullem, provided the basic support he needed to keep himself upright, and prevented him from being washed away in a sea of grief and self-pity. Gradually, a third, reinforcing stilt grew under Ryan's existence, and if Kelly and Fullem saved the interior from toppling, this last support shored up the exterior, allowing those around Ryan to see a house in order, assuring all of its structural integrity.

This third pillar of John Ryan's existence was the job. He had been a decorated detective before the accident, and he was always good at what he did. But after Joey and Linda were killed, and he gradually reinserted himself back into the world, Ryan's job had become the conduit through which he restored order to his life. The police psychologist he was forced to see for three visits before he was allowed back on the street, and with whom he had shared absolutely nothing, saw Ryan's newly intense passion for the job, and theorized that it resulted from a desire to forget about Linda and Joey; that it served as an intense distraction from having to deal actively with his overwhelming grief.

In a way she was right, as Ryan certainly did everything he could to avoid dealing with the reality of his wife and son's death. But she had been mostly wrong, because Ryan's absolute determination to solve every homicide case he was assigned, was born of one single motive. He wanted to prevent any other family from ever having to suffer the added, intensifying grief of never seeing the face of the person who caused the death of their loved ones, and seeing that person punished.

Despite a monumental effort, waged over a period of years, Ryan had never been able to find the driver of the car which had run Linda and Joey off the road. He had interviewed and re-interviewed the witnesses dozens of times; had run motor vehicle checks on every car even remotely fitting the description given, and had spent hours upon hours parked alongside the spot on the Schuylkill where it happened, hoping against hope that the driver might pass that way again and somehow be recognizable to Ryan as the man responsible for the deaths of his wife and son.

Recognizing however, over time, the futility of his quest, Ryan channeled all of that energy and anger and determination into his job, working Herculean hours, refusing to give up on even the most inscrutable murders. It became his peculiar passion pursuing murderers, to the point where it fueled his desire to live. Once he learned who the victim was, about the life he or she led, and the family and friends left behind, Ryan would not rest until the person responsible was caught and behind bars.

Perhaps it was this single-minded determination that justice be done which kept Ryan from eating a bullet when he heard of his daughter's murder. Maybe somewhere deep within him he felt he must be around to see justice for his daughter. The police psychologist would have thought so. But although she would have been a little bit right, again, she would have been mostly wrong.

When the Police Commissioner and the priest showed up at his door that morning and told Ryan of Kelly's murder, Ryan did in fact cease to exist. Whatever was left of the man tumbled noiselessly out to sea, dead and drowned, even as the condolences were being offered. He accepted them politely of course, and thanked them for coming as they left, giving no outward sign of his complete immolation.

*   *   *   *

He never seriously considered suicide. After speaking with Ash Wilson a few days after the murder, and being shown all the Commonwealth's evidence, Ryan shared Wilson's confidence that Darnell Cooper had murdered and raped his daughter, and he believed that Wilson would be true to his word and convict Cooper of his crimes.

As much as he really wanted to no longer live with the pain, Ryan did not kill himself for the simple reason that if he did, he would desecrate the memory and lives of his dead family. He was all that remained of the clan Ryan, and were he to end his life, it would effectively end the existence of those whom he had held most dear, even if their existence was only in his memory.

He believed Linda, Joey and Kelly Ryan to have been the three most extraordinary people he had ever met, and the love he had for them would always be alive as long as he was. So despite the fact that every second, of every minute, of every day, his heart felt as if there were a fist clenched around it, squeezing it like a grape, wringing it of his desire to live, Ryan soldiered on, and in his pain, honored the lives of his wife and children.

CHAPTER 16

▼

"Lionel, we've got him by the short hairs…literally."

Sciolla and Lionel were standing outside of the small interrogation room in which Darnell was being held. Lionel had spent a few minutes alone with Darnell, but all he'd done was reassure him that everything would be okay.

"I'm listening," he said to Sciolla, his arms folded across his chest, his head down.

"We know he was with the dead girl last night just before the time of the murder. We have a witness who heard her say 'don't touch me' to him and then she screams at him, calling him a 'motherfucker.' He denied having sex with her. But you and I both know that's going to turn out to be lie, and when it does, that's the ball-game."

Lionel could not accept what he was hearing. But he was not a criminal defense lawyer, and he didn't know what questions to ask. "He loved that girl," he said. *He can't have done this.*

Sciolla put a reassuring hand on Lionel's shoulder. "I take no pleasure in this, Lionel. By all accounts he's a good kid. So the sooner he gets out in front of this, the sooner we can start figuring out how we're going to handle it."

It suddenly dawned on Lionel that Sciolla was suggesting Darnell confess. Criminal or not, Lionel was lawyer enough to know not to let that happen.

"Thanks, Detective," he said politely, "but I'd like to actually see the evidence before we make any decisions."

Sciolla held up his hands. "Fair enough. Here's my card. Give me a call when you're ready. I'll do the same. As soon as I know what we've got."

What they got over the next few days was overwhelming. Despite Lionel's protests, there had been nothing he could do in the face of Sciolla's warrant to prevent the samples of Darnell's blood and hair from being taken. Within a week the lab returned the positive comparison for both. There was a one in three billion chance that someone other than Darnell had deposited that semen. He had lied about them having sex, and the roommate had heard them arguing, followed by a thud and silence. Darnell's hands were big enough to have caused the bruising on her face, and he was certainly strong enough to have broken her jaw with a punch. On the strength of all this evidence, he was arrested and charged with first-degree Murder, Rape, and all the lesser included offenses.

The press frenzy had begun immediately the first day after Kelly's murder, when it had been leaked that Darnell was being questioned. Every network, from the big three networks to ESPN to MTV, assigned reporters to the story. Camera crews and people with microphones swarmed over the city, bombarding everyone from the Mayor down to the security guards at the Palestra, all seeking to put their own unique spin on the situation. Every local newspaper, magazine, and broadcast news channel ran daily stories about the murder, and about the life of Darnell Cooper.

The only universal church in America today is the one in which the false gods of celebrity are overtly worshiped. But just beneath the surface of our outward reverence for their ascension, lie our secret prayers for their fall from grace, a reality which has become the driving force behind the way information is presented to the public in the twenty-first century. This country may love a winner, but it roots for failure. As soon as the news of Darnell's involvement in the murder investigation and the fact that he was a suspect became public, the search was immediately begun within the Fourth Estate to uncover the dirt underneath the fingernails of the story. After his arrest, those efforts were quadrupled.

Within days, the focus of many of the published articles and news reports centered around Darnell's mysterious upbringing prior to showing up at the age of eleven at a center city middle school. The only paper trail which existed belonged to Darnell Cooper. In an effort to thwart this discovery process, Lionel sent a threatening letter to each school the boy had attended, and every doctor and dentist who'd ever treated him, including Charles, letting all of them know they would be sued for every asset they owned if they released any of Darnell's private records. Seeing the letterhead on which the letter was sent was threat enough, and the administrators of each organization took the prudent steps of sealing Darnell's records within secure locations.

Except Dr. Charles. He was the only person with access to his office, which was where he kept Darnell's file, and he certainly had no intention of sharing its contents with anyone.

The one person Lionel could not threaten though was Clark. But having not heard from Clark in so long, Lionel was convinced he was dead. And if he wasn't, Lionel decided he'd just have to cross that bridge when he came to it. The bottom line was that if Clark surfaced, he would be doing so as a drug dealer and pedophile, two characteristics which cut against his credibility just a bit.

Having come up empty with their investigation of Darnell, several reporters also dug into Lionel's background. He had been a basketball star himself, plucked from the ghetto, and when his athletic ability failed him, had blazed a trail through academia as well, securing a position in one of the best law firms in the world, where he was now a partner.

Multiple interviews with local attorneys revealed Lionel's reputation amongst the bar for tenacity, talent, and integrity. His own partners at

Cohen & Elson raved about both Lionel and Darnell, whom they had come to know well. In fact, Darnell was a point of pride at the firm as many of the attorneys there had helped Lionel over the years in various ways in his solo parenting effort, adopted as it was.

But the media were not the only ones interested in finding out about Darnell's early childhood.

A few days after Darnell was arrested, Ash Wilson had called Tony Sciolla into his office for a chat. The frumpy detective sat in the D.A.'s sparsely decorated office, puffing on his ubiquitous pipe, waiting for his marching orders.

"This is going to be the toughest case this office has ever handled, Tony," Wilson had said as he looked out of his fifth floor window onto Arch Street, which even at that moment was clogged with reporters, news trucks and satellite vans, as it had been since the case had broken.

Sciolla tamped down his Burly Kentucky tobacco that he had shipped to him by the pound from some backwoods tobacconist he had found on the internet. Smoking was prohibited in the building, but Wilson's inner office had sort of a don't ask-don't tell policy in that regard. Even though at Noelle's urging Wilson had sworn off his beloved cigars, he did not begrudge Sciolla his vice. The detective did not offer a response to Wilson's comment.

The D.A. turned from the window. "We're going to be under a microscope here," he said while flopping down into the worn leather chair he had inherited from his predecessor. "I want all the i's dotted and the t's crossed."

Sciolla didn't need to hear that to know it, and he waited without comment for whatever it was that Wilson wanted to tell him.

Wilson sensed Sciolla's understanding of the situation, and was glad for it. The two men were more than just professional colleagues, they were friends, as were their wives. It had been a friendship borne of two things: first, the belief that they were not just bureaucrats, but actual instruments of justice, and second, the willingness to put in the work to effectuate what they believed justice to be.

Each had seen both qualities in the other almost immediately, and over time, initial respect had developed into affection, and then into trust. It was because of the latter that Wilson had called him into the office alone, without the rest of the vast investigative team assigned to the Cooper case. Sciolla was one of only three people alive with whom Wilson dared share the fears he was about to express. But his wife, and an ailing George Cohen, were not in a position to do anything to allay them. Sciolla was.

Wilson sat forward in his chair and folded his hands on the desk. "This is an extraordinary young man we've charged with murder, Tony."

Other than a raised eyebrow, Sciolla offered no response.

"Don't get me wrong, I think he did it. Hell, I've put men on death row on far less evidence than we've got against this kid."

Sciolla finally took the pipe from his mouth. "You havin' doubts, Ash? Maybe you shouldn't be the one who tries the case."

Another reason Wilson liked Sciolla so much was his directness. In his position, Wilson was rarely able to have a frank and open discussion without worrying about the subtext of what he, or the other person was saying. But with Sciolla there was no such worry. Each man knew that whatever was said was truly meant, and said for a constructive purpose. There were never any hard feelings, and the words spoken never left the room.

"No, I'm trying the case." Wilson had made that decision immediately. Not only did he believe himself to be the best qualified to do it, but it would simply have been unfair to put that kind of pressure on an assistant. "But I would be lying to you, Tony, if I told you I didn't have a doubt about his guilt simply based on what I know about this kid. It's just so totally out of character for him. And if I have that feeling, imagine how a jury's gonna' feel."

"I hear you. So what do you want to me to do?"

"We have to find out where Cooper came from."

Sciolla chortled. "We've been tryin', you know that. Hell, we've got the full weight of the American media on that detail with us. There just ain't nothin' there. Besides, you think that finding out about this kid's true background is gonna' change the evidence?"

"Maybe," Wilson replied wistfully.

"What the hell does that mean?"

"It means, Goddammit, that I've got to make a decision about whether or not to seek the death penalty against this kid, and if there is some mitigating factor out there, I want to know about it." If there isn't, Wilson didn't say, he would have no choice but to invoke the penalty, as he had in every single other murder case in which there had been a rape since becoming D.A. If he made an exception in this case, the perception would be that Cooper was getting preferential treatment because of his celebrity status.

Sciolla knew all of this, and intuitively sensed Wilson's struggle. "You don't want to believe he did it, do you?" he asked softly.

"Do you?"

The pipe went back into Sciolla's mouth. "I don't know," he said after a few thoughtful puffs. Like every other sports fan in the country, he had certainly heard of Darnell before the murder. But since then, after delving into his life with as fine an investigative comb as he possessed, Sciolla was impressed. "I mean, on the one hand, he appears to be just about as perfect a human being as you'll ever meet. Brilliant, handsome, supremely athletic, gregarious, popular with his classmates and professors. This is the kind of kid who, if we're all lucky, grows up to be President or something."

Even as he was speaking, Sciolla was beginning to see Wilson's point. It suddenly dawned on him what the D.A. had been struggling with internally since the morning of the murder. Darnell Cooper did not just appear to be the perfect human being…he appeared to be the perfect human being, who also happened to be black. He was a walking, talking, breathing symbol of hope. And yet there they sat, talking about the very real possibility that the oft-criticized American justice system, with its historical and at least statistical bias against African-Americans, was about to kill him.

Wilson saw the light bulb going off behind the silky blue smoke around Sciolla's face.

"See what I mean?"

Sciolla nodded his woolly head. "Yeah, I think so, Ash. So what do you want me to do?"

Wilson smiled at the strangeness of what he was about to say. "I want you to do your job, just like I'm going to do mine. Right now, all the evidence we have points beyond a reasonable doubt to Cooper. So I am going to do everything within my power to see that he is convicted of murder. But this case won't go to trial for another three months. Our case is a simple one from an evidentiary standpoint. Delegate the mop-up duty to others. I want you to focus solely on uncovering this kid's background."

"Okay…," Sciolla was a little confused.

Wilson leaned forward even further. "I don't want to see this kid executed, Tony, okay? Find out for me why he did it. Just for me. From this point on you are working on this one issue, and there are to be no written reports. What I am asking you to do is convince me that it is okay not to seek the death penalty here."

"You sure you want no reports?" As much as he trusted Wilson, a Philadelphia Detective's CYA instinct is powerful.

Wilson nodded. "Yeah, I'm sure, and not because I'm trying to hide anything. The only reason is I don't want anyone, except you, to know how much I am struggling with this. Intellectually, I know he did it. Emotionally, I just can't accept it. But I wasn't elected to prosecute cases emotionally, nor is it in my job description. So that is what you are doing. And don't worry about not making any reports. The defense has the burden of proving mitigating circumstances, so what I'm having you do is essentially their job."

Wilson stood up. "By the way, if you should happen to uncover any exculpatory evidence, which, between you and I, I hope you do…then I will happily turn it over to the other side."

Sciolla smiled at the irony of it all as he stood to leave. Wilson was about to prosecute Darnell Cooper for capital murder. In doing that, he would do his best to make sure that everyone watching believe that he believed Cooper was one hundred percent guilty. Meanwhile, the whole time he was doing that, Wilson would be sending Sciolla out on a stealth mission to save the kid's life.

"Justice must be blind *and* stupid," Sciolla said over his shoulder as he left.

*   *   *   *

"Why me?" Asked Roger Queenan.

Lionel sat across from the former prosecutor in Queenan's sparsely furnished office on the fourth floor of the historic Bourse Building at 4th and Chestnut Streets in the Old City section of Philadelphia.

As he looked around, Lionel began to wonder the same thing.

"Because I've been told you're a good criminal lawyer, and that's what Darnell needs right now."

Queenan smiled patronizingly. "C'mon, brotha,' let's be honest with each other. You can afford any lawyer in this town and beyond. Shit, I bet you got guys calling you to offer their services for free knowing the publicity this case'll generate. So…why me?'

They both knew the uncomfortable answer, even if Lionel was the only one who was uncomfortable with it.

Lionel understood perfectly what Queenan wanted him to say. "Okay, Roger," he said, "there are three reasons I want you. First, you're black. Second, the evidence is overwhelming. And third," Lionel leaned forward to underscore the importance of number three, "I need a lawyer who is not going to let the evidence get in the way of getting that boy acquitted."

"Well all right," said Queenan with a satisfied grin. "Now we're calling a spade a spade…so to speak."

Lionel did his best not to allow the disgust he felt register on his face. As a black lawyer, he had been aware of Roger Queenan and his ilk, operating on the fringes of the bar, espousing conspiracy theories and racial discrimination in every case they handled.

To lawyers like Queenan, black men were never guilty of the crimes with which they were charged. Rather, they were victims of a racist justice system and segregated society, the inequities of which were visited solely upon the black man. Lawyers like Queenan had no problem arguing, zealously, for the acquittal of their clients based on the color of their skin alone.

As distasteful as that concept was to Lionel though, he knew that Queenan was exactly the type of lawyer he needed.

"You've read the papers, I'm sure, so you know what Darnell is facing," said Lionel.

"If I know Ash Wilson, that boy's facing the needle!" replied Queenan.

Lionel ignored his inappropriate jocularity and the contempt he felt. "If I hire you to defend Darnell, how would you attack the evidence?"

Queenan smirked. "I wouldn't."

He stood up and walked over to a filing cabinet, on top of which sat a cold pot of coffee. He poured himself a cup, but did not offer any to Lionel.

"Evidence has nothing to do with this case, Lionel. That boy is in jail for one reason, and one reason only…the color of his skin. So I will not attack the evidence because that's not what put him where he is. I will attack the prejudice that did."

Even though it was this precise posture of Queenan's that had brought Lionel to this office in the first place, it literally turned his stomach to hear such talk. He rejected the idea of one's skin color being an excuse or reason for anything. He had pulled himself up by his own bootstraps, he felt, why couldn't everyone else?

But once again, at a pivotal moment in his life, Lionel was haunted by that old lingering guilt. He was a successful black man who had made a lot of money and had gained a glowing reputation, due largely to his ability to operate in a white man's world, largely on terms dictated by white men. He had assuaged his guilt in this regard once before, long ago, with his reclamation of Darnell. But since then, Lionel had to admit, he had given himself a pass on "keepin' it real."

But more than his philosophical differences with Queenan's stance, he was skeptical of its practicality.

"You don't really think playing the race card, in this day and age, will really work, do you?"

Queenan raised an eyebrow. It was bad enough he had to exploit white guilt to win cases, he thought, now I gotta' deal with black guilt too.

"It'll work. It always does."

Lionel's face registered his doubt. He had always dismissed the claims of lawyers like Roger Queenan as ploys by black men to get other blacks on juries to disregard the law. He thought such tactics were insulting, not just to him, but to jurors as well.

But even though his heart was telling him Darnell was innocent, his brain was telling him that the kid was guilty. It wasn't just the evidence. It was the years of learning from and working with Dr. Charles, trying to quell the demons which had been insidiously implanted into Darnell's psyche by his tortuous childhood. The crime with which Darnell was now accused was Lionel's worst fear realized, that despite his best efforts to leave it behind, Darnell's past had reached out and yanked him back to it.

Words he had fooled himself into believing he need not remember, taught to him so long ago by Dr. Charles, came flooding back the moment he'd hung up the phone after Darnell's call from jail. Words and phrases like 'Borderline Personality Disorder,' and 'inappropriate sexual behavior,' and 'impulsivity.' Even though Dr. Charles had always warned that Darnell's emotional problems would remain with him forever, the boy's meteoric successes had blinded Lionel to that reality. His heart broke to know that no matter how extraordinary

Darnell's life had been or could be, he simply could not escape what had been done to him when he was young.

Lionel knew what strong feelings Darnell had for Kelly. He also knew how devastated he'd been at her recent rejection of him. These were new and volatile emotions for any young man to experience, much less one who was predisposed to reacting explosively to them. So while Lionel knew it was truly not Darnell's fault that he did so, Lionel had no doubt that he had in fact killed Kelly Ryan.

He was sitting there in Roger Queenan's office because Lionel realized he simply did not care...it was irrelevant to him. He loved the boy too much. There wasn't anything, or anyone, Lionel wasn't prepared to hide the truth behind.

Understanding at least some of Lionel's inner struggle, Queenan decided the moment was right to take him on a tour of Independence Hall, which was directly across the street from his office. It was a pre-canned excursion that he took many of his clients on.

"Let's go for a walk," he said.

Ten minutes later, they were standing in front of a framed copy of the Declaration of Independence.

"Did you know, Lionel, that Thomas Jefferson wanted to include a denunciation of the slave trade in the Declaration, but the Continental Congress voted to delete the section because South Carolina and Georgia wanted to continue the importation of slaves?"

Lionel shook his head. "Didn't know that."

Queenan lowered his voice and leaned a little closer to the much taller, younger man. For his clients, this little tour was not just a way to inflame their passions, but also, and perhaps more importantly, a way for Queenan to show that he was smarter than they were, that he had a deeper understanding of the world, and that they should therefore trust him to know better than they how their case should be handled.

Given Lionel's stature in the legal community, Queenan relished the opportunity to show just how smart he was, and he was pulling out all the stops. In preparation for this meeting, Queenan had come earlier in the day to rehearse some added features to the normal lecture.

"Do you know what you're looking at?" he whispered.

"The Declaration of Independence," he replied flatly, already weary of Queenan's company.

"That's right," said Queenan, as if Lionel had deduced something especially clever. "Have you ever read it?"

"I'm sure I have," said Lionel, although he couldn't readily remember ever actually having done so.

Queenan raised an eyebrow up at Lionel. "You know, we as lawyers are taught that the most important document in our country's history is the Constitution. Which makes sense given that the Constitution lays out the framework for all the laws upon which our civilized society is meant to rest. But the truth is, this document right here," Queenan nodded towards the glass case, "this is the basis for everything our country is, and ever will be. You see, Lionel, America is not a place, or a thing, or a person…it's an idea."

Lionel feigned interest, hoping that Queenan would come to the point soon in this obviously rehearsed speech. He was beginning to wonder why the hell he was there.

Sensing Lionel's impatience, but unwilling to cede the floor, Queenan said, "Time is precious, I know, Lionel. But I am hoping that I can explain to you why I believe that Darnell cannot ever be allowed to be convicted of any crime, much less the murder of some white girl."

Suddenly, Lionel was interested again.

Turning to the case, Queenan read aloud. "*When in the course of human events, it becomes necessary for one People to dissolve the Political Bands which have connected them with another, and to assume among the Powers of the Earth, the separate and equal Station to which the Laws of Nature and of Nature's God entitle them, a decent Respect to the Opinions of Mankind requires that they should declare the causes which impel them to the Separation.*"

Queenan looked up at Lionel. "Read it to yourself, Lionel," he said, "but this time, instead of old, fat, rich, white guys saying it about themselves…think about every black man, woman and child in this country declaring the same thing."

Lionel did. "Okay," he said when he was finished.

"Those are the words used by men who were sick and tired of living in a world they did not have the power to control, nor could they ever hope to. They were a colonized people. They lived here, they worked here, they died here, all for the pleasure of a King who neither cared for them, nor feared them. They had no voice in the government of their own land, and no access to its resources. Their existence was entirely dependent upon the largesse of others in power, as was their physical well-being. Most importantly, they had no justice…the law did not apply equally to them."

"You're suggesting a revolution?" Asked Lionel, as he began thinking about other lawyers he could call. Queenan was just a bit too radical for his tastes.

"Yes!" replied Queenan emphatically. "But not in the way you're thinking."

He grasped Lionel's arm and squeezed. "I do not mean to suggest that we, as a people, should seek to violently overthrow the government. In fact, I think such ideas are foolhardy, myself. I know you're losing patience with me, but just hear me out.

"Lionel, America is an idea which is just as viable for African-Americans today as it was for those rich, white guys back in the eighteenth century. The only problem is, we do not have the core group of leaders that they did, who have both the courage of their convictions and the confidence of their leadership. Think about it. How easy is it for white America to dismiss black causes when the face of our fight belongs to adulterers, thieves, and militants? They do not take us seriously because our leaders, our face, is a joke. Our cause has no credibility because they have no credibility.

"And why don't the very best of us take the helm of our ship and sail us into our rightful equality? Why aren't we, as a unified people, standing up and refusing to accept any less than that each opportunity available to every white child born in this country, be equally available to every black child? I'll tell you why. Because for two centuries now, freedom and equality and opportunity have been doled out to us in drips and drabs, like the proverbial carrot enticing the horse. There's always been just enough to allow most of us to get by, with some of us even achieving incredible success."

Lionel was suddenly embarrassed, and felt a rush of heat to his face. He was one of the successful ones, he knew, and he knew Queenan was talking about him.

"And that piddling bit of freedom which we've been allowed to taste has mollified us as a people. It has splintered our resolve, because for some of us, life is good, and for many others, it's not so bad. But the fact is that until all of us enjoy the same freedoms and the same opportunities, none of us should be willing to accept any less. And the only way we are ever going to achieve these things is not through violence or rhetoric, and not through handouts. No, the only way we, as a people, can ever hope to have the idea of America apply equally to us, is if we truly believe it can."

Knowing he'd finally gotten Lionel's attention, Queenan turned back to the glass case. "All experience hath shown, that mankind are more disposed to suffer, while evils are sufferable, than to right themselves by abolishing the forms to which they are accustomed."

Both men stood silent for a few seconds, one in contemplation, the other for effect.

"Do you see the point?" Queenan asked softly after a spell.

Lionel was honest. "I see *a* point, Roger, but I'm not sure I see *the* point."

Queenan smiled. "The point is simply this…America is an idea that we as a people never had the opportunity to embrace the first time around, because back then, we weren't even considered human beings.

Because of the way we were brought here, and because of the way we have been oppressed since, black people have been fighting to be recognized in a system not of their creation. The fight for equality has taken place on their home court, by their own rules. Under those parameters, we could never hope to win equality, because they wrote the rules, and they can always change them.

"But the time has long since passed for us to assume the powers of the Earth, and the separate and equal station to which the laws of nature and of nature's God entitle us.

"In order for us to do that, though, just as the colonists did, we need our Thomas Jefferson, our Benjamin Franklin, our George Washington. We need black leaders who, just like those men, are not only leaders by words, but by actions. We need leaders who not only believe themselves in the inevitability of equality, but who can make the rest of us believe in it as well.

"Darnell Cooper can be that kind of leader, Lionel. I feel it in my bones. I know you do too. He is everything any human being could possibly hope to be, white or black. He is a living, breathing, walking, talking embodiment of the very qualities that we as a people must learn to not only strive for, but believe we can achieve.

"Darnell's acquittal can be the beginning of our own peaceful revolution, Lionel. I think it can have the same rallying effect on our people that the Boston Tea Party did back then. I want to serve notice on the world that it can no longer subjugate black America to its laws, when those laws do not afford us the same protections as all Americans. That it's system of justice is no longer applicable to us, so long as justice remains unavailable in equal measure to us. And, that they cannot use their racist system of laws to continue to rob us of the very people who might one day rise up against it, and rid it of it's racial bias."

Queenan turned to face Lionel as he reached up to grab hold of both of his broad shoulders. "The bottom line is, Lionel, that I don't give a good Goddamn whether or not Darnell is guilty. He's not going to jail."

*   *   *   *

As they walked back to Queenan's office, Lionel considered everything that had been said. It had certainly been what he wanted to hear. He didn't think he believed a word of it though, and he still wasn't sure that Queenan did either. But the fact was, in the face of overwhelming evidence of his guilt, Darnell needed a defense based on something. Lionel figured Queenan's was about the best he was gonna' do.

Lionel had been surprised at Queenan's office, and it's lack of the usual accouterments. His own office, in a fifteenth floor corner of the Cohen building, overlooked Center City, his giant, oak desk surrounded by valuable art on the walls, a wet bar in the corner, and leather couches to relax upon. The guilty flush began to rise again in his belly.

"Have you thought about a fee?" asked Lionel, hoping to change the subject in his mind, but realizing that the question he asked had not done so.

Queenan hid his emotions behind a stone face. Aside from the hastily added historical touches to his normal client lecture, pretty much all he had thought about since Lionel's call was the fee. Normally, when a client, or the client's family, asked 'how much,' Queenan's response would be 'how much you got?' Often, a negotiating session would ensue, whereby a fee would be agreed upon, with a percentage up front as a retainer. He could count on one hand the number of times he had successfully collected on the full amount of his fee.

But sitting before him in his humble office, Queenan had a junior partner of the most successful law firm in the city, somebody who was probably making over a quarter million dollars a year. Since becoming a criminal defense lawyer, Queenan had always dreamed of having the same resources to defend a first-degree murder case that the D.A.'s office had to prosecute it. He could get the best experts, the best investigators, jury consultants, same-day transcription of trial testimony, and myriad other things with which to combat the massive machinery of the state. Of course, he had no idea how much all of that would cost. So he made it up.

"I'll require a retainer of $100,000.00, payable before I begin work. My time, billed at a rate of $250.00, per hour, will be billed against that retainer. Once the amount of time I spend exceeds the retainer, I will provide monthly bills which are expected to be paid timely. Costs, as they are incurred, will be billed separately."

He had spoken in a rehearsed rush, not knowing what the reaction would be. Lionel hardly blinked. He was prepared to pay anything. His own hourly rate of $400.00 even made Queenan's asking price seem reasonable.

"Okay," he said, as he reached into his briefcase and retrieved his checkbook. "But I have one condition."

Queenan could scarcely believe he was about to be handed a check for that much money, and was prepared to accept just about any condition it came with. "Shoot."

"I sit second chair."

In any other case, with any other client, Queenan would have laughed and said no way. But there was a lot of money about to be handed to him, and this case was going to make him famous, win or lose.

"No problem," he said, as he accepted the check from Lionel. Queenan rationalized that he would be able to control Cooper, and at the same time use him for legal research and brief writing on motions.

For his part, Lionel needed to be as close to Queenan as possible. He was happy about the man's zeal…it was necessary. But Lionel was worried about the ways in which Queenan might exercise that zeal if unchecked. He intended to be that check.

CHAPTER 17

▼

"You've been drinking," said Ryan as he stepped aside to let Fullem into his house.

They hadn't seen each other since Kelly's funeral. His friend's absence had been okay with Ryan. He knew that Fullem had loved Kelly almost as much as he himself had, if that was even possible. They had both needed time.

Fullem flopped down into the soft leather of Ryan's couch in the living room. He looked terrible. His eyes were bloodshot, he was unshaven, and his clothes were unkempt and dirty. He looked as if he hadn't slept in days.

"You look like shit," Ryan said as he sat down in the love seat across the coffee table.

Fullem smiled ruefully. "Yeah? Then I'm looking a whole heck of a lot better than I feel."

Ryan waved his hand in front of his nose. "I can smell the Ol' Granddad from here. When did you start drinking again?"

"Does it matter?"

There had been a time in his life when Ryan had considered it one of his greatest accomplishments to have convinced Fullem to stop drinking. But rather than be angry with his friend for falling off the wagon, he was oddly jealous. If only it were that easy to make the pain go away, he thought.

"Where have you been? I called your apartment a couple of times, but never got an answer?"

At first, Fullem said nothing. Rather, he shifted his heft forward, put his elbows on his knees, and hung his head down between his enormous shoulder blades. It looked as if there was something he was trying to say, but his mouth couldn't quite form the words.

"What is it, Joe?" asked Ryan softly. Reflexively, he said, "Maybe I can help."

With that, an emotional damn broke somewhere deep inside of Fullem, and he began to loudly sob, tears flowed down his cheeks, and his massive chest heaved with sorrow. "I'm so sorry, John...I'm sorry...," he couldn't continue, as the sobbing overtook his words.

Ryan was shocked by Fullem's display. In even the darkest moments of the man's life, Ryan had never seen him so vulnerable. It touched him deeply, and he went to his friend's side to comfort him.

"I know, big fella, I know." He rubbed his hand on Fullem's muscular back. "I know."

Fullem looked bleary-eyed over his shoulder at Ryan. It was surreal seeing him as he sat there. He was neatly dressed in slacks and a golf shirt, sitting up straight as always. His hair was combed and his face shaved. He appeared perfectly normal. Fullem looked around the room, and realized that the place was as spotless as ever, with everything neatly arranged as it always had been. It seemed almost tranquil.

"How can you be so...calm?" He asked, his own raging insides having prevented him a moment's peace from the torture of his own torment since Kelly's murder.

Ryan eyed Fullem for a second as he pondered the question. The truth be told, he *was* calm, and had been since the very moment he learned of Kelly's rape and murder. More so, in fact, than he had been at any moment in all the years since Linda and Joey's accident.

When his wife and son died, Ryan had died as well. The life he had planned, the life he had wanted, had ended, and he was bitterly angry about it. Every moment of every day, he privately railed at the injustice of it all, at the unfairness of his continued existence without his wife and son. He had wanted his life back, dammit! When he realized he could never get it back, all he had wanted to do was curl up in a ball and stop living, and it infuriated him that everything else around him didn't. The sun still came up, the newspaper still got printed, and traffic was just as bad. The indifference of the world was maddening.

But it also served a purpose. It forced Ryan to realize that he still had a daughter to raise, a daughter whose very existence depended solely upon his ability to stay in the real world, precisely *because* of its indifference. Without him, Kelly would be lost, and as much as it pained him to go on, the thought of harm befalling his little girl because he was wallowing in self-pity, spurred him to at least pretend to be living a normal life.

It was this same feeling which made him appear so normal now. After learning of Kelly's murder Ryan had not screamed and cried, he had not crawled into a bottle, and he had not sought counsel with anyone else about his grief. Instead, he retreated to the refuge of memories inside of his own head, and simply stayed there. He did not return to work, he did not watch television, he did not read the newspaper. He simply woke up every day, showered, shaved, ate regular meals, and thought about his family. He cleaned the house daily, went out only to buy food and basic supplies, and made sure to preserve everything exactly as it had been when his family was still alive.

He had used the phone twice, both times to call Fullem. These were moments of greatest weakness for Ryan, when even he could bear the weight of his grief alone no longer. But Fullem had not answered, and Ryan had gotten through those times alone.

"I'm okay," he said, his voice devoid of emotion.

Fullem wiped his face and watched his friend, who seemed to be lost in thought. "Seriously," he whispered, "aren't you angry?"

Ryan gave a half-heartedly sardonic smile. There was no way he could explain to Fullem how he truly felt, so he didn't. "It wouldn't do any good, Joe. So the answer is no, I'm not angry."

Fullem had come there expecting to find a raving maniac, a man destroyed, a man…like himself. He had come there prepared to confess to such a man. But seeing Ryan so, so…normal, fooled Fullem into thinking that Ryan was somehow okay. And because he so desperately needed it to, Fullem mistakenly believed that because Ryan had recovered so quickly, maybe their friendship could too. Ryan's approval was the only thing left in Fullem's world worth living for, and the possibility that he might yet keep it, however slim, eradicated from Fullem any intention of coming clean.

"Aren't you worried that he's gonna' get away with it?" he asked, hoping to reestablish their connection over something they could presumably both agree upon.

Ryan shook his head. "No. Wilson called me. We spent a lot of time talking about it. He'll get convicted."

Fullem did not share his confidence. For days since the funeral, he had kept himself in a drug and alcohol induced stupor, not because he felt guilty, but because he dreaded the inevitable moment when Ryan found out about what he had done. In fact, he had expected that as soon as his fingerprints were found, he would have been the number one suspect.

So he had waited in his apartment, drinking non-stop, ready to eat a bullet when the knock on the door came. But all that had come was a visit from Tony Sciolla, to whom Fullem had lied to with surprising ease. Sciolla had mistaken his guilt for grief, and dismissed him as a suspect because he already believed Darnell had done it. In fact, all the attention was focused on Cooper from the start, and with his arrest, no other suspects were even being mentioned. It never once even crossed Fullem's mind to be worried that an innocent man was behind bars.

It was only after it had finally become apparent that the cops weren't considering other suspects, that Fullem had ventured out to see Ryan, fully expecting *him* to have seen the truth. It was clear though that Ryan too believed not only in Cooper's guilt, but also in the likelihood of his conviction.

But because deep down like most cops, disgraced or not, Fullem believed that the system really does work, he suddenly felt the need to prepare Ryan for the possibility that the murderer of his daughter might get away with the crime.

"You haven't been watching the news have you?" Fullem asked, as Ryan went back to his seat on the other couch.

Ryan shook his head. "No."

"So you haven't heard what's going on?"

Again Ryan seemed non-plussed. "What's going on?"

Ryan's passivity was maddening. "John, this whole country has been split right down the middle by this case. The kid's got some sort of foster brother who's a big time lawyer, and he's gone out and hired Roger Queenan. You remember Queenan, right? That fuckin' schwoog who used to be a D.A.? He's been holding press conferences like every day, talking about how this whole prosecution is based on race, how Cooper is only being charged with the crime because he's black and somehow a threat to whites because he's educated.

"All anybody's talking about is race and whether or not he can get a fair trial and all that bullshit. You know what's gonna' happen, John, don't ya'? They're gonna' get twelve niggers on that jury and their gonna' do the same thing they did for Cheeseboro."

"I don't think so." Ryan was like a robot.

"C'mon, John, don't be naïve. In all the murder cases you testified in, how many jurors were white? At the very least there's gonna' be a predominantly black jury in this case. The whole country'll be watching, and they'll acquit him. Shit, if they don't, the riot here will make the L.A. riots look like a peace demonstration."

Ryan leaned back into his seat and thought about the possibilities. He had not been witness to the intensity of the debate amongst the media that had been raging over his daughter's alleged killer, so he did not have a true perspective on the situation.

"The evidence is too overwhelming. He was there, they argued, he…," he still had not even formed the word 'rape' in his mind, much less said it. "His DNA and fingerprints are in the room, he lied about it to the cops. What else could there possibly be?"

Plenty, thought Fullem.

As soon as some anonymous source within the police department had leaked the fact that Fullem's fingerprints had been found in the room, the videotaped beating of Frank Cheeseboro had been immediately dusted off and played ad nauseam. Fullem's brutality was no less revolting and shocking, even after all these years, and a growing voice in the black community believed that the videotape alone presented reasonable doubt of Darnell's guilt.

"John, do you know that the Cheeseboro tape has been all over the news for the last week? They found my fingerprints in Kelly's room."

Ryan smirked. "So what? My fingerprints are in that room, too. I told Wilson and Sciolla that we helped her move in for Christ's sake. What's that got to do with the murder?"

"Absolutely nothing!" Fullem exclaimed. "That's my point, John. But the dumb coons they put on that jury aren't going to be smart enough to realize that. They're going to see me sitting there in the courtroom and that'll be the ballgame.

"They'll acquit Cooper just because Kelly knew me. That's the way it works with those people, John, you know that. All they care about is getting over on the system. They don't care about the facts, or the law. They won't care that Cooper's guilty, they'll acquit him just because he's black."

Ryan stood up and began to pace the room. "That's ridiculous, Joe. The evidence is too overwhelming."

Fullem shook his massive head and pursed his lips derisively. "You know, John you've always been real naïve when it comes to those people, and you're being naïve now."

Ryan held up his hand. "I'm not in the mood for this, Joe, really. I know how you feel, but it's got nothing to do with Kelly, and it's got nothing to do with the case."

"Oh c'mon, man! You cannot be that stupid! The color of that boy's skin has everything to do with it, starting with why he did it, and ending with why he's gonna' get away with it."

Ryan sat back down and rubbed his face. He hadn't even considered any of this. All he had wanted to do, all he in fact had done, was contemplate all the happy times, all the love, all the good. He had deliberately blocked out all the rest. Now he was being confronted with the bad from every conceivable angle all at once, and it was overwhelming. He didn't know what to say.

In the absence of a reply, Fullem felt emboldened to filibuster. "How many criminals have you arrested over the years, John? I'm not talking petty thieves or small-time hoods. I mean stone-cold, hardened criminals, the kind of motherfuckers who'd just as soon stick a shiv in your ass as they would say hello to you. How many? Hundreds?"

Ryan simply stared back, trying not to listen.

"How many were white?"

He hadn't expected the question, and didn't have time to think of an answer.

Fullem didn't need one. "And why is that, John? Don't tell me it's because of oppression, or racism, or freakin' slavery! They choose to be criminals. They choose to be unemployed. They choose to have ten fuckin' kids out of wedlock when they're teenagers. They fuck each other like animals with no self-control, and then they expect the government to pay for their upkeep. Then they blame the white man for their station in life. You put a dime in a poor white man's pocket, you know what he does with it, John? He saves it. Or he invests it. Or he uses it somehow, someway, to make his life better.

"You know what a poor nigger does with a dime? He goes and buys somethin' shiny! How many coons have you arrested wearing three thousand dollar suits, driving a fuckin' Mercedes, living in public housing? They're squawkin' about reparations! You know who's most in favor of reparations? Every purple suit-maker, chrome hubcap dealer, and jeweler in America, that's who.

"And by the way, when's the last time you heard of a young black kid with a father? The next time I see some gap-toothed monkey makin' four million dollars a year because he can jump real high and dunk a basketball, look into a television camera and thank his *father*, I'll shit myself."

Ryan couldn't take anymore of the diatribe. "Joe, shut up," he said quietly.

Fullem blinked, the last vestiges of his inebriation slipping away. He looked back at Ryan with a blank stare, as if he'd not realized he was even speaking aloud.

"I said I'm not in the mood. I was never in the mood for that shit when we worked together, I'm certainly not in the mood now. Unless you have something constructive to say, something that has some relevance to anything, you better leave."

Fullem slumped back into the couch and studied his friend. "What I'm saying is constructive, John. I've got a point."

Ryan sighed deeply and rubbed his temples. "Go ahead."

"The point is this. You can call me a racist, you can call me ignorant, and you can dismiss what I say. You don't have to listen to me because you, like everyone else, have been so goddamn politically correcticized that you're afraid to even *think* bad thoughts about black people. And do you know why that is, John? Because every time someone in this country opens up his mouth to criticize a black person, no matter how justified the criticism, he's immediately branded a racist. Whenever someone points out that maybe some of the bad shit that happens to black people may, just may, have something to do with their own choices and their own values, that person is literally destroyed.

"And why is that? Because white guilt has swept the nation, man, that's why. Deep down inside, every white person in the world knows that black people are their own worst enemies, but we have all been trained to feel guilty for feeling this way. So when one of us makes the mistake of saying something out loud, and gets labeled a racist, we all feel compelled to agree, or else maybe we might be found out too."

Ryan shook his head. He had heard these speeches from Fullem before. "I thought you said there was a point?"

"There is. As soon as Cooper was arrested, niggers all across this country have been spouting off about how poor Darnell Cooper is getting railroaded by a racist and oppressive justice system that only protects white people. They have been on talk shows, and news programs, and the covers of magazines. USA Today has conducted polls that say that seventy-two percent of black Americans think Cooper's being framed.

"And no one's saying a word. There is not any real, intelligent opposition out there. The supposedly respectable news commentators are afraid to say anything at all because they're afraid they'll be branded racist. The cops and the D.A. ain't saying a word to anybody. The only people who are dumb enough to open their mouths are illiterate rednecks on Jerry Springer, who just like me, are dismissed as idiots, and at the same time, held up as examples of what white Americans really think."

"Well what am I supposed to do about that, Joe?"

"You can stand up, dammit! You can get out there, and tell the world who Kelly was. Explain why it is that they should be upset that a beautiful, intelligent young girl was raped and murdered, rather than be worrying that this moolie might not get picked first in the NBA draft because he killed her."

Ryan had no intention of doing any such thing. "No way. Do you really think for one second that I would demean the memory of my daughter by participating in such nonsense? Believe me, I would rather see Cooper walk. Besides, any jury'll see right through that crap."

"Yeah, well, I'd like to believe in Santa Claus," said Fullem bitterly. "But I don't, because I know he's too good to be true."

The discussion never really got any better, and soon enough, there was none at all. His sobriety nearly returned, Fullem left in order to go chase it away again. Ryan was left, once again by himself, alone with his thoughts.

He thought about what Fullem had said. Not the racist diatribe, but the ultimate point he was trying to make. *Maybe I should be out there,* he thought. *Maybe if I don't, people will forget about Kelly altogether, and the case will be only about Cooper's life, rather than Kelly's death.* He had failed Linda and Joey in his quest to hold someone responsible for their deaths. He couldn't fail Kelly too.

Ryan walked into the kitchen where there was a little desk upon which sat the family's computer. In the top drawer to the desk he found what he needed. It was a little scrap of paper with Ashland Wilson's cell phone number on it. Ryan hadn't ever considered using it up until that moment.

"Hello?" asked the D.A., expecting to hear the voice of his wife, one of his boys, or George Cohen, as they were the only other people who had the number.

"Mr. Wilson? This is John Ryan."

Wilson sat up in his chair behind his desk in the D.A.'s Office. Even though it was after ten o'clock at night, he still had work left to do. "Yes, Detective, what can I do for you?"

"You can be straight with me," said Ryan.

"Unfortunately, I don't know any other way to be."

"Are you gonna' convict Cooper?" Ryan asked, his tone low and suspicious.

Wilson thought briefly of Tony Sciolla, who had yet to uncover anything about Darnell's background. "Yes," Wilson replied honestly.

"What about the racial stuff, is that going to be a factor?"

The D.A. hesitated before answering. He knew exactly what he wanted to say, but he wanted to use the best words possible to say it. "No, it won't, John. Here's why: I believe that the people of this city are a whole lot smarter than the press and the defense are giving them credit for. I think that ultimately, this strategy of theirs will backfire badly. So rather than try and throw sand on that fire, a fire by the way that all the sand in the world couldn't extinguish, we're letting it burn out of control. In the end, I think the only person who'll get burned by it is Darnell Cooper."

Ryan snorted. "You sound like me. A friend of mine would call you naïve."

Wilson nodded to the empty room. "Maybe I am. Shit, I know I am. But I would much rather believe that the good in people will ultimately win out over the bad. I'll tell you something else. If I didn't think like that, there's no way I could be a prosecutor. If I don't believe that ultimately good will be done, then I would be losing the war before I even put on my uniform. I know you have to feel the same way about your job.

"You ask me if I will convict Darnell Cooper? I say yes. The evidence shows that he's guilty. But more importantly, I believe that a jury, no matter what it's racial make-up, will follow the law and their duty, and accept the evidence, regardless of his color. And by the way, if we can't depend on that to happen in every case, we're all fucked anyway."

The extended silence on the other end of the line made Wilson think that he'd lost the connection. Finally, Ryan said, "Okay, I believe you. Thank you."

But he'd lied. Something in Wilson's voice betrayed a doubt as to his ability to convict Cooper. And more than he had been by anything in his life, John Ryan was suddenly terrified that the man who had killed his daughter, might actually get away with the crime.

He vowed at that moment never to let that happen.

CHAPTER 18

▼

"The war starts today, Lionel."

Queenan and Lionel were standing alone in the fourth floor men's room of the Criminal Justice Center, the twelve-story concrete rectangle where all criminal cases in Philadelphia are heard.

It was the morning of the preliminary hearing. People had been lined up for days to get a seat in the courtroom, which held room for seventy-two people in the seating section. From the seventy-third person on down, people were ordered away from the overcrowded lobby and out onto the sidewalks along Filbert Street. Of the people being allowed in, fifteen were media representatives from all four networks, all three cable news channels, ESPN, Sports Illustrated, the Daily News, Inquirer, USA Today, the Wall Street Journal, Time and Newsweek Magazines, and MTV.

The murder had happened three weeks before, to the day. The first listing of the hearing had been continued a week before by Wilson, who needed more time to get completed and confirmed laboratory results on the DNA evidence. There was no question, from a scientific point of view anyway, that it had been Darnell's sperm inside of Kelly Ryan.

The extra week had only given Queenan more time to fan the flames of the racist conspiracy he claimed was the sole cause of Darnell's troubles. While the story of Darnell's arrest had been a fairly big one, the racial angle made it huge.

Lionel knew that it was going to be a war. Hell, high-stakes litigation always is. But they were going into battle severely outgunned. The evidence was overwhelming. Lionel had spent hours upon hours with Darnell at the prison, begging him to come clean, all the while promising the boy that he would not blame him, or love him any less. But Darnell had been adamant in his denials, his anger and bitterness increasing exponentially each time Lionel even suggested that he was guilty.

And as his anger and bitterness towards Lionel increased, Darnell gravitated towards Queenan's inviting acceptance. Queenan did not challenge Darnell, and he never even seemed to consider that he might actually be responsible for Kelly's murder. Or if he did consider the possibility, it obviously did not matter.

While Lionel understood Darnell's desire to be believed, he was a bit disappointed that his younger brother so quickly went from proclaiming his innocence, to simply avoiding his guilt. It made Lionel all the more secretly convinced that Darnell was guilty, and made him like Queenan even less.

"Let's just make sure we remember what we're fighting for," said Lionel into the mirror as they both checked their suits. Queenan had gone all out for the hearing, wearing his finest, Italian-made, three-piece number. It was a nice suit, and despite his beer belly, it actually made him look dapper. But standing next to Lionel, he just couldn't compete. It was like Denzel Washington standing next to Sherman Hemsley.

"What do you mean by that, Lionel?' asked Queenan as he turned away from their reflections.

Lionel stared into the mirror. "I mean don't forget that your job is to make sure Darnell is acquitted, not to preen for the press or grandstand, or make this in any way about you. The war today is against the evidence, not the white man."

Queenan chuckled humorlessly as he walked toward the door. "That's what I've been tryin' to explain to you, Lionel. In this case, those two things are exactly the same. If we can kill either one of them, we win." Queenan smiled over his shoulder as he strutted out the door, proud of himself for believing he had said something clever.

Well, Lionel thought to himself, I can always fire him after the prelim.

The courtroom was a zoo. Every inch of bench space was taken. Courthouse employees, most of whom had been around forever, stood along the walls. The cacophony of opinions being expressed by all in the room was deafening, and the reporters busied themselves taking notes. The crush of bodies raised the temperature at least ten degrees. The late November air, kept at bay by the sealed shut windows, offered no relief.

Darnell was led into the room in handcuffs from the side door. All motion and conversation immediately stopped. Every eye in the room turned to him, sizing him up. He was very tall, and his muscular arms and shoulders strained the thread of his well-worn orange jumpsuit. He did not lower his head or avert his gaze in any way. Instead, he looked imperiously and defiantly over the room, just as Queenan had instructed.

The cuffs were removed so he could be seated between Queenan and Lionel at the defense table. With their height, Lionel and Darnell dwarfed Queenan, and made the sturdy oak piece of furniture before them look like a card table.

Wilson sat by himself at the prosecution table, just a few feet away. He busied himself with papers on the table, seemingly oblivious to everything going on around him.

Municipal Court Judge Colin MacDuffie, who was to preside over the preliminary hearing, would not be the trial judge. His only job was to determine whether or not there was prima facie evidence of guilt, and bind the case over for trial. Like most judges in Philadelphia, he was just another lawyer who had contributed enough money to the right politicians and ward leaders to have gotten himself elected to the bench.

"All rise," said the court crier as Judge MacDuffie strode to the bench. He was a short man with a runner's build, a shiny, bald head, and big ears.

"First case is number 1463-02, Judge," said the crier.

"Commonwealth ready to proceed?" asked the Judge.

Ash Wilson stood up. "Commonwealth is ready, Your Honor."

MacDuffie looked over at Queenan. "Defense ready?"

"Yes, judge. We would just ask for sequestration of all witnesses."

"Already done, your Honor," said Wilson.

Queenan looked over at Wilson. "I'm assuming that means that Detectives Sciolla and Ryan won't be testifying today?" Sciolla was seated on the bench behind Wilson's table, his unlit pipe hanging loosely from his lower lip, and Ryan was next to him.

Wilson began to speak, but MacDuffie held up his hand. "The detectives can stay. All other fact witnesses to be sequestered."

Queenan considered arguing the point, but knew it would ultimately be futile. He sat back down with a theatrical shake of the head.

"Commonwealth calls Anita Levine, your Honor."

A side door across from where Darnell had entered opened, and Kelly's roommate was led into the room by a deputy sheriff. Levine was a little girl, almost mousy. She had short black hair and chubby little legs that were clad in too-tight, but very stylish black pants. A bulky sweater covered her top half, and expensive looking thick-heeled shoes announced her walk. She looked terrified.

After being sworn in, Anita took her seat in the witness stand, her attention focused solely on Wilson, as he had instructed her to do when briefly preparing her testimony earlier that morning.

"Ms. Levine, you were Kelly Ryan's roommate at Penn, is that right?"

Queenan jumped from his seat and shouted, "Objection!"

It was so abrupt and energized an interjection that the Judge chuckled in surprise. "Yes, Mr. Queenan?"

"Judge, this is a Commonwealth witness. Mr. Wilson is asking leading questions on direct. He should not be allowed to testify for her, Judge."

It was a silly objection, at least after one question, a fact of which Queenan was fully aware. But he hadn't made the objection so that it would be sustained. When he shouted, he looked directly at the witness. He wanted her to hear his voice right away, to put into her mind the first bit of apprehension about his upcoming cross-examination.

"Sit down, Mr. Queenan," said the Judge with annoyance.

"Ma'am, you were in fact Kelly's roommate?" asked Wilson, completely ignoring Queenan's expected theatrics.

"Yes," Levine responded, her voice cracking just a bit as she cast a quick glance towards Queenan.

"Were you at home on the evening of October 28th of this year?"

Anita nodded yes.

Before Wilson could say anything, Queenan jumped from his chair diagonally, so it looked like he was leaping towards the witness. "Please remind this witness that she is to answer verbally, Judge!" he shouted at Anita.

Wilson had only been able to spend a few minutes with the girl that morning. She had been traumatized by her roommate's death, and her parents had sent her to stay at the family's vacation home in Aspen to recover. Wilson had only persuaded them to bring her back when he threatened to have Tony Sciolla fly out to Colorado and hand her a subpoena personally. It was a threat which had not endeared Wilson to Mr. Levine, who was a six-term Congressman from Northeast Philadelphia. He also happened to be one of the few politicians in Philadelphia that owed no allegiance to George Cohen. Levine was a self-made millionaire in his own right. The last thing the Congressman said to Wilson when he dropped his daughter off that morning was "do not let anything happen to my little girl."

Wilson had no intention of letting anything happen to Al Levine's little girl, but the only way he had of protecting any witness was exhaustive preparation. For trial prep, the sessions would last for days. For a preliminary hearing such as this, Wilson would liked to have spent at least a few hours preparing Anita for the circus she was about to enter, but her father's obstructive attitude had prevented that from happening.

As it was, Wilson simply warned Anita about Queenan and what he was likely to do in order to intimidate her. She was a smart girl, but naïve. She thought because she got a 1580 on her SAT's and had watched a few episodes of *Law and Order*, that she knew what to expect and could handle it. But sitting there, with the eyes of the press fixed upon her, Queenan's sudden burst in her direction had obviously unnerved her.

Sensing this, Wilson moved directly into Queenan's line of sight.

"Anita," he said very softly, with a warm smile. "Please make sure that all of your answers are verbal so that the court reporter can take down what you say, okay?"

Anita nodded, then said "yes" as she realized what she was doing.

But Queenan was on his feet again. "Judge, Mr. Wilson is standing in my way."

"And I'll be there until his client is convicted, your Honor," said Wilson, as he walked back to his chair. The reporters, loving the exchange, scribbled furiously.

MacDuffie, in the meantime, simply shook his head and said nothing.

"Now, Ms. Levine, were you in your apartment on the evening of October 28th?"

"Yes, I was." She was now looking at Queenan after each answer, waiting for his next eruption.

"Was Kelly Ryan home as well?"

"She got home around 9:00 I guess. She and Darnell came in together."

Wilson got up and pointed at Darnell. "Are you referring to the defendant?"

"Yes."

"Your Honor, may the record reflect the identification of the defendant?"

Before the Judge could respond, Queenan was on his feet. "Darnell, stand up," he said. Darnell rose to his feet, looking directly at the Judge. "Your Honor, I am proud to let the record reflect that this young man standing to my left is Darnell Cooper."

Even Lionel rolled his eyes at that one. "Sit down, Mr. Queenan. You too Mr. Cooper. Go ahead, Mr. Wilson," said the judge wearily.

Wilson acted as if Queenan wasn't even in the room and continued asking his questions in the same maddeningly calm manner. "Were Ms. Ryan and the defendant together?"

"Well, yeah," said Levine, "they came in together and went into Kelly's bedroom."

"When is the next time you saw Kelly after that?"

They had rehearsed the answer to this question. "When I found her dead on her bed about three hours later."

It had the effect Wilson was looking for. Titters rippled throughout the spectators, causing the judge to bang his gavel and shoot a stern look at the crowd. Ryan remained stone-faced.

"Between the time that you saw Kelly and the defendant enter her bedroom, and the time, as you say you found her dead, did you hear anything from inside the room?"

"Objection!" shouted Queenan, on his feet once again. "Calls for hearsay."

Surprised at hearing a legitimate objection, the judge looked to Wilson for a response.

"It's a yes or no question, Judge," said Wilson. "Doesn't call for what was said."

"Overruled. Answer the question."

"Yes, I heard them having sex."

Wilson hid his smile as Queenan literally leapt from his chair. "Objection! I demand that it be stricken! I demand that this court...".

The judge had had enough. "Sit down, sir!" he bellowed at Queenan. "*I* demand that you begin to exercise some decorum in this courtroom or you will be excused and co-counsel will finish this hearing. Do you understand me?"

Queenan sat down with a chastened look on his face, but inside he was pleased. Wilson had unwittingly opened the door and given him a legitimate reason to ask a question that might otherwise have landed him in a jail cell for asking. He was going to ask it no matter what, but not having to spend a night in the Roundhouse was an added bonus.

"Now, Mr. Wilson," said the judge, "if you want this young lady to testify regarding an opinion she formed based on what she heard, you're going to have to lay a foundation."

"That's okay, judge, I'll move on." Wilson certainly didn't want to question Anita Levine about what experience she had that would have allowed her to understand that what she heard in that room was two people having sex. At trial he would, but it was not necessary at the moment.

"Ms. Levine, what else did you hear?"

"Well, after I heard them..." she looked over at Queenan, "you know, I heard them arguing."

Wilson waited for the objection, but none came.

"Go ahead."

"I heard Kelly say 'don't you touch me,' and then she called him a...," Anita looked nervously, but Wilson nodded that it was okay. "A Motherfucker.

"Then I heard a really loud thump, and then it was real quiet. I waited for awhile, hoping Darnell would leave so I could see if Kelly was all right. But it was so quiet that I went and knocked on the door. When I didn't hear an answer, I opened the door a little bit, and that's when I saw her."

"Thank you, Ms. Levine, those are all the questions I have."

"May I cross-examine the witness, Your Honor?' asked Queenan sweetly as he rose from his chair and buttoned his jacket.

The judge nodded wearily.

"Ms. Levine, good morning," he said with a smile. "My name is Roger Queenan, and I represent Darnell Cooper."

Levine smiled involuntarily back at him, relaxing just a bit with Queenan's suddenly friendly demeanor.

"I just have a couple of questions for you, okay?"

Anita nodded. "I mean yes," she said in a smiling rush. Queenan laughed, as if her earlier faux paus was but a fond memory for the both of them.

Queenan got up and walked toward Levine without asking for permission from the court. He showed her a two page document. "Anita, is this document the statement you gave to the police when they interviewed you?"

"Yes, it is," she said after reading over it briefly.

"Take the time to look at it carefully. Is everything in that statement true and accurate?"

She spent more time pretending to read it. She was so nervous her legs were shaking. "Yes, sir, it's all true."

"Thank you," said Wilson as he took the paper back from her and returned to his seat.

"You said that you heard Ms. Ryan say 'don't you touch me,' and then she called someone a 'motherfucker'?"

Levine nodded. "Yes."

"But you also said that you heard them having sex, correct?"

"Right."

"So it's your testimony that Ms. Ryan had sex with Darnell, *and then* told someone not to touch her?"

Levine hesitated for a second. "Well…yeah, that's what I heard."

Queenan shifted his weight so that the reporters in the front row could see him rolling his eyes. He then turned back to the witness.

"Now, Anita, you had an abortion when you were fifteen years old, did you not?"

"Objection!" Now it was Wilson's turn to explode. "Sidebar, Judge!"

"Counsel, in my chambers!" snapped the judge as he stormed off the bench into his robing room.

"You've got exactly five seconds to convince me why I shouldn't throw your ass in jail for contempt right now!" yelled the judge when all three lawyers were assembled in the small robing room behind the courtroom.

Queenan appeared non-plussed.

"Certainly, Judge. Mr. Wilson elicited a conclusion from the witness that she had heard my client and the dead girl having sex. You allowed that testimony to remain on the record, even though counsel chose not to lay a foundation for it. Notwithstanding Mr. Wilson's failure to do so, I am certainly entitled to explore the foundation of this girl's opinion as to what experience she has that would allow her to draw the conclusion that two people she cannot see are having sex.

"I have information that this girl had an abortion when she was fifteen years old. She was impregnated, Judge, as I understand it, after having been raped. Since that time, I am given to understand she has not had sex with any man, and in fact has expressed on many an occasion to fellow classmates her absolute disdain for it. She has absolutely no basis in her personal experience by which to gauge whether or not two people are having consensual sex, because the only frame of reference she has is sex as rape."

It was total bullshit, and everybody in the room knew it. The question had been asked for one reason, and one reason only, to intimidate the witness and scare her off from testifying at trial. Wilson was livid both because his own team of investigators had failed to turn up the little nugget about Levine's abortion, and because he knew that the question would most likely have its desired effect.

Unfortunately, so much of the practice of law is simply putting one-self in a position to spout the right bullshit at the right time, and no matter who in the room knows it's bullshit, you have to live with it because it's the law.

"Judge, I don't know how he found all of this out," seethed Wilson with barely controlled fury, "and I am certainly going to investigate whether or not this girl's privacy was illegally invaded. But that's not the issue for the moment. Forget relevance, that line of questioning is so beyond the pale of professional ethics that Mr. Queenan ought to be sanctioned immediately. I am disgusted by this man's behavior. His sole intent was to intimidate this young girl, and I shudder to think what she is experiencing right now in that room out there. If you don't put a leash on this guy right now, this whole hearing will be a joke, which is exactly what he wants."

"Put a *leash* on me! You racist bastard!" hissed Queenan.

"Goddammit, that's enough!" yelled the judge as he pounded his fist on the small desk in the middle of the room. "Both of you shut up." The judge sat down hard in his chair and rubbed his chin angrily.

"On the one hand, I agree with you wholeheartedly, Mr. Wilson."

He looked at Queenan. "You are a disgrace, sir, and I am sorry to call myself a member of the same bar as your ilk. It is men such as yourself who are the reason for every lawyer joke there is."

Queenan said nothing, not because he didn't want to, but because he knew there was a "but" coming up that would make everything the judge said before it totally meaningless.

"But," said the judge to Wilson, "technically speaking, you did open the door to at least give him an argument that the question was reason-able."

As much as Wilson wanted to scream at the judge what a fool he was, he didn't. It was a point of pride with Wilson that he had never deliberately shown disrespect to a judge in his whole career, regardless of how much it might have been deserved. He could get as down and dirty with his opponents as any lawyer in the city, but the D.A. had always felt that the robe, if not the man wearing it, deserved deference, even in the heat of battle.

"Respectfully, your honor," he said through clenched teeth, his hands clasped behind his back, "I disagree."

"I know you do. But there's no sense arguing about it now. Mr. Queenan, I know you think you're clever. But regardless of the technical reasons you asked that question, it was your last of this witness. You are foreclosed from asking this girl any more questions. You pull one more stunt remotely like that one with any of the other Commonwealth's witnesses, and I'll end the hearing immediately and bind the case over for trial. Got it? Now get out."

Queenan bowed his head, not because of his repudiation, but mostly to hide his smile. The questions he had asked of Levine were the only questions he had wanted to ask. Everything he had done, from the angry objections to the sweetness with which he approached her had been calculated and pre-planned. From the moment Lionel's investigator had uncovered the abortion story from an old boyfriend embittered by his inability to bed his classmate, Queenan had envisioned with glee the moment he would ask Levine about it.

Levine's father was a conservative Republican and outspoken critic of abortion rights. He would also be facing re-election at just about the time Queenan expected the case to go to trial. The defense lawyer relished the possibility of not only eliminating one of the key witnesses against Darnell, but also derailing the campaign of one more white politician, whose voice in Congress reflected only the perspective of his white constituents.

Out of the corner of his eye Queenan searched for the expression on Lionel's face. But the younger man's square jaw was firmly set and his hazel eyes were cast towards the floor. Lionel had expressed strong distaste for just about all of Queenan's tactics, and had argued vociferously against this one. Aside from the moral pangs he felt, which were considerable, Lionel thought that Queenan's attacking style would alienate the public against Darnell, and should he somehow be acquitted, make him a pariah and laughingstock along the lines of O.J. Simpson. Queenan had disagreed of course, and ultimately convinced Lionel to go along with the plan by reminding him of his original mandate…get the boy acquitted, no matter what it takes.

Although he was still committed to that goal, Lionel was just now realizing what it would take, and for the first time, wondered whether it was worth it.

As the three men shuffled back into the courtroom, they were struck at first by the absolute quiet of the crowd, and second, by the uniform consistency of the direction in which they were all staring. They all three turned and saw at the same time what everyone else had been looking at for the previous five minutes they had been in the robing room.

Anita Levine appeared to have emotionally disintegrated. Seated still on the stand, she was weeping, without sound but uncontrollably, into the chest of Tony Sciolla. Her entire body seemed to be racked with sobs, and she softly pounded her fists into the detective's back. He was whispering something into her ear in an attempt to soothe her, or perhaps convince her not to simply get up and run away. She was not permitted to leave the stand because in his haste to get off the bench, the judge had not excused her.

As soon as MacDuffie came back out though, he realized his error. "Ms. Levine," he said softly after retaking the bench, "you are excused. Detective, will you escort the young lady out of the courtroom?"

After a murderous look in Queenan's direction, Sciolla gently pulled the still sobbing girl from her seat and led her back out the side door through which she had come. It had been a powerful scene, and had angered everyone in the room. All of that animosity was directed towards Queenan, and by extension, Darnell. But, as he had been instructed to do before the hearing had started, Darnell looked over at Queenan after Levine was gone, and shook his head with an exaggerated look of disgust. Every reporter in the room saw it, and dutifully noted that Darnell clearly disapproved of his lawyer's tactics.

Tony Sciolla reentered the room almost immediately. He caught Wilson's eye as he returned to his seat, and tried to communicate with his glance just how badly he wanted to destroy Roger Queenan. Wilson averted Sciolla's gaze, though, ashamed that he had allowed his courtroom to be taken over by his opponent.

Sciolla noted Wilson's reaction, and burned even more. *The D.A.'s too soft on this kid,* he thought. *He needs to be in kill mode, not worried about making sure justice is done. The system doesn't expect one side or the other to be worried about such things,* thought the detective. *It's geared so that both sides beat the crap out of each other with everything they've got, and ultimately, whatever passes for justice will emerge. But that's not going to happen in this case if Wilson gets teary-eyed every time he looks at Cooper.*

It was at that moment that Sciolla decided he had to even the playing field, even if Wilson was unwilling to. If that meant breaking some of the rules, well so be it. The citizens of the Commonwealth deserved not to be taken advantage of by a shark like Queenan. While Wilson might be able to sleep with himself if Cooper got acquitted, Sciolla would not.

"Call your next witness, Mr. Wilson."

"The Commonwealth calls Dr. Maury Templeton."

Into the room strutted a short, bald, old man, with tufts of white hair that jutted out over his long ears. His suit was ill-fitting but his shoes were comfortable. At the age of sixty-eight, his best years as a medical examiner, and as a witness, were well behind him. Templeton had in fact been semi-retired for a few years, and only filled in as an on-call emergency replacement for full-time staff members.

Wilson would have preferred any of the other very able assistant medical examiners in the office to have been his witness for this case, but, as luck would have it, Templeton had been on call that very early morning when Kelly's body was brought to the morgue. And because Wilson had insisted on an immediate autopsy, the task had fallen to

Templeton, who eagerly jumped at the chance to inject himself into a potentially juicy case.

Templeton took his time getting to the stand. When he was finally seated, and after being sworn, Wilson asked him where he was employed.

"Several places," Templeton intoned imperiously. "Where would you like me to start?"

If Wilson's eyes could have shot fire, Templeton would have been brisket. But before he could ask his next question, Lionel stood up.

"Your Honor," he said, "I will be handling the cross-examination of Dr. Templeton, and to speed things along, I will certainly stipulate to his qualification as an expert." It was standard operating procedure, but clearly showed Lionel to be the good cop to Queenan's bad.

Wilson accepted the stipulation gladly. The less time Templeton was on the stand the better.

"Doctor, did you perform an autopsy on Kelly Ryan in the early morning hours of October 29th of this year?"

Templeton picked a piece of non-existent lint off of his immaculate herringbone suit trousers. "Yes, I did."

Wilson rose from his chair and dropped a packet of papers in front of Queenan. He then handed an identical set of papers to the witness. "Doctor, looking at what I've marked as Commonwealth's exhibit 1, a copy of which has just been provided to defense counsel, is this the report you prepared detailing your autopsy findings?"

Templeton eyed the papers suspiciously, intent on showing the crowd that he was not simply the D.A.'s puppet. "Yes, it is," he said after leafing through the report several times and pretending to read portions of it.

Wilson ignored the unnecessary theatrics. "Doctor, what did you determine the cause of death to be?"

Templeton located the relevant portion of the report and pretended to read it, as if this were just another case, and he hadn't spent all night memorizing every word of the report.

"Asphyxiation," The medical examiner said finally, leaning into the microphone when he answered, but not uncrossing his legs.

"And did you determine the manner of death?"

"Manual strangulation."

"What led you to that conclusion?"

Templeton cleared his throat. "A couple of things. There was petecchial hemorrhaging in the eyes, disc-like finger-tip bruising around the neck, and larynx damage."

"What if anything else did you find?"

He lifted his leg and crossed it with the other.

"The poor girl had been raped. There were vaginal abrasions as well as the presence of sperm, and her jaw had been broken. The pattern of bruising on the neck and face were clearly made by someone who was very strong and who had very large hands."

Instinctively, Darnell lowered his hands and hid them under the table. It was a move missed by no one in the audience, and more than one newspaper article would later point to that simple act as clear evidence of guilt.

"Did you have the sperm that you found tested?"

"Yes, we had it sent to our State Police Crime lab in Lima."

"Lastly, Doctor Templeton, were you able to ascertain a time of death?"

"Ah, yes, death occurred anywhere between 10:30 and 11:30 p.m."

"Thank you Doctor, I have no further questions."

At trial, Wilson would have to spend a great deal of time laying a foundation for asking all of these questions, and would have to elicit testimony from the doctor as to exactly how it was he was able to make his conclusions, detailing the scientific method behind all of them. But for the purpose of the preliminary hearing, the conclusions were enough. Besides, the less Templeton was allowed to say, the better it was from Wilson's perspective.

Lionel stood up slowly, buttoning his blazer as he did so. At trial, they would attack the bases for his conclusions. But that would be for the jury only, as they would be the only twelve people in the world that mattered. Plus, Lionel had no interest in giving the state a sneak preview of what was to come at trial. He only wanted to establish one point at this hearing.

"Dr. Templeton, good morning sir. I just have a couple of questions. You testified that you found vaginal abrasions. Am I correct then that the principal evidence you are relying upon to conclude that the decedent had been raped is the presence of those abrasions?"

Templeton smiled, thinking Lionel had asked him a silly question. "Well, that and the fact that she was beaten and murdered, and that there was sperm deposited in the vaginal canal, I would say all of those factors were what I relied upon to conclude that Ms. Ryan had been forcibly raped prior to her death."

Lionel hung his head briefly and smiled sheepishly, as if to acknowledge that he'd asked a silly question.

"But isn't it possible, sir, that the abrasions you found could have occurred in the course of a consensual sexual encounter, if for example, Ms. Ryan had been a virgin?" The press corps tittered, causing the judge to bang his gavel lightly for quiet.

It was something Templeton had not even considered, and he took a moment to ponder it. "I suppose so, but then again, why would someone have consensual sex and then strangle and beat their partner to death afterwards? It doesn't make any sense."

It was Lionel's turn to smile. "I agree with you wholeheartedly, doctor, that conclusion makes no sense at all. No further questions." He'd had five or six more to ask actually, but Templeton's answer was too good not to end on.

Ash didn't even look at Templeton as he left the stand. The last thing he wanted to see was the Doctor's proud grin, believing he had shown Lionel up with his smug answers. Wilson had long before in his career realized that the main problem with people who think they're smarter than they are is not that they do things like Templeton had just done on the stand, it's that nothing could ever be done to convince them they had done something stupid.

"Any more witnesses, Mr. Wilson?" asked the judge. Clearly he had heard enough to bind the case over for trial, and his question was aimed at communicating just that message to the District Attorney.

"May I have just a moment, your Honor?" Wilson didn't wait for an answer. He pretended to be digging around into his trial bag, but really all he was doing was considering whether or not to call anymore witnesses. The technician from the State Police crime lab was on hand to testify about the matching DNA between Darnell's samples and the semen found in Kelly's vagina. And there was Sciolla to testify that Darnell had lied about having had sex with Kelly that night.

But he hadn't had sufficient time to prepare as good a direct exam of the lab tech as he otherwise would have, given more time to do so. He was not yet fully educated about the DNA evidence and the way it had been preserved and tested, and the last thing he wanted to do was ask an ill-informed question, the answer to which might hurt him at trial.

Whether or not to put Sciolla on the stand was an altogether different question. All he really had to offer at this point was Darnell's lie about the sex. But once up there, everything about his investigation was in play on cross. What Wilson wanted to avoid, if possible, were questions about Joe Fullem, especially at this early stage.

Levine had told the police about the call from "Joe" earlier in the evening when Kelly had been killed, and his promise to call later. His cell phone records reflected the call that Levine took, but there was no record of any second call, and no one besides Darnell and his defense team knew about that. Fullem had explained to Sciolla that he had simply been calling to check up on his best friend's kid, and that he had forgotten to call her again as he had said he would. There really was no evidence suggesting that Fullem was lying. In fact, all of the physical evidence was pointing to Darnell, which by implication, supported Fullem's story.

Like all good lawyers, Lionel had not allowed the police to have any further conversation with his client than they'd already had. There was no possible benefit to be gained by telling them about the second call, or even Kelly's revelation to Darnell that she had helped Fullem sell drugs. The cops already believed Darnell was guilty, and rather than see that information as leading to any other suspects, they would simply do whatever was necessary to eliminate that evidence as helpful to Darnell's defense.

So these two nuggets of information were tucked safely away in the defense team's ammo bag like sensitive explosives. The trick was going to be how to set a match to the explosives during trial at just the right time.

Even without knowing what Lionel and Queenan were keeping from him though, Wilson was well aware that the Fullem issue could blow up in his face. For that reason, he wanted to minimize in any way that he could the ability of the defense to interject that name into the proceedings.

"No further witnesses, Your Honor. The Commonwealth would ask that Doctor Templeton's report be admitted into evidence. With that, the Commonwealth rests."

MacDuffie glowered towards Queenan. "Any witnesses or evidence, Mr. Queenan?"

Queenan was surprised that Wilson had chosen not to call the lab tech, if for no other reason than to show the press corps just how dead to rights the State had Darnell. It's what Queenan would have done had he been the prosecutor. He leaned across Darnell and whispered to Lionel. "Wilson doesn't get it. He thinks the trial hasn't started yet."

Queenan then stood up. "No witnesses, Your Honor."

"Do you wish to make any argument?"

"Oh, yes, Judge. My argument is this. There has been no evidence offered by the Commonwealth today which suggests anything other than a consensual sexual encounter between Darnell Cooper and the deceased. There has been no evidence presented as to a motive, nor has there been any testimony directly linking Mr. Cooper to this girl's murder. The State is asking you to draw inferences based upon conjecture, and were it not for the color of my client's skin, Judge, this prosecution would not even be happening."

"Enough of that crap," said the judge crossly, holding up his hand. MacDuffie stared angrily at Queenan for a few seconds, collecting his thoughts and trying not to explode.

"Let me just say for the record, Mr. Queenan," he said finally, "that I believe you to be doing your client a disservice when you attempt to inject matters which are irrelevant and inflammatory into these proceedings. It draws attention from the facts of the case, and one can only assume that is your intention. The only person, it seems to me, who is making the color of your client's skin an issue in this case is you, sir. Again, one can only wonder why. The matter is bound over for trial on all charges. Arraignment will be held on," the judge checked his calendar, "December 18th. That is all."

MacDuffie strode from the bench before Queenan could respond directly, so the fuming lawyer held court outside the courthouse a few minutes later.

"Judge MacDuffie's comments are representative of the mind set of our judiciary, and the justice system as a whole," he said to a throng of reporters and news cameras.

"Both of the witnesses who testified today, and those who will testify at trial, see the world from the perspective of their own biases and prejudices. The conclusions they draw are therefore colored by those biases. My client is a straight A student at one of the world's finest universities. He is an All-American athlete who has passed up millions of guaranteed dollars so that he could finish his education at that university. He is a pillar of his community who volunteers his time to help those less fortunate than he. He has no criminal record nor any previous involvement in any criminal activity. And yet, simply because he made the mistake of having a wholly consensual sexual encounter with the white daughter of a Philadelphia Police Detective, he is automatically the number one suspect in her death.

"If the young man I just described were white, we would not be here. Judge MacDuffie says that the color of my client's skin is irrelevant, and that my comments are inflammatory? I ask you, who is it really that's trying to divert your attention from the truth?"

"Mr. Queenan!" shouted a Philadelphia Inquirer reporter from the back of the crowd. "Why did Darnell lie about having had sex with the victim if he did nothing wrong?"

From his stance to the far right of Queenan's position, Lionel gritted his teeth and hoped that he would have the sense not to comment directly on the evidence. Queenan however, did not get the telepathic message to shut up.

"First of all," Queenan boomed, "let me say that we heard no evidence from the Commonwealth today that my client has done anything other than cooperate fully with the authorities in their investigation of this poor girl's death. More importantly, however, let me suggest to you that any young black man, when torn from a sound sleep and accosted by a Philadelphia detective in his own living room, with accusations of having made love with the white daughter of one of their fellow detectives, would be a fool to admit having done so.

"Because in this town, when a young black man has sex with a white girl, he must have raped her, right? And if anything bad happens to her, he must have done it, right? The bottom line message is that young black men are animals, devoid of self-control, who will rape and pillage and steal and murder at will."

Queenan reached up, grabbed his lapels, and puffed out his chest and lips mockingly. "It don't matta' how smart he is," he said in his best step n' fetch it voice. "It don't matta' how much education he got, how well-spoken he might be, ultimately, he ain't ever goin' to be allowed to be anything more than a nigger in the eyes of this racist system of so-called justice we have in this country."

CHAPTER 19

▼

Queenan was still holding court with the press corps by the time Ash Wilson and Tony Sciolla returned to the D.A.'s office. A small television in the corner with the sound turned down showed Queenan gesticulating wildly as he spoke, and an eager press corps eating up every word.

Alone together finally, Sciolla closed the door, glanced briefly at the TV, and then let his boss have it.

"What the fuck are you doing?" he asked angrily.

"Huh?" responded a surprised Wilson.

"What the fuck are you doing? That hearing was for shit. You let him score all the points, and you didn't even put up our best evidence. You refuse all interview requests and you answer no questions from the press. What the fuck are you doing? Are you trying to lose this case because you like this kid?"

Wilson sat down as Sciolla was talking. He had learned long ago from George Cohen that a truly effective boss never gets angry at an employee for speaking his mind, especially when the employee is being passionate about doing his job. Many powerful men get so wrapped up in their own egos, counseled Cohen, that they view dissent from subordinates as somehow traitorous and disrespectful. In fact, it should be seen for what it is, a desire to see the goals of the enterprise, be it a law firm or a grocery store, fully achieved. Wilson prided himself on following this philosophy, and it was one of the many reasons those who worked for him always remained loyal to him.

Still, nobody likes to be told they're doing a bad job.

"First of all, I never had any intention of putting our best evidence on the record. We didn't need it. The sole goal was to get the charges bound over for trial. I knew MacDuffie was going to do it anyway, so it would have been stupid to let them take potshots at you or the DNA evidence just to prove to the press that we have a solid case."

Sciolla interrupted. "Ash, I know that you're smarter than that. The jury is out there, man, reading the papers and watching the news. They're out there listening to Queenan spew his garbage. It's one thing to refuse to speak to the press about the case, but it's entirely different when you don't take an opportunity to show them what we've really got. I think you're sitting so far up on that high horse of yours that you're forgetting what your job really is."

"What's that supposed to mean?" Wilson snapped.

Sciolla sat down and pulled out his pipe, which he began to load angrily with tobacco from a plastic bag he fished from his jacket pocket. "I'll tell you what it means. How many times have you and I talked about the whole perception versus reality thing? Hundreds? You always say that you don't care about perception, that what you're concerned about is the truth, right?"

"Not in so many words, but yeah, generally that's correct."

Sciolla stuck the pipe in his mouth and started to light it. "What I've always found vaguely disconcerting about that philosophy is something that I today, for the first time, realized is totally fucked up about it. You feel that men who are wrapped up in simply creating a perception, regardless of the reality, are that way because they're egotistical. In your mind, they care less about who they really are, than they do about how others see them. They define themselves through others eyes, not their own.

"But you see, Ash, the fatal flaw in your philosophy is the presumption that you, Ash Wilson, know what's real and what isn't."

Wilson raised an eyebrow. "Okay, you lost me."

"I don't want to talk esoterically, so let me be very clear about why I'm telling you this. You believe the reality to be that Darnell Cooper is guilty of raping and murdering Kelly Ryan. You believe that it is your job to ultimately reveal that truth to a jury."

"I guess that's right."

Sciolla grabbed the pipe from his mouth and sat forward. "But that's where you're wrong. The truth about who murdered Kelly Ryan has yet to be created. The truth will be whatever the foreperson of the jury stands up and announces it to be at the end of the trial. The jury will create the truth based on everything they've heard and read and seen starting three weeks ago. All they're getting right now is Queenan's bullshit, but in the face of no alternatives, they're going to believe him. What's truly egotistical is to expect that the jury will ultimately come to accept your version of the truth, simply because you believe it to be correct."

The D.A. looked at his friend quizzically. "You don't really believe all that, do you?"

"I sure as shit do."

Wilson smiled patronizingly. "I freely admit that the truth is not an absolute. But you said you weren't interested in an esoteric discussion. And that's good because we are not dealing with a philosophical question. We can either prove beyond a reasonable doubt that Cooper killed the girl, or we can't. Those are the two truths from which the jury will have to choose.

"You're right, I do believe the truth to be that he killed her. And I allow for the possibility that my ego is telling me that I will be able to convince a jury of that no matter what Roger Queenan does.

"But you're wrong when you say that the truth has yet to be created. The girl is dead, and someone killed her. The evidence shows the killer to be Cooper. I believe that if I do my job, the way it's supposed to be done, the jury will see the truth, and Cooper will be found guilty of the crime based on that evidence."

Sciolla interrupted again. "Does the saddle on that horse chafe at all?"

"C'mon, man, will you stop breakin' my balls?"

"No, I won't. Queenan's right about one thing, you know. Everything we do is colored and motivated by the way we see the world. You have an essentially optimistic view of the world and mankind. I don't know if it's because of all that religion nonsense you were taught as a kid or what, but there is no cosmic payback, there is no scorecard being kept by some imaginary being in the clouds with a long white beard and flowing robe. You think that living life in accordance with your principals will ultimately earn you some special reward.

"But it's time to stop living life like a third grader, Ash. If you don't say your prayers at night, nothing will change. If a tree falls in the forest and no one hears it, guess what? It hasn't made a sound. If Ash Wilson does the right thing, and no one knows it, guess what? Darnell Cooper gets away with murder."

Wilson had heard enough. "Whattdya' want me to do Tony? Hold daily press conferences and tell the media about every piece of evidence we have? You want me to go on talk shows and say that I believe Cooper's guilty? You want me to tell everyone what an asshole Roger Queenan is? Well, I can't do those things. It's simply not the way I practice law, I'm sorry."

"And if we lose because of it?"

Wilson pursed his lips and turned his chair towards the window. "Well, then we lose. But at least I'll be able to sleep at night."

Sciolla jumped from his chair and slammed his fist onto to the D.A.'s desk. "You egotistical motherfucker! It *is* all about you, isn't it? You don't care about justice. All you care about is how you feel about what it is you're doing. That's no different than the guys who only care about what others think about them. You get to think less of them because they define themselves solely through others' perception of them. But it's just as bad, Ash, if you refuse to accept that how others perceive you is still important. The fact is, you don't care about the truth any more than they do. Just like them, all you care about is yourself!"

Sciolla stormed from the room before Wilson could respond. Not that he would have. He never turned his chair back around to face his friend. Instead, the D.A. stared past his reflection in the window…wondering if Sciolla was right.

*   *   *   *

Back in Queenan's office Lionel was able finally to tell Roger how he felt about his performance at the preliminary hearing.

"You're fired," said the younger man matter-of-factly.

Queenan smiled as he leafed through some mail on his desk. "Aw, C'mon, Lionel, did I offend the delicate sensibilities of the uptown lawyer? What do you think this is, croquet? There are no points for politeness here, Li. Nobody's gonna' suddenly offer us some money to go away. There are two possible outcomes to this case. Either your boy gets acquitted, or he gets the needle. You hired me to prevent that from happening, no matter what it takes. Don't lose your nerve now. Our hands are going to get a lot dirtier than they got today."

Lionel let the 'uptown lawyer' comment go. "Don't you care that people are calling you a shyster? That they think you're a clown?"

Queenan laughed. "Do you? As long as I'm the clown, and as long as I'm the one being called names, what do you care?"

"Because I'm sitting next to you, and it makes me look bad too."

"Oh…I'm sorry. I thought the goal was to get Darnell acquitted, not make you look good."

Lionel reached out and grabbed Queenan's jacket lapel. The strength of his grip lifted the much shorter man onto his tippy-toes. "Fuck you, you little turd," growled Lionel. "I love that boy more than you'll ever know…," Lionel let go of Queenan's jacket and turned away to hide the tears which had unexpectedly filled his eyes.

"Then why are you questioning my tactics?"

Lionel moved towards the window and glanced across the street at Independence Hall. "Because there's a line, Roger. There has to be, a line that we won't cross no matter how much we might need to in order to get what we want."

"And what makes you think I've crossed it?"

Lionel turned. "You can't be serious. Asking that girl about her abortion? All the unnecessary objections? The diatribes on race? If you don't know that all of those things crossed the line, then you really are fired, because you're crazy."

Queenan sat down behind his desk and with a wave of his hand invited Lionel to sit down, which he did.

"Let me address all three of those things in order. First, how can you suggest that my question about abortion was improper when the judge himself ruled that it wasn't? Second, the objections were all thought out in advance and strategically made. And they were effective. Lastly, the 'racial diatribes' as you call them. I made very clear to you from the very beginning that I believe race to be the critical factor in this case. And not just because I can make it look that way.

"Do you really think that your protégé would be sitting in jail right now if he was white? No matter how wonderful he is, the color of his skin carries with it a presumption of guilt. It may be difficult for some-one like you…and I do not mean any insult by this…who has not had to deal with the daily inequities of racial discrimination for a very long time, to understand, but it is true. All the cops really do know at this point is that Darnell had sex with that cop's kid the night she was mur-dered. If it had been a white kid, he would have been questioned and released while the investigation progressed."

Lionel didn't believe that, but mostly because, and he hated himself for it, he believed Darnell to be guilty. Queenan had not been made privy to the diagnoses of Darnell as a child which made him feel that way. Not that it would have mattered to Queenan's way of thinking.

"Oh, and by the way, if Darnell were white, the investigation would be focusing on Fullem a whole heck of a lot more. The only reason the D.A.'s detectives haven't gone after him as a suspect is because they don't want to give me the opportunity to argue it in court any more than I already will. If Darnell were white, that wouldn't be a problem, would it?"

Queenan went to the file cabinet for a cup of coffee.

"Don't get me wrong. I don't mean to suggest, just between you and I, that these decisions are being consciously made because Darnell's black. I don't seriously think that anyone in the police department said, 'hey, this kid's black, she's white, he must've killed her.' That would be silly. What I am absolutely one hundred percent sure of though is that subconsciously, for every cop on the case and the D.A. himself, the unseen glue holding all of their circumstantial evidence together is the color of that boy's skin. It's what allows them to draw the otherwise absurd conclusion that Darnell Cooper is a murderer.

"So, you see, Lionel, even though it may be technically correct to say that this prosecution is not necessarily *motivated* by race, it is certainly being *propelled* by it. And I assure you that the only way we will get this boy acquitted is if I manipulate the jury into blurring the distinction between those concepts. People may call me a clown, or a race-baiter, or even say that I'm cheating. But I don't care. Everything I do is within the bounds of the law. It may be distasteful, it may be crass, hell it may even be morally wrong. But that is not my concern. I am simply taking the very same system of laws that have been so brutally wielded against us as a people for two centuries, and using them to club the shit out of the system itself. Actually, I think it's some pretty sweet irony when you think about it. If it works anyway."

"Ah, but what if it does work? What will Darnell be left with? Everyone will look at him like he's a murderer anyway."

Queenan nodded. "I admit, there is that possibility. I think if I do my job right though, that won't happen. But if that's really what you're worried about, go ask OJ at his next tee time where he'd rather be. Ultimately, Lionel, if we don't take this affirmative action on Darnell's behalf, he'll stay exactly where he is right now, and then he'll die. At least if he gets out, he'll have a chance."

Lionel left Queenan's office without having decided one way or the other whether or not he would fire the man. Instead of taking a cab, he walked up Chestnut Street, back towards City Hall and his own office. He needed to think about everything that was happening, and what he should be doing to control it all.

Lionel had long understood that amongst people of high intelligence, there is a certain feeling that the general rules of life don't really apply to them as they do to everyone else. People like this go through life believing that they have a deeper understanding of the world around them, and that the social constrictions that we as a human race impose upon ourselves are arbitrary and meaningless in and of themselves. Because of this, they feel no obligation to follow these rules, because the rules are meant for people who, rather than question their environment, simply choose to exist within it.

Some people call this feeling egotism. Others call it selfishness. Boiled down to their essential meaning, both of those adjectives describe the same state of mind.

Whatever it was called though, Lionel was keenly aware of this character trait because he was guilty of it himself. It was a feeling that manifested itself in his every day life so simply, like parking right in front of the grocery store in the no parking zone while he ran in for a few quick things, instead of finding a parking space like everyone else.

Early in his career as a lawyer, it had also manifested itself in the way he conducted business. The law is a myriad of technical rules, especially when it comes to the process itself. When he first started out as a lawyer, Lionel would often find himself ignoring the technical procedural requirements of his cases, believing ultimately that the only important thing was that he would prevail in the end, not because his was the right position, but simply because it was his position.

In essence, it was a feeling that gave Lionel the confidence to believe that details are unimportant, because he had the capacity and the foresight to grasp the big picture.

Over time though, Lionel came to realize the hard way that no matter who you are, the rules, arbitrary or not, meaningless or not, do in fact apply to everyone. Not always equally, not always fairly, but across the board nonetheless. In fact, it is essential that they do, lest we as a society lose our ability to bring order and predictability to our lives, which is why laws and rules were formulated in the first place.

This realization had come to him in a funny way he'd never admit to publicly, or privately for that matter. He had been flipping the channels at home late one night and started watching "Lethal Weapon II." In one scene, Mel Gibson's character jumps into a movie shoot and starts beating the crap out of a totally innocent actor who was pretending to hold Danny Glover's daughter hostage. When the movie's director rightfully complains and then fires the daughter, Gibson beats the crap out of him and humiliates him until he agrees to hire the daughter back.

As Lionel watched it, he was struck by the fact that Mel Gibson's character was a total asshole, and that the movie director was the victim of a brutal and unprovoked assault. Yet the scene was meant to make the audience fall all the more in love with Gibson's character, and despise the movie director. If the movie had actually been about the movie director though, instead of Mel Gibson, Lionel realized, the audience would have hated Gibson's character and seen him as the bad guy.

Lionel realized at that moment that in the real world, every person on the planet is the star of their own perpetually running movie. Once he realized that in any situation he just might be a bit player in someone else's movie, Lionel resolved to stop seeing the rest of the world as simply his supporting cast.

He crossed 11th Street and buttoned up his overcoat against the cold. Lionel recognized that Queenan was the kind of person who was incapable of seeing anyone else's movie but his own four star feature. And while he was smart enough to write a great script for himself, he was too narcissistic to read any others, or even recognize that another script even existed. It was a tragic flaw that might serve to make Queenan as famous as he expected to be. But it would also just as surely destroy him…and maybe Darnell too.

CHAPTER 20

▼

"Turn that TV off," rasped George Cohen to the people gathered around his hospital bed. The coverage of the Cooper preliminary hearing was entering its fifth hour. The hearing itself had lasted less than forty minutes.

"Well, look who's awake," said the junior Republican Senator from Pennsylvania. "You ready for some birthday cake?'

Cohen eyed the man with irritation. He knew he was dying. He'd been unable to buy off the cancer in his lungs. But worse than the pain in his chest was the torture of having to put up with the sycophants and ingrates who were buzzing around his soon to be carcass.

He let out a long, painful cough. "Yeah, cake sounds great. How about a cigar while we're at it?"

The senator laughed heartily, as if everyone in the room didn't think he was a jackass.

"You'll be back on your feet in no time, George," said the chief judge of the eastern district. "We'll have cigars for your ninety-first."

"Here here," mumbled the Mayor of Philadelphia.

After another sharp cough, Cohen looked around at all of them with hollow, red eyes. God he hated them. "If I live to be ninety-one, I promise that none of you will be invited to the party."

They all laughed at that one, forced to believe he was kidding. When Cohen died, he was going to leave a lot of money behind. Money that they wanted. They were willing to put up with however much shit Cohen had left in him to get it, too.

Ironically, they were in fact shit out of luck. Because the only person George Cohen was leaving his money too was sitting alone in the back of the room, waiting for them all to leave.

"I think George probably needs some rest, folks," said Wilson. "Whattya' say we give him a chance to do that?"

After everyone had finally shuffled out, Wilson came to his mentor's bedside and sat down.

"Don't you want people to actually miss you when you're gone, George?" asked Wilson, deeply saddened that there weren't more people who loved this man for more than just his money.

The old man coughed up some phlegm that Wilson caught in a tissue and threw away.

"Why would I want that?" He asked in a thin, raspy voice.

Wilson shrugged. "I don't know. If people miss you when you're dead, it means that you were loved, I guess. Isn't it important to you that you were loved at least?"

Cohen laughed-coughed. "I know that *you* love me. I know that your wife and sons love me. Why on Earth would it be important to me that anyone else love me? You of all people should know, Ash, that the love of strangers is nothing but a mirage in the desert. It looks appealing, often maddeningly so. But in the end, it's never more than an empty promise. We have both been very successful besting men who sought the approbation of all."

Wilson was in no mood for a philosophy lesson. Cohen's illness, combined with a sudden feeling of inadequacy in his work, had drained him of his will to contemplate deep thoughts.

Cohen appreciated this better than anyone. He had of course followed the Cooper case closely, and the turmoil it was creating at his alma mater, in Philadelphia and the country, and most of all, within his friend's heart, not to mention within his own firm. Many of the partners had been split about allowing Lionel to devote his time and energy to representing Darnell while still drawing a paycheck from Cohen & Elson.

It had been Cohen's decision to allow it. He was a big fan of the boy's, and had been since first intervening on his behalf to have him declared an emancipated minor. But having also met him personally, both through Penn Basketball and Lionel, Cohen believed him to be a extraordinary young man. He did not tell Wilson any of this, and he also did not say that as much as he wanted Wilson to succeed, he secretly hoped that Darnell would be acquitted.

In fact, Cohen had deliberately refrained from even discussing the case with Wilson, not wanting to suggest that he had anything less than total confidence in his ability to handle the situation. But as events had unfolded, Cohen sensed in Wilson a growing dissatisfaction with the direction the case had taken. Noelle had shared, in confidence, the internal struggle within her husband against accepting Darnell's guilt in the first place.

Cohen reached out a bony hand and covered Wilson's. "I love you, son, you know that?" Both men's eyes filled with tears. Cohen said the same thing every time Wilson came to visit him, just in case.

"I love you because you have always done things the right way. You have always stood up for what you believe, and have never let me down. You're struggling over this Cooper case, I know. But you're focusing on the wrong thing. You have a job to do. It is your job to gather evidence and present it to a judge or jury. As long as the evidence is gathered fairly and by the rules, and as long as it is presented within the rules, you have done your job."

Wilson grasped Cohen's hand. "I wish it were that simple, George. I wish I could treat this like just any other case and simply present the evidence and be confident that I was doing my job. But I know this kid, George, or at least I feel like I do. I've been around him. Hell, you have too. I've talked to a lot of people who know him. I just can't believe he would do such a thing."

Cohen understood that much of Wilson's internal struggle really revolved around Cooper's race, and the mere suggestion, from any source, that he was treating the case differently because of it. From the very beginning of his first term as D.A. when Roger Queenan had accused Wilson of racism, it had been the one area of sensitivity that even his own mentor dare not delve into with Wilson. It had been a deep, personal insult, and the wound left by it had never healed. But fearing that he might never get another chance, the old man felt he had no choice but to address the subject.

Cohen retracted his hand and eyed the younger man with a bemused grin.

"You're not a racist, Ash. I know you're not, because I am, and you don't think the same way I do."

Wilson shot Cohen a disapproving glance. "What are you talking about? I've never known you to be a racist, George. Hell, if you're a racist, then everybody's a racist."

Cohen tried to chuckle, but it was subsumed by another coughing fit. "I didn't say I was proud of it, Ash," he gasped finally. "I have always known, or at least I have always hoped, that the racist thoughts I have are wrong. And I am certainly aware, as are you painfully, that our society has evolved to the point where expressing what others even perceive to be racist thoughts is met with swift and drastic reprisals. So do not be surprised that even you, the person in the world who knows me best, does not know the darkest thoughts contained in my heart."

Wilson shook his head to clear the cobwebs that were forming. "So what racist thoughts do you have, George? What makes you a racist?"

Cohen sat quiet for a few seconds, collecting his thoughts. He knew that he would be dead soon, and he was determined to leave his earthly existence with the respect and love of Ash Wilson intact. The last thing he wanted to do was reveal a part of himself which might jeopardize either of those things. But he also felt that what he had to say might help Wilson in his battle against self-doubt. Ultimately though, he knew that he would do whatever it took to help Wilson, even at the expense of his own legacy.

"Ash, in the annals of history, has there ever been a more consistently despised or oppressed race of people than the Jews? They have never, never, had a land that they could peacefully call their own. Forget the Holocaust, you can go back thousands of years, and the one constant in Jewish history is pain and suffering at the hands of others who believe Jews to be parasites and meddlers. They have been systematically murdered, exiled, and reviled by not just individuals, but by entire nations.

"Despite all that, somehow, someway, Jews have managed to not only survive, but to flourish. Why is that? How have they been able to overcome seemingly insurmountable obstacles? How have *they* battled and overcome racism?

"I'll tell you what they haven't done. They haven't relied upon the goodwill of those in power to give them things. They haven't used the oppression occasioned by their race as an excuse for anything. What they *have* done is band together and rely upon only each other to help themselves. Whatever resources they have managed to accrue to themselves, they find a way to infuse their own people with access to the same resources. They have a strong faith in God, and they abide the principals of their religion. By that I mean that they do not indiscriminately spread their seed, they do not leave their children fatherless, and they always work hard.

"Ash, you ask me what makes me a racist? It is the fact that I have never been able to understand why blacks are any less capable of overcoming racism than the Jews. I am a racist because even though I do not know the answer, and even though I have never taken any steps to study the differences between the two, I have always just assumed that the reason the blacks are so much worse off than Jews in the world today, is because they must be an inferior race of people.

"I look at the continent of Africa and cannot understand why the place with the most natural resources in the world, a place with the most diamonds and gold and silver in the world, the place literally where civilization was born, is also the poorest, most disease-ridden, and technologically regressed continent on Earth. I look at the poorest cities in this, the richest country in the history of the world, and see nothing but black faces. I hate myself for thinking it, Ash, believe me I do, but I attribute these things to race. Because no matter what outside forces have operated upon these people, they should have the ability, as did the Jews, to band together and rise up against their oppressors, and take what is rightfully theirs."

Wilson looked down at Cohen with an expression of, if not disgust, then certainly distaste.

"I see the look on your face," said Cohen as he turned away. "Believe me, it expresses exactly what I feel in my heart when I admit to myself that I have these feelings. I am ashamed. I know that I am wrong, or at least I assume that I must be wrong. But I am unable to change how I feel. I have given millions of dollars to black causes. I have volunteered my legal services, and those of my employees, to the black community. I have used my influence in politics to help enact legislation specifically designed to help black causes. But none of it has seemed to help, none of it has been able to change my darkest thoughts, and none of it has been sufficient to assuage my guilt for having them in the first place."

Cohen's words had sapped his strength, and when he had finished speaking, his body was racked with yet another violent fit of coughing. It was evident that there would be no more discussion on this evening, as Cohen's private nurse came into the room and ushered Wilson out.

Not that Wilson would have known what to say had Cohen been able to listen. He was by no means shocked to hear his mentor's words. And they did not change the way he felt about the man. Everybody has feelings and thoughts of which they are ashamed, but cannot control. The important thing from Wilson's perspective was that Cohen was ashamed of these involuntary emotions, and did things above and beyond the call of duty to atone for them. George Cohen was a great man in Ash Wilson's mind, and nothing he had said changed that.

But Cohen's words did have a jolting impact. Wilson had intended to head home after leaving the hospital, but changed his mind. *If George Cohen's a racist*, he thought, *then everybody's a racist, including me.* Wilson was less troubled by that notion though, than he was by the realization that, unlike Cohen, he had ignored the possibility of his own racism. He had spent so much time denying that race ever played any part in his decisions, that he had never actually considered that it might actually have. What scared him most about this thought was the sudden prospect that Roger Queenan might actually have a point.

After calling Noelle on his cell, he had his driver take him back to the office. Wilson knew that he had to immediately re-review every piece of paper in the Cooper file, and try to look at it not like Ash Wilson, but like…well, like Roger Queenan. He was suddenly energized, feeling focused for the first time since the morning he received the call about Kelly Ryan's murder. He was newly determined to steer himself and the case onto the right course. If he felt, after looking at the evidence yet again, that Cooper's race was a factor in his having been charged, he would immediately make a motion to allow bail, and then determine whether or not the charges should be dropped, or reduced.

If however, he convinced himself that Cooper was simply guilty, he would announce immediately thereafter his intention to seek the death penalty.

Wilson bounded through the halls of the deserted and darkened District Attorney's offices, feeling positive for the first time that he was ready to do right by both his job, and Darnell Cooper. He was getting that old feeling back again, the one that made his stomach flutter like a teenager after his first kiss. Justice was a very real concept to Ash Wilson, and nothing had ever excited him more than the opportunity to make it happen.

But as he threw open the door to his personal office, and saw Tony Sciolla's face staring back at him through a cloud of pipe smoke, he knew it wouldn't be that simple.

CHAPTER 21

The attorney-client conference rooms at the Curran-Fromhold Correctional facility on State Road in Northeast Philly are eight-by-eight concrete cubicles with thick metal doors, an aluminum table, and two folding chairs. Prior to Darnell's arrest, Lionel had never been in such a room, nor had he ever even visited a prison. Since the arrest though, he had visited Darnell almost every day, sometimes with Queenan, most times without. On the occasions of his solo visits, Lionel had found that he had little to say to Darnell.

Lionel was angry with the boy, but not just because the evidence forced him to believe Darnell to be guilty. No, the fact of the murder disappointed and saddened him really, more than it made him angry. What truly made Lionel furious was the fact that Darnell had wasted the opportunity he'd been given. The boy had been literally plucked from the depths of depravity and handed everything that any human being needs to succeed: education, physical and emotional nourishment, financial freedom, and love and encouragement. He had been given these things simply because he was in the right place at the right time to have received them, and not because he had done anything special to earn them. And now, with one stupid, rash, and selfish act, he was throwing all of that away.

What made it especially galling to Lionel was the fact that he too had been handed the same opportunities, and had flourished as a result. He could not comprehend why he had been able to become the man he was, and Darnell, so close to becoming even greater, had allowed that possibility to slip away.

The young man was led into the room in which Lionel had already found a seat at the table, in the same red jumpsuit he'd worn in court earlier that day, but sans handcuffs. He sat down heavily across from Lionel, and as was his wont as of late, avoided eye contact.

"How you holdin' up?" asked Lionel after the guard had left them alone.

Darnell shrugged his massive shoulders. "Okay, I guess."

Lionel stared across the table, his mind suddenly empty of soothing words. He wondered where the boy he loved had gone, and whether or not one terrible act could serve to remove all that was good about him and turn him into a truly bad person. If that was so, then Darnell had never been a good person to begin with. Lionel felt as if he was at a very real crossroads in his relationship with the boy. Although he would never withdraw his support, Lionel could not abide being lied to, and unless Darnell told him the truth right at that moment, he knew he would no longer be able to love him the same way.

"I think you killed that girl," he said, in as calm a tone as he could muster.

Darnell's eyes flashed with anger as he finally returned Lionel's gaze. "There's a surprise," he said sarcastically.

"Why?"

Darnell smiled sardonically. "Why do you think that? Or why did I do it?" He didn't wait for an answer. "I'll tell you why you think I did it. Because deep down, no matter what your skin color, you're a racist."

"What the fuck are you talking about?" Lionel spewed. "You know, it's your total willingness to run and hide behind that bullshit that makes me think you did it in the first place."

Darnell snorted. "You can call it bullshit, Lionel, but it's not. Think about this. You know me better than anyone else in the world ever has or ever will, even my own momma. You raised me, made me what I am, turned me into the All-American boy. Every single quality I have as a human being is the direct result of you're guidance. If there is any person in existence I ought to be able to look in the eye and say I didn't do it, and have them believe me, it's you. No matter what the cops say, no matter what the evidence says, you should believe in me. But you don't. And the only reason I can think of for that is your basic distrust of your own people."

"What do you want me to do, Darnell, ignore the evidence, ignore the facts?"

"Yes, Goddammit! That's exactly what I want you to do! If someone were to walk in here with a fucking videotape of me killing Kelly, I expect you to believe me when I say I didn't do it. You've always told me that you trusted me unconditionally. Well, that's what unconditional trust is. And the fact that you think I am lying to you now makes me wonder if everything you've ever told me is a lie. What other parts of our relationship come with strings attached?"

Darnell was too angry to cry, but he did anyway, with small sobs followed by deep breaths.

Lionel was about to automatically respond by saying that he did trust the boy, and that his trust came without strings. Before he opened his mouth though, he heard the word 'but' trailing that sentence in his mind. The 'but' of course, would necessarily change everything about the sentiment, and essentially prove Darnell's point. So he sat quietly instead for a few seconds, wondering what to think.

"I am ready to trust you, Darnell," he said finally as he leaned forward and rested his elbows on the table.

"*But...* I am not interested in hearing that you are the victim of a racist conspiracy. What I want to hear from you are facts which will make me believe you, facts that I can rely upon to know that my trust is not being taken advantage of. It's a two-way street, bud. Now, talk to me."

Darnell wiped the wetness from his face. Since being arrested, he had done nothing but think about how Kelly could have been raped and murdered after he left that night. He had come up with a scenario in his mind, but had been afraid to share it with either Lionel or Queenan. He was afraid that by pointing fingers blindly, he would only make himself look even more guilty. He was happy to have Queenan tilt at his racist windmills, or do and say whatever else it took to get him acquitted. Darnell knew that he was unjustly accused, and he certainly had no qualms about fighting fire with fire. But now that Lionel had finally sought his own version of the truth, he was anxious to share it.

"Okay, here it is," said Darnell as he too leaned forward onto the table. "I think it was Fullem who called Kelly that night while I was in the room. I think that he maybe even knew that I was there. I think Kelly asked me to leave because, for whatever reason, she didn't want him to see me there. I think that he came in the back door that night after I left. It would be so easy to get in and out of that room through that door without being seen. Hell, nobody saw me leave, and I wasn't even tryin' to be inconspicuous.

"I think that Kelly must have told him that she told me about helping him sell drugs. Or maybe she threatened to go tell the cops about it. Or maybe he just killed her because she had been with me. I don't know. I can only guess that he," Darnell took a deep breath, "raped her, and then killed her. Or maybe he didn't rape her and Templeton's wrong like Roger says he is, that I caused the abrasions in her…you know, because it was her first time and all."

Lionel had focused on Darnell's eyes as he spoke. It was clear the boy believed what he was saying. "But what about the fact that yours was the only semen found?" he asked, hoping that Darnell would have an answer.

"I don't know," shrugged Darnell with exasperation. "Maybe he didn't finish. Maybe he wore a condom. I don't know. All I know for sure is that I did not rape Kelly…I loved her."

Darnell sat back in his chair and slumped down. He couldn't tell if he had convinced Lionel or not. It was exhausting trying to figure out how to look innocent, much less how to sound it. His favorite television shows as a younger kid had always been the ones involving lawyers and trials. Darnell could remember now how he could always tell if someone was guilty just by the way they testified on the stand, or spoke to the police when being questioned. He could always tell the innocent guys because they were the ones who didn't seem to care that the police were questioning them. Heck, most of the time, they were too busy to be bothered. No, the guys the cops were wary of were the ones who seemed nervous, or the dead giveaway—sweated—during an interview.

But sitting there at that moment, a completely innocent man, trying to convince the one person in the world he thought would believe in his innocence, Darnell was sweating profusely and his stomach was doing somersaults. He almost wished he were guilty. It would probably be easier to look innocent that way.

Although he did not believe that Fullem killed the girl (too convenient), Lionel found that his belief in the boy had been strengthened somewhat. Not by his story, but by the conviction with which he told it. Though he'd been a trial lawyer for years and had cross-examined hundreds of witnesses, Lionel had no better system than Darnell in identifying liars.

"D," he said finally, "I told you when all of this started that no matter what, I will always love you just the same. And I know that when I express doubt about you, you see that as a betrayal. But I have never lied to you, son, about anything. I will always love you, no matter what. It would have been dishonest for me to tell you that I believed you from the start, because I didn't. Ultimately, though, it doesn't really matter what I believe. You know that, right?"

Darnell let out an exasperated sigh. "Lionel, don't you realize that that's the *only thing* that matters to me? The world thinks I'm a murderer and a rapist, and I don't really care because those are opinions I can't control, and I don't want to.

"Don't you remember what I was when you found me? That seventy-eight pound bag of bones, covered in piss and shit, teeth rotted out, barely able to string a sentence together? That was me. And the only thing that changed me from that was the totally unexplainable faith you had that I could actually be transformed into a human being. Without your blind faith I was dead. If you're telling me that I can't have it now, especially after I've demonstrated over and over again that I deserve it, I might as well be dead."

He was right of course, and Lionel knew it. There was no rational basis upon which to believe that the wild animal he had pulled from the streets ten years earlier could ever be a functional human being, much less everything Darnell had actually become. Lionel never had been able to figure out specifically why he had helped Darnell. But he fully appreciated it as the most rewarding, and important, thing he had ever done.

Looking at the boy now, it was apparent that he had come full circle. Everything was suddenly the same as it had been that day outside Temple Law School, only now Darnell was bigger. It was simply his prison that had gotten smaller. So even though his doubts about Darnell's innocence had not been erased, Lionel decided, once again and once and for all, that it didn't matter. He had made a commitment to the boy, and now it was time to honor it, no matter how difficult, no matter how unpopular it might be. His word had to be his bond, or else he was not the man he believed himself to be. Sometimes, he decided, a man's character is not defined by simply who he is, but what he makes himself do.

No physical contact was allowed between prisoners and visitors, but the guards were also not allowed to watch lawyers and their clients talking. The prison board probably figured there wouldn't be too many lawyers touching their clients anyway. The only way that Lionel could figure out how to show Darnell that he was sorry for doubting him and also that he was newly recommitted to setting him free, was to get up from his chair and hug the boy as tightly as he could. Darnell met him halfway. Their embrace was joyfully silent and intense, only the sound of each man's muffled sobs breaking the silence. They hugged for at least a minute, neither wanting to let go of the other. Finally, Lionel pulled away first and they sat back down.

"Okay," said the lawyer as he wiped away some tears that had sneaked down his cheeks. "Now that that's out of the way, I guess I've got to go get you a real criminal defense lawyer."

Darnell sat up straight in his chair. "Why? What's wrong with Roger?"

"C'mon, D, the man's a total clown. He's a one-note tune. Sure, all that race-baiting makes great headlines, but trust me, a jury will see right through what he's trying to do."

"What he's trying to do is get me acquitted, Lionel. He sure as shit scared the hell out of that little brat at the preliminary hearing. And he's got the D.A. scared to even put on evidence because he knows Roger's gonna' cream 'em with the Fullem stuff. I think he's doing a damn good job so far."

Lionel shook his head from side to side. "No, what you're seeing is nothin' more than bells and whistles and sound effects. There's no substance to anything the man's saying. His only shot with the tack he's taking is for jury nullification, and that simply won't work."

"What's jury nullification?"

"It's where the law says the jury should do one thing, like convict you of first degree murder for example. But the lawyer asks the jury, usually in a subtle way, to ignore the law and acquit you anyway because of some other reason.

"Like, for example, you're black and you're smart, and you're handsome and you're a superstar and you can do great things, and the girl was white, and the cops are white, and the D.A.'s white, and too many potentially great black men have been wrongfully destroyed by the white system. So even though it looks like Darnell's guilty, and under the law he should be convicted, give him a pass this time, if for no other reason than to pay back the white man's system of justice for all the wrongfully convicted brothers who have come before you. It's the classic O.J. defense."

Darnell ran his hands over his head and rubbed his face, but his pained expression did not go away. "I'm not allowed to watch T.V. in here, Lionel, but the last time I saw O.J. on it, he was playing golf."

Lionel understood perfectly what Darnell was saying.

"But what is he?" he asked in response. "Everyone thinks he's a murderer and a scumbag. Every white person in America thinks that he got off just because he was black and the jurors were black. You don't want that, do you?"

Darnell let out an little angry laugh. "Two things. First, I don't care what has to be done or said, or who has to be fooled, bribed or hoodwinked, I do not want to spend one more minute in this shithole, and I sure as hell don't want to go to state prison.

"Second, the very last thing I will ever be concerned about again, is what any fucking white person thinks of me. Fuck white people. They're all racist, they all think they're better than we are, and they're afraid of us. As far as I'm concerned, white people put me in here for no reason. If black people take me out for no reason, I'm okay with that."

"Don't you want everyone to know you're innocent?"

Darnell shrugged. "I *am* innocent. As long as you know it, what the hell do I care what people think? You know, I don't even read the newspapers because I don't want to know what people are saying. It's irrelevant."

Lionel sighed. "That would be a great way of looking at things if you didn't have to live in the real world. How can you possibly expect to succeed in life from this point on, if everyone you meet thinks you're a murderer and a rapist who got away with it? You'll never be able to get a job, in basketball or anywhere else. You'll never be able to find a place to live. You'll be ostracized wherever you go. No, we have to prove that your innocent, straight up, or else you'll never get your life back."

"Who's not living in the real world now, Lionel?" said Darnell bitterly. "You know as well as I do that as soon as I got arrested, every white person in the world convicted me in their heads. No matter what I do now, nothing's going to un-ring that bell. Shit, if we showed up in court with a videotape of this Fullem guy killing Kelly, that still wouldn't change their minds." Darnell looked down at his hands, weighing whether or not to speak his mind fully. Finally, he decided that he had to.

"You know what's funny, man? Ever since I met you, I've watched you, and tried to act just like you. I could see how you acted around white people differently than you do around your own people. When I watched you in court, I saw how you talked and dressed and carried yourself. Whatever I saw you do, I did.

"All the while, although I saw it, I never consciously understood it until all of this happened. Whenever you would be who you were around white people, they would act as if you were one of them. But the funny thing is, it was always so obvious that you were pretending, and that they were too, and everyone pretends like they're not pretending, but at the same time, everybody knows everybody's pretending. You act like you're not black, and they act like they don't care that you are. Don't you know by now that you've only gotten as far as you have because you've acted the way they want you to act, done things the way they want them done, and talked like they want you to talk? Because you've done all that, they've pretended to let you in to their club, pretended to let you be one of them. It's all a giant fucking charade, Lionel."

Seeing the devastated look on Lionel's face, Darnell realized immediately his mistake. He had not in any way intended to insult him. In fact, he had been about to insult himself.

He reached across the table and grabbed Lionel's shaking hand.

"Yo, bro, you didn't let me finish. I was about to say that I know all of these things because I have been guilty of doing the same thing. Every day since you started me in school ten years ago, I have slowly learned how to manipulate every situation I am in. When I'm with white people, I know that they are intrinsically scared of me physically, not just because I'm big and strong, but because I'm black.

"So when I'm with whites, I shrink myself. I sit down, or I bend my knees or I smile real wide and I keep my hands in my pockets or at my sides. At first, I didn't even realize I was doing these things. But over time, I came to see that when I am around my own kind, I'm always standing up, I talk louder, I use my hands when I speak, and I don't measure my words.

"That's why all these Ivy League pricks think I'm the greatest thing since sliced bread. On the one hand, I jump around and marvel them with my animal athleticism, but at the same time, make them believe that they've still got dominion over me."

"You learned that from me," said Lionel, his heart broken by his own shame. "All this time, I've been congratulating myself for teaching you how to be this great person that you've become, and all I've really done is show you how to step and fetch." He buried his head in his hands, unable to look Darnell in the eyes.

Darnell got up from his chair to go kneel by his attorney's side. He put his arm around the older man's back and leaned in close to his ear.

"Bullshit," he said with a whispering smile. "You taught me how to survive in a world just as dangerous as the one I had come from. You taught me how to be a human being. Even though I could see the hypocrisy of what I was doing, I always felt it was for a larger purpose, I really did. And I don't mean just being the number one pick in the draft or becoming socially acceptable in order to get endorsement deals. I mean, I always wanted to put myself in a position to be given everything that a young black man in this society is allowed to have…and then simply give it back."

Darnell got back up and went to his seat. "Lionel, look at me," he said quietly. Lionel reluctantly returned the gaze from across the table.

"I have never told you this before. In fact, I haven't ever told any-body because I didn't know if I would ever have the courage to really do it, much less see it all the way through to success. From the day I said I would go to Penn, up until the day I got arrested, I had what, at first anyway, was just a fantasy, but as time went on, and it all actually appeared like it could happen, I made it my goal in life.

"First, my plan was to get my Ivy League degree. Then, it was to put myself in a position where I was one of the best college basketball play-ers in the country, and work myself into becoming a lottery pick, with all the guaranteed millions that brings waiting for me.

"Now, because of my education and my degree and my smile and my seeming…*safeness*, I would get all sorts of endorsement deals, with all those millions waiting for me, too. I would be the most famous young, single, black man in America, and I would be held up as a role model for all young black men in this country. And as crazy as it sounds, I was well on my way to making all of that happen. But do you want to know what my ultimate dream has been, Lionel?"

Lionel shook his head yes.

"To turn it down. To stand up there on the podium with the Com-missioner, shake his hand, and say 'no thanks.' To stand in front of the press of the world and say 'I don't want to be a millionaire slave to bil-lionaire white guys. I've just graduated from an Ivy League school, and I don't have to jump around like somebody's pet to make something of myself.'

Then, my plan was to turn around and go to Harvard law school, because every great leader this country has ever had has done one of two things: been a lawyer or gone to Harvard. Then, when I was twenty-five and graduating summa cum laude from Harvard, and the best basketball player in the world not in the NBA, and everyone was begging me to play, I would say no again. I would then pick up the phone, call you, and convince you to start a new firm with me.

"We would have represented only our own people, and we would have employed only our own people. And we would have made millions of dollars for them and for us, and we would then become important, because the true color of power in this country is green. And then, when I turned thirty-two, I would have run for Congress. Then, after two or three terms, Senator. Then, every four years thereafter until I was elected, I would run and run and run until I became the first black President of the United States.

"Then, and I think only then, could I, and every other brother in America, finally stop pretending. And if that had happened, Lionel, you would be the one who had made it all possible."

Lionel looked back at Darnell and was stunned. Not at all though because of the sheer magnitude of the boy's dreams, but because he had been well on his way to actually making them happen. Lionel was at once fiercely proud of the boy, and at the same time shattered beyond comprehension with the realization that his wonderful fantasy could not ever happen. Because Darnell was right.

No matter how it happened, if he was acquitted, the perception would be amongst a large segment of the population that he had gotten away with murder. That perception would prevent the boy from ever actually becoming what he was already well on the way to achieving.

"Wow," said Lionel softly, his sadness palpable in the air between them. "I had no idea you had all those plans. I would have loved," he bit his quivering bottom lip to stem the tears, "to have been your partner someday."

Darnell sagged a bit in his chair. Although he believed that he had no future, regardless of the outcome of the case, it was still difficult to hear Lionel accept that fate for him as well.

Sensing Darnell's thoughts, Lionel said with as reassuring a smile as he could muster, "It can still happen, kid. Let's not give up hope that justice will prevail. Don't tell Queenan I said this, but I've got a sneaking suspicion that the D.A. isn't as sold on your guilt as everyone else is."

"What makes you say that?" asked Darnell.

Lionel shrugged. "Honestly I don't know, I can't quite put my finger on it. But we haven't heard a word from him or his office in the press. He seemed to be going through the motions at the prelim. Maybe it's just the fact that I used to see him at all the Penn games and I know he likes you. I bet you don't even remember, but when that group of business leaders and politicians came to you and asked you to stay in school, he was there."

"No shit?"

Lionel smiled. "Yeah, no shit. For all we know, he sees the possibility of Fullem as a suspect, and simply needs to be convinced. I think I'll suggest an off-the-record meeting between the two of you. Maybe he's still star-struck enough to agree to it. Hopefully we'll be able to plant a seed of doubt in his brain. Who knows what could happen then."

"With my luck, it's anybody's guess," said Darnell wearily.

*   *   *   *

Lionel drove down the long driveway leading away from the prison towards State Road. To the left was the way to I-95 and the route back to his apartment in center city. To the right though, was the way to Fullem's apartment, the address of which was in his file, tucked inside the briefcase in the trunk.

He hesitated at the end of the driveway, unsure of which way to turn. He still could not accept that Fullem had killed the girl, mostly because he thought there was no way Darnell couldn't have. But he thought about Darnell's dreams, and the look in his face when he finally believed he'd lost them forever.

He turned right.

Fullem's apartment was on the third floor of a square, five story cement building just off Roosevelt Boulevard near Cottman Avenue in the Northeast section of the city. Lionel parked his car in the parking lot, having no idea what he was doing. Lionel desperately wanted to believe Darnell was innocent, wanted to believe that it was the right thing to do to get him acquitted by any means necessary. But he knew, deep in his heart, that in order to convince himself, he needed to put a face to the murderer other than Darnell's. He wanted that face to be Fullem's. But still, Lionel was scared that he was just picking the most convenient scapegoat. He was also scared of what he knew Fullem to be capable of, whether he killed Kelly Ryan or not, and Lionel was secretly hoping Fullem wouldn't answer the door.

He had no such luck. Fullem opened the door almost immediately upon Lionel's light knock.

"What the fuck could you possibly want?" Fullem demanded in drunken surprise. He was wearing a greasy white undershirt and dingy blue jeans. His feet were bare and he had a beer in his hand.

The man was huge, and his sheer size took Lionel's breath away. Almost as tall as him, but twice as wide, it was all Lionel could do not to just apologize and walk away.

But instead, he said the first thing that popped into his head.

"I know you killed her."

Fullem's eyes narrowed for a split second, but then he let out an evil laugh. He looked Lionel up and down with naked contempt. "You got a lot of balls, nigger, I'll give you that."

Fullem stepped backwards and pulled the door all the way open. They stood facing each other head on. "Come on in," he whispered, "I'll kill you too."

Everything about Fullem was familiar to Lionel, from his clothes, to his giant beer belly, to his voice. He was the living, breathing, embodiment of Lionel's most intimate feelings about white people. He wanted nothing more than to walk straight ahead and kill Fullem with his own bare hands.

"All right, mothafucka,'" Lionel growled as he took a step forward. "But just remember...I ain't no little white girl."

Something in Fullem's eyes changed suddenly. Looking back on it, Lionel wouldn't call it fear so much as doubt.

Fullem suddenly slammed the door shut. Lionel, who was practically inside the apartment at that point, was pushed backwards by the force of it almost to the balcony. He stood there, breathing hard, his heart pounding in his ears.

Even as the adrenaline which had surged through his body at the prospect of physically attacking Fullem quickly began to drain away, Lionel stood on the balcony fuming at Fullem's closed door. But although he was enraged, he was still rational. He calculated his options, number one of which was to rush forward, kick down the door, and see just how tough Fullem was. But as enticing as that was, Lionel knew it wouldn't help Darnell. He calmed himself as best he could, and looked around to see if anyone had seen him. Seeing nothing, he rushed back to his car, dialing his cell phone as he ran.

"Roger, wake up," he said before Queenan even said hello. "Roger, I do not give a shit about the truth anymore. I want Fullem's ass. You're right, man, he represents everything that's wrong with the world, and I want to *hurt* that cracker…bad."

Queenan laughed out loud. "Cracker? Did you just say cracker? Don't talk like that, son, it'll put a crease in your suit. I'm glad you're on board though. Now maybe we can start working together on how we're going to win this case."

CHAPTER 22

▼

Thirty minutes after slamming the door on Lionel, Fullem sat on his couch and fingered the trigger of the CZ .380 acp Blue Pistol that was otherwise being swallowed by his trembling right hand. He was certain that Lionel had seen him for who he really was, and he would rather be dead than have Ryan learn that truth.

Fullem expected that he would ultimately be exposed as Kelly's killer. But if he offed himself before being exposed, there would always be doubt in Ryan's mind as to the truth, and Fullem was prepared to take the benefit of that doubt into the afterlife. Hell, it couldn't be any worse than the tortured existence he had been living.

But he was a coward, and he knew it. That was the worst part. Fullem was well aware that he had no courage…that for all of his physical strength, he was too weak to accept the consequences of his actions. Be it losing Kelly's money and lying to Ryan about it, or guilting her into helping him sell drugs so that he could hide the truth even longer, or killing her. Ever since Cheeseboro, he realized that his life had been one long scramble from the truth, hiding from it no matter what the cost.

The knock on the door startled him from his self-pitying stupor. He wiped the tears from his cheeks, quickly slid the gun under the cushion of the sofa and walked to the door.

"Who is it?" he asked nervously, fearing it was Lionel again, this time with the police in tow.

"It's John. Open up."

Fullem's heart leapt forward in his chest as if it was going to reach out and turn the doorknob itself.

"Hey," he said with obvious relief upon opening the door. Ryan barely acknowledged him as he walked into the small kitchen just off the living room and opened the refrigerator. After retrieving a beer, Ryan walked over to the couch and sat down heavily.

Ryan had not seen Lionel leave, but he clearly had something specific on his mind. Fullem stood by the door, half wanting to run away. "How'd the hearing go, John?" he asked finally.

"Haven't you turned on a television today? Christ, it's been on every goddamn channel all freakin' day."

Obviously, the beer in his hand was not Ryan's first of the evening.

Fullem had assiduously avoided any contact with the television coverage of the preliminary hearing. He had expected it to be bad for him, and he assumed that Ryan was there to tell him just how bad it had gone.

The behemoth went and grabbed a beer of his own and sat down next to his friend. "I couldn't stand to watch or listen to anymore of the crap."

Ryan shook his head bitterly. "I can't figure it out, Joe, I just can't. Wilson comes off all gung ho about puttin' that motherfucker away, but today at the hearing, he totally lets Queenan walk all over his witnesses. He didn't even put Sciolla on the stand, for cryin' out loud. And he lets that prick lawyer get away with saying the most outrageous shit I ever heard in a courtroom. Everything's about race and the fact that Cooper's black, blah, blah, blah."

Fullem's eyes narrowed. "How much have you had to drink tonight, John?"

Ryan raised an eyebrow. "You're kidding me right? You haven't been sober for three weeks and now you're going to try and begrudge me one load? Fuck you."

"C'mon, John, you know a prelim don't mean jack shit. Wilson's smart, he knows what he's doing. Did any of the charges get tossed?"

Ryan shook his head no as he finished the last of his beer and retrieved another from the fridge. "Not that it matters. Everybody in the country, except you apparently, saw what a show Queenan put on. Where does Wilson think the jury's gonna' come from, for Christ's sake?"

"Tell me what Queenan said."

Ryan laughed bitterly. "Do I really have to? Let's just say you were right. I hate to say it, Joe, but that fuckin' nigger is gonna' get away with murdering and RAPING MY BABY!"

He was shouting, spittle flying from his lips. Fullem couldn't ever recall actually having seen Ryan drunk, much less spouting off like this. But Ryan's mood and sentiments raised an interesting dilemma for Fullem. On the one hand, he needed John to feel anger towards Cooper. He needed him to be so girded for the racism defense that he would dismiss out of hand any suggestion that Fullem was the real killer.

But on the other hand, he felt the need to tread carefully. Fullem knew, better than anyone, that Ryan didn't mean what he had just said. In fact, Ryan was the only cop Fullem had ever met whom he had never heard say the word "nigger." The booze and the grief and the frustration were teaming up inside the man though, and together they were making him feel things he had never allowed himself to feel before.

Fullem decided that if he was ever going to get his friend back, he had to exploit that rage. "So what do you want to do about it, John?" he asked quietly.

Ryan's face remained expressionless as he stared through bloodshot eyes at the worn carpet in front of the sagging couch. "I want him dead, Joe."

Silence erupted between them. In most situations, when one buddy says to another buddy that he'd like to kill a guy, it's understood as blowing off steam. But it's different when it's two cops, drunk or not. And it's especially different when the comment is made to a man like Fullem. Ryan knew that. But more importantly, Fullem knew Ryan knew it.

"Are you serious?"

Fullem turned his head and waited for Ryan to turn his. When he finally did, a chill ran down Fullem's spine. John Ryan had made no idle comment. He was asking his friend to kill Darnell Cooper.

"John," said the man-giant, "I'll do it in a heartbeat, you know that. I just want to make sure it's not the booze talking."

Ryan nodded. "Fair enough," he said. "I'm going to sleep on your couch tonight. When I wake up in the morning. Ask me again if I'm serious."

Later that night, as he lay awake in his own bed staring at the ceiling, Joe Fullem fantasized about killing Darnell, and what a fitting end it would be to all of his crimes. It truly did not matter to him that Darnell Cooper was an innocent man sitting in jail for his crime. Because for the first time in many, many years, Fullem's heart was aflutter with the excitement of what the next day might bring. If Ryan was serious, and was asking him to kill Cooper, it would solve everything.

Meanwhile, John Ryan sat up on Fullem's couch, his mind unable to rid itself of the image of Cooper raping and beating and choking his daughter, over and over and over again. Ryan had fought so hard to keep those images from crystallizing, but the day's events had been too much. Once the vision was there, he knew it would never go away.

He wanted Darnell to die, slowly and painfully if possible. He gave silent thanks that the one man with the capacity to act out the cruelty Ryan felt in his heart was asleep in the next room, prepared to do exactly what needed to be done.

When the sun did finally come up, Fullem wasn't awake to see it. He had fallen asleep with dreams of murderous redemption in his head. He didn't open his eyes until he felt Ryan sit down at the edge of the bed.

"Wake up, sunshine," he said cheerlessly.

Fullem rubbed his eyes and looked up at his friend. "How are you feeling?" he asked.

Ryan waited for Fullem to get the sleep out of his eyes so he could see clearly. "Can you see me, Joe?" he asked.

"Yeah," said Fullem as he propped himself up on the pillows.

"Good, because it's important you see my face when I say this. I want you to kill Darnell Cooper. Do it for me, Joe. Do it for Kelly. I want you to take him and make what you did to Frank Cheeseboro look like a slapfight. Do you understand what I'm saying, Joe? This is it. I'm calling my chit. You owe me."

A tear escaped from the corner of Fullem's right eye. It is an over-whelming feeling to be needed by someone you love, especially when you love someone as much as Fullem loved Ryan.

Neither of them spoke. They didn't have to. Ryan knew that Fullem would not let him down.

CHAPTER 23

▼

"I hope you're not here to give me more shit about how I'm not doing my job, because I'm really not interested in hearing it right now," said Wilson as he tossed his keys onto the desk and sat down.

Removing the pipe from his mouth, Sciolla pursed his lips as if to stop the words that wanted to come out. Instead of responding he reached down to his side and picked up an expandable file folder that was stuffed full of documents. He handed it over the desk without a word.

"What's this?" asked the D.A. as he held the file in his hands. But then he saw the answer to the question.

He placed the file down onto the desk, gingerly, as if it were explosive. "What did you do, Tony?" asked Wilson angrily.

"I got you what you asked me to get. You couldn't understand why Cooper would kill and rape a young girl with all that he's got going for him? Well, there's your answer."

Wilson looked at the file laying in front of him. The name "Darnell Cooper" was printed in capital letters on the upper left corner of the front cover. "Clint Charles, M.D." appeared in the right cover. Sciolla had somehow gotten a hold of Darnell's psychiatric records, and he had obviously read them.

"I thought we didn't cheat," Wilson muttered, more to himself than Sciolla.

"We don't, Ash, that's why we're the good guys. But I couldn't stand by and let you be taken advantage of. It's one thing to live your life by your principals, but it's quite another to assume that everyone else will too."

Ash fingered one corner of the file. "How'd you get this?"

"After I left here earlier I went to CHOP and broke into Charles' office. I've got to get it back before the office opens at 8 tomorrow morning."

"Have you read it?"

"Have I read it? Yeah. And I still can't believe it. This kid's life reads like a Kafka novel that's been turned into a movie by Frank Capra. I guarantee that after you read this, you'll be left with two conclusions. First you'll realize that Darnell Cooper is an extraordinary human being. Second, you'll understand what demons this kid has that allowed him to rape and kill that girl. You might not necessarily blame him for doing it, but you'll believe that he did."

Wilson stared at the file, wondering what could possibly be contained in there that would warrant the description of its contents given by Sciolla. He stroked his chin, debating whether or not to read it.

"It's not cheating, Ash. You're not going to use it against him. All you're doing is confirming for yourself that he has the capacity to kill. Believe me, after what this kid's been through, it's a miracle he went as long as he did without exploding." Sciolla stood up and headed to the door. "Call me on the Nextel when you've finished."

The file lay there on the desk, waiting to be read. It was what he'd asked for. Something to convince him, either way. But if he read this, he'd be doing something he had sworn never to do—break the law in pursuit of winning.

Funnily, for a man determined not to worry about perceptions, he still felt the need to search his brain for the just the right rationalization to read the file before actually doing so. Despite the fact that he knew it would be wrong, and illegal, to read the file, he also knew that he was going to do it. Still, he felt the need to create a legitimate reason for himself to read it, as if himself would be fooled. Ultimately, Wilson decided that because he would not use any of the contents to prove his case, it would be okay.

Three hours later, Wilson put the last piece of paper back into the folder. His cheeks were wet and his dress shirt was drenched in sweat, and he had never felt so sad. Sciolla had been exactly right. Darnell Cooper was an extraordinary human being.

That he had even lived past the horrid first eleven years of his life was unbelievable. The sexual abuse of the monster Clark, the crack-induced oblivion of his mother, and the total absence of human-ity in the boy's existence, should have killed him outright. But his unexplained redemption by Lionel Cooper, the astounding ways in which he blossomed, and the extraordinary success he had achieved academically and athletically, were true, honest to God miracles. Even Frank Capra would have rejected the boy's story as too preposterous and sappy to be believed.

But even though he didn't want to, Wilson also saw Sciolla's point that the reports of the psychiatrist showed ineluctably why it was almost…understandable…that Darnell had eventually committed the crimes of which he was accused.

He read about Darnell's score on the Trauma Symptom Inventory, and Charles' conclusions: "Minor difficulties or frustrations can pro-voke contextually inappropriate responses," and "Darnell is easily excitable and less functional under stress." But most damning was Charles' discussion of the likelihood that Darnell would "externalize distress through aggression and inappropriate sexual behavior."

The reports indicated that Charles had treated Cooper with therapy and medication steadily, up until the time of his matriculation at Penn. Thereafter, the therapy sessions became less frequent, and it was unclear to Charles whether or not Darnell was continuing to take his medication. Their last session took place three days before the murder.

Cooper had apparently told Charles that he was desperately in love with Kelly, and he had thought she felt the same. But Wilson recently had learned through other witnesses that she had been avoiding him in the weeks before the murder, and Darnell had expressed to Charles a determination not to let Kelly get away. The stress of losing the girl you love can be enough to drive any normal man over the edge, much less a ticking time bomb like Darnell apparently was.

Wilson flipped open his cell phone and chirped Sciolla. "C'mon back."

"Amazing, isn't it?" asked Sciolla rhetorically as he sat across from the D.A.

"Tony, the first thing I want you to do, starting tomorrow morning, is find out who this 'Clark' motherfucker is," hissed Wilson through gritted teeth, "and bring him to me. You understand?"

Sciolla punched some tobacco into his pipe and nodded. "Way ahead of you. I've already made some calls. You know those projects were torn down about three years ago, but I've got some old sources still around who used to live there. They remember hearing stories about this guy named Clark. Apparently, about ten years ago, he just appeared out of nowhere and took control of the drug trade in that area for about a year.

"Apparently, Clark wasn't his real name. The story is that they called him that because he was like Superman, no one would go near him. Everyone was scared shitless of him. Clark was short for 'Clark Kent.' Anyway, my guess is he's dead or in jail. If he's alive though, I'll find him."

Sciolla waited a respectful few seconds before making sure Wilson's head was now where it needed to be.

"So...now that we know he did it...are you going to invoke the death penalty?"

The D.A. sighed at his friend, and got up to face the window so that Sciolla would not see his pained expression. Unfortunately, his own reflection did not spare him that visage. "How can I?" he asked himself. "I know that there are mitigating factors."

Wilson could see the detective shaking his head in the glass.

"Wait a minute, Ash. When you sent me on my little secret mission to find what I've now given you, you told me that it wasn't your job to prove mitigating circumstances, and that if they existed, the defense would bring them out. As horrible as this kid's life was, and as extraordinary as we now both believe him to be, let's not forget that the beautiful and innocent daughter of my fellow officer was raped and killed by that kid. Your job is to convict him. We both know that a death-qualified jury gives us a better shot at doing that."

He was right of course, and that very point had been made in his own mind several times over already. Wilson had promised himself when he left George Cohen's bedside that if he felt convinced the boy was guilty, he would do everything within his legal power to convict him. If he couldn't keep his own word to himself, what kind of man would that make him?

"You better get that back," Wilson said flatly to the window.

Sciolla knew better than to say anymore. He had done all that he could, and was confident that his friend would do the right thing.

*   *   *   *

The jarring blare of the telephone startled Lionel, but it did not wake him. He was laying in bed, staring at the ceiling. He noticed the clock on his night stand as he reached out to pick up the receiver.

"Hello?" he said in a clear voice.

"Lionel, it's Ash Wilson. I'm sorry to call so late, but this can't wait. Can you come to my office...now?"

"It's three o'clock in the morning."

"I know. I'll be waiting."

It took longer for Lionel to catch a cab than the ride to the District Attorney's Office actually took. It wasn't that there were none available. It was just that none wanted to stop at three A.M. for a six foot seven black guy in jeans and a hooded sweatshirt.

"Thanks for coming, Lionel," said the D.A. as he held open the heavy oak door in the lobby of the building. They rode in the elevator in silence, and neither man spoke until Lionel was seated in the chair across from Wilson's desk. They had not been alone in a room together since the day Wilson had hired him as an associate at Cohen & Elson.

"Lionel," said the D.A. finally, "I'm going to announce tomorrow that I intend to seek the death penalty against Darnell."

This was not unexpected news to Lionel, and he wondered why the hell he'd been dragged out of bed in the middle of the night to hear it. So he said nothing, figuring there had to be more.

"I have a very strong suspicion, however," continued Wilson, "that you will be able to prove mitigating circumstances. I know Darnell is an extraordinary young man. The reason I've asked you to come here now, Lionel, is because I want to give you the opportunity to share with me the true mitigating circumstances. If they are what I think they are, I may be in a position to offer Darnell a plea to Third Degree Murder and rape. I'd recommend the maximum sentence, but he'd be out in 15 years. As tough as that might be to accept, it's better than life in prison."

Lionel looked back at Wilson, trying to figure out what was really happening. For the first time in a long time, Lionel miscalculated. He thought that what he was seeing was confirming his earlier suspicions, that the D.A. either didn't believe Darnell did it, or didn't think he could prove his case.

"I appreciate the offer, Ash, I do, but Darnell didn't do it. He's innocent. Fullem did it. I know you don't believe that, so I'm not going to waste time trying to convince you of it. But that racist motherfucker did it, Ash, and we're going to prove it."

Wilson let out a deep sigh. The worst part about being a lawyer is that you can never stop being one.

"Lionel, I didn't drag you out of bed at three o'clock in the morning to dick around. I'm trying to tell you something here that I hope to God you'll understand as genuine and not just some adversarial trick. I *know* Darnell did it. There is not a doubt in my mind about that. What I'm telling you is that I also believe very strongly that there are things about Darnell's background, his early life, that may mitigate against my need to see a First Degree Murder conviction here.

"If such things do exist, I am giving you the opportunity to tell me now, because tomorrow morning I'm holding a press conference to announce that I'm seeking the death penalty in this case. You know as well as I do that I'll be able to weed out in the death qualification process any potential juror who I think might be swayed by Queenan's line of bullshit. So tell me now, because after tonight, the offer's off the table."

Lionel sat back in his chair, his tired mind trying to speed up to contemplate all the angles. Working backwards, he wasn't concerned about the death penalty in and of itself because the mitigating circumstances were overwhelming. No jury would vote for the death penalty based on the strength of Darnell's character alone, much less after they heard about his early childhood. But Wilson was right about a death-qualified jury. What he was really saying was that because black people generally tend to disfavor the death penalty, he'd be able to strike many of them for cause. The jurors that were left would more likely be white, and convinced of Darnell's guilt from the beginning.

But Lionel didn't care.

"I appreciate the offer," he said, unable to hide his sarcasm. "And because you've been so honest with me, I will be honest with you. There isn't going to be any plea in this case." Lionel stood up. "I'll allow you to drop the charges, but only if you issue an apology with it."

Wilson sat alone in his office for awhile, his mind so full it was blank. He finally collected his things and made his way home, satisfied that he had done everything he could for Darnell.

"Why so late?" Noelle mumbled through closed eyes as he crawled into bed next to her.

Ash snaked his right arm under his wife's head and pulled her close to him. "Remember that first night I found out about Cooper's arrest?"

"Mmhmm," said Noelle as she burrowed into his chest. "You said you were about to charge the American dream with murder."

"Yeah, well, watch the news tomorrow, because I'll be announcing my intention to kill it altogether."

CHAPTER 24

▼

The announcement the next day that the District Attorney's Office would be seeking the death penalty against Darnell Cooper added a new layer, and fervor, to the national debate which had been raging throughout the country since Darnell's arrest and Roger Queenan's inflammatory pronouncements.

But it barely caused a ripple in Lionel and Queenan's defense plans. Queenan held his own press conference forty minutes later in which he handed out glossy brochures containing facts, figures, graphs and pie charts, from all across the country, showing that the death penalty was sought almost exclusively against black men accused of killing a white person. Also included were blurbs about each of the cases in the last five years in which the death penalty had been overturned due to DNA testing ruling out the convicted man as the killer.

Queenan finished his press conference by calling Wilson's decision just one more example of a racist system of justice railroading an innocent young black man.

As usual, Wilson did not respond. He had a homicide case to prepare for. He dropped all of his other cases and focused exclusively on the Cooper trial. Darnell was formally arraigned on charges of first degree murder and rape, and a trial date was set for February 1st. Wilson would spend the time before trial learning his evidence cold, preparing exhaustively each and every witness, and drafting his opening and closing arguments. He also had to figure out how to combat the negative inferences that Queenan would be asking the jury to draw about race, and Joe Fullem in particular.

As soon as Lionel had left his office that night before the press conference, the D.A. had decided once and for all that no more thought would be wasted on Darnell Cooper the person. From that moment on, his entire focus was placed on how to convict Darnell Cooper, the defendant, of murder in the first degree and rape, and how to convince the jury that he should die for those crimes.

He had said as much to George Cohen in his last visit with the old man before his death.

It had been the night before the arraignment, and it was clear to both of them that Cohen was not going to last more than a day or two longer. Like an exploding star though, Cohen had rallied his last bit of strength to see and say goodbye to Wilson.

He was the last man to be alone with Cohen, just as the old man had wanted. He had managed to control everything in his life up to that point, and as long as he breathed, he would continue to do so.

His effort to be seen as unwaveringly strong throughout his entire life, but especially in his last days, had been a monumental one. When left alone with the man he considered his son, though, he finally allowed himself to show weakness.

"Ash," he whispered, "we haven't spoken about what I told you a few weeks ago. I don't want to die believing that you think less of me."

Wilson grasped Cohen's gray and withered hand where it lay on the bed at his side.

"George," he said, trying not to cry, "you are the most important man I have ever known. I truly believe that. I love you with all my heart and I always will. Not because I ever thought you were perfect, but because you always tried to be."

"But I have admitted to you that I have feelings you abhor. I have revealed a part of me to you that no one else in the world has been privy to, my deepest shame. How can you not think less of me?"

The old man's voice was a wheezing whisper, and every breath was like a knife in his chest. But he needed to die with Ash Wilson's love as pure as it had ever been, and no amount of pain was going to prevent him from earning that last prize.

Wilson smiled sadly. "George, every man has thoughts he is ashamed of. Every man has impulses and instincts he cannot stop from occurring within his brain. In my mind though, it is the good man who can control these thoughts and not act on them. And it is the great man who recognizes that they are wrong, and atones for them."

Cohen shook his head no. "But have I atoned, Ash? Have I done enough?" A violent fit of coughing interrupted him. "Tell me about the Cooper case," he said when he could, "do you still have your doubts?"

"No, I don't. He did it," Ash said sadly but firmly.

"The tragedy is that if this kid had had the opportunities from birth that I had, there is no doubt in my mind that he would have been able accomplish as much, if not more, than you or I put together. Despite the absolutely horrific and unimaginable things this kid was put through, he still made it out, he was on his way. But the chains of his past could simply not be shed, and he now finds himself right back where he started."

Cohen wheezed to clear his throat. "Your opposing counsel would say that the chains of his past are nothing more than his skin color, and that it is you and our system of justice that hold the key which keeps the chains fastened. Are you now confident that is not the case?"

"You mean am I confident that Cooper's race has nothing to do with his prosecution? Or are you asking me if I believe his race played a factor in leading him to commit the crime in the first place? The answer to both is yes."

Since reading Charles' file, Wilson had thought of little else.

"I think that like most young black Americans, he was born into a world which offered him few, if any, of the chances and opportunities to which young white Americans are born. He needed the generosity and patience of someone much more fortunate than he to lift him from the abject station into which he had been thrust, through no fault of his own. And yet, somehow, he almost made it.

"So I believe his race played a factor in his committing this crime in the sense that I know if he had been born white, he would not be where he is right now. But I can't let that change the fact that he committed a crime for which our system of laws prescribes death as the penalty. I am not prosecuting him because he is black. I am prosecuting him because he is guilty—even if he is not to blame."

"What do you want to see happen?" Cohen rasped.

Wilson shrugged and shook his head. It was an impossible question to answer.

"I would say justice, but that is a silly concept in this case. Ultimately, all I can hope for is that the system works like it is designed to work, and that it is not perverted by those whose sole goal is subverting it."

"Do you think that's possible in this case?"

"Yeah, I do. As long as I do my job the right way. And as long as we get a judge who can somehow be immune to the immense pressure that Queenan's antics are going to bring into that courtroom, I think that the right outcome can be achieved."

Cohen's eyes were closed as Wilson spoke, so it was impossible to tell if he was still listening. The younger man leaned forward and kissed his mentor on the cheek and the forehead.

"I love you, George. I have always been and always will be proud of you. Thank you…for everything," he said, unable to hold back the tears any longer.

Although he didn't open his eyes again, Cohen managed to squeeze Wilson's hand with more strength than should have been possible. The end of his life would not come for another twenty hours, long after he and Wilson had said their final goodbyes, and long after George Cohen had made two last phone calls.

*   *   *   *

Cases are assigned to Judges in Philadelphia through a computerized rotation program. The system is designed to blindly pick the judges who will hear a particular matter. After Darnell's arraignment, at which a formal plea of not guilty was entered on his behalf, the case of the Commonwealth versus Darnell Cooper was plugged into the system. Out came the name of Judge Abram Jefferson.

As soon as the assignment was announced, all of the pundits in the media proclaimed it a huge boon for the defense. Judge Jefferson was black, and had been serving on the Court of Common Pleas bench in Philadelphia for twenty years. He was, by universal agreement, the most liberal of any judge on the bench. He was hated by prosecutors for what they believed to be his lenient sentences and skepticism of police testimony. He had presided over thirteen death penalty trials in his career. Four had ended in outright acquittals, seven had ended in plea bargains to lesser charges of murder, and two had concluded with the juries rendering verdicts of death. In both of those cases, Judge Jefferson had overturned the verdicts on post-trial motion of the defense attorneys.

He had also given numerous speeches over the years in opposition to the death penalty, and was particularly active in fund raising for African-American causes. Jefferson was a graduate of Howard University and Penn law, and had held his season tickets to the Penn basketball games for over twenty years.

If there was any one judge in the city who might be receptive to the conspiracy theories of Roger Queenan, it was Abram Jefferson. Or so they said on Court TV and CNN and MSNBC and ESPN.

What the experts and the defense didn't know though, was that as a senior at Howard University, a twenty-one year old Abram Jefferson had been accepted to the law school at the University of Pennsylvania, but had no way of paying the tuition. No bank would loan him money, and his three jobs were all low paying, manual labor efforts that barely paid his and his mother's rent.

Desperate, he had sent letters to every law firm in the city with his college transcript and a resume. He was graduating in the top five percent of his class, was an All-American in the 400 meter hurdles, and was the president of the Howard University chapter of the NAACP. He asked in his cover letter for a part-time position and assistance with tuition. It was an unusual request in that he couldn't really offer a law firm any real benefit commensurate with the compensation he was seeking. It was really just a shot in the dark.

Only one firm responded. In fact, only one lawyer responded. George Cohen had called young Abram at home and asked him a series of simple questions: why do you want to be a lawyer? Because I'll be good at it, was Jefferson's off-the-cuff response. Who else did you send your resume to? Everyone, he had said. How many interviews do you have scheduled? Well, none, sir. Why not? You are the only firm who's called. And that was it. Cohen had said thank you, and hung up.

But apparently Jefferson had given the right answers, because two days later, he received a letter at his mother's second-story apartment in Powelton Village from the Dean of the law school at Penn. It said that his tuition had been pre-paid for all three years, but that his benefactor wished to remain anonymous. That day, Jefferson went to Cohen's office to thank him, and find out what he had to do in return for his generosity, but the great man was unavailable to be seen, according to the receptionist and his secretary.

So Jefferson waited across the street, determined to thank the total stranger who had for no apparent reason simply given him the possibility of a career. At eight o'clock that night, as usual, Cohen had emerged onto Market Street and headed towards the concourse under City Hall, where he could catch the subway home.

"Mr. Cohen?" Jefferson had asked nervously as he tried to catch up to Cohen's pace.

Cohen looked over his shoulder without slowing down. "Yes?"

"Sir, I'm Abram Jefferson."

"Do I know you, son?"

Jefferson was almost running to keep up. "Well yes, sir," he stammered, "I think you just paid my tuition to Penn law. I would like to say thank you."

Cohen didn't slow at all. "Do you really want to thank me, son?" The older man asked to the air in front of him.

"Um, yes, yes, I do, very much."

"Then do two things. First, never mention to anyone what I've done, because it's nobody's goddamn business but yours. Second, make the most of what you've been given."

And that was the sum total of the conversations Abram Jefferson had ever had with George Cohen. He never told anyone of Cohen's extraordinary gift, and as far as he knew, neither had Cohen. But every day since that brief meeting, he had done exactly as Cohen had asked. He had finished at the top of his class at Penn.

After graduating, Jefferson spent ten years as an assistant public defender in Philadelphia, defending those for whom justice was simply too expensive to be available. During his time as a P.D., he had represented hundreds of defendants, less than a third of which had been white. Gradually, his front seat view to the economic disparity between the races, and their relative access to justice as a result, became the thing that most shaped his view of the practice of law.

But no matter how many times he tried to bring the inherent unfairness of the system to the attention of judges and juries, no matter how many Bar committees he headed, and no matter how much of his meager savings he contributed, Jefferson never felt as if he was having any impact in righting the wrongs he saw every day. But always conscious of George Cohen's mandate, he never stopped trying.

On the wall of his tiny office hung a framed paraphrase of Oliver Wendell Holmes' famous quote. It said "The law is what any given judge, on any given day, says it is." It was something he had said to his mother one day after a particularly absurd result in court. His mother had embroidered the words onto a small piece of fabric, which Jefferson had framed. It was positioned so that it was the last thing he saw every day as he headed to court.

After ten years in the trenches, Jefferson came to believe firmly in the truth of Holmes' observation. No matter what the lawyers said or did, ultimately, the judge was the ultimate arbiter of justice. So he decided to try and attack the problems he saw from the other end.

When he decided to run for the Bench, however, Jefferson found himself in a similar predicament as his clients. He simply couldn't afford it. In order to mount a legitimate campaign for the bench in Philadelphia, at the time, one needed at least twenty thousand in cash to even get on the ballot. That money went to committeemen and ward leaders and poll workers, all of whom controlled the electorate in the city. They decided a candidate's position on the ballot, ushered the right voters into the polls, and prevented the wrong ones from entering. But the initial outlay of cash only served to get you into the race. On election day, in order to win, an additional fifty to eighty thousand in cash was needed to pass out at the polls.

But this wasn't the only impediment to Jefferson getting elected. He not only had no money, he had no political base too. The man was simply not a politician. He was gregarious and intelligent and handsome, but he had neither the ability nor the desire to fake sincerity. And amongst politicians, the man who is unwilling or unable to do that is viewed with disdain, like he's a snob.

Recognizing this reluctance of Jefferson's to play the game by which they all survived, the party leaders, the men who decided what names got on the ballots, refused to even consider Jefferson. After all, what good would it do them to put a judge on the bench whom they couldn't control?

It was a hallmark of Jefferson's character that despite the obstacles in his path, he still expected to overcome them. He had no idea how, but he knew he would. And he did. On the day after his meeting with party leaders about getting his name on the ballot, when they had told him in no uncertain terms that he would never be a judge, he had received at his tiny row house in West Philly a short, unsigned note on plain white paper. It had been hand-delivered to his mailbox as there was no postage, nor return address on the envelope.

The note said, "You've done well. But you're not finished. Remember, if you want to thank me, keep this to yourself, and make the most of what you've been given."

Along with the note, inside the envelope, was a check for fifty thousand dollars, drawn on the personal account of George Cohen. The memo at the bottom of the check said it was for the election campaign of Abram Jefferson.

He had rushed to the phone and called Cohen's office immediately. Cohen was in, but unavailable to talk. Abram finally was able to get his benefactor's personal secretary on the phone.

"I must speak to Mr. Cohen!" he had said, his excitement and his gratitude overwhelming him. "Please tell him that it's Abram Jefferson. I know he'll want to talk to me immediately. I have to thank him for something very important!"

The secretary put him on hold for about two minutes. When she came back on the line, she said, "Mr. Cohen is on another call. He said that there is no need for you to speak with him. He said to tell you…wait a minute, I wrote it down. Mr. Cohen said to tell you that you need not speak with him. He said to read his note again, and keep up the good work."

So twice in Abram Jefferson's life, George Cohen had anonymously propelled him into his future, for no apparent reason. Of course, Jefferson had no way of knowing that Cohen had made similar gifts to countless other young African-Americans who somehow managed to find their way onto his radar screen.

There were teachers and veterinarians and doctors and engineers, and people in every other profession and job imaginable, all over the city, who owed their careers to George Cohen. There were also many people who had accepted Cohen's gifts and squandered the opportunities they represented.

For his part, not a day had gone by since Jefferson had received the first note that he hadn't thought of George Cohen, and what he could do that very day to make the man proud. But when his phone rang the morning that Darnell Cooper was to be arraigned, the very last person in the world Judge Abram Jefferson expected to be calling was George Cohen.

"Abram?" asked a whispery voice when Jefferson answered.

"Who is this?" he asked brusquely.

A pained cough was the response, and Jefferson almost hung up. "It's George Cohen."

He was stunned. "My God, Mr. Cohen, how are you feeling, sir? What can I do for you?" Jefferson didn't know what to say, but was prepared to do anything the man needed, and had been so prepared for over thirty years. At least he thought he was.

"I don't have much time, Abram, so I'll be brief," wheezed Cohen. "You are going to be assigned the Darnell Cooper case today. I will be dead before the trial." Cohen stopped talking for a brief but excruciating cough.

"I expect that you will put your personal feelings aside, and be fair to both sides," he whispered as soon as he could. "You have done more with my gifts than I could ever have hoped, Abram. You are a passionate and talented lawyer and judge. But your passion will make you want to favor the Cooper boy and his lawyer. Do not give in to that temptation. You owe yourself, your office, and everyone who will be watching, your complete objectivity. I choose you to do this because the appearance of justice in this case is as important, if not more so, than actually seeing it done for this boy and our city. Only a man of your stature, and unfortunately, your color, can make that happen.

Will you promise me to put your personal feelings aside when presiding over this case?"

Jefferson was still too stunned to think straight. "Uh, yes, of course, Mr. Cohen, I mean, I try to do that in every case so I don't see why I wouldn't do it for this one."

"C'mon, Abram," wheezed Cohen, "I've watched you all these years. I've heard your speeches, followed your rulings. I know what you must feel about Cooper. I'm not saying you're wrong, but it will affect your ability to be fair. What I'm asking is that you let me go to my grave knowing that I can count on you to put those feelings aside. Let the jury decide this case on its merits. Let the system work as it is supposed to."

He was suddenly offended by the request. No matter what this man had done for him, he had no right to make Jefferson a token. That's exactly what he had worked so hard not to have to become.

"Mr. Cohen," he said icily, "I am always fair. But I refuse to be anyone's token. I have to admit I'm surprised you're asking this, since it was you who gave me the opportunity I needed to avoid becoming one in the first place. Why are you asking me to do it now?"

Cohen coughed violently into the receiver. "Now you listen to me, goddammit!" he said finally with more strength than Jefferson realized he had. "I am not asking you to do anything more than uphold the oath you took when you became a judge. I am not suggesting that you do anything improper…I'm asking just the opposite.

"You're not anyone's token, Abram. I chose you when you were twenty-one years old because I recognized your potential. I am choosing you now because you have realized that potential, and are the most qualified person to do the job that is necessary. I and you both know what your true abilities are. The fact that you are black has nothing to do with the truth, only with the perception."

But that is my only concern, thought Jefferson. What the hell difference does it make for me, and a soon-to-dead George Cohen, to know the truth, when everybody else in the world is making decisions based on the perception?

"I can't talk much longer, Abram," said Cohen in a fading voice. "I need to have your answer."

Jefferson sighed deeply. He was torn between what he owed the man, and what he owed to himself. "I will do my best, Mr. Cohen," he said finally, giving the only honest answer he could.

"That is all I've ever asked of you, Abram. Thank you." The line went dead before Jefferson could say goodbye.

The last call George Cohen made before he died was to the Court Administrator of Philadelphia, who was just another in a long line of city government employees who owed their jobs to George Cohen and his phalanx of flunkies. A two-minute conversation was all that was necessary. Within an hour of hanging up, Abram Jefferson had been assigned the Darnell Cooper case, and George Cohen was dead.

*   *   *   *

Cohen's death was hard on Ash Wilson. He loved the man deeply, an emotion not shared by many toward the old man. Which is not to say that he wasn't admired and respected. His funeral was one of the grander affairs anyone in Philadelphia could remember. The memorial service was held at the Kimmel Center for the Performing Arts, with dignitaries from all over the world attending. The President of the United States sent a videotaped message, which his Vice-President hand delivered to Ash Wilson. Neither man would hold the office they did without the financial backing of George Cohen.

"I am almost fifty years old," Ash had said haltingly in his eulogy to the mass of gathered mourners, "and today, for the first time in my life, I feel old. I was a child when I met George Cohen, and he made me a man. Yet as long as he lived, I was still, in many respects, his child. Now that he is gone, so is that child. I would guess that there are many among us today, and scores more who could not be here, who feel the same way."

Watching the service on TV at home, Abram Jefferson wiped away a tear, and agreed with the D.A. But no matter how much he loved Cohen, Jefferson was just as sad that he would not be able to honor the old man's final wish.

From the moment he'd learned of Cooper's arrest, he'd worried that the case would be assigned to him. He was worried because he wanted to see the boy acquitted, and wasn't sure he could be fair at all.

CHAPTER 25

▼

It took three and a half weeks to seat a jury. Eighteen men and women were selected; twelve jurors, plus six alternates. Eight of the first twelve were black, one was white, one Asian, and two Hispanic. Four whites and two blacks comprised the alternates.

The selection process had not been a pleasant one. It started off ugly when Roger Queenan submitted his proposed voir dire questions for the prospective jurors.

All judges conduct jury selection differently. Abram Jefferson preferred to have the lawyers submit proposed questions to be asked of the panel, and he himself would conduct the questioning. A death penalty case was different, though, in that each potential juror had to be questioned specifically on the issue of whether or not they could impose a sentence of death, if the law and the facts called for it.

So Jefferson asked for a list of questions which he would ask of the entire panels of people. These were general questions to weed out those who simply could not serve, regardless of the type of case it was. He decided that after they had culled two hundred from the general panels, he would allow individual questioning in a separate courtroom, where it would be only the lawyers, the defendant, the judge, and one juror at a time. He asked for proposed questions for the individual process as well, although he had originally contemplated allowing the lawyers to conduct that questioning.

Queenan's first proposed question was, "do you think Darnell Cooper has been charged in this case because he is black?" That turned out to be his most innocuous query.

The first meeting with counsel to go over the questions had quickly devolved into a shouting match between Queenan and Wilson about the propriety of injecting race into the case. Queenan obviously felt as if he was the home team in this regard because of Jefferson's presence. Despite an overwhelming desire to let Queenan run rampant, a feeling he was not necessarily proud of, Jefferson had to shut him down early.

"You know, son," he said to Queenan in his baritone voice at the final pre-trial conference, "you've got no subtlety. You don't even try to dress your arguments up. You just paint them with black face and put 'em out there on stage. You expect me to just go along with that program? Why? Because I'm black? You think I don't know the law? You think I'm stupid? I would be offended if I thought for a second you'd comprehend why. Forget it. I'll ask all the questions, and I'll decide what they are. That is all."

Testamentary to each man's perspective were Wilson and Queenan's respective takes on what the Judge had said. Wilson thought Jefferson was going out of his way to show that he wasn't going to toe the company line with the defense. Queenan of course, thought the Judge was simply putting on a show for Wilson, and that he would be there for Queenan on the important issues. They were both right, of course.

The jury that was ultimately selected was satisfactory to both men, but for different reasons. After decades spent in various courtrooms, trying all types of cases in front of all kinds of jurors, Wilson had come to accept the fact that there was no science, or even art, to picking a jury. Jury selection was about one thing from Wilson's perspective, stereotyping.

An older white, professional male is supposed to be pro-prosecution. Young black males, good for the defense. Overweight women? No good. And there were a thousand other reasons for why a particular type of person would be a good or bad juror for either side that had been taught to every young litigator by every old litigator, who had been taught the same things themselves when they were young.

Wilson had dutifully learned the rules, read the books by the experts, and spoken with countless jury consultants. But every jury he had ever picked surprised him anyway. Not necessarily with their verdicts, but by the way he would learn they had arrived at them. Rather than their personal or professional backgrounds influencing their deliberations, Wilson found that the credibility of his witnesses, and the sum total of his evidence, were the things most focused upon.

It was the genius of the jury system really. Twelve strangers thrown into a room together, told they have to make a decision, invariably find a way to wash out their personal prejudices and preconceptions, and make the decision warranted by what was presented to them. That was why Wilson never wasted a lot of time worrying about jury selection. Perhaps it was naiveté, but he believed, ultimately, that the system would work on its own, regardless of his efforts to manipulate it to his purposes.

Queenan, on the other hand, felt the way that ninety-nine percent of trial lawyers do. He believed that every case was won and lost in jury selection, and that he could control, with careful planning and pruning, just who got to sit on his juries. Going into the selection process in the Cooper case, he'd had one goal—get as many black jurors, men or women, as he could.

He certainly wasn't naïve enough to believe that blacks would acquit Darnell just because of their skin color, but he felt strongly that only his own people could truly appreciate the message he was trying to send, and needed to be sent. He'd fought hard throughout jury selection to limit Wilson's ability to strike black panel members for cause, and forced him to use many of his allotted peremptory strikes on blacks. Every time he did though, Queenan made a *Batson* objection, to the point of absurdity at times.

One elderly black lady had said under no circumstances could she find Darnell Cooper guilty. When asked why by the Judge, she said, "Because I believe he's innocent and that he's been framed by the police."

Wilson of course asked that she be excused for cause. Queenan approached the bench and objected.

"Judge, I'm making a *Batson* challenge to Mr. Wilson's request to strike this juror."

Jefferson peered down over his bifocals, his bushy gray eyebrows clouding his eyes.

"Mr. Queenan, have you actually read the *Batson* case?" he asked with a patronizing smile.

"Yes, sir, I have, and it is clear in that a juror may not be excused on the basis of their race."

Jefferson's smile disappeared. "What does the *Batson* case say about excusing a lawyer for sheer stupidity? Now step back, and the next baseless objection you make, I'm fining you a thousand dollars." It frustrated Jefferson to no end that Queenan's minstrel show was the only thing standing between Darnell Cooper and a lethal injection.

In the end, Queenan got the best jury he could hope for, and so did Wilson.

Another major battle had not even come directly from Wilson or Queenan. All of the major networks, cable news channels, and major newspapers around the country, had filed petitions with Jefferson seeking to have television cameras allowed in the courtroom. His first, and second instincts had been to forbid any such distraction.

After hearing from all the high-priced legal talent from New York and elsewhere argue in favor of the camera, he really saw no legitimate reason why they should be allowed. But after careful reflection, Jefferson relented. The cameras were necessary, if for nothing else than to allow the perception of justice to be created. The question was, of course, how to shape the perception.

Because of his decision to allow cameras, Jefferson was forced to do something he had never done in his twenty plus years on the bench; sequester a jury. As much as he may have privately wanted them to be influenced by the rhetoric of the media, he simply could not justify letting the jurors go home every night to watch the six o'clock news. His decision in this regard was helped considerably by Wilson's promise that the Commonwealth's case would take less than a week to present.

All of the networks immediately announced plans for uninterrupted (except for commercials), coverage of the trial, with all the usual suspects lined up as expert commentators. These experts consisted uniformly of men and women with little or no trial experience.

Fortunately, what they lacked in informed experience, they more than made up for with unfounded opinions. As Jefferson derisively explained to the attorneys during a conference on how the media crush would be handled inside the courtroom, "they are often wrong, but never in doubt."

Unfortunately, it quickly became impossible to even turn on the television without hearing from one or more of these so-called experts. Even worse, people watching at home viewed these second-rate Monday morning quarterbacks as insiders, and they were often the recipients of sensitive information from court personnel with access to it and a desire to be part of the story.

On the Sunday morning of the second week of jury selection, Noelle Wilson had sat at the kitchen table, reading the Inquirer and eating a bowl of cereal with the boys. Wilson was upstairs in the bedroom, getting ready to go into the office.

"Ash, turn on channel six," she shouted up to him.

On the screen was a local lawyer who Wilson recognized as a specialist in Trusts and Estates law, who as far as Wilson knew, had never tried a case of any kind, much less a capital homicide. He was of course billed with the title "legal expert." The thought of a podiatrist commenting on open-heart surgery jumped into Wilson's head.

The man was speaking with one of the local hairdos that passed for a television news reporter. "Apparently, Congressman Levine has been unreachable as well. The whole family appears to have left the country with him."

Wilson sat down on the edge of the bed just as Noelle entered the room.

"Obviously this suggests that Anita Levine, who is the lynchpin of the prosecution's case, is not going to testify. How will that affect the case against Darnell Cooper?"

The Trusts and Estates lawyer wagged his head sagaciously. "Oh, I think it will have a devastating affect. Levine is the only witness who can offer direct evidence of Cooper's presence in the apartment at the time we know she was murdered. Without her, the case is totally circumstantial."

The hairdo turned to face the camera. "Well, an interesting development in the Darnell Cooper murder and rape trial, currently in the midst of jury selection. Congressman Arnold Levine and his entire family, including his daughter Anita Levine, the star prosecution witness in the case, have left the country on an extended vacation. Word from the Congressman's office is that they are scheduled to be gone for two months. There has been no official comment from the District Attorney's Office. We will follow the story as it develops, and keep you updated."

Wilson turned off the set with the remote, and flopped backwards onto the bed.

"What?" asked Noelle. "She can't just run away. Can't you have her arrested and brought back for disobeying a subpoena?"

Wilson grimaced. "I haven't been able to serve her with a subpoena yet. Tony's been asking and asking the Congressman's office to accept service because she's been holed up at their estate. He's been stonewalling. I told him on Thursday that if he didn't accept service on behalf of his daughter, that Sciolla would personally climb the gate and crawl through her bedroom window. I guess he decided to hightail it out of town before I could do that."

Noelle cringed as she sat beside her husband on the bed. "Still, isn't it obstruction of justice or something? He can't just whisk her away like that, can he?"

Wilson sat up. "Levine knows I can't touch him. Christ, I could spend the next six years fighting his lawyers on those issues, and still never get her back here. Bottom line is we screwed up, because she's gone and not under subpoena. I should have had Sciolla serve her at the prelim like I do every other goddamn witness I've ever had."

Mrs. Wilson rubbed his leg. "C'mon, Ash, that girl was a wreck at that hearing. Hell, I can't say I blame her old man for not wanting her to be put through that again. But what does it do to your case? I mean, she is your star witness. Is that guy right, that without her the case is all circumstantial?"

Wilson shook his head disgustedly and got up to finish getting dressed.

"Any time you ever hear anybody say that a case is weak because it's based on circumstantial evidence, it's a tip-off that he's an idiot. Circumstantial evidence is the best evidence there is."

Noelle began making the bed. "Wait a minute, F. Lee, care to explain that to the wife?"

Ash smiled as he combed his hair in the bathroom.

"Picture a scenario. You walk into your house on a bright sunny day, not a cloud in the sky. The windows are closed and the shades are drawn. An hour later, some stranger walks in and tells you that a freak rain shower just blew through that lasted for twenty minutes, but now everything's sunny again. That's eyewitness testimony, direct evidence.

"Now, picture the same scenario, except after an hour, you walk outside your house, and although the sun is shining, the grass is wet, there's mud puddles in the yard, the cars are soaked, and it smells like a summer shower outside. All of that evidence is totally circumstantial.

"Now, which of those two types of evidence would you find more persuasive that it had rained?"

"Okay, you made your point," said Noelle. "But still, isn't Levine an important witness?"

Wilson shrugged. "Not really. The most important thing she gives me really is that Cooper was there at the time we know Kelly was killed. But that's hardly a contested issue. Cooper admitted he was there until 10:30, and the DNA proves they had sex. Cooper's denial of that is more important than anything Levine would have testified to.

"If anything, her failure to appear hurts them more than it hurts me, because now I can allow the jury to draw the inference that, like my other witnesses will say, Cooper was chasing Kelly that night, and that maybe she didn't really want him in her house at all."

Noelle could see that her husband was annoyed, so she stopped herself from asking why he felt it was okay to create an inference he knew to be contradicted by Levine's statement.

"But if she's not an important witness, why are you so pissed?" she asked instead, hoping he would tell her anyway.

"Because I hate being in the position I'm going to be in now. If Levine showed up and testified consistently with what she told Tony the night of the murder, she would tell the jury that Kelly appeared to have invited Cooper into the house. The problem is that I've got two witnesses whose testimony contradicts that, and the written statement that Levine gave, which is all we are left with if she doesn't show up, is really silent on that issue.

"So although I'm perfectly within my rights, hell my duty as a prosecutor, to argue to the jury that Cooper was essentially stalking this poor girl and had basically followed her unwanted into her apartment, in the back of my head I've got to deal with the nagging guilt that I'm misleading the jury."

Mrs. Wilson put her arm around the D.A.'s shoulder. "I thought you said you had resolved all your doubts about Cooper's guilt?"

Wilson had told his wife that he'd learned information that convinced him beyond all doubt of Cooper's guilt, but had not told her what that information was or how he'd obtained it.

"I have," he said as he shrugged her arm off. He was annoyed at himself for having allowed Sciolla to show him the Charles file in the first place. Now, with Levine apparently having taken a powder, he felt like it would be cheating again to argue to the jury as he now could with her absence.

"I'm sorry," he said to his wife as she tried to get up in a huff. He pulled her back down onto the bed and kissed her. "I don't have any doubts he did it. It just seems that everybody's trying to make this trial about something other than the crime itself, and I don't want to get caught up in the hype."

Noelle sat quietly for a few seconds. "But all you're doing is your job, Ash. You can't worry about anything else."

He looked at his wife. She was always prettiest to him on Sunday mornings, with her hair loose at her shoulders, her naturally pretty face devoid of make-up.

"I'm trying, babe. I'm trying."

In the office later, Wilson and Sciolla confronted the damage that Levine's absence might possibly have on their case. They both agreed that it was not devastating by any stretch. Sciolla bristled at Wilson's reluctance to seek the admission of Levine's written statement, and the argument that could flow from it. After a heated debate, Wilson agreed that he was within his rights to argue all inferences available from the evidence. It was Queenan's fault Levine was gone, anyway.

As for Levine's apparently willful avoidance of a subpoena to testify, the D.A.'s Office had no official comment, but unofficially expressed disappointment in the Congressman's behavior. The House of Representatives launched an internal investigation of its own, but it went nowhere when it was revealed that the Levine family trip was to Germany and Austria to visit their ancestral homeland, and specifically the concentration camp where most of Congressman Levine's family had been killed in World War II.

So rather than waste time worrying about Anita Levine, Wilson went about the business of preparing the case for the execution of Darnell Cooper.

*   *   *   *

In the living room of John Ryan of course, the case had already been made. The disappearance of Levine only served to solidify the verdict in his mind. He had discussed for weeks with Fullem how they might accomplish their execution of Cooper. Ryan had not returned to work since the murder and rape of his daughter. His full-time job was revenge.

At first, Ryan had wanted to do it himself. But Fullem was adamant that that not happen.

"You've got to go on, John, for Kelly," he had said late one night in the beginning. "If you do it, this kid will have effectively ended not just her life, but yours as well. It's not what she would've wanted. I have to do it."

The question was how. Cooper was in twenty-three hour lock-up at the prison. His only contact with outside visitors was with his jailers and his lawyers there, or with his guards in the van on the way to court. The van transport drives directly into the Criminal Justice Center, and prisoners are taken up to the courtrooms by a back elevator accessible only to uniformed personnel.

They spent days following the transport van on its runs back and forth to the CJC, mapping its routes, figuring out the schedule of drivers, and the number of guards. Their thought was to hijack the van on the way to court. But the risk of danger to other people was too great, and even though he was hell-bent on revenge, Ryan wasn't crazy.

"I recognize that driver," Fullem said as they watched the van pull into the underground garage beneath the CJC. "I bet we could slip enough cash to get him to fake a breakdown, maybe on the Vine Street Expressway somewhere. We pull up, I charge the van, shoot Cooper through the window."

Ryan shook his head no. "Too many variables. Too many things could go wrong. No, we're only going to get one shot at this, Joe. I want to make sure we do it right the first time."

They were quiet for a few minutes while Fullem navigated his way out of Center City and onto I-95 North back to the Northeast.

"It'll have to be at close range, then," said Fullem finally. "I'll do it right in the courtroom, in front of cameras. Let's let the whole world see that monkey get what he deserves."

Ryan liked that idea…a lot. "But how do we get a gun into the courtroom?"

Post 9/11 security measures made smuggling even a cell phone into the CJC practically an impossibility. Everyone who entered the building, besides cops, had to pass through a metal detector, and also pass whatever bags they were carrying through a conveyor belted x-ray machine. A full-time officer was assigned to each checkpoint, of which there were four total.

"Isn't Donny Moxley the one who watches the attorney line?" Fullem asked.

"Yeah," said Ryan, "he was there when I went to the prelim. He's a good egg."

"You and he are pretty good friends aren't you?'

Ryan nodded yes.

"All right then. You know those moolies are going to subpoena me as a witness, right?"

Ryan grimaced. Queenan had been widely quoted as saying that Fullem would be a major factor in the case. "Yeah?"

"Well, I'll shoot that nigger right between the eyes when they call me to the stand."

Ryan was getting frustrated. "You still gotta' get the gun into the building, Joe."

"No problem. On the day I'm set to testify, you and I walk into the building together. You know how crazy those guys get when they see a gun on the x-ray machine, right? You leave your service pistol in your bag and feed it through on the conveyor belt. I will walk through the metal detector at the same time. I'll have my little .380 in my pocket. As soon as Moxley yells gun, I step through the detector. No one will even notice me beeping, as long as you're right behind me walking through."

Ryan pictured the scenario in his head.

"That just might work," he said after a few seconds. "You know what I'll do? I'll call Wilson and just kinda' give him the idea that I'm thinking about taking care of Cooper myself. That way they'll be looking for me to try something like that."

Fullem was excited by their plan of attack. "I like it. But I think if it's going to work, I think it's best if I don't come to the trial until I'm called as a witness. I'll be way too much of a distraction anyway."

CHAPTER 26

▼

"How do you feel," asked Tony Sciolla. It was the morning of opening arguments.

"Nervous," Wilson replied honestly.

Despite the cartwheels his stomach was doing, Wilson viewed this as a good sign. He always got nervous before a trial, second-guessing his preparation and his ability. For a long time in the beginning of his career, he had thought his nervousness meant he was a bad lawyer. All of the guys he saw trying cases who were considered great trial lawyers, never appeared the least bit nervous.

But then he read an article about Bill Russell, the great Boston Celtics Center, the winningest basketball player of all time. Even though he was arguably one of the best players in history, Russell would get so nervous before every game that he actually threw up. It even became a ritual, one that his teammates and coaches came to rely upon. If Russell was in the bathroom throwing up before a game, everything was cool.

Wilson felt the same way, though he never had to throw up. He took his jitters as a sign that he had prepared well, and that his focus was in the right place. He embraced his apprehension and used it for fuel.

*   *   *   *

"You ready?" Lionel asked Queenan. They were in Queenan's office, packing their trial bags.

Queenan smiled confidently. "Born ready, brotha."

But he was nervous too. Unlike Wilson though, he didn't acknowledge it, even to himself. He had tried hundreds of criminal cases. Queenan told himself that he had seen it all and that he was prepared for anything. He couldn't let himself feel nervous, because if he did, it would mean he didn't have total faith in his own abilities. He was a man who needed to be able to count on himself.

"How 'bout you, you ready?"

Lionel just nodded.

He wasn't nervous, he was petrified. The stakes were too high to even fully comprehend. He had rescued, and nurtured, and protected Darnell for too long to even contemplate letting him down now. Despite their countless hours of preparation, Lionel was still not entirely convinced that Queenan could pull it off. But he was prepared to do whatever it took to help him do just that, and his fear was in part based on his recognition of just how far he was willing to go in that effort.

*   *   *   *

"Big day, today, Darnell," said the van driver.

Darnell said nothing and just stared out the window.

They were on their way to the CJC. Darnell sat in the first seat in the fifteen passenger van, directly behind the steel cage barrier between the driver and his charges. There were ten other inmates seated sporadically throughout the vehicle. Darnell was the only one not dressed in an orange jumpsuit, clad instead in a brand new Armani suit Lionel had bought just for the trial.

Everyone on the van was quiet, which was unusual. All of the men on it, including the driver, were black, and for different reasons, each identified with Darnell's situation, and were worried for him.

Darnell was worried too, but mostly he was tired. Ever since he had been a very little boy, he had felt very old. That's what fear does, it ages you emotionally. He had lived in fear from the moment of his birth. Somehow, miraculously, Lionel had appeared one day, and gradually over time, the fear had dissipated and been replaced by hope and optimism. His arrest though had erased the hope and brought back the fear. And it aged him all the more, like a recurrent cancer. No matter what happened, Darnell just wanted to stop being afraid.

*   *   *   *

"We're still a go, right?" asked Fullem.

Ryan was on his way to the courthouse, speaking to Fullem on his cell phone while sitting in standstill traffic on 95.

"Yeah, Joe, we're still a go. I'm not changing my mind."

Ryan was bitterly angry. Although he had deliberately continued to try and avoid the media overkill surrounding the trial, it was so pervasive that there was really no missing it altogether. In every story he had heard or read, Kelly had appeared as nothing more than a footnote. The media was tripping all over itself to either lionize or demonize Darnell, with barely any consideration to his victim. This infuriated Ryan, and made him all the more glad that the sentence he truly deserved was going to be inflicted.

"Good," said Fullem as he ended the call.

After all that had happened, Fullem felt nothing. He was guilty of too many things to feel ashamed of them all, and his grief had taken a backseat to the task at hand. He no longer felt hopeful of ever regaining his friendship with Ryan, because his friend was no longer the man that he loved. That too was Fullem's fault. He had destroyed everything he had ever touched, including his own sense of remorse. He had kept from Ryan so many secrets, the last of which was his intention to kill himself immediately after killing Darnell.

*   *   *   *

The large courtroom on the sixth floor was filled to capacity. Unlike the scene at the preliminary hearing though, this was Judge Abram Jefferson's province, and he was in absolute control.

He ascended to the bench with a flourish, his long black robe billowing out behind him as he strode to the high-backed leather chair behind an imperious oak bench. Jefferson was a man of average height and average build. What distinguished him physically though was his shockingly white beard and hair, which he wore in the afro style of the seventies. Against his dark skin and surrounding sharp features, it gave him a strikingly handsome countenance. His deep bassoon-like voice, combined with the confidence exuded by his physical presence, gave the judge a commanding presence.

"All rise!" shouted the court crier. "This court is now in session. The Honorable Abram T. Jefferson presiding."

"Be seated," said the judge as he took his own.

The jury was assembled to his left. Wilson sat alone at the prosecution's table in front of him, and Queenan, Lionel and Darnell were at the defense table to Wilson's left. Darnell's suit was dark blue, complimented by a bright white shirt, and deep red tie. His hands were folded on the table in front of him.

Jefferson had given the jury its preliminary instructions on the final day of jury selection.

"Mr. Wilson," he said over a pair of bifocals perched at the end of his nose, "is the Commonwealth ready to proceed?"

Wilson stood up and buttoned the jacket of his gray suit. "Yes, your Honor, we are."

As he had carefully planned, Wilson took a series of precise steps from behind his table until he was standing three feet in front of the jury box, directly in the center.

"On October 28th of last year, at approximately 9:30 PM, Darnell Cooper, the defendant," Wilson turned and pointed to Darnell, "followed an eighteen year old classmate named Kelly Ryan, back to her college apartment after she had literally fled from his presence at her campus dining hall. The defendant followed her all the way to her bedroom. The defendant is six feet, eight inches tall and weighs two hundred and thirty pounds. He was over a foot taller and well more than a hundred pounds heavier than Kelly. I say 'was' because once the defendant managed to get inside Kelly's room that night, he brutally raped her." Wilson paused for effect. "After he raped her, the defendant then punched Kelly so hard in the face that he broke her jaw…he then wrapped one large powerful hand around her fragile throat, and choked the breath from her body until she was dead.

"Your Honor," Wilson half-turned and nodded to the Judge. He then turned to his right to look at John Ryan, who was seated in the front row of the gallery, and nodded deferentially. "Mr. Ryan," he said, and Ryan nodded back in acknowledgment.

He then turned back to face the jury. "Ladies and Gentlemen. As you know, my name is Ashland Wilson. I represent the Office of the District Attorney, the Commonwealth of Pennsylvania, the County of Philadelphia, and all of its citizens, in our case against the defendant, for the brutal rape, and first degree murder of Kelly Ryan. In this trial, I will present evidence to you, evidence that will convince you beyond a reasonable doubt…that the defendant is guilty of the crimes with which he has been charged."

Wilson took two careful steps to his right with his head bowed, and clasped his hands behind his back, like a college professor giving a lecture.

"Before I tell you about the evidence you're going to hear and see, though, I first want to thank you for being here." He eyed the jury out of the corner of his eye and pretended to be suppressing a smile. "I know you're all probably thinking that you didn't have much choice, aren't you?" A couple of jurors smiled back and nodded, always a good sign. Wilson acknowledged the smiles with one of his own and faced the entire panel again.

"The fact is you did have a choice. Let's face it, everybody knows what to say in order to get out of jury duty. But each and every one of you," Wilson took his time to pan each face in the box, "chose to answer honestly the questions posed to you. Each and every one of you chose to accept the extraordinary and momentous duty of being a juror. Most importantly though, each and every one of you have sworn under oath to uphold your sacred duty as a juror, which requires that you leave whatever preconceptions and prejudices you may have, outside of this courtroom. It requires of you that you listen to all of the evidence that is presented, that you weigh that evidence fairly, and that you apply the law as Judge Jefferson instructs you to the facts as you find them to be based on the evidence.

"And for swearing to do that, I thank you.

"Now, what will the evidence be? First, you'll hear from a witness who saw the defendant and Kelly Ryan arguing at dinner the night she was murdered. This witness will tell you that Kelly began crying as the result of something the defendant said to her. You will hear from a witness who saw Kelly running up campus immediately after that and that she appeared afraid. You will hear from witnesses who will tell you they saw the defendant following Kelly back to her apartment, and that they saw Kelly run away from the defendant, who chased her onto the front steps of her apartment building.

"You'll hear from Dr. Maury Templeton, who is the Medical Examiner for us here in Philadelphia. Dr. Templeton performed the autopsy on Kelly's body. He will tell you that, based on scientific evidence collected from her body, Kelly was raped and murdered, and that she died between 10:30 PM and 11:30 PM. He will show you the pictures of Kelly's body, specifically the deep, purple and black bruises that the defendant left on her jaw when he punched her there, and on her neck when he choked her to death. The size, pattern, and severity of the bruising, Dr. Templeton will tell you, shows that Kelly's killer had very large, very strong hands."

Wilson turned and walked over to the defense table until he was standing directly in front of Darnell. He stared down at Darnell's hands which were folded in front of him on the table.

As he had been instructed repeatedly to do, Darnell stared straight back at Wilson, his head held high, and this time kept his hands where they were.

Wilson turned back to the jury. "Dr. Templeton will also tell you that he performed a physical examination of Kelly's genital area. This showed that Kelly had been sexually brutalized before her death, as evidenced by lacerations and bruising on the interior of her vaginal wall, and blood on her bed sheets." Wilson lowered his head and approached the jury box.

"Dr. Templeton also performed what's known as a 'rape kit' to search for bodily fluids. With this he found semen in Kelly's vagina. He carefully collected the samples, and had them analyzed by Pennsylvania State Police Crime Laboratory. There, two different sophisticated types of DNA testing were done on the semen sample taken from Kelly's body. The first is called Restrictive Fragment Length Polymorphisms, or RFLP, and the other is called Polymerase Chain Reaction, or PCR. These tests identified the specific DNA that is unique to Kelly's killer.

"A sample of the defendant's blood and hair was also tested using the same exact methods, and compared to the semen found in Kelly's body. A state certified criminalist who did the testing will tell you that the samples were identical. There is no doubt. It is scientifically and statistically impossible for any human being other than the defendant to have left that semen inside Kelly Ryan's dead body."

He turned and walked back towards Darnell, looking at him now as he spoke.

"The scientists however, are not the only people who tell us that the defendant was with Kelly Ryan on the night of her murder. You see, the defendant himself has admitted that he was with Kelly on the night she was killed. In the early morning hours after the murder, the defendant was visited by Detective Tony Sciolla, of the district attorney's office detectives squad. Detective Sciolla asked the defendant directly if he had been with Kelly the night before." Wilson wheeled back to the jury.

"The defendant said yes, and even admitted that he'd been with her until 10:30 PM. The detective then asked the defendant if he'd had sex with Kelly…The defendant said no. Ladies and gentlemen, the scientific evidence in this case is unimpeachable. There is no doubt that it was the defendant's semen inside Kelly's body. The defendant lied about having sex with her because, as all liars do, he was trying to hide the truth…which was that he had raped, and then murdered Kelly Ryan."

Wilson paused briefly and repositioned himself directly in front of the jury.

"The evidence in this case is overwhelming, ladies and gentlemen. Eyewitnesses place the defendant and Kelly together just before the murder. Eyewitnesses saw the defendant chasing Kelly towards her apartment. The defendant's semen was found in Kelly's body just a few hours after she had been raped and murdered by someone with large hands who was physically powerful. And of course, the defendant himself has admitted that he was with Kelly at or near the time of her death.

"I've told you what your job is. You have the obligation to uphold your sworn duty as jurors. This duty compels you to find the defendant guilty of first-degree murder and rape if the evidence warrants it. Now, Judge Jefferson will tell you certain things at the end of this trial. He will tell you that I have the burden of presenting the evidence which will prove beyond a reasonable doubt, that the defendant is guilty.

"I promise you, ladies and gentlemen, that I will do my job. And if you do yours, as you have sworn to do, you will find the defendant guilty of first-degree murder, and rape.

"Thank you."

Wilson walked deliberately back to his seat. It had been a strong opening and the gallery was buzzing. He had been determined to send the message that Cooper was just another murder defendant to him, and not some icon. Wilson wanted the jury to start getting themselves into the same frame of mind. The evidence was simple and straightforward, and that was how the D.A. intended to present it.

"Mr. Queenan, do you wish to make an opening argument?" asked the judge, who hoped it would be a good one.

"I do, your Honor," said Queenan somberly as he rose from his seat.

He was dressed in a double-breasted, dark blue suit that Lionel thought to be an unfortunate choice. Men with big bellies do not belong in double-breasted suits. Hell, from Lionel's fashion perspective, the only men who do belong in double-breasted suits are yacht captains and bellhops. But Queenan didn't care. He told Lionel that he was purposefully showcasing his girth for the jury. He wanted them to see him as larger than life, literally bursting at the seams. Queenan wanted this jury to feel him coming at them, not just hear him.

"Ladies and gentlemen, good morning," he said in a low, muted tone as he ambled up to jury box. He paused for a few seconds, his head bowed, giving the appearance that he was thinking of what to say as he stood there. But he wasn't. He and Lionel had ordered and studied every opening argument Wilson had ever given in a capital case. They were, but for minor variations, uniformly the same.

"Before I tell you that Darnell Cooper is absolutely, one hundred percent, without any doubt innocent of these crimes, and stands before you wrongfully accused, I want to address something that the D.A. asked you to do in his opening statement. He suggested to you that you should leave your prejudices and your preconceptions outside of this courtroom, and only bring with you your common sense. I think that's what he said, right?"

Juror number 4 nodded yes.

Queenan turned to her.

"Well, let me tell you that I disagree with everything the D.A. said, especially that part. After all, what is your common sense? What is it? I'll tell you. It is the sum total of your life experiences, combined with your prejudices and preconceptions. If you exclude any one of those components from your decision-making process in this case, you will not be giving Darnell Cooper the fair trial he deserves. Darnell is an innocent man, ladies and gentlemen, and the only way you will be able to see that truth is if you come into this courtroom every day with the full benefit of every life experience you've ever had, and every prejudice and preconception you own.

"I promise you that the D.A. and his police squad did not exclude their prejudices when they charged Darnell with the rape and murder of this white girl."

Wilson had to literally hold himself down from jumping up and objecting, even though it was anathema to him as a professional to object during the opening or closing argument of another attorney. He knew that was exactly what Queenan wanted. Queenan wanted the jury to see Wilson exercised about the accusations of racism, he wanted the D.A. to be seen as vehemently offended when even subtly accused. After all, everyone knows that it's only the truth that hurts. So Wilson just rolled his eyes, shook his head disappointedly, and snorted quietly.

Jefferson glanced over at Wilson, waiting for the objection. He was relieved when it didn't come, because he would have had to sustain it.

Not hearing any objection, Queenan continued. "Now, having cleared that up, let me address all of the other factual inaccuracies of the D.A.'s opening argument. As I do, I want you to consider why it is that you're being misled. Why does it seem that the D.A. and his police squad are so hell-bent on convicting this boy, that they will lie and obfuscate to see it happen?"

Wilson rolled his eyes again and re-crossed his legs. He was determined not to object. It was a dangerous strategy, he knew, to let Queenan run amok in front of the jury like this. But Wilson felt strongly that two things would necessarily happen if he did. First, Queenan's lack of subtlety would eventually alienate the jury, who would realize that Queenan thought they were stupid. Second, Wilson was convinced that if allowed to spew whatever invective and hyperbole he wanted, unchecked, Queenan would eventually say something incredibly stupid that would hang himself, and his client.

When no objection came this time, Jefferson recognized Wilson's oratorical rope-a-dope for what it was. It infuriated him because he saw immediately that it could be effective. He had to restrain himself from interjecting though, because his doing so would only make Wilson's strategy even more effective. It would show that Wilson could care less about Queenan's wild accusations because they were so silly as to not require response, and that what Queenan was saying was so outside the bounds of decency and decorum that the judge had to rebuke him on his own initiative.

With no roadblocks from either the D.A. or the judge, Queenan started to get rolling.

"First, and foremost, the D.A. deliberately failed to tell you that Darnell and Kelly were very much in love. You will hear from fellow students of theirs at the University of Pennsylvania, who will tell you that Darnell and Kelly were inseparable in the months leading up to her unfortunate death.

"You will hear from other witnesses who were present in the dining hall that night that Darnell told Kelly he loved her, and that he left the table first. They will tell you that it was Kelly who ran after Darnell and that they embraced and kissed. As for this person who will supposedly tell you that Darnell 'chased' Kelly? The D.A. is deliberately creating a false perception. Kelly was not running because she was afraid. She was running because she was horsing around. She wanted him to chase her.

They were laughing and smiling the whole time. She wanted him to come back to her room. And that's what he did.

"Now, let's talk about this supposed rape. Darnell and Kelly made love that night. It was consensual, and it was loving. There was no rape, and the medical examiner will not be able to tell you that it was rape. What he will tell you is that there were abrasions found on the inside of Kelly's vagina, and that based on the fact that she was later murdered, he assumes that she was raped by the person she had sex with.

"Again, I urge you not to forget what I said about prejudices and preconceptions. It was exactly because Darnell is all too familiar with the prejudices and preconceptions of the Philadelphia Police force that his first instinct was to lie about having had sex with Kelly. Here it is, 5:30 in the morning, and a detective rousts him out of bed, demanding to know if he had sex the night before with the white daughter of another Philly cop."

Queenan looked directly at juror number three, a middle-aged black engineer from South Philly. "What would you have said?" Number three just raised his eyebrows as if to acknowledge a point well-taken.

Queenan began to stroll slowly back and forth in front of the box. "Ladies and gentlemen, this is a sad story all around. Kelly Ryan was a very lonely, depressed girl whose family situation was very unfortunate. Her mother and older brother had been killed in a car accident when she was just a little girl. She was very nervous about being in a relationship with Darnell, afraid of being in love with anyone for that matter. Because of that fear, she had remained a virgin until the time she fell in love with Darnell.

"The night she was unfortunately later murdered, Kelly Ryan made love for the first time. The abrasions that the medical examiner will tell you about are one hundred percent consistent with those one would normally expect to see when a narrow vaginal canal such as the deceased had, is penetrated for the first time. I will present the testimony of Dr. Vincent Curran, a Board Certified gynecologist, who examined the reports of the medical examiner, and who will tell you that the deceased was in fact not raped at all."

Queenan began walking towards his table and didn't stop until he was standing directly behind Darnell's chair, and had both hands resting on his shoulders. "Now, you're going to hear from a lot of witnesses in this case, on both sides. None, however, will be more important than this young man right here.

"Darnell is going to tell you himself that he loved Kelly Ryan with all of his heart. He will tell you himself that for a short time before her death, Kelly had become scared because she loved Darnell and was afraid he would leave her the way her mother and her brother had left her. That night at dinner, Darnell will tell you that he simply told Kelly that he loved her, and that she should take her time in deciding what she wanted to do. When he left, she began to cry, and then she ran after him. When she caught up with Darnell up campus, she hugged him and kissed him.

"They then walked up campus, hand-in-hand, until they reached the point where he would go towards his apartment, or she towards hers. Kelly then asked Darnell to come back to her apartment with her. She very happily and very playfully told him to try and catch her as she ran to the front steps of her building. Ask yourselves why this supposed witness, who will apparently tell you that she saw a six foot eight black man chasing a tiny little white girl down a street in the middle of West Philadelphia, didn't call the police? Or didn't try and help her? The answer is because she knew that what she was seeing was two people kidding around, not a girl in any danger.

"Again, ask yourselves why the D.A. is trying to paint that picture for you?"

Queenan came back around the table and approached the box. "The fact is, Darnell left Kelly's apartment at approximately 10:30 PM that night when she was very much alive. They had plans to eat breakfast together the next day. The reason he left, ladies and gentlemen, is because at around that time, Kelly received a telephone call. Whoever was on the phone was obviously someone Kelly knew, because the person on the other end said that they were coming over. Darnell will tell you that Kelly was not happy that this person was coming, but acted as if she had no choice in the matter. She asked Darnell to leave. Her last words to him were 'I love you too.'

"The person who called Kelly that night, ladies and gentlemen, was a man named Joseph Fullem."

Wilson gritted his teeth. He knew what was coming, but steeled himself from making any objections. He wanted the jury to hear Queenan's crazy conspiracy theory and see it for what it was…crazy. Once Queenan came up empty on his promise to prove his conspiracy, the jury would hold it against him. Or so Wilson hoped.

"You may recognize that name because Fullem is something of a legend in this town. He's a giant of a man physically, who was kicked off the Philadelphia Police force fifteen years ago after a series of brutal, racist attacks against black suspects. He stabbed one unarmed black man to death, and he methodically beat another brother named Frank Cheeseboro almost to the same fate. That second incident was caught on videotape, and Fullem is clearly heard calling Cheeseboro a 'filthy nigger' as he breaks literally every bone in the man's body."

Jefferson was aghast, not just at Queenan's audacity, but at Wilson's refusal to object. None of what Queenan was saying was remotely relevant. The judge knew it was certainly within his authority to stop Queenan without an objection, but, as he ashamedly had to acknowledge to himself, he didn't want to.

"Joseph Fullem is the best friend and former partner of Kelly Ryan's father, detective John Ryan." Queenan looked over at Ryan, whose red face and twitching legs betrayed his unspoken fury.

"We know that it was Fullem who had called because earlier in the evening, when they had arrived at the apartment, Kelly's roommate told…

"Objection!" said Wilson as he thrust himself from his seat. This one he couldn't let go. "May we approach, Your Honor?"

Jefferson waved them forward and turned on the white noise machine to drown out what was being said at sidebar. "Glad to see you're paying attention, Mr. Wilson," said the judge sarcastically as the two lawyers arrived at the side of the bench.

Wilson ignored it. "Judge, Mr. Queenan is about to tell the jury what Anita Levine said in her statement to the police. As the court is well aware, Ms. Levine is out of the country, and is deliberately avoiding a subpoena to testify in this case. The only way that statement comes in therefore is through hearsay testimony. Mr. Queenan should not be allowed to slip it in during his opening when he knows there is no way it comes into evidence."

"Mr. Queenan, what do you have to say for yourself?"

Queenan smiled. "Judge, I agree with the D.A. that the witness is unavailable. However, she testified under oath at the preliminary hearing that what she said in that statement is true and accurate. Therefore, it's not only admissible as a prior-recorded statement, but it qualifies as a prior-recorded statement under oath, which, as your Honor knows, comes in for the truth of the matter asserted."

Wilson just shook his head in lieu of a response. Jefferson mistook it to mean that the D.A. was acknowledging that Queenan's argument was legitimate.

The judge arched his eyebrows at the unexpectedly cogent argument from Queenan. "Overruled. Step back."

"As I was saying," continued Queenan back in front of the jury, "when Kelly and Darnell came home that night, Anita Levine…that's Kelly's roommate, whom Mr. Wilson also neglected to tell you about…told Kelly that her father's friend Joe had called and that he would call her back later that evening.

"That's what he did. He called her later and told her he was coming over.

"And that was when Kelly told Darnell to leave. She knew that Fullem is a violent racist, and that if he found Darnell in Kelly's room, he would do to Darnell exactly what he had done to Frank Cheeseboro. He must have seen Darnell leave though, that we can be sure of. That's why Kelly Ryan was killed."

Wilson was steaming, but he couldn't object now. He'd let it go on too long. He also had no choice but to dismiss Queenan's claim of a second call from Fullem as untrue or irrelevant.

"Mr. Wilson didn't mention a word to you about Joseph Fullem, did he, ladies and gentlemen?" Juror number nine nodded no.

"Ask yourselves why not. He also didn't tell you that Fullem's fingerprints were found in Kelly's room. Ask yourselves why he didn't tell you that."

Queenan started to walk back towards his seat. "You know," he said with his back still to the jury, "I don't blame the D.A. for asking you to leave your prejudices and your preconceptions outside of this courtroom." He turned to face them one more time.

"Hell, that's the only way he can hope to win this case."

*   *   *   *

Judge Jefferson adjourned the case for the day after openings. He had several other minor matters on his docket that had to be disposed of and he didn't want to interrupt the presentation of evidence to do it.

The reporters and talking heads were abuzz with criticisms of the lawyers. Former prosecutors called Wilson's opening 'deplorable' and 'weak', and criticized him for not objecting to virtually all of Queenan's opening. Former defense lawyers called Queenan's argument 'over the top' and 'a stretch,' and criticized him for so blatantly playing the race card.

Wilson went back to his office and ignored the stack of mail on top of his desk. Since he'd begun preparing in earnest for the trial about a month and a half before, he had turned the day-to-day operation of the office to his assistants. It was a testament to the strength of his people that the office had not missed a beat.

Sciolla followed him in. "John Ryan would like to speak with you," he said as he pulled out his pipe and sat down across from Wilson.

Wilson nodded. "What did you think?"

Sciolla shrugged. "I thought your opening was fine, Ash. You hit all the strengths of our case. We knew what Queenan was going to come with. I'll admit I was a little surprised that he outright accused Fullem of the crime, but other than that, he gave us what we expected. Right?"

Wilson swivelled his chair toward the window. On the street below a gaggle of news vans and reporters swarmed over each other hoping to get some official comment from the office. He certainly didn't have any intention of giving them one. His desire to keep everything he did confidential was also the reason he was trying the case alone, with only Sciolla's full-time help. He wanted no leaks.

The D.A. had to admit that Queenan had done better than he'd expected him to do. He was a dirty player, but he was effective. Because he was so effective, Wilson regretted not having addressed the Fullem issue in his opening.

"What about Queenan saying Fullem called again while Darnell was there. Any truth to that at all?"

Sciolla shrugged. "We checked Fullem's phone records…apartment and cell. The cell phone showed the first call, but there weren't any others after that."

"Okay," said Wilson, satisfied that all of the bases had been covered to refute the argument. "Where's Ryan?" he asked.

"Right outside," said Sciolla as he got up and opened the door so that John Ryan could come into the room.

"John, you okay?" asked the D.A. as Ryan took the chair next to Sciolla's.

Ryan was fuming mad, although not necessarily at Wilson. He'd been prepared for Fullem to be an issue, but he had not expected Queenan to outright accused his friend of the murder.

"I'm fucking incensed, Ash, I'll tell you that much. How can you just sit there and let him spew that fucking nonsense? Don't you think that if you say nothing, the jury'll think you don't disagree?!"

Wilson shook his head and ignored Ryan's challenging tone. "No way, John," he said calmly. "People are wise to these kinds of stunts now. I'm glad that Queenan's already beating them over the head with Fullem. It's a mistake. He's got nothing to back it up with, and when the jury realizes that there is nothing to it, they'll reject it out of hand. What's more, they'll hold it against Queenan that he led them down the primrose path for no payoff, and they'll convict Cooper because of it."

Although Ryan had planned this little scene with Wilson in advance of the trial, he was genuinely outraged at Queenan's accusations. So although his words were rehearsed, they were deeply heartfelt.

"I'll tell you what, Ash," he seethed, "I don't care what happens in that courtroom. There's no way I'm letting that kid walk out of this thing without the death penalty."

"Take it easy, John," said Sciolla soothingly. "Don't go making threats like that. You'll get yourself in trouble."

"Fuck you," said Ryan, who turned and stormed out of the office.

"He's upset," said Sciolla to Wilson, "don't pay any attention to him."

Wilson nodded. "I won't. But keep your eye on him. The last thing we need is for him to do something stupid."

*   *   *   *

Across town, Lionel stood in Queenan's office, admiring the view of Independence Hall, marred as it was by all of the post-911 barricades. In spite of himself, he had to admit that he had been favorably impressed by Queenan's opening. The circumstantial evidence was such that people's perceptions had to be challenged. On the face of it, the Commonwealth's case looked strong, and if believed, Darnell's guilt was obvious. But Darnell needed a lawyer who could somehow convince the jury that everything, and nothing, were both exactly as they seemed.

And he certainly had done that. They had worked well together once Lionel had come to believe that he had no other choice but to support Darnell...and point the finger at Fullem. It had been Lionel's idea to come right out and accuse Fullem in the opening, put the ball in Wilson's court, and see if he would try and hit it. Lionel and Queenan agreed that no matter how Wilson tried to handle their pitch, he could do nothing better than foul it off.

The opening had been just as effective the night before in Queenan's office as it had been in court the next day.

"Well, Lionel," said Queenan as he entered the room, "we're on our way."

Lionel nodded, his eye on the Liberty Bell. He was still incredibly afraid of what might happen, and would be until he heard the words "not guilty."

"I just hope we know where we're going."

"Aw, c'mon, we knocked 'em dead today. Wilson doesn't know what hit him. I wouldn't be surprised if he decides to call Fullem in his case-in-chief now just to refute what I said today. If he does that, that'll be all the proof we need that he's a viable suspect. And that's reasonable doubt right there."

"I hope you're right. I'm not sure that just making the accusation is enough though, especially if Wilson doesn't take the bait and just ignores the whole Fullem angle. We're going to have to put on some evidence that points to Fullem as the killer in our case."

Queenan sighed. He had never loved one of his clients, so he did not fully appreciate Lionel's consternation. But he was getting tired of having to constantly lift the man's spirits.

"Okay, just for the sake of argument, let's say Wilson doesn't address Fullem at all in his case. Easy solution...we put him on as our first witness. That motherfucker'll be on the stand for three days. You heard how much shit Jefferson let me get away with in my opening. The jury now knows all about Fullem. If Wilson tries to object at that point to all of the extraneous bullshit, they'll know he's now scared for them to hear it, and wonder why.

"And if he doesn't object, and continues to let me do whatever I want, we'll convince that jury that Fullem not only killed Kelly Ryan, we'll have 'em convinced he killed JFK and Jimmy Hoffa too."

Lionel was still not convinced. Although he had come to respect Queenan as a trial lawyer, he still doubted that he could cross-examine Fullem as effectively as he would need to.

"I guess you're right," said Lionel, as he turned away from the window. They were still a week away from having to call any witnesses. Lionel decided to just relax for the moment and wait and see what Wilson did with his case.

CHAPTER 27

▼

Wilson's first few witnesses were stage-setters. The first officer to arrive at the apartment after Levine's initial, frantic call to 911; the paramedic who declared her dead at the scene; the landlord of Kelly's building to show the jury a blown-up diagram of the layout of the apartment and the rooms, including the back door to Kelly's room. Their testimony had taken up that second day, with Queenan not doing any damage on cross. The "senior legal correspondents" of the major networks all confirmed that none of these witnesses were crucial to either side's case.

The first witness of day three was a Penn sophomore, a member of the rowing team, who had been eating dinner after practice at the table right next to the one where Darnell and Kelly had sat. His name was Seth Rosenberg, and he had the height and long muscles of a rower. He was a handsome kid with deep blue eyes and shaggy hair, and he was not at all nervous to be in the spotlight. After establishing who he was and how he came to be sitting near Darnell's table, Wilson's examination began in earnest.

"Mr. Rosenberg, how close was your seat to where the defendant was seated?"

"About five or six feet away, I guess."

"Were you close enough to where the defendant and Ms. Kelly were seated that you could hear what was being said between the two?"

"Yes, I could hear what they were saying."

"What did you hear the defendant say?"

"Well, he sat down at Kelly's table and she was like giving him the cold shoulder, because he like wrapped his arms around himself and said 'it feels really cold in here all of a sudden, doesn't it?'"

"What did Ms. Ryan say?"

"Objection! Hearsay," said Queenan from is chair without even looking up from his notepad.

"Res Gestae, Your Honor, it's not offered for its truth," replied Wilson.

"Overruled. Answer the question," said Jefferson to the witness.

"She said that winter might be coming early this year, like she was trying to tell him…".

"Objection!" shouted Queenan loudly so the jury couldn't hear what the witness was saying.

"Sustained."

"Mr. Rosenberg, please confine your testimony to what was said."

Rosenberg sat back in his chair, a little miffed because he was only trying to help. "Okay. She said that winter was coming early this year."

Wilson stood up to ask the next question, anticipating the objection. "Were you able to see as well as hear Ms. Ryan as she spoke?"

"Yes."

"How did she appear to you?"

"Objection! Your Honor, calls for a conclusion."

Jefferson peered over his spectacles at Wilson. "Mr. Wilson?"

"Judge, the question certainly calls for a conclusion, but it's one any lay witness is capable of making. I could lay a foundation to establish that Mr. Rosenberg has actually seen human beings interact with one another before, and thus has a basis upon which to draw a conclusion about a person's body language, but I do not want to waste the court or the jury's time."

This was why Jefferson hated speaking objections. He fixed Wilson with an icy stare. "Please confine your arguments, sir, to the law. Objection overruled. Answer the question."

Rosenberg sat forward in his chair and leaned into the microphone. "She appeared to not want Darnell to be sitting there."

"Objection!" shouted Queenan from his seat.

"Overruled."

"What else did the defendant say?" asked Wilson.

The witness was starting to feel comfortable. "Well, he got up to leave, because of the way she was acting, I guess…"

"Sustained," said Jefferson as Queenan rose from his chair. "Mr. Rosenberg," said the Judge patronizingly, "I remind you to confine your answers to the questions that are asked of you. Don't tell us what you think, tell us only what you saw. Understand?"

The witness' face reddened. "Yes, sir, I'm sorry." The boy turned back to Wilson. "Darnell got up to leave, and he was crying, and he said, 'I love you, Kel, please call me. And then he walked away."

"And did Ms. Ryan say anything?"

"No."

"Thank you, Mr. Rosenberg. I have no further questions, Your Honor."

Queenan jumped up from his chair and stood between the two lawyer tables. "Mr. Rosenberg, you came to the police and offered your assistance to them about two months after my client was arrested, isn't that right?"

Rosenberg leaned in again. "Um, I don't really remember when it was."

"Oh," said Queenan, "well was it the day after the murder that you contacted them?"

"No."

"Was it some period of time after Darnell had been arrested?"

Queenan's aggressive attitude was making the youngster nervous. "Um, yes, I believe it was."

"That was helpful of you," said Queenan sarcastically. "Do I take it then from the fact that you waited until well after Darnell was arrested, that you placed absolutely no significance on what you heard at the time you heard it?"

Rosenberg looked to Wilson briefly for help. "I'm not sure I understand what you mean."

"Oh, okay, well let me explain it to you, son," said Queenan as he inched closer to the witness stand. "You found out that Kelly Ryan had been murdered the day after it happened, right?"

"That's right."

"And you didn't go to the police that day to tell them what you heard, right?"

"No, I didn't," said Rosenberg.

"So therefore, in your mind, nothing you heard or saw made you think 'Oh, wow, I heard Darnell say this last night, I bet he did it', right?"

"Um, I guess not," said Rosenberg with another glance towards Wilson.

"In fact," said Queenan more loudly, "the only reason you came forward at all was because you wanted to get on television, isn't that right?"

"Objection. Argumentative," said Wilson.

Queenan turned towards Jefferson. "Your Honor, it is not an argumentative question, and if the court will permit me some latitude, you will see that my question goes directly towards this witness' credibility."

"Go ahead, Mr. Queenan," said the Judge, who was interested in hearing where the defense lawyer was going.

"Didn't you tell your girlfriend just the other night that you were anxious to testify because you want to pursue a career in acting after college and that being a witness in this case would get you on the cover of every magazine and newspaper in the country?"

Rosenberg looked genuinely shocked by the question, with his mouth literally hanging open. Ironically, it was this expression that was plastered on the cover of every magazine and newspaper in the country the next day. He couldn't believe his girlfriend would betray him like that.

When Rosenberg didn't answer right away, Queenan hammered him. "C'mon, Mr. Rosenberg, a whole bar full of people heard her say it, you're not really going to deny it now are you?"

"Objection," said Wilson. He was surprised, but not shocked. Something like this always happens at every trial.

"Overruled," said Jefferson, trying to hide his excitement that Queenan was about to score major points with the jury. "Answer the question."

Rosenberg shifted in his seat. "I was only kidding around," he said quietly.

"Well I'm not laughing, Mr. Rosenberg. It is true that you want to be an actor, right?"

"Yes."

"Well, you've done a nice job today acting like you're telling the truth."

"Objection!" shouted Wilson.

"Sustained," said the Judge with disgust, and a sidelong glance at Lionel. Jefferson wished the much more distinguished lawyer sitting quietly taking notes next to Cooper was the one trying the case. Queenan's lack of subtlety really prevented him from making the most of a good opportunity. "Mr. Queenan, ask a question."

"After Darnell left the table, Kelly got up and ran after him, didn't she?"

Rosenberg was angry for having been embarrassed, and he wasn't about to agree with anything Queenan said, even if it was true. "I don't know where she went when she left. And I certainly didn't see her running." It was the first conscious lie he had told.

"Darnell didn't seem angry when he was speaking to Kelly, did he?"

Rosenberg now wanted to damage Queenan's case. "I would say he appeared hurt, like a spurned lover."

"Objection, non-responsive," said Queenan, annoyed that he was losing control of the witness.

"Overruled," replied Jefferson before Wilson could argue. "You asked how Mr. Cooper seemed, Mr. Queenan. Just because you didn't like the answer, doesn't mean it wasn't responsive to the question."

Jefferson loathed embarrassing lawyers in front of the jury, but Queenan was really pissing him off. He was going to get Cooper convicted on the strength of his own incompetence, regardless of the evidence, and Jefferson wanted to reign him in to try and stop it from happening.

Recognizing finally that he was only losing whatever points he'd scored, Queenan backed off. "No further questions," he said, breaking the cardinal rule that you never end an examination on a sustained objection, especially your own.

"Any redirect, Mr. Wilson?" Jefferson asked.

Wilson stood up. "Just one question, sir. Mr. Rosenberg, have you told this jury the truth today?"

Rosenberg nodded forcefully. "Yes, totally."

"I'm satisfied, Your Honor. I have no further questions."

Only Lionel's firm hand on Queenan's thigh prevented him from getting up and asking more stupid questions. "No further questions," he said glumly from his seat.

After Rosenberg was excused, the court took a fifteen minute break. Because that wasn't enough time to take Darnell back to a cell, Queenan, Lionel and their client congregated in a conference room behind the courtroom.

"You ignorant fool!" hissed Lionel at Queenan when the door was closed.

Queenan smirked back at his employer. "Hey, screw you. I got what I needed to get out of that kid. The jury ain't buyin' what he's selling. He didn't hurt us, and that was the point."

Lionel could barely contain his anger, both at Queenan for his stupidity, and at himself for sticking with the imbecile.

"No, that's not the point, genius. You had an opportunity there to make the Commonwealth's witness look like a liar. Your whole theory is that this prosecution is based on the fact that Darnell is black, that he wouldn't even be a suspect if he were white. You just had the chance to make hay on that argument with Rosenberg's testimony, but all you threw was the haymaker."

Lionel began to pace the room around his suddenly quiet co-counsel. "You know, you remind me so much of all the homies I used to play hoops against in the playground when I was a kid. They could be losing a game by fifty points, but all they cared about was getting off a cool dunk or dribbling the ball behind their back or making some other flashy play. They'd jump up and down and hoot and holler with excitement and fall all over themselves congratulating each other, all the while the other team's out there making their lay-ups and their short little jump shots that win games."

Lionel walked up to Queenan and towered over him. "Listen up, asshole. I don't give a shit how you look. Start taking the lay-ups and stop trying to do a fancy dunk every play. Got it?"

Queenan may have been a fool, but he was no dummy. He knew Lionel was right, so much so that he didn't even feel the need to point out to Lionel that what he had just said was blatantly racist. He had blown a golden opportunity with Rosenberg because he'd been impatient. "I got it, Lionel," he said, properly chastised. "It won't happen again."

Darnell didn't say a word. Although he too agreed that Queenan had not done as good a job as he could on cross with Rosenberg, he liked the fact that Queenan was swinging for the fences, and didn't want to him to lose that aggressiveness.

When court resumed, Wilson called Janet Kegler to the stand. Kegler was one of the night cleaning crew at Steinberg-Dietrich Hall, where the famous Wharton School of Business was located, in the heart of campus on Locust Walk. She testified that she had just gotten off her bus at 40th and Spruce Street when she saw Darnell chasing after some white girl.

"So you recognized the defendant?" Wilson asked.

The older black lady blushed. "Oh, yeah, I would recognize that boy anywhere. I'm a big fan of his." She smiled over at Darnell, to let him know she was on his side.

Wilson ignored the look. "Was the girl you saw running away from the defendant?"

"Well," she hesitated, "that's hard to say. They might have been horsing around."

Her answer to this question had been different during the prep sessions. But Wilson was unfazed. He had fully expected Kegler to go south on him. The D.A. reached into the thick, three-ring binder that lay on his table in front of him and pulled out a one-page document. He pretended to be reading it for a second, then looked up at Kegler with a look of feigned confusion. "Mrs. Kegler, do you remember giving a statement to the police about what you saw that night?"

The witness nodded. "Yes."

"Do you remember telling the police that the girl was running away from the defendant when you saw them?"

"Objection. Judge, Mr. Wilson is impeaching his own witness."

Wilson looked at the judge as if to say 'so what?'

"Overruled. Answer the question."

"Yes, I did say that then. It's just that now that I look back on it, they were probably just kidding around."

The D.A. returned to his seat. "Ma'am, have you had a chance to watch any of the television coverage of the trial so far?"

"Just the first day," she said nervously.

"You don't want to see the defendant convicted, do you, ma'am?" Wilson asked sweetly.

"Objection," shouted Queenan. "The District Attorney is now arguing with his own witness."

"Overruled," sighed the Judge.

Mrs. Kegler, missing the point entirely, turned towards the jury. "No, I most certainly do not want to see that young man convicted of anything," she said earnestly.

Wilson smiled. "Nothing further."

He had gotten what he wanted from her, which was to introduce her statement into evidence so he could use it in his closing argument. Every question of every witness had been pre-scripted, and all were designed to elicit some fact that Wilson would ultimately argue to the jury showed Cooper's guilt. The fact that this older black lady was so obviously changing her story to help Darnell was yet one more nugget the D.A. planned on including in his close. He wanted the jury to be embarrassed by her behavior, and see Kegler as representative of what Queenan would not so subtly ask them to do.

Queenan remained in his seat, sensing that he had to distance himself from Kegler physically if he was going to be able to reestablish her credibility.

"Mrs. Kegler," he asked somberly, "when you saw Darnell running after Ms. Ryan, were you able to see either of their faces?"

Kegler shook her head. "No, sir, they were running away from me."

"So you don't know if they were smiling or not, correct?"

"That's right."

"Were you able to hear if they were saying anything as they ran?"

Kegler scrunched her face in thought. "No, I was about half a block away when I saw Darnell."

"So you don't know if they were laughing, correct?"

"No, I don't," she said.

Queenan now stood up at his table. "Mrs. Kegler, do you carry a cell phone around with you?"

She was surprised by the question. "Why yes I do."

"Did you have it with you that night?"

She smiled. "I always have it with me. My husband worries about me working at night."

"You didn't call the police when you saw Darnell and Ms. Ryan running down the street, did you?"

Again she shook her head. "No, I did not."

"And that's because you did not think there was any danger to the girl based on what you saw, isn't that right, ma'am?"

She was beginning to catch on to Queenan's lead. "That's right."

Queenan pretended to leaf through some notes on the table. "In fact, you never called the police to tell them what you saw that night, did you?"

"No, they came to me."

"Could you explain that?"

She shifted her weight in her seat and leaned back. "Well, about a month and a half ago, detective Sciolla came knocking on my door. He said that he found out I always get off the 37 bus at 9:13 every weeknight at the corner of 40th and Spruce. He wanted to know if I knew who Darnell Cooper was, and whether or not I had seen him chasing some poor white girl down the street that night. I told him what I've told everybody here today, and he wrote up that statement that Mr. Wilson showed me, and I signed it."

"At the time you saw Darnell running down the street, you didn't think he was chasing that girl to do her harm, did you?"

Kegler shook her head vigorously from side-to-side. "Oh, no sir. He's a good boy."

Again she smiled at Darnell, who couldn't help but return it.

"No further questions." Queenan sat down. Lionel's admonition had settled him down nicely. He had been sorely tempted to ask Kegler why it was that Detective Sciolla forced her to sign a statement he knew to be misleading, and why the D.A. was relying on that misleading information to charge Darnell with murder. But instead, he just took the lay-ups, content to wait until closing arguments to slam it down Wilson's throat.

"Brief redirect, Your Honor," said Wilson. "Mrs. Kegler, you said to Mr. Queenan that you don't believe, based on what you saw, that the defendant intended to do any harm to Ms. Ryan, right?"

"Yes, sir."

"So, if it had been some other individual, someone you didn't know and admire, chasing Ms. Ryan down the street, would you have thought differently?"

"Objection, calls for speculation and it's leading," said Queenan.

"Overruled. Answer the question," said the Judge.

"I don't know," said Mrs. Kegler with a nervous glance at Queenan. "I would only be speculating."

Wilson had to stop himself from snorting sarcastically. "Nothing further, your honor. Thank you, Mrs. Kegler."

Although Queenan had made some valid points, Wilson still felt he would be able to argue that what Kegler saw was not horsing around, but a prelude to murder. The fact that she didn't call the police could easily be chalked up to the fact that she either did not want to believe that Darnell Cooper could be doing something wrong, or that she simply didn't want to get him in trouble. Either way, she had been an effective witness for the Commonwealth.

The D.A. was no longer troubled with arguing that Cooper had been chasing and stalking Kelly into her apartment that night, even though it was at odds with the way Anita Levine had characterized what she had seen in her conversation with Sciolla. The evidence that was available was only Levine's written statement. If it turned out that the girl's actual presence might have benefitted Cooper, that was tough shit as far as Wilson was concerned.

Cooper's own lawyer was to blame for Levine's absence, and it was only by his design that the statement was all they had. If Cooper was made to look more guilty than less by virtue of his lawyer's tactics, then he should have chosen a better lawyer.

The lunch recess the judge called after Kegler's testimony was welcomed because it gave Wilson and Sciolla a chance to go over his testimony one more time. He would be Wilson's afternoon witness.

"Remember, we're not going to deal with the Fullem bullshit at all if possible," said Wilson. The stack of unopened mail on his desk was almost as tall as his youngest son. Both had been equally neglected since he'd begun preparing for trial in earnest.

"You sure we don't want to just deal with Fullem up front? I mean, what are we afraid of?" asked Sciolla between puffs on his pipe.

Wilson rocked back in his chair. "C'mon, Tone, we've been over it. Our case is exceedingly simple and short. We only muddy the waters unnecessarily if we try and head off every racial innuendo Queenan's going to make. Plus, we only lend the whole Fullem line of reasoning credibility by talking about it. If we make Queenan do everything in his case-in-chief though, the jury will realize that he's just using it to distract them. Trust me, in the end, they'll hold it against him."

Sciolla smiled at his friend and shook his head. "You're the boss, Ash. I just hope that jury deserves all the faith you have in them."

Wilson laughed. "Me too, buddy, me too."

An hour later, his pipe tucked safely in the inside pocket of his tattered sport coat, and his white sweat socks showing at the bottoms of his khaki trousers, Sciolla settled himself into the witness stand. After establishing his experience as a detective, Wilson got down to business.

"Detective, were you assigned to investigate the death of Kelly Ryan?"

"Yes, I was," said Sciolla.

"As part of your investigation, did you interview Kelly's roommate?"

"I did."

"May I approach the witness, your Honor?" Wilson asked Jefferson, who nodded yes.

The D.A. showed Queenan what was in his hand and then walked over to Sciolla. "Detective, I'm showing you what's been marked as Commonwealth's exhibit 14. Could you identify this document for the jury."

Sciolla put on his glasses and pretended to read. "This is the two-page statement I took from Anita Levine, who was Kelly's roommate, about two hours after the body was found."

In light of Queenan's opening argument to the jury, Wilson had decided to use Levine's statement for all it was worth.

"Now, detective, there are a series of questions, followed by answers on this document. I am going to read the questions that are written, and I would like you to read the answers, okay?"

"Sure."

"Question: What time did Kelly come home last night?"

"Around 9, 9:30."

"Question: was she alone?"

"No. She came in with Darnell Cooper, the basketball player."

"Question: was that unusual?"

"Yes and no. It was unusual in that Kelly had never had anyone over as a guest before, guy or girl. It was not unusual in the sense that everyone knew that she and Darnell had been seeing a lot of each other."

"Question: did they appear to be fighting?"

"Not then, although Kelly seemed a little nervous."

"Question: how did Darnell appear?"

"Normal."

"Question: where did they go?"

"They went into Kelly's room and closed the door."

"Question: Does anyone else live with you two on the first floor?"

"No. There's my bedroom at one end of the hall, and Kelly's at the back of the house. There's a hall bathroom and a kitchen."

"Question: did you have any conversation with Kelly or Darnell before they entered the bedroom?"

"I told Kelly that a friend of her father's named Joe had called earlier, and that he said he would call her back later tonight."

"Question: what happened after Kelly and Darnell went into her bedroom?"

"I didn't really hear anything for awhile. Then it sounded like they were having sex, then Kelly screamed 'don't you touch me,' then she called him a 'motherfucker.' There was a loud thump. Then it was quiet."

"Question: did you see Darnell leave?"

"No."

"Question: Is it possible that he left by the front door and you didn't see him?"

"No. My door was open the whole time and I was studying in a chair right by my door. I would have seen him if he had left that way."

"Question: what did you do after you heard the loud thump?"

"Nothing at first. Kelly is a very private person. I do not know her very well. I did not want to intrude. After a while, I did not hear anything, so I went and knocked on her door. There was no answer. I thought that they might be sleeping. For some reason I knocked again, louder. When they did not answer I opened the door just a crack. That is when I saw her laying there. I called the police."

"Question: is there anything else you would like to add?"

"I would like to say that I am sorry for not calling the police sooner."

Sciolla lowered the document. "Detective, did Ms. Levine have the opportunity to read over that completed statement and sign it?"

"Yes, she did. She initialed and signed both pages."

"As a result of your interview with Ms. Levine, what did you do next in the course of your investigation?"

Sciolla shifted his weight so he could directly at the jury. "At approximately 5:30 AM that morning, I, along with two unformed officers of the University of Pennsylvania Police Department, went to the campus apartment of the defendant. The defendant let me inside and I informed him that Kelly had been raped and murdered."

"How did he react?"

"He was upset, visibly agitated."

"What did you do next?"

"I asked the defendant to come with me to the station so that we could collect a sample of his blood and hair. He agreed. While en route in my car, I asked the defendant if he had been with Kelly the night before. He said yes and admitted that he'd been inside her apartment until at least 10:30. He was also very adamant in that he wanted me to know that he loved Kelly very much and that he would never do anything to hurt her. I asked him if he and Kelly had had sex the night before. He said no."

"Were you able to collect hair and blood samples from the defendant?"

"We have a registered nurse technician at the station who took blood and a hair sample. I secured the samples in sealed evidence containers and transported them both myself to the Pennsylvania State Police Crime Lab in Lima."

"Did you interview any other witnesses besides Ms. Levine?"

"Yes, I interviewed several other students who saw the defendant and Kelly at dinner and on campus as they headed back to her apartment. I also performed canvasses of the neighborhood over the course of the next three weeks interviewing all of the neighbors."

"At any point did you receive information from any witness that led you to believe anyone other than the defendant had been in the room with Kelly the night she was killed?"

"No."

Queenan jumped up. "Objection. Hearsay your Honor."

Jefferson peered over his glasses. "Too late Mr. Queenan, he already answered the question."

"No further questions, your Honor," said Wilson.

"Mr. Queenan, you may cross-examine," said the judge.

Queenan jumped up from his chair. "Detective, take a look again at C-14. That statement that is recorded there, that's all your handwriting, isn't it?"

"Yes it is," said Sciolla.

"Do I take it therefore that you would write the question, and then write the answer that was given?"

"That's about right."

"So this is not a word-for-word recitation of the conversation you had with Anita Levine?"

"No, sir, it is not."

"So you only wrote down what you thought was important?"

Sciolla shook his head no. "I wrote down the answer to the questions that were posed. I may have paraphrased certain things here or there. You've got to understand, this girl was extremely upset and this statement was taken over the course of a couple of hours while she was composing herself. In the end though, she did read what was written and confirmed that everything that was written was accurate."

Queenan held up his hand to show that Sciolla had misunderstood where he was going. "I don't mean to suggest that anything in this statement is inaccurate, Detective. What I am suggesting is that it is incomplete. The fact is, Anita Levine told you that Darnell had very clearly been invited into Kelly's room, didn't she?"

"Objection! Hearsay." Shouted Wilson.

"Overruled," said Jefferson. He wanted the jury to hear everything, especially if it was helpful to Darnell.

Sciolla and Wilson exchanged surprised glances at the ruling. "Yes," he said, "she told me that."

"Funny that you decided to leave that out of the statement," said Queenan.

"Objection. Argumentative."

Jefferson was happy to sustain this objection, as the damage had already been done.

"Now, you told Mr. Wilson that nothing you came across in your investigation suggested to you that anyone else was in that room on the night of the murder, is that correct?"

"That is what I testified to, yes."

"Well, correct me if I'm wrong, but didn't you find the fingerprints of a man named Joseph Fullem inside that room?"

"No sir, I did not. I did not do any processing at the scene."

Queenan smirked. "Okay, but you know that Fullem's fingerprints were found, don't you?"

"All I know is what I've read in the report of the crime scene investigators."

Queenan reached into his three-ring binder and pulled out a seven page document. "Your Honor, I'd like to mark this document as Defense Exhibit 1."

"Objection, your Honor," said Wilson almost apologetically as he rose slowly from his seat. "May we approach the bench, sir?"

Jefferson hated sidebar conferences, but he hated speaking objections more.

"What's your objection," he asked with irritation when the lawyers had approached.

"Judge, Detective Sciolla did not prepare the crime scene report. Mr. Queenan is going to be asking him questions about things that appear in the report, and that's hearsay. My crime scene guys will be testifying later on and they will authenticate the report and Mr. Queenan can ask them any questions he wants about what they found. If, after that, he wishes to call Detective Sciolla in his case-in-chief and ask him about those things, he is free to do that. But as it stands now, that report is hearsay.

"In addition, Judge, while we are up here, Detective Sciolla did in fact take a statement from Fullem in the course of his investigation. Any questions about the contents of that statement would also be hearsay. There is no evidence that Mr. Fullem is unavailable as a witness."

Queenan's eyes narrowed. All Wilson was doing was delaying the inevitable, and it was increasingly clear that he was avoiding all mention of Fullem in the Commonwealth's case.

"That's fine, Judge," he said with a dismissive wave, "I'm happy to call Sciolla *and* Fullem in my case. I'd ask that you order the detective to remain under subpoena."

He really could have put up a legitimate fight and probably gotten the judge to allow him to question Sciolla on the report, but it wasn't worth it. He would have to couch everything in a hypothetical, which would make the questioning unwieldy, and more than anything else, he wanted everything about his cross of Sciolla to be streamlined and focused. It was going to be all about Joe Fullem and his checkered history on the police force.

The more he thought about it, Queenan actually saw Wilson's objection as a gift, because now he'd be able to put Sciolla in as a witness in his case wherever it would be most effective, and not have to rely on the jury's ability to remember everything he had said earlier.

"Okay," said Jefferson as the lawyers returned to their seats. "Detective Sciolla you are excused but you remain under subpoena. Do you understand?"

"Yes, sir," said the pudgy detective as he exited the witness box.

"Call your next witness, Mr. Wilson," said Jefferson with a glance at his watch. He knew who the witness would be, and was concerned that they might not finish his testimony that day.

"The Commonwealth calls Dr. Maurice Templeton."

It had been the most excruciating witness prep Wilson had ever conducted. He had spent five straight days browbeating, cajoling, insulting, complimenting, and finally begging, all to get Templeton to testify like a normal human being.

Wilson had discovered two universal qualities in doctors which made them absolutely impossible witnesses. The first was that they all feel they are the smartest participant in every conversation they have. Second, and much worse, was that they also feel the need to prove that fact to whomever they are speaking. Maury Templeton suffered severely from these afflictions. It had taken five days, but Wilson felt somewhat confident that he'd finally convinced Templeton to simply do as he was told.

Wilson spent a considerable amount of time establishing Templeton's qualifications as a board certified pathologist and tendered him as an expert, to which Lionel, who would be handling the cross, had no objection. None had been expected. The problem was not that Templeton was not qualified as a pathologist, it was that he believed himself qualified to be the lawyer as well.

"Doctor, did you have occasion to perform an autopsy on Kelly Ryan's body on October 29th of last year?"

"Yes, I did."

"Based on your examination, were you able to make a determination as to the manner of death?"

Templeton cleared his throat. "Manual strangulation."

"And what was the official cause of death?"

"Asphyxiation," replied Templeton.

Wilson got up from his seat and retrieved from behind him a very large piece of poster board which was covered with a plastic trash bag. He removed the covering to reveal a black and white picture of Kelly Ryan's dead body, from just above the breasts to the head. It was the only picture of the body Jefferson would allow the jury to see, but they were appropriately shocked by the sight, much to Wilson's satisfaction.

John Ryan had been forewarned by Wilson of what was to come, and had been offered the opportunity to leave the courtroom. He stayed.

"Dr. Templeton, showing what's been pre-marked as Commonwealth's Exhibit 15, does this show the upper chest, neck and head area of Kelly Ryan's body as it appeared at the time of your autopsy?"

"Yes it does," replied Templeton.

"Does this picture show the external evidence of strangulation?"

"Yes."

Wilson handed the witness a laser pointer. "Please tell the jury, using this picture, what you mean?"

Templeton fumbled with the pointer, even though they had spent hours working with it, but he finally got it to work. He pointed the beam at the neck area of the picture.

"As you can see, there are several disc-like bruises that are consistent with finger-tips here, here and here." He moved the beam higher. "Here, you can see hemorrhages under the skin and bruising of the strap muscles, which are these here. All of these are classic external signs of manual strangulation."

Wilson sat back down. "What other signs, if any, did you find of manual strangulation?"

"Your Honor," interjected Lionel before the witness could answer, "if counsel is finished asking questions related to C-15, I'd ask that it be taken down."

Jefferson was only too happy to have the picture removed. When it had been, Templeton answered the question.

"In examining the body, I found blueness of the tongue, pharynx, and larynx, as well as damage to the superior horns of the thyroid cartilage and the greater horns of the hyoid bones."

"What does all that mean, doctor?"

"Well, essentially, it means that her throat was crushed, that oxygen was prevented from getting to her brain, and she died as a result."

Wilson was glad Lionel had asked him to take the picture down, because it gave him an excuse to parade it back in front of the jury when he needed it again. "Based on the bruising that you saw, were you able to draw any conclusions about the person who caused them?"

Lionel intentionally did not object, even though these conclusions were not proper. It was actually because they were improper conclusions to make that he wanted Templeton to testify about them.

"Um, yes," said the pathologist as he picked up the laser pointer. These bruises were caused by an individual with extremely large hands, as you can plainly see from the circumference of each individual bruise. The person was also obviously very powerful, because there appears to have been only one hand used to commit the strangulation, and given the level of damage to the bones in Kelly's throat, this person would have to have been extremely strong."

"What other observations did you make about the portion of the body shown in C-15"?

Templeton pointed the beam at Kelly's mangled jaw. "As you can see from the bruising and swelling here, this poor girl's jaw was badly broken. The fact that some swelling occurred tells me that this happened shortly before she was killed. I say shortly because given the level of the fracture, one would expect to see considerably more swelling than actually occurred. The heart had obviously stopped pumping blood soon after the break occurred, and thus only a minimal amount of swelling is seen."

Wilson took the picture down without being told this time. Templeton was doing well, and he wanted to keep it simple and short.

"Did you perform a physical examination of Ms. Ryan's genital area, Doctor?"

"Indeed I did," said Templeton as he sat back in his chair and folded his legs.

"Tell us what you did and what your examination revealed."

"Well, I physically inspected the vagina and vaginal canal for any damage associated with rape. I was able to see, very plainly, abrasions and fissures inside the canal, which are classic signs of rape." Templeton got more comfortable in his chair, holding on to the lapels of his lab coat as he continued.

"Having found these objective signs of vaginal trauma, I performed what's known as a 'rape kit,' which is utilized to detect semen, blood, hair and fiber evidence. I also used long-wave ultraviolet light that lends a faint fluorescent glow to semen."

"Did these tests help you find anything?"

Templeton nodded with a sly smile. "Oh, yes. I was able to find a rather sizable, microscopically speaking of course, semen sample, which I collected as evidence and had sent to the crime lab for analysis."

"Doctor Templeton, based on your physical examination of Kelly Ryan's body, do you have an opinion, to a degree of scientific certainty, as to whether or not Kelly Ryan had been raped before her death?"

Templeton crossed his legs the other way and glanced at Lionel. "Oh, there's no question that she was. The fissures and abrasions inside the vaginal canal, along with the semen, and the fact that she was brutally beaten and strangled shortly thereafter, all lead me to the rather inescapable conclusion that the deceased had been raped prior to her death."

"And lastly, Doctor, based on your examination, were you able to make a determination as to the time of death?"

Templeton always enjoyed this part of testifying. He felt it made what he did appear truly magical. "In fact I was. I place the time of death between 10:30 and 11:30 in the evening of October 28th."

Wilson sat down. "And how were you able to draw that conclusion?"

Templeton sat forward finally to deliver his lecture and turned towards the jury for the first time. Wilson had instructed him to do this throughout his testimony, but Templeton thought doing it his way would be more effective.

"As we all know," he said in a professorial tone, "the body has a normal temperature of 98.6 degrees. At death, the body's temperature starts to drop by a factor of 3 degrees for the first hour, and a factor of 1 degree each subsequent hour. The body in this case was taken directly to my office for immediate autopsy. At exactly 4:12 a.m. the temperature of the body was 91.6 degrees. This means that death had occurred approximately five hours earlier."

"Were there any other factors which went into your consideration of the time of death?"

"To a lesser extent, the fact that rigor mortis, or stiffening, had not yet set in confirmed that death had occurred between five and six hours earlier, because that is the outside time frame for rigor mortis to occur."

Wilson would normally liked to have dressed up the testimony of the medical examiner in more dramatic fashion, but he was afraid of Templeton. After spending five days in a room with the man, Wilson had gotten everything out of him he needed to get, and nothing that hurt his case. He decided to simply end the direct testimony then, rather than risk Templeton saying something stupid.

"Thank you, Doctor Templeton, I have no further questions for you, sir."

The judge had been told before the trial started that Lionel would be cross-examining Templeton. "Mr. Cooper?"

"Yes, sir, thank you," said Lionel to Jefferson as he closed his notebook and stood at the table.

"Dr. Templeton, my name is Lionel Cooper. I represent Darnell Cooper. Good afternoon, sir."

"Hello," replied Templeton congenially.

"Doctor, you are not a full-time member of the medical examiner's staff, are you?"

"No, I'm not."

"You are in fact 'semi-retired', isn't that right?"

"Yes."

Despite the doctor's body language, Wilson was glad at least to see he was following the D.A.'s advice and answering with as few words as possible.

"And the only reason you were the one who performed the autopsy in this case is because the office was running short-staffed around that time last year, and they asked you to stay on call for any emergencies, right?"

"Well, I don't know if that's entirely correct. I was on call when the request for an autopsy came in, so I performed it."

Lionel came out from behind the table. "But you do agree that this was termed an emergency request—in other words, the D.A.'s office wanted the autopsy done immediately, right?"

Templeton leaned into the mike. "It was certainly an emergency request. Who made it and why it was made I don't really know."

"If it had not been an emergency request, the autopsy would have been performed later that day by an actual member of the medical examiner's staff, wouldn't it?"

Templeton bristled noticeably at the suggestion that he was not an actual member of the M.E.'s office. "No, that is not correct," he said tersely.

"You're 68 years old, are you not, doctor?"

"I am."

"And the last autopsy you had performed before this one was almost three years ago, correct?"

Templeton crossed his legs away from Lionel and towards the jury, to whom he said, "I don't know how long it has been. However, I have been called in to consult on many, many autopsies over the past three years, and have lectured at Hahneman University Hospital to pathology residents for the past fifteen. I certainly know what I'm doing."

Wilson tried not to roll his eyes. He could sense Templeton heading south.

Lionel held up is hand. "Oh, I'm sorry, doctor, I didn't mean to suggest that you aren't qualified. I'm just wondering if maybe you were a little rusty when you performed this autopsy."

Templeton smirked. "I don't think so."

Lionel took two steps towards the witness stand and stopped. "Doctor Templeton, what is a colposcopic examination?"

Templeton sat back in his chair again and offered a dismissive arch of his brow. "A colposcopic exam is one way to document internal damage to the vagina where rape has occurred."

"A colposcopic exam produces actual pictures of any damage, like fissures or tears or abrasions, isn't that right?"

"That's correct."

"You did not perform a colposcopic exam here, did you, doctor?"

Templeton nodded. "No."

"So, rather than being able to show us pictures of the microscopic fissures and abrasions inside the vaginal canal, all we're left with is your word that they were there, right?"

"I suppose so," snorted Templeton.

"And of course, we are prevented from showing any of the evidence that you say you observed to our expert pathologist for that same reason, right?"

"Objection," said Wilson. "Argumentative."

"Sustained," said Jefferson.

"Doctor, are you familiar with the acronyms S.A.N.E. and S.A.R.T.?"

"Yes of course. SA.N.E. stands for sexual assault nurse examiner, and S.A.R.T. stands for sexual assault response team."

"These are technicians and medical professionals who are specially trained in observing, detecting, and recording evidence of rape, right?"

Templeton was getting bored. "Yes, that's right."

Lionel took one more step. "Was either a S.A.N.E. nurse or S.A.R.T team present during the gynecological portion of your exam?"

"No. I didn't need them. I was perfectly capable of detecting all the signs of rape."

Lionel nodded. "I guess we have to take your word for that," he said quietly. "You've been a practicing pathologist for about forty years, is that right?"

"That's right," said Templeton, his chest puffing out unconsciously.

"I would imagine it's difficult, after so many years, to incorporate new technologies into your practice."

"Oh, I disagree. I stay abreast of all the useful advances available and incorporate them whenever I can."

Lionel took one more step forward. He was now about five feet from the witness stand. "I recall from your report in this case that you measured the 'distensibility' of Ms. Ryan's vagina. What does that mean?"

Templeton recrossed his legs in the other direction. "Distensibility is the measurement of the vaginal orifice itself."

"And how did you take that measurement?"

"Well, with my fingers of course," replied Templeton as if it was a silly question.

It probably was a silly question, as it was a common practice to measure distensibility in this fashion. But to the average juror, it would surely seem a bit anachronistic to handle a female body in such a cold way.

John Ryan could not stand to listen anymore. He very noticeably got up from his seat and left the courtroom. Every reporter in the room scribbled furiously.

"How many fingers were you able to pass through the vaginal opening without difficulty?"

Templeton cleared his throat with a cough. "One."

Lionel took one more step. "I take it therefore, that Ms. Ryan had an extremely narrow vaginal opening?"

Templeton thought for a second. He knew where Lionel was going. "You could certainly say that."

"Doctor, Templeton, what is the hymen?"

Templeton sighed. "The hymen is a thin flap of skin inside the vaginal canal that most women have until their first sexual encounter, when it is broken away."

"In other words doctor, the hymen is what gives way when a virgin has sex for the first time?"

"Typically, yes. In many girls, the hymen may give way through participation in rigorous athletics, or masturbation, or simply by every day activity."

"When the hymen is torn away, is there bleeding that can occur?"

"Certainly," said Templeton.

"What is a hymenoscope?"

"It's a device used to measure the size of the hymenal opening."

"You didn't use one of those either, did you?"

"No."

Lionel turned and walked back to his seat. "Doctor, if Kelly Ryan was a virgin, and given the narrow vaginal orifice she had, could the fissures and abrasions that you observed have come from a nervous first-time sexual encounter, entirely consensual, especially with a man who had a very large penis?" Lionel hated the last part of the question, just for the imagery it conjured. But it was necessary to make his point.

Templeton removed his glasses and unconsciously began cleaning them on his lapels. "As I've said before, Mr. Cooper, it's possible, but not likely, given the totality of the evidence."

Lionel nodded. "The totality of the evidence being that this poor girl was eventually beaten and killed on the same night the sexual encounter took place."

"Yes, of course."

"So, you're assuming, doctor, that whoever had sex with Kelly Ryan that night, is necessarily the person who killed her, isn't that right?"

"It's a natural assumption to make, given the timeline."

"So this whole case is based on your assumptions, isn't it?"

"Objection," said Wilson.

"Sustained."

"You used the word 'timeline' a few seconds ago," said Lionel as he gathered his notes in front of him. "What did you mean by that?"

Templeton cleared his throat. "I'm not sure what you mean."

"It was your word, Doctor. What did you mean?"

Templeton glanced at Wilson before answering. "Well, just that given the approximate time of death and the fact that Mr. Cooper had been with the victim very close to that time…

"Aha," said Lionel as he sprang from his seat. "Now we get to the heart of it. You were told before you even looked at the body that Darnell Cooper had been with the decedent earlier in the evening, and that her roommate believed them to have had sex, correct?"

"Objection, hearsay," said Wilson, just to break up Lionel's rhythm.

"Overruled," replied Jefferson.

Templeton glanced at Wilson with an irritated look before answering. "I don't remember."

Lionel's eyes narrowed and he stepped closer to the witness. The Doctor had given him an unexpected opportunity to score even more points than he had expected. "You don't *remember*?" He asked incredulously. "Doctor, you're a sports fan, right?"

Jefferson glanced at Wilson for an objection, but none was forthcoming.

"I enjoy sports, yes."

"In fact, you enjoy sports so much that you're a season ticket holder for the Penn basketball team aren't you?"

"Objection," said Wilson weakly.

"Overruled. Answer the question, Doctor," said Jefferson, who knew the answer by virtue of the fact that Templeton's seats were three rows behind his at the Palestra.

"I do have tickets to the games, but I find that I have less and less time to attend."

Lionel nodded. "But you've been to enough games to know exactly who Darnell Cooper is—I mean, you had watched this boy play basketball on more than a few occasions, had you not?"

"Your Honor," started Wilson, but Jefferson held up his hand to stop him.

"I've seen him play," said Templeton.

"Mmmh-hmm," muttered Lionel with a smirk. "You've seen him play, and you knew prior to the night of this murder, as did even the most casual sports fans in the country, much less Penn season ticket holders, that Darnell Cooper is one of the best college basketball players in the country, didn't you?"

"Objection."

"Overruled. Answer the question."

Templeton leaned forward and folded his hands in front of him. "I was certainly aware of who Mr. Cooper was, yes."

"Thank you, Doctor," said Lionel as he turned to the jury. Still facing them he asked, "So, is it really your testimony that you don't remember being told that the most famous college basketball player in the country, who you've just happened to see play on several occasions, was the prime suspect in the rape and murder of a Penn student upon whom you were about to perform an autopsy?"

Templeton looked to Wilson, who hoped there was not actual steam coming from his ears.

"Well, I guess I was given the information about Mr. Cooper sometime prior to performing the autopsy, but I just don't remember when specifically that was."

Lionel gave the jury a look as if to say, 'whatever,' and returned to his seat. "Just so the jury is clear, Doctor, when you performed your autopsy, you knew that Darnell Cooper was a suspect, correct?"

"Objection, Your Honor. Dr. Templeton never used the word 'suspect,' only defense counsel did," said Wilson in a blatant attempt to coach his witness.

Jefferson peered over his glasses disapprovingly at Wilson. "I will sustain that objection, Mr. Wilson, but I will remind you of this court's feelings about speaking objections."

Ash nodded, accepting the rebuke.

Lionel sighed. "Okay, Doctor, you knew before you performed the autopsy, that Darnell Cooper was last seen with the decedent at or near the time of her death, and that a witness believed them to have had sex, correct?"

"I would say yes, that's correct."

"So when you discovered the bruising patterns on the neck that you described earlier, and saw that they were made by someone with large hands who was very strong, you simply assumed that it had been Mr. Cooper who had left those marks, knowing as you did that Mr. Cooper is a big, strong boy. Isn't that right?"

Templeton sat back and crossed his arms, the absolute worst posture for a witness to take. "I assumed nothing, counselor," he said icily.

"Well, I'm confused then, Doctor Templeton. If you assumed nothing, then why didn't you, or anyone else for that matter, take fingerprints from the decedent's neck?"

"Objection," said Wilson. "May we approach?"

Jefferson waved them forward to the sidebar.

The D.A. spoke first. "First of all, Judge, Doctor Templeton did not process the scene, and that question, if it was proper, should be directed to the crime scene technician. Secondly, Mr. Cooper is well aware of the fact that fingerprints from skin is at best, an experimental and inexact science, which has not been admitted into any court in this jurisdiction. He is creating a false impression in the jury's mind."

Jefferson looked to Lionel. "Well?"

"Your Honor, addressing the first issue, the medical examiner has the authority to order that prints be taken from the skin, and in my opinion, should be able to do so himself. The fact that fingerprint evidence from skin has not been deemed admissible as of this date does not relieve the government from utilizing every tool at its disposal in attempting to catch the real killer, so I think it was a proper question."

Wilson was about to speak again, but Jefferson held up his hand. "No more questions about that subject, Mr. Cooper. Objection sustained. You may step back."

Of course, Lionel didn't care that the objection was sustained. The jury had already heard the question. Not having an answer made it more effective.

Wilson was now stuck. "Your Honor, I request a limiting instruction be given to the jury that they disregard the question, and further, that they be told that it is not possible for fingerprints to be taken from skin in any reliable fashion."

A vision of George Cohen suddenly popped into Jefferson's head as he considered Wilson's request. A ruling either way would not be incorrect.

"Denied," he said with a pang of guilt.

"Any further questions, Mr. Cooper?" Jefferson asked when the lawyers had stepped back to their tables.

"Just one, Your Honor. Doctor, please assume for me that the person who killed Kelly Ryan is someone different than Darnell Cooper. Is it possible that all of the evidence you observed in your genital exam is perfectly consistent with Darnell and Kelly having had a consensual, virginal, sexual encounter?"

Templeton sighed. "As I've said, counselor, anything's possible."

Lionel fought the urge to pound it home in his cross-examination that Templeton had simply made a series of assumptions during his autopsy, and that he considered the evidence only through the prism of those assumptions. But he knew he'd gotten enough that Queenan could argue it in his closing. "I have no further questions."

Wilson eschewed redirect. He'd gotten what he needed from Templeton, and so had Cooper. The rape charge was not really all that important to him. In reality, even though Wilson was convinced that Cooper was guilty, he still did not believe the death penalty was deserved.

But it was his job to seek it. If he lost the rape charge, obviously there would be no aggravating factor, and the death penalty would be removed from the jury's consideration. He was okay with that. The possibility of the death penalty had gotten Wilson the jury he wanted, and that was plenty. As for Templeton's assumptions, they were all reasonable, and Wilson would tell the jury that in his closing.

The Commonwealth's next few witnesses were called simply to establish the chain of custody of the crime scene evidence, especially the semen samples taken from Kelly Ryan's body. Given Jefferson's previous ruling on the fingerprint issue, Queenan had few questions for them, given that their testimony centered mostly on establishing exactly whose fingerprints had in fact been found in Kelly's bedroom. Queenan simply emphasized the fact that Fullem's prints had been one of the sets found.

Given that the scientific evidence would be next, the Judge ended the day's session in order that the jury would have fresh ears and eyes for what was to come.

Not that fresh ears and eyes mattered, given the dryness of the evidence. The next morning, after it had been firmly established that what was taken from the body and what was taken from Darnell had been securely transported to the crime lab, Wilson called the criminalist who had done the DNA testing.

Because Queenan had conceded in his opening that Darnell had in fact had sex with Kelly on the night of her murder, the science wasn't all that important to the Commonwealth's case. Wilson still wanted it in though. He'd tried enough cases to know that juries deliberate as much on what they didn't hear as what they did. He feared that if he didn't put the DNA into evidence, one or more of the jurors would use it as an excuse to say there was reasonable doubt. But it was not easy stuff to process, and there really was no way to make it interesting.

The State Police criminalist very excitedly and exhaustively explained the entire DNA process, about the gels and the Southern Blot, and the A, T, C, and G bases of the DNA strand. He explained how the x-rays of the DNA results which Wilson had blown up on the overhead projector eliminated conclusively the possibility that the semen found at the scene belonged to anyone other than Darnell.

It was lengthy and boring testimony, and rather than have the witness testify about the PCR testing that was done as well, Wilson cut him short by simply asking him what the statistical probability was that some other person could have had the same DNA sequence as Darnell.

"One in three billion," was the answer.

"No more questions," said an exhausted D.A. He could only imagine how the jury felt. The direct testimony alone had taken virtually the entire morning.

Jefferson appeared to have been startled from a daydream by the abrupt end to the direct examination. "Oh, um, you may cross-examine, Mr. Queenan."

Queenan laughed out loud as he stood. "Judge," he bellowed, "I would cross-examine this witness, if I understood a word he said!" He looked straight at the jury and smiled broadly. Jurors number nine and four laughed out loud, nodding their heads to show they too didn't understand a word of the criminalist's testimony.

"I'm sorry, your Honor," said Queenan obsequiously in response to Jefferson's reproachful glare. He jammed his hands in his pants pockets and looked at the jury, but spoke to the witness. "I actually only have a couple of questions, since I think he just spent a great deal of time telling this jury something I already told them...which is that Darnell Cooper made love to Kelly Ryan on the night she was later killed."

"Is there a question in our future, Mr. Queenan?" asked the judge.

Queenan smiled conspiratorially, as if he and the judge were in on a secret.

"Yes, Judge, sorry." He turned to the witness. "Sir, can any of the tests you've talked about here today tell this jury whether or not the semen that was found was left as the result of a consensual sexual act?"

The witness shook his head. "Of course not."

Queenan shook his own head from side to side and returned to his seat. "Well, I guess there's really nothing you can tell us that's of any importance. No more questions."

Wilson smirked at Queenan's gratuitous remark and stood to face the Judge, buttoning his suit coat as he did. "Your Honor, the Commonwealth would move for the admission into evidence of exhibits C-1 through C-27. And with that, the Commonwealth rests."

The Judge adjourned court for the day after that, announcing that the defense would present its first witness the next morning. The early end to the court day meant that millions of people watching at home had to endure the post-mortem by the media and their expert commentators, all of whom were in agreement that Wilson had tried a very boring case. They also agreed that it had been far too short. Everyone had expected an O.J.-like marathon.

One thing that all of the commentators agreed upon however was that as dry and as boring as the evidence had been, it was compelling. Any hopes of Darnell being acquitted, they all said, rested solely on Queenan's ability to make Fullem a viable suspect.

Tony Sciolla agreed with them in at least one respect. "Kind of dry, don't ya' think?" he asked Wilson as they shared a Luigi's pizza back at the office after court.

"Hey, I'm telling Luigi that you said that."

"Funny," said the detective. "Seriously, how do you feel about our case?"

Wilson shrugged as he wiped some marinara sauce from his cheek. "Good, I guess. Let's face it, our case is what it is. There is no eyewitness testimony. Queenan has admitted his boy had sex with her, so the science I wasted so much time on today is pretty irrelevant. This is the rare kind of case where the defense essentially agrees with our evidence, just not our conclusions about it.

"The bottom line is, this case is going to come down to whether or not the jury buys the defense theory that a rogue, racist cop snuck, unseen and unheard, into Kelly's room after she had just finished having consensual sex with Cooper, and killed her. He then somehow managed to sneak back out of the room without being seen. Oh, and by the way, the girl is also the only living child of the man's lifelong best friend. I tell you buddy, if the jury buys that crap, then nothing I did was going to make a damn bit of difference."

Sciolla snorted. "You might have a point. Anyway, one thing's for sure. This trial's about to get a whole lot more interesting."

CHAPTER 28

▼

Fullem knew that Queenan had been trying to serve him with a sub-poena. The process server was a pimply young kid in his twenties who was not very subtle about stalking. It had been easy to avoid the boy. But when Wilson had told Ryan the day before that the Common-wealth's case was about to wrap up the next day, Fullem appeared at the car door of the boy's beat up red camaro, parked conspicuously down the street from Fullem's apartment, and simply asked for his subpoena. Scared shitless by his prey's surprise appearance, the process server literally threw the paper at Fullem, and peeled away.

The subpoena instructed Fullem to come to court the next morn-ing, and remain until excused. "It's me," he said into the telephone when he returned to his apartment. "I got the subpoena. I go in tomor-row."

Ryan had been waiting for his call, but was somewhat surprised that Queenan obviously intended for Fullem to be amongst his first wit-nesses. "Okay," said Ryan, "we still on?" he asked nervously.

Fullem had not slept since the trial had begun, and had been steadily drunk since. "Yeah," he whispered, "we're still on. I owe you, John. Damn right we're still on."

Ryan's eyes began to water. Fullem was so blindly loyal, so devoted to him, that he was almost overwhelmed with his love and appreciation for the man. "Joe," he said haltingly, "I don't deserve a friend like you."

It was Fullem's turn to well up. "Just don't forget the plan," he said over the lump in his throat. "I'll meet you on the corner of Broad and Filbert at 8:55." Fullem hung up so his friend wouldn't hear him sobbing.

They met the next morning as planned. Neither said a word. Together they walked towards the lobby doors of the CJC and the line of people waiting to get in that was snaking out onto the sidewalk. That line of people was waiting to go through a set of metal detectors on the west side of the cavernous lobby. On the East side, a much smaller line was moving more quickly, as it was the line for lawyers and court personnel.

It was the metal detector and x-ray machine at the end of this line which was manned by Donny Moxley, and it was this line Ryan had been using since the trial had started.

"Hey, John, how's it goin'? You hangin' in there?" asked Moxley upon Ryan and Fullem's approach.

Ryan nodded as he placed his leather satchel onto the conveyor belt, and walked through the metal detector, with Fullem directly in front of him. "Yeah, Donny, I'm doin' okay. Thanks for…"

"Gun!" shouted Moxley suddenly, cutting Ryan off.

Just as the shout went out, Fullem was crossing through the metal detector himself. In the rush of officers to the area, no one had heard the beep caused by the .380 automatic tucked securely in Fullem's belt under his light jacket.

Ryan threw his hands up to his forehead as Fullem sidled towards the elevators. "Jeez, Donny, I forgot it was in there! I'm really sorry, man. I haven't even carried that bag in about a month. I totally forgot it was in there."

Donny waved away the other cops who had run over. He reached into the bag and pulled out Ryan's service revolver. "C'mon, John, what are you trying to do, give me a heart attack?" Moxley did not mention the visit he'd received from Sciolla, instructing him to be extra careful with Ryan. "Go put it in a locker before you get me fired."

Ryan took the gun with a melancholy grin, and shook Donny's hand. "Thanks for being so cool about this, Don. I've just had a lot on my mind lately. You know."

Donny nodded and pulled Ryan towards him so he could whisper in his ear. "I know, John, believe me, I know. We all can't wait for that deuce to get the fuckin' needle."

Ryan patted the officer on the back. "Thanks, man, I appreciate that." And he wasn't lying.

*   *   *   *

As Fullem and Ryan entered the building, Lionel and Roger Queenan were already upstairs in a small conference room, waiting for Darnell to be brought down. The jury was not allowed to see him in handcuffs, and every morning before court, and at every recess, the jury was held at bay while Darnell was led in and out of the courtroom. Because there were hundreds of other prisoners being transported, by a handful of sheriff's deputies, it was not uncommon for there to be a long wait.

"You ready for this?" Lionel asked. They had talked for so long about how their defense would be presented, had fought bitterly, and prepared hard. Any chance Darnell had for freedom lay in their hands now. It was an awesome, and fearsome, responsibility, and despite his personal feelings for Queenan, Lionel felt a warrior's kinship with the man as the fight drew near.

Always the bombast, Queenan nodded his head emphatically. "Oh, yeah. We're gonna' knock 'em right out of the water with Fullem, Lionel, I'm telling you. The jury's gonna' hate that motherfucker when I'm done with him."

"Remember, Rog, take lay-ups, especially with Fullem," said Lionel, hoping to quell Queenan's adrenaline just a bit.

Queenan smiled. "I got it, coach. Just call me Larry fuckin' Bird."

At that moment Darnell was led into the room. When his shackles were removed, he hugged Lionel and shook Queenan's hand. He had lost about twenty pounds in jail and he looked gaunt. The media had been commenting throughout the trial that he looked sick, with worry some said.

On this day, he also looked scared.

"Hey, little brother," said Lionel reassuringly, "don't worry. Now's our time to show the world what we've got. Have faith, okay?"

Darnell managed a weak smile. "I do have faith in you guys. It's them out there I don't have a great feeling about."

Queenan walked towards the door. "Well, let's go on in and convince them then."

It took another fifteen minutes for the courtroom to get settled, with John Ryan claiming his customary seat in the front row. When all the lawyers and gallery were in place, Abram Jefferson strode to the bench, waving everybody to sit down as soon as they had all stood up in honor of his presence.

"Mr. Queenan," said Jefferson when he had settled into his own seat, "you may call your first witness."

All of the witnesses had been sequestered from the first day of trial, and Fullem had been instructed by the bailiff not to enter the courtroom until called. He had been pacing outside in the hallway since his arrival twenty minutes earlier. Most of the arriving media recognized him immediately, though none were brave enough to approach and ask for an interview.

Throughout the trial there had been many different police officers watching the trial in a quiet show of support for Ryan. They too recognized Fullem. None of them approached him either. He just looked pissed off, and the cops who knew him were all too familiar with all the bad stuff that could happen when Joe Fullem got mad.

But Fullem wasn't angry, he was actually excited. In his own twisted mind, he felt extremely proud that he was about to do something for

Ryan that no one else in the world could, or would, do for a friend. It never occurred to him to think about how he had arrived in that position in the first place. All Fullem knew for sure was that he was just a few minutes from killing Darnell Cooper in front of the whole world, and he felt good about it. He reached inside his jacket and pulled the gun so that it was loose inside his belt. It would have to be quick, and he didn't want to get snagged up drawing the weapon.

"Your Honor," announced Queenan from inside the courtroom, "the defense calls Joseph Fullem to the stand."

A buzz rippled through the gallery as the bailiff headed towards the rear doors of the courtroom to summon Fullem inside. Even the jurors straightened up in their chairs, anxious to for the show to begin. Jefferson banged his gavel lightly for quiet.

Unlike everyone else in the room, including the lawyers, who had turned to look at the rear door, Ryan just stared at Darnell from across the room. He wanted to memorize the face of the man who had done such unspeakable things to his daughter. He wanted to see every expression on the bastard's face as his own life ebbed away.

"Joseph Fullem?" asked the bailiff to the hallway.

Fullem turned and nodded.

"Come this way, sir."

The bailiff entered first, with the hulking Fullem looming directly behind. Every face in the gallery was turned to look at the man entering the room. Every face that is, except Ryan's, who was still staring intently at Cooper.

Because of whom he was facing, Ryan was the first to see Darnell's reaction to Fullem's appearance.

The boy's smooth brown face turned almost white, and immediately a wet stain began expanding across the front of his pants. He started to slide down his chair as he fainted, but remarkably, the boy's eyes, wide as saucers, remained locked on Fullem, who was slowly approaching now the gate in front of the gallery.

Lionel was watching Fullem walk up the aisle. When Fullem crossed in front of Ryan though, Lionel's eyes were drawn to where Ryan was looking, and saw also the quizzical expression on his face. He whipped his head around to Darnell, who by now was almost off his chair and about to fall on the floor. The entire front of his pants was soaked, and the smell of feces began to waft up from his body.

"Your Honor!" yelled Lionel as he dropped down to gather the disintegrating young man into his arms. Alerted to what was happening, the crowd came alive, and the court officers rushed to help the obviously stricken defendant.

Fullem stopped at the gate, his hand inside his jacket, about to flip the safety off of the .380. He looked over at Ryan, and with his facial expression asked what he should do. Ryan nodded his head no, unsure as to what he was seeing.

Jefferson banged his gavel and shouted for calm. "Quiet! Everybody stay seated!" He looked at Darnell, who now had his arms around Lionel and was sobbing violently, his face buried into his protector's chest.

"Darnell!" gasped Lionel into Darnell's ear, "what's the matter, son? What happened? Are you sick? Are you hurt?"

But Darnell would not answer. All he could do was grip his friend tighter, and sob.

Lionel looked up to the bench, his eyes begging for help.

"This court is in recess!" shouted Jefferson as he stood up. "Clear the courtroom. Now!"

As he watched the jury hustled from the room and supervised the reluctant exit of the crowd, Jefferson saw Fullem still standing at the gate to the well of the courtroom, with a confused, lost look on his face. "The witness is excused as well," he said to Fullem.

Lionel and Queenan forced Darnell to his feet, amazed at what they were seeing. Each of them put one of Darnell's arms around their shoulders and started to drag him towards the door. His eyes were becoming hooded and Lionel wasn't even sure if he was conscious.

"Darnell," he whispered into the boy's ear, "can you tell me what's wrong?"

Tears streamed from his eyes, his entire face a blanket of fear. He shook his head no.

"C'mon, buddy," said Queenan, who was struggling with the much larger Darnell, "was it Fullem who scared you?"

Darnell's eyes blazed suddenly with anger as he pulled himself away from Queenan to lean solely on Lionel. He stood on his own so he could cling only to him. With his face buried in Lionel's shoulder, Darnell finally said something, but Lionel hadn't been able to hear him. The court officers were crowding around them, and Judge Jefferson was standing behind the bench, surveying the scene.

They were almost to the door of the side conference room. Lionel extracted himself from Darnell's clutch and opened the door, which he closed after only the two of them had entered the room. Knowing they had only a few seconds alone before paramedics would arrive, Lionel sat Darnell in a chair, grasped both of his shoulders and stared into his face.

"Darnell!" he yell-whispered, "look at me!"

His head down on his chest, Darnell lifted just his eyes.

"What happened!? I didn't hear what you said."

Darnell started to speak, but the words couldn't get past the tears, and he leaned forward to hug Lionel's legs. Lionel rubbed the boy's head and shoulders. "It's okay, I'm right here, it's okay," he cooed. "I'm not going to let anyone hurt you, Darnell, I promise…now tell me why you're so upset."

Lionel could feel Darnell's chest pounding inside his chest. He decided to be quiet for a few seconds, and hope he would calm down enough to speak.

Still clutching Lionel's legs, Darnell said finally, "I didn't know who he was."

"Who?"

"Fullem."

"What do you mean?"

"That's...Clark."

Lionel felt suddenly weak in the knees and he sat down hard. His mind was racing in a thousand different directions at breakneck speed, trying to arrive at one coherent thought. One though came screaming over all of them.

"I thought he was *black*," he said, more to himself than to Darnell.

The boy's face crinkled in pained confusion and fear. "Why?"

Before Lionel could answer, the door burst open, and two paramedics carrying a stretcher rushed into the room, with two sheriff's deputies right behind. They literally picked Darnell up out of his chair and made him lay down on the stretcher, slapping handcuffs to his right wrist as he did.

He was gone before Lionel knew what to say.

CHAPTER 29

▼

Lionel didn't know what to do. One thing he was certain of though was that he could not allow himself to do nothing. If he did, the cruel invective in his head that he was spewing towards himself would consume him totally. He had mistakenly allowed himself to believe that the spark of recognition he felt when he confronted Fullem was due to his own fears, rather than his own innate racism. Lionel had assumed Clark was black from the moment he'd learned about his actions, and had never once considered that he was white. He suddenly hated himself for the assumption.

Almost on autopilot, he snuck out of the building's west entrance and walked around the swath of reporters who were swarmed around Queenan on the sidewalk at the East doors. Vaguely he heard Queenan saying something about food poisoning.

Not knowing why he was there, Lionel stormed into the lobby of the District Attorney's Office, and demanded to see Ash Wilson.

Sciolla opened the door to Wilson's office as Lionel bulled into the room.

His fury was palpable. "Do you know who that…that monster is?" he seethed.

Wilson, seated behind his desk, had no idea what Lionel was talking about. "Who?" he asked.

"Fullem!" shouted Lionel, causing Sciolla to both close the door and unfasten the holster holding his service revolver.

Lionel didn't wait for anymore questions. He had to get it out. "When Darnell was a little boy, before I met him, he was raped and beaten, repeatedly, by a man named Clark. I never knew who this motherfucker was until today, when Darnell saw him in court."

Wilson jumped to his feet. "Fullem is *Clark*?!"

It was not the reaction Lionel was expecting. It was apparent that Wilson knew about Clark.

Ash saw Lionel's confused look. "I know all about it, Lionel. I know everything that kid's been through. That's why I made you come here that night to try and make a deal. He's an extraordinary human being."

Lionel threw his hands up in the air. He'd truly heard it all. "Well why the fuck have you been trying to kill him, you piece of shit!" he yelled, his fury having found a target.

Sciolla stepped forward and put his hand inside the much larger man's elbow. "Take it easy, Lionel. Don't do anything stupid."

Lionel jerked his arm away, but didn't otherwise move. "So what are you going to do about it now?" he challenged.

Wilson scratched his head. "Are you sure? I mean, how do you know it's him?"

Wilson left unsaid the fact that he had assumed Clark was black as well.

"You saw what happened to Darnell when Fullem walked in didn't you?"

He had a point. Along with everyone else in the room, Wilson had been absolutely stunned by what had happened to Darnell. He and Sciolla had been puzzling over that very fact when Lionel had arrived. The explanation made perfect sense, and Wilson believed him.

Lionel saw in Wilson's face acceptance of Fullem's true identity. "So?" he demanded again.

The D.A. picked up his suit coat off the back of his chair. "Let's go get him," he said as he strode towards the door. Sciolla followed closely behind, as did Lionel. He was going along whether he was wanted or not.

*   *   *   *

Ryan and Fullem rode in silence back to Fullem's apartment. It was clear that there would be no more court that day. In his mind's eye, Ryan could not erase the terrified look he'd seen on Darnell's face when he first spotted Fullem. It was a totally inappropriate reaction, and Ryan simply could not understand it.

They arrived at the apartment where Fullem removed his tie and jacket and went to the refrigerator. He pulled the gun from his belt and threw it onto the couch. Ryan went there too and flopped down.

He looked straight ahead at nothing, obsessing over the meaning of Darnell's reaction. "You know that kid, Joe?"

Fullem said nothing for a few seconds. "Whattya' mean?" he said finally as he emerged from the kitchen with two cans of beer.

Ryan accepted his beer and cracked it open. "I mean he looked like he...recognized you from somewhere all of a sudden, and that was why he went batshit."

Fullem drained his beer and shrugged. "He's probably seen me on TV or something.'"

Ryan shook his head. "Nah, it was different than that. As soon as he saw you, his eyes got huge and he literally pissed himself." Ryan turned to face his friend, who had sat down on the other end of the couch. "There's something you're not telling me, Joe."

"I need another beer," he said as he started to get up.

Ryan reached across the couch and put his arm on Fullem's leg to stop him. "C'mon, Joe, you can tell me. What don't I know?"

A slight, rueful smile crossed briefly over Fullem's lips then disappeared into a deep frown. His eyes flitted towards the gun which lay on the couch between them. He had expected to be dead by now, and was sorry he wasn't.

Ryan caught Fullem's peek towards the gun and every instinct in his body suddenly told him that Fullem was a danger to him. For the first time since he'd gotten the news, he wondered if Fullem could have actually killed his daughter.

As nonchalantly as he could, Ryan slid his hand across the cushions and picked up the gun. He held it in his lap.

Fullem saw what he had done, and welcomed the gesture. He needed it to be over.

"What don't I know?"

The huge man seemed to shrink a bit as he slouched forward until his elbows were resting on his knees and his giant hands were rubbing his bald pate. He turned his head to look at his friend. "Everything," he said quietly.

✻   ✻   ✻   ✻

Sciolla was driving his own car, with Wilson in the front and Lionel in the back seat. It had occurred to neither the D.A. nor the detective to tell Lionel not to come, because as they all three walked towards the car, Lionel was telling them everything he knew.

He told them about how he had met Darnell in the first place, what he had been. He told them about the early struggles, and then the astounding procession of successes. He told them about Clark's extortion, and even his own crimes in forging Darnell's records. And with great shame he admitted that he'd always assumed Clark was black.

Sciolla and Wilson said nothing to that, each acknowledging within himself the shame of having made the same assumption.

It was too much to absorb. Neither of the men in the front seat were able to even speak. They were too stunned. Not just by what they were hearing, but by the fact that they had each been so convinced that Darnell was the real killer. Wilson especially felt a hole forming in the pit of his stomach, as he confronted the monstrosity of his own determination to send an innocent boy to the death chamber.

The car screeched to a halt in the parking lot directly below Fullem's third floor apartment. To that point, none of them had actually considered what they were going to do. But none of them cared.

Sciolla was the first to the door. He removed his .45 from its holster and banged on the door to announce his presence. "Fullem!" he shouted. "It's Tony Sciolla! Open up!"

They stood there for a brief second, waiting for a response.

BANG!

All three of them instinctively duck down. Against all of his training, and common sense, Sciolla kicked in the door and rushed inside. Wilson and Lionel charged in right behind him, too startled into action to be afraid.

"Put the gun down, John," they heard Sciolla say softly.

Seated on the couch in front of the television, John Ryan was holding Fullem's .380 pistol, a thin trail of blue smoke wafting from the end of the barrel. Tears streamed down his face. Fullem lay sprawled against the other end of the couch, half his giant head a mottled mess of blood and brains.

"He killed her," whispered Ryan. He was staring at Fullem, still holding the gun straight out. He turned to face Sciolla. "He told me...he killed them all, Tony. He killed them...all." Ryan dropped the gun and curled up into a ball. For a few moments, his sobs were the only sound in the room.

For the first time since the murder of Kelly Ryan, Ash Wilson was one hundred percent certain about what he had to do to make justice happen. He walked over to the couch and picked up the .380 from the floor. Very deliberately, and without a word, the District Attorney wiped the gun down with the flap of his suit coat.

He then stepped over to Fullem's body, and placed the gun into its lifeless left hand.

Nobody in the room said a word.

EPILOGUE

▼

Wilson withdrew the charges against Darnell the next day and Jefferson ordered him released from jail immediately. Fullem's confession to the crime and subsequent suicide were the bases offered by Wilson to the court and the press. Neither Sciolla nor Lionel, nor Ryan, ever said a word to anyone about what they had seen Wilson do.

Not that he ever asked them to stay quiet. Two weeks later Wilson resigned his position as District Attorney. After a two month vacation, and much soul searching about who he was and what justice truly meant to him, he realized what he was meant to do.

Upon the recommendation of Judge Jefferson, Wilson created a non-profit advocacy group whose sole function was to monitor every case in the country in which the death penalty was being sought. He still believed that the system could work, and he accepted that the death penalty was a valuable prosecution tool, and a valid sanction under the law for murder. His was not an anti-death penalty group. Rather, it was designed to act as a check on the system, making sure that the evidence in every case was being examined in a race-neutral manner.

The group also employed a full-time staff of social workers, psychologists, and grief counselors, whose sole function was to work with family members of the murder victims. It was called the LK Ryan Justice For All Project.

John Ryan spent three months after the death of Fullem in an exclusive rehabilitation facility in Colorado Springs, paid for by Ash Wilson. He would not ever be the same man. But Ryan learned that he still wanted to live, if for no other reason than just to spite Joe Fullem. He eventually retired from the police force, and accepted a full-time position as Wilson's chief investigator for the project named after his wife and daughter.

*   *   *   *

Although he had missed all of the first, and most of the second semesters of his junior year, Darnell was able to get right back into class after his release from prison. By taking two full summer sessions, he was able to get back on track to start his senior year on time. The NCAA, on its own volition, enacted special legislation which granted Darnell an extra year of eligibility if he wanted it. He didn't.

Darnell was the consensus college player of the year the next season, leading Penn to an undefeated Ivy season, and the Sweet Sixteen of the NCAA tournament. There was no question that he would be the number one pick in the NBA draft the following season. Speculation ran rampant as to which of the major sneaker companies would be able to pay him enough millions to endorse their products.

Agents called him non-stop, offering money, women, jewelry, cars, and whatever else they thought a soon-to-be multi-millionaire, twenty-one year old black kid from the city might want out of life. He returned none of their calls, and they, along with the sports cognoscenti, all assumed that Lionel would act as Darnell's agent.

When he took the law school admissions exam in April of his senior year, no one seriously considered for a second that he intended on going to law school. It was widely reported in the press as a negotiating ploy, an effort to raise the bidding by his various suitors. No one knew for sure, because since his release from jail, neither Lionel nor Darnell had granted any interviews with the press.

Even when he applied and was accepted, with a full scholarship, to Harvard Law School, everyone applauded and made jokes about how he'd be the smartest rookie in the NBA since Bill Bradley.

And when the NBA Commissioner called his name on draft day as the number one pick in the NBA draft, Darnell shook the man's hand, stepped up to the microphone, and politely declined the offer.

He faced the banks of cameras and microphones, and ignored the glare of the flashbulbs going off in his face.

"I want to thank the NBA and the Commissioner for the opportunity to be here today," he said in a firm voice. "But I will not be playing in the NBA. There is too much for me to do. The time for playing games is over."

All noise in the room stopped.

"In my short life so far I have seen the worst and the best that we as a society have to offer one another. I have made it this far for one reason, and one reason only." Darnell turned to his left and caught Lionel's eyes. "Because a brother, *my* brother, simply decided one day that he was not going to let my life be wasted." A tear escaped down Darnell's cheek as he turned back to face the cameras. "Well now it's my turn to make sure that none of the lives of all my little brothers out there are wasted either. And I'm not going to do that by dribbling a ball and telling them what kind of sneakers to wear. I'm going to do it by showing them that there are more opportunities available to them than just being a fancily dressed show pony. Thank you."

With that said, Darnell, left the stage.

In the waiting room behind the podium, Lionel smiled at the shocked and horrified faces on the other athletes (all black), their agents (all white), and their families.

"That's a first," muttered one agent sardonically.

Lionel picked up his coat to leave and smiled brightly at the man.

"You ain't seen nothin' yet."

THE END

978-0-595-36967-0
0-595-36967-7

Printed in the United States
203420BV00003B/68/A